THE RINCE

Puzzle House

Story by **AARON EHASZ**
and **JUSTIN RICHMOND**

Written by **PETER WARTMAN**

Illustrated by **FELIA HANAKATA**

graphix

An Imprint of

SCHOLASTIC

ISBN 978-1-338-79437-3

10 9 8 7 6 5 4 3 2 1   23 24 25 26 27

Printed in China   62

First edition, August 2023

Edited by Katie Woehr and Conor Lloyd

Book design by Martha Maynard

Colors by Arley Nopra

Letters by Olga Andreyeva

Creative director: Yaffa Jaskoll

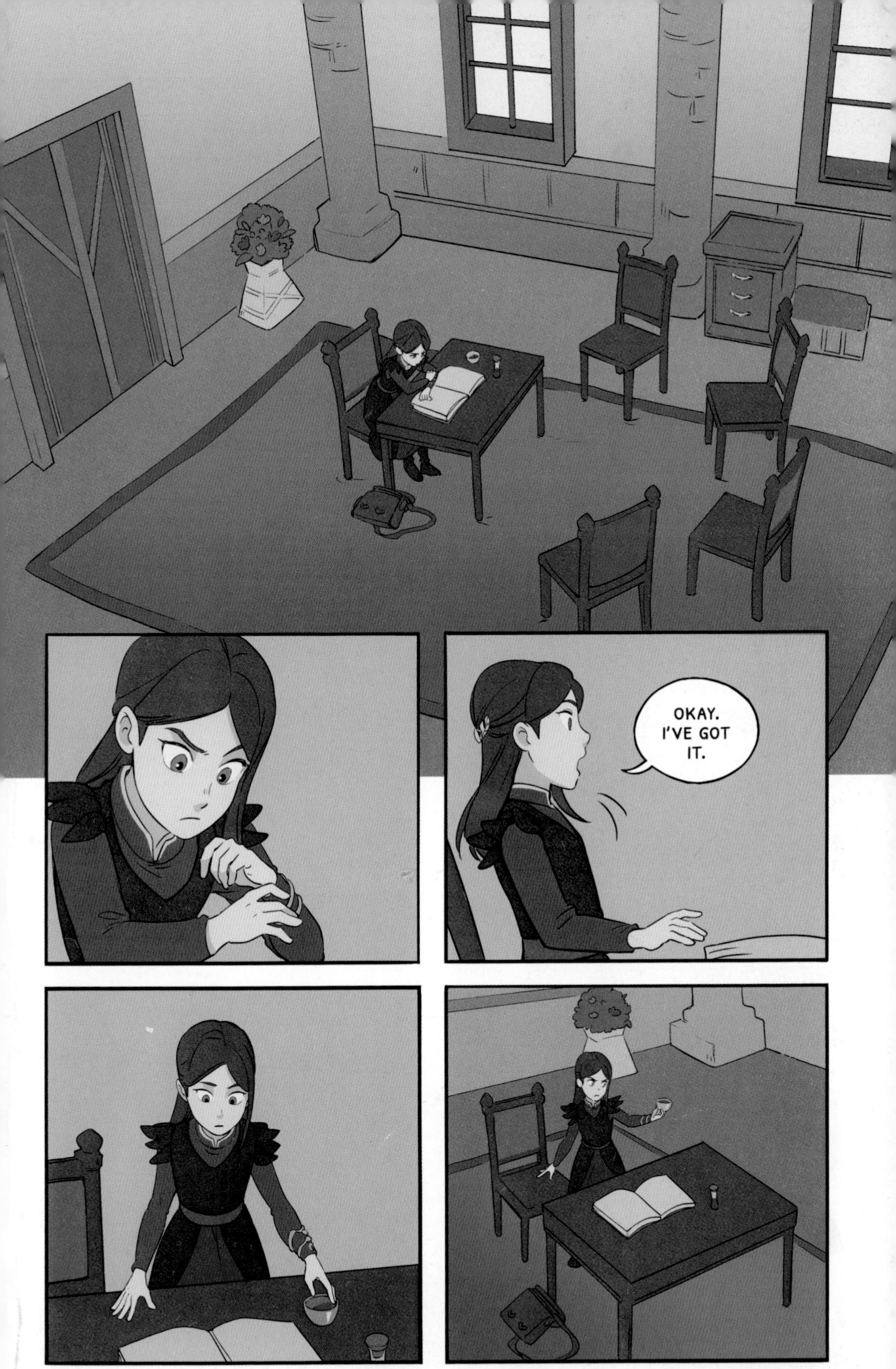
OKAY.
I'VE GOT
IT.

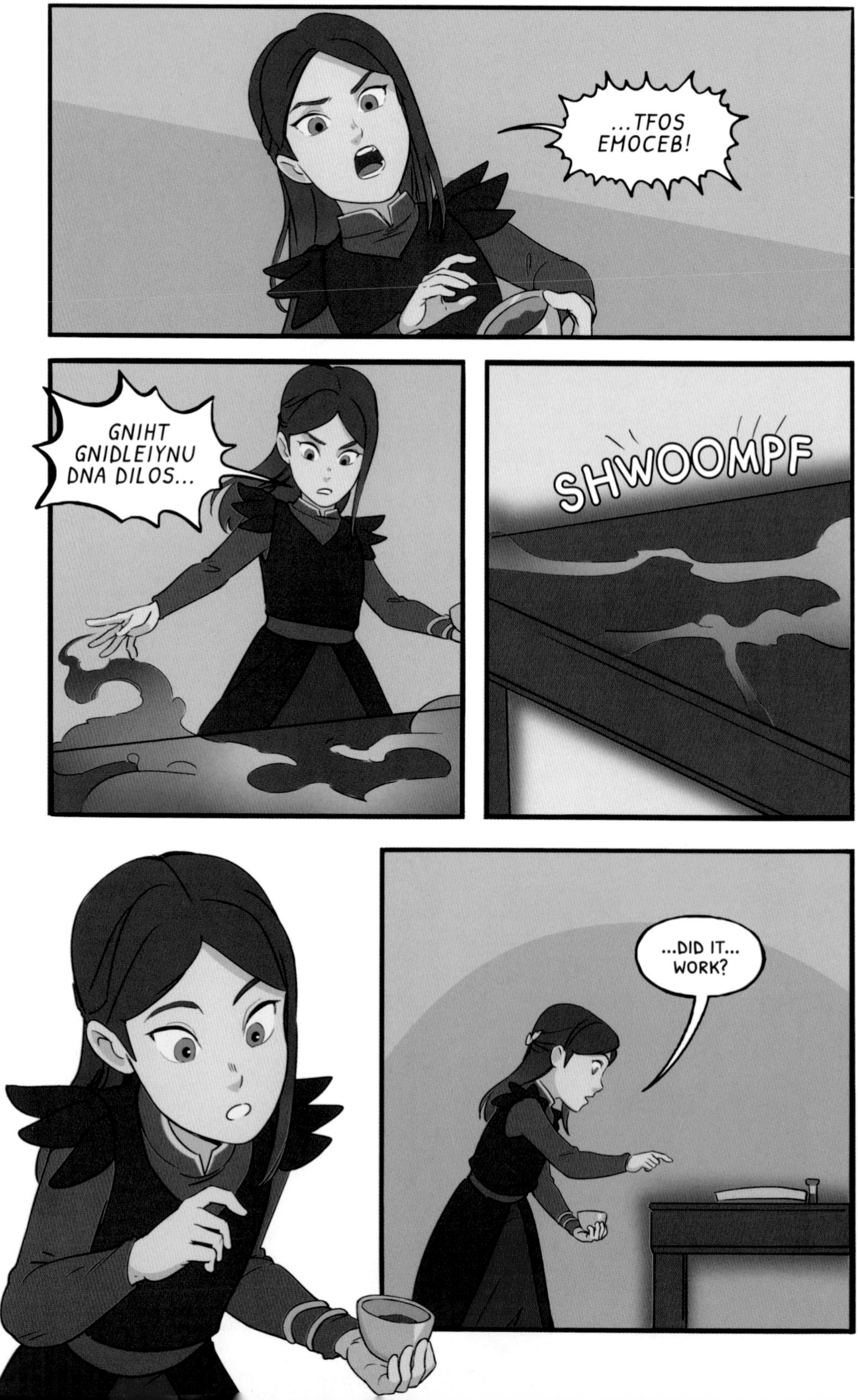
...TFOS EMOCEB!
GNIHT GNIDLEIYNU DNA DILOS...
SHWOOMPF
...DID IT... WORK?

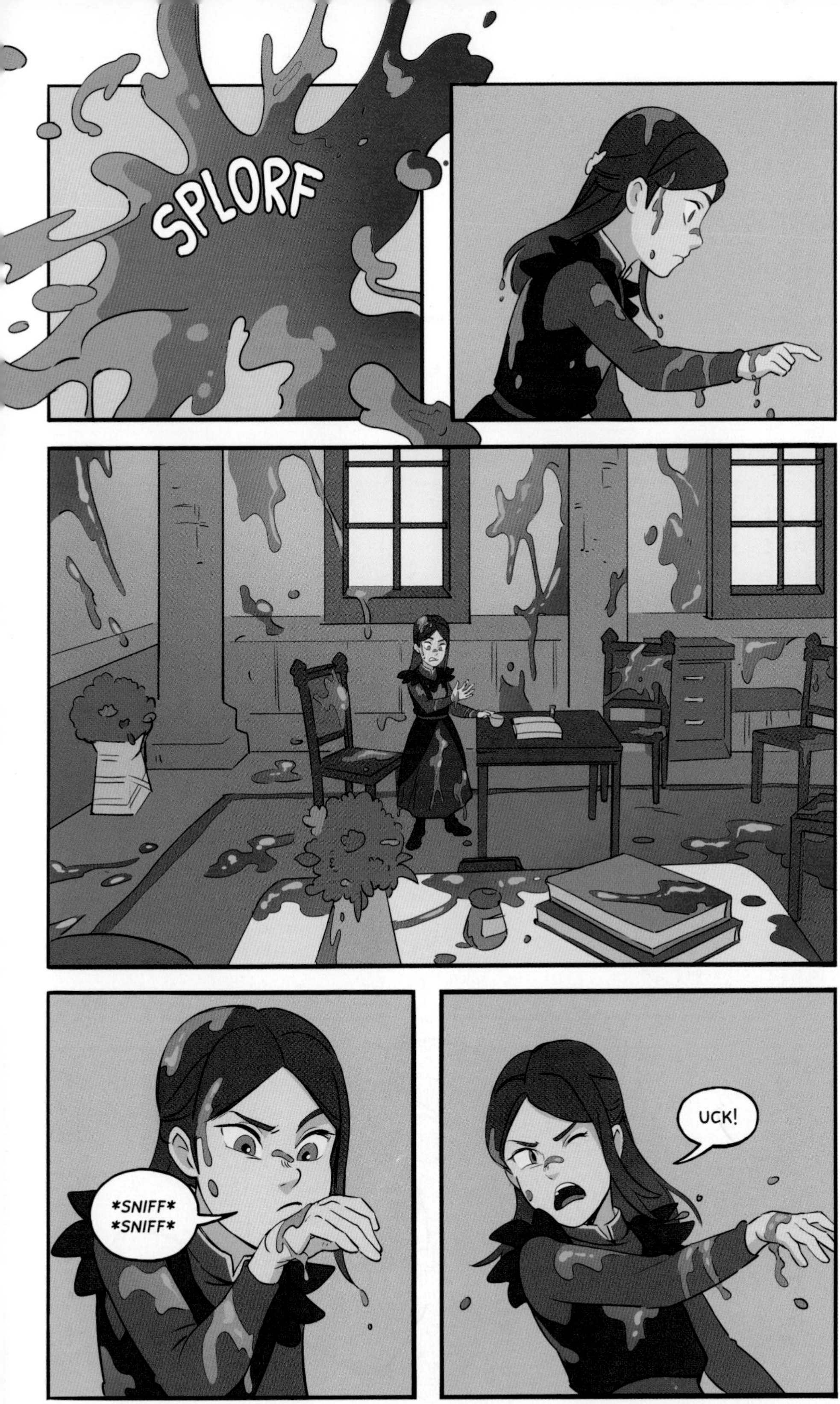
SPLORF
SNIFF *SNIFF*
UCK!

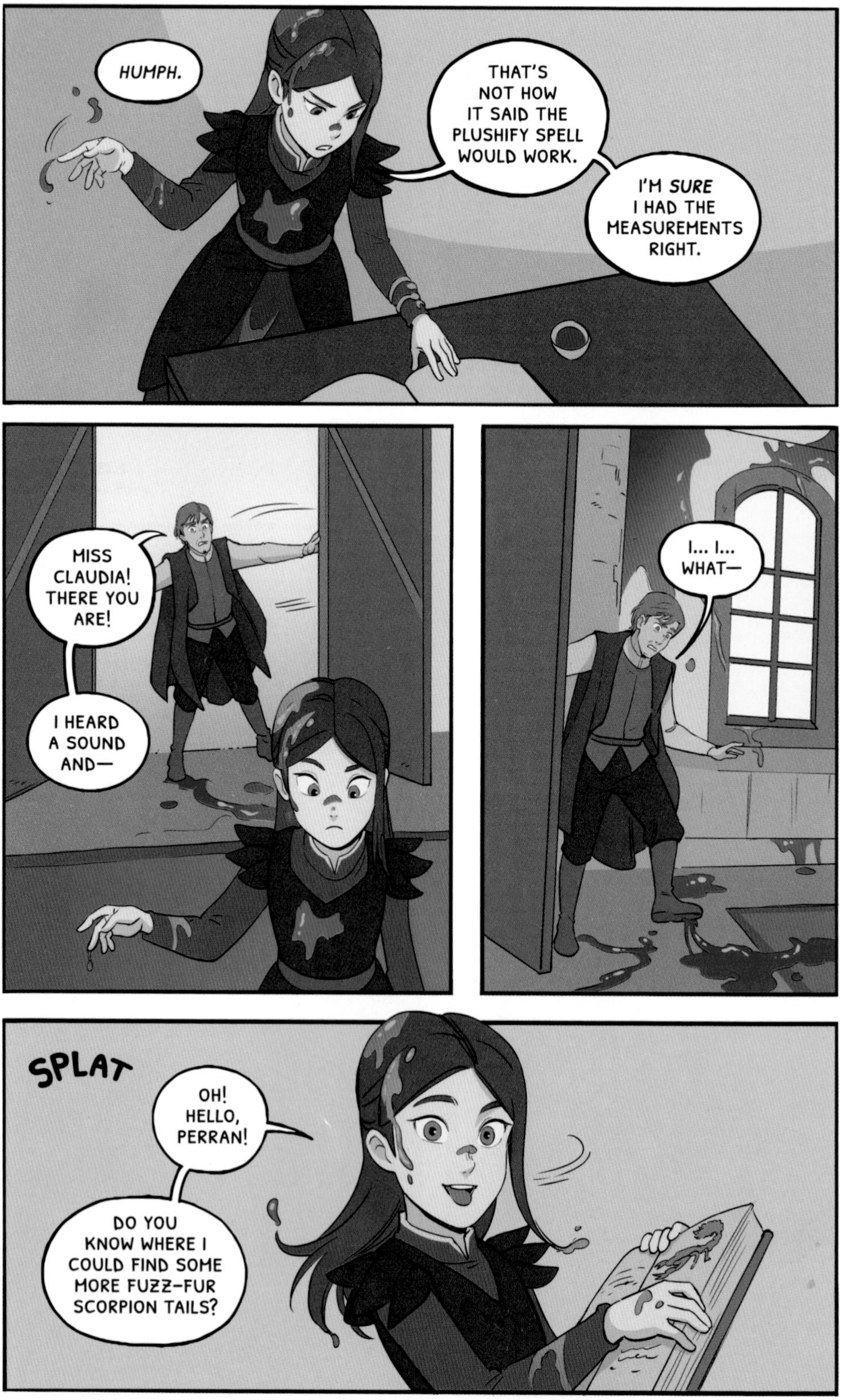
HUMPH.
THAT'S NOT HOW IT SAID THE PLUSHIFY SPELL WOULD WORK.
I'M *SURE* I HAD THE MEASUREMENTS RIGHT.
MISS CLAUDIA! THERE YOU ARE!
I HEARD A SOUND AND—
I... I... WHAT—
SPLAT
OH! HELLO, PERRAN!
DO YOU KNOW WHERE I COULD FIND SOME MORE FUZZ-FUR SCORPION TAILS?

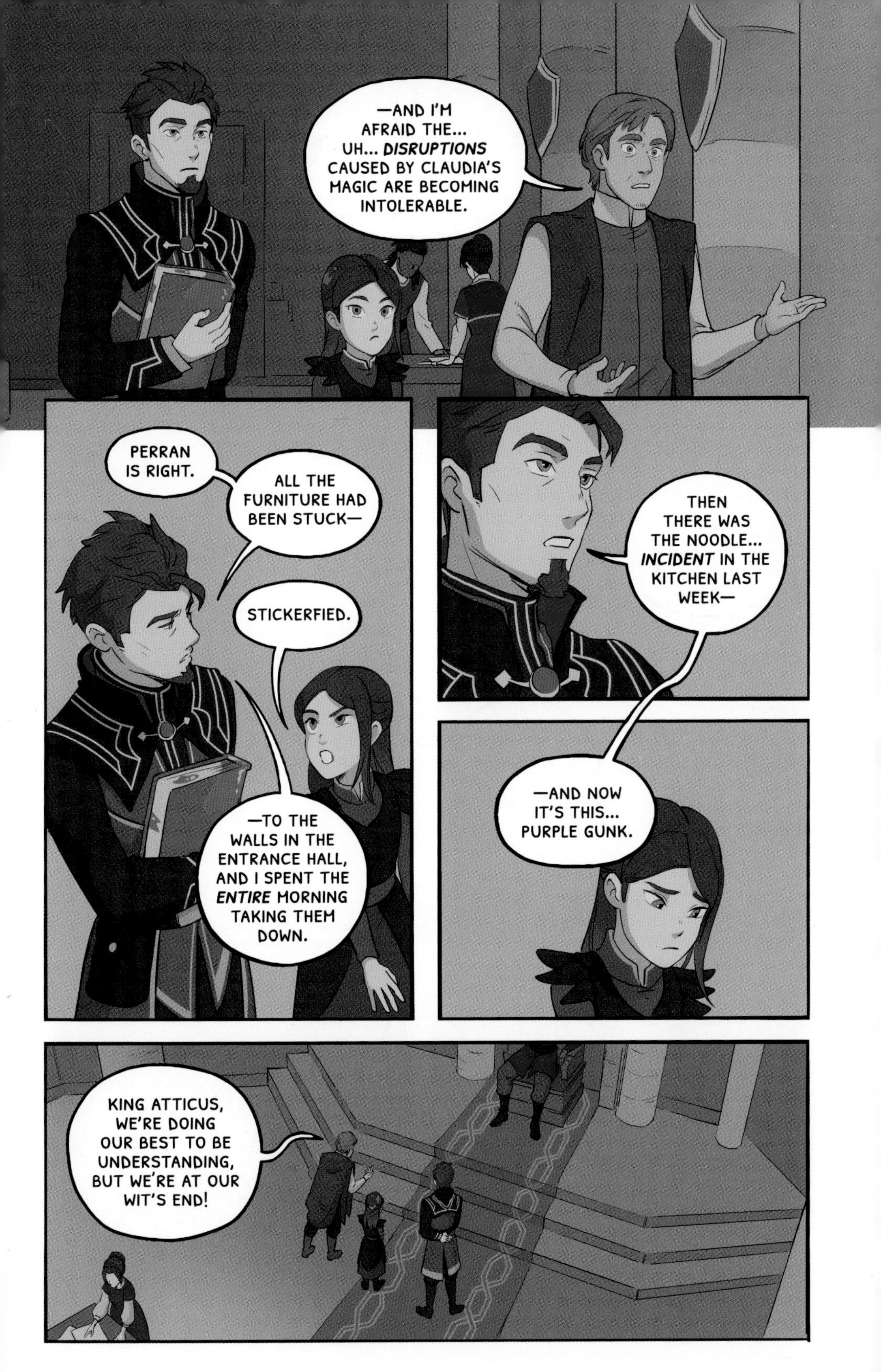
—AND I'M AFRAID THE... UH... *DISRUPTIONS* CAUSED BY CLAUDIA'S MAGIC ARE BECOMING INTOLERABLE.
PERRAN IS RIGHT.
ALL THE FURNITURE HAD BEEN STUCK—
STICKERFIED.
—TO THE WALLS IN THE ENTRANCE HALL, AND I SPENT THE *ENTIRE* MORNING TAKING THEM DOWN.
THEN THERE WAS THE NOODLE... *INCIDENT* IN THE KITCHEN LAST WEEK—
—AND NOW IT'S THIS... PURPLE GUNK.
KING ATTICUS, WE'RE DOING OUR BEST TO BE UNDERSTANDING, BUT WE'RE AT OUR WIT'S END!

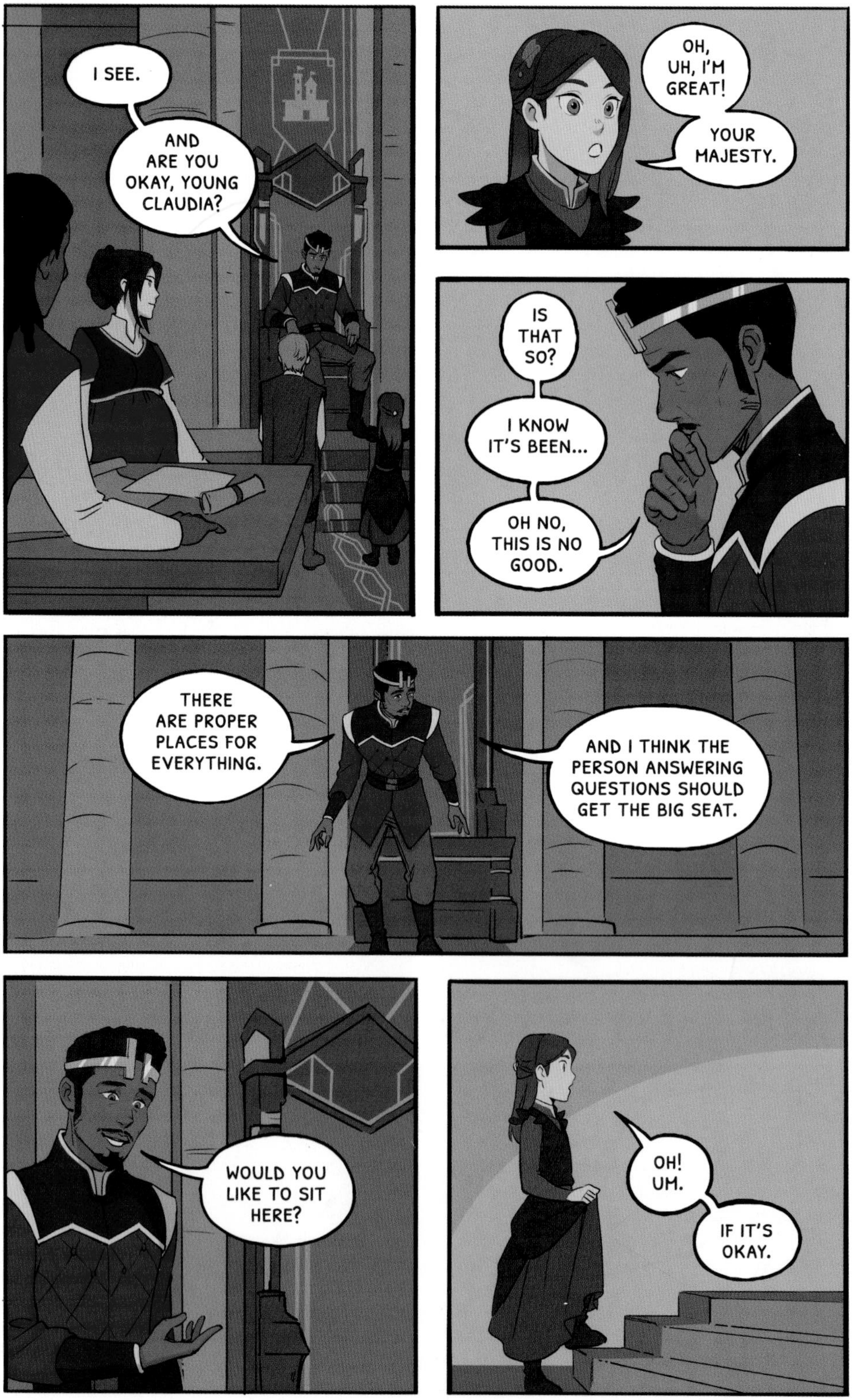
I SEE.
AND ARE YOU OKAY, YOUNG CLAUDIA?
OH, UH, I'M GREAT!
YOUR MAJESTY.
IS THAT SO?
I KNOW IT'S BEEN...
OH NO, THIS IS NO GOOD.
THERE ARE PROPER PLACES FOR EVERYTHING.
AND I THINK THE PERSON ANSWERING QUESTIONS SHOULD GET THE BIG SEAT.
WOULD YOU LIKE TO SIT HERE?
OH! UM.
IF IT'S OKAY.

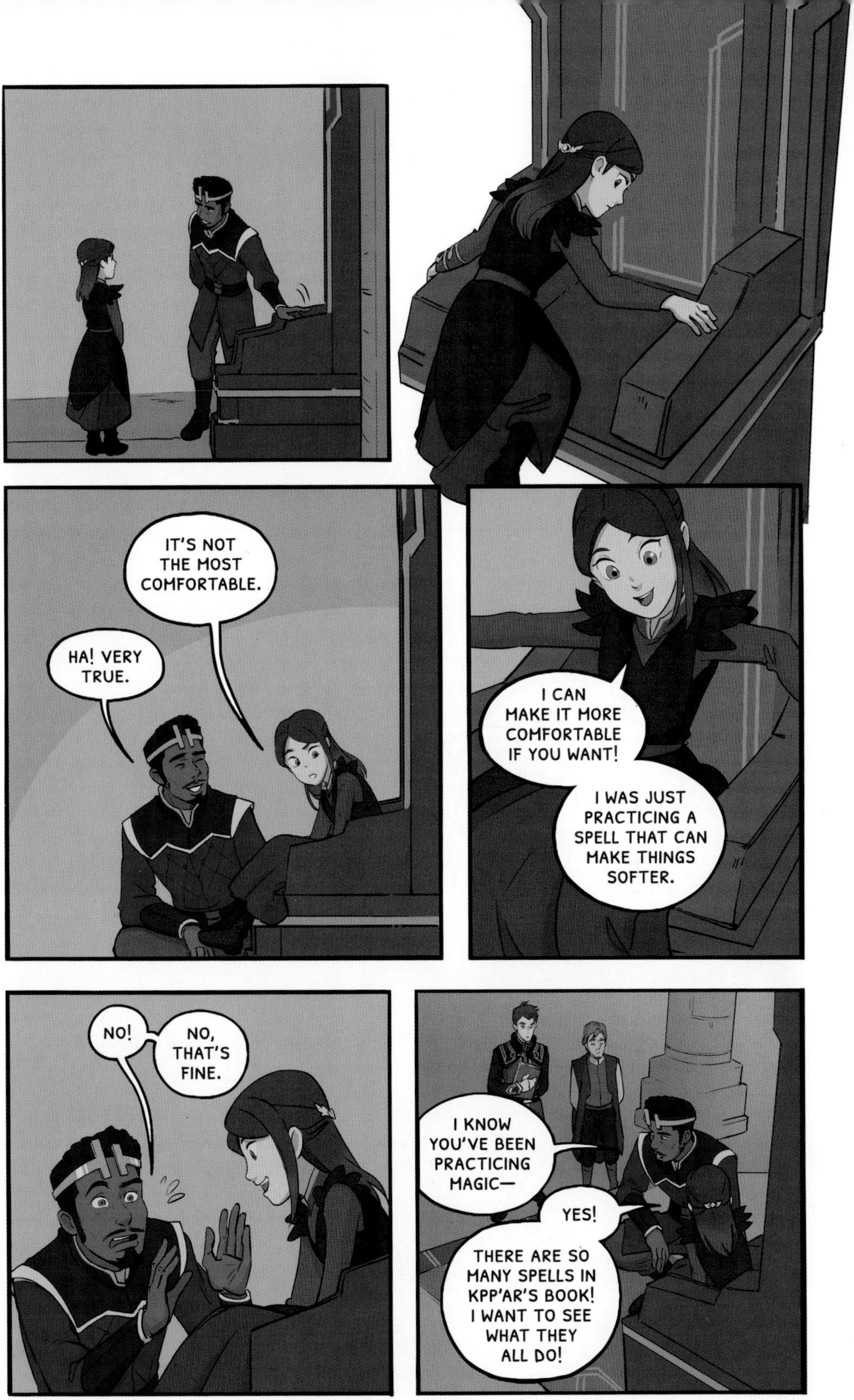
IT'S NOT THE MOST COMFORTABLE.
HA! VERY TRUE.
I CAN MAKE IT MORE COMFORTABLE IF YOU WANT!
I WAS JUST PRACTICING A SPELL THAT CAN MAKE THINGS SOFTER.
NO!
NO, THAT'S FINE.
I KNOW YOU'VE BEEN PRACTICING MAGIC—
YES!
THERE ARE SO MANY SPELLS IN KPP'AR'S BOOK! I WANT TO SEE WHAT THEY ALL DO!

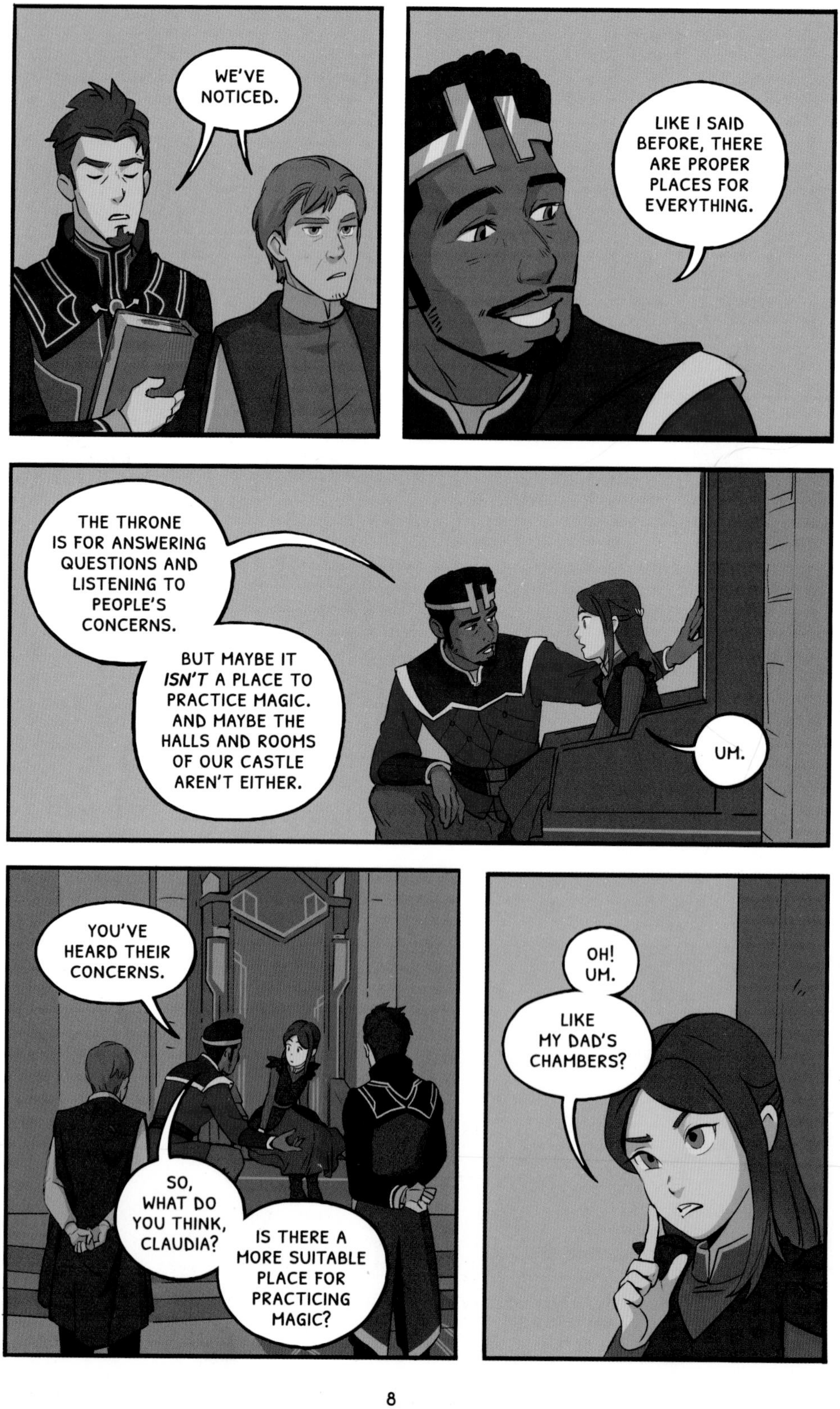
WE'VE NOTICED.
LIKE I SAID BEFORE, THERE ARE PROPER PLACES FOR EVERYTHING.
THE THRONE IS FOR ANSWERING QUESTIONS AND LISTENING TO PEOPLE'S CONCERNS.
BUT MAYBE IT *ISN'T* A PLACE TO PRACTICE MAGIC. AND MAYBE THE HALLS AND ROOMS OF OUR CASTLE AREN'T EITHER.
UM.
YOU'VE HEARD THEIR CONCERNS.
SO, WHAT DO YOU THINK, CLAUDIA?
IS THERE A MORE SUITABLE PLACE FOR PRACTICING MAGIC?
OH! UM.
LIKE MY DAD'S CHAMBERS?

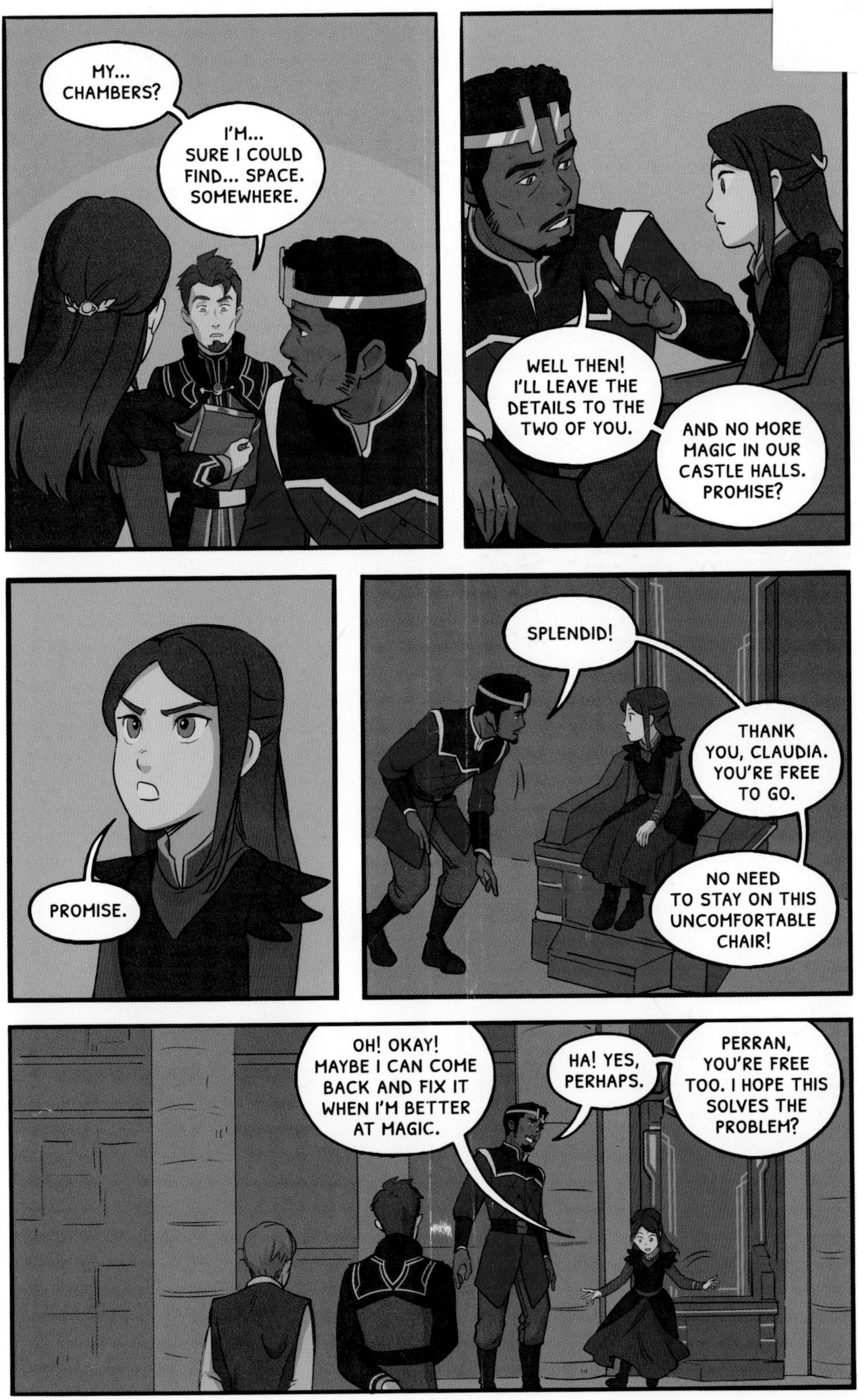
MY... CHAMBERS?
I'M... SURE I COULD FIND... SPACE. SOMEWHERE.
WELL THEN! I'LL LEAVE THE DETAILS TO THE TWO OF YOU.
AND NO MORE MAGIC IN OUR CASTLE HALLS. PROMISE?
PROMISE.
SPLENDID!
THANK YOU, CLAUDIA. YOU'RE FREE TO GO.
NO NEED TO STAY ON THIS UNCOMFORTABLE CHAIR!
OH! OKAY! MAYBE I CAN COME BACK AND FIX IT WHEN I'M BETTER AT MAGIC.
HA! YES, PERHAPS.
PERRAN, YOU'RE FREE TOO. I HOPE THIS SOLVES THE PROBLEM?

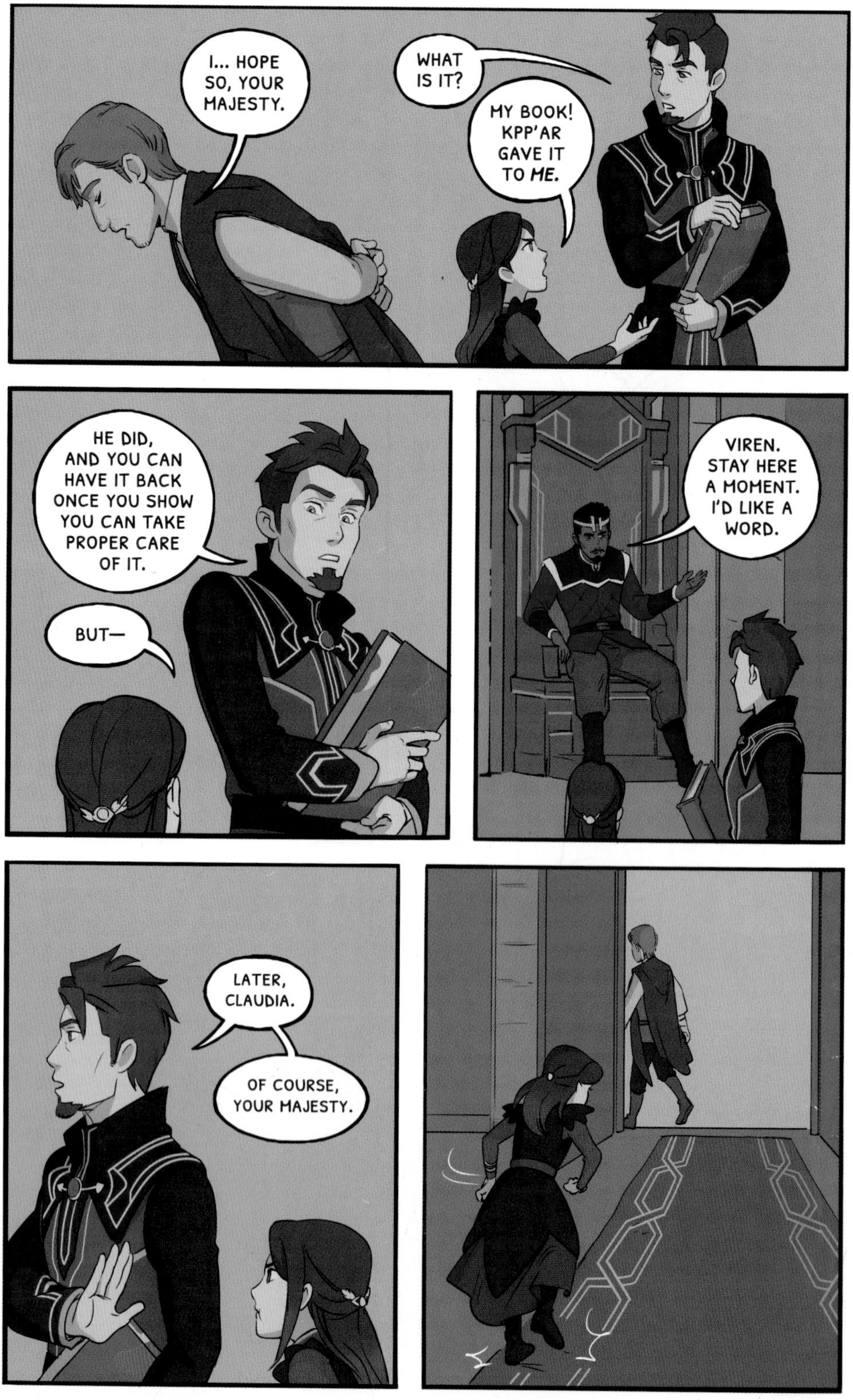
I... HOPE SO, YOUR MAJESTY.
WHAT IS IT?
MY BOOK! KPP'AR GAVE IT TO *ME.*
HE DID, AND YOU CAN HAVE IT BACK ONCE YOU SHOW YOU CAN TAKE PROPER CARE OF IT.
BUT—
VIREN. STAY HERE A MOMENT. I'D LIKE A WORD.
LATER, CLAUDIA.
OF COURSE, YOUR MAJESTY.

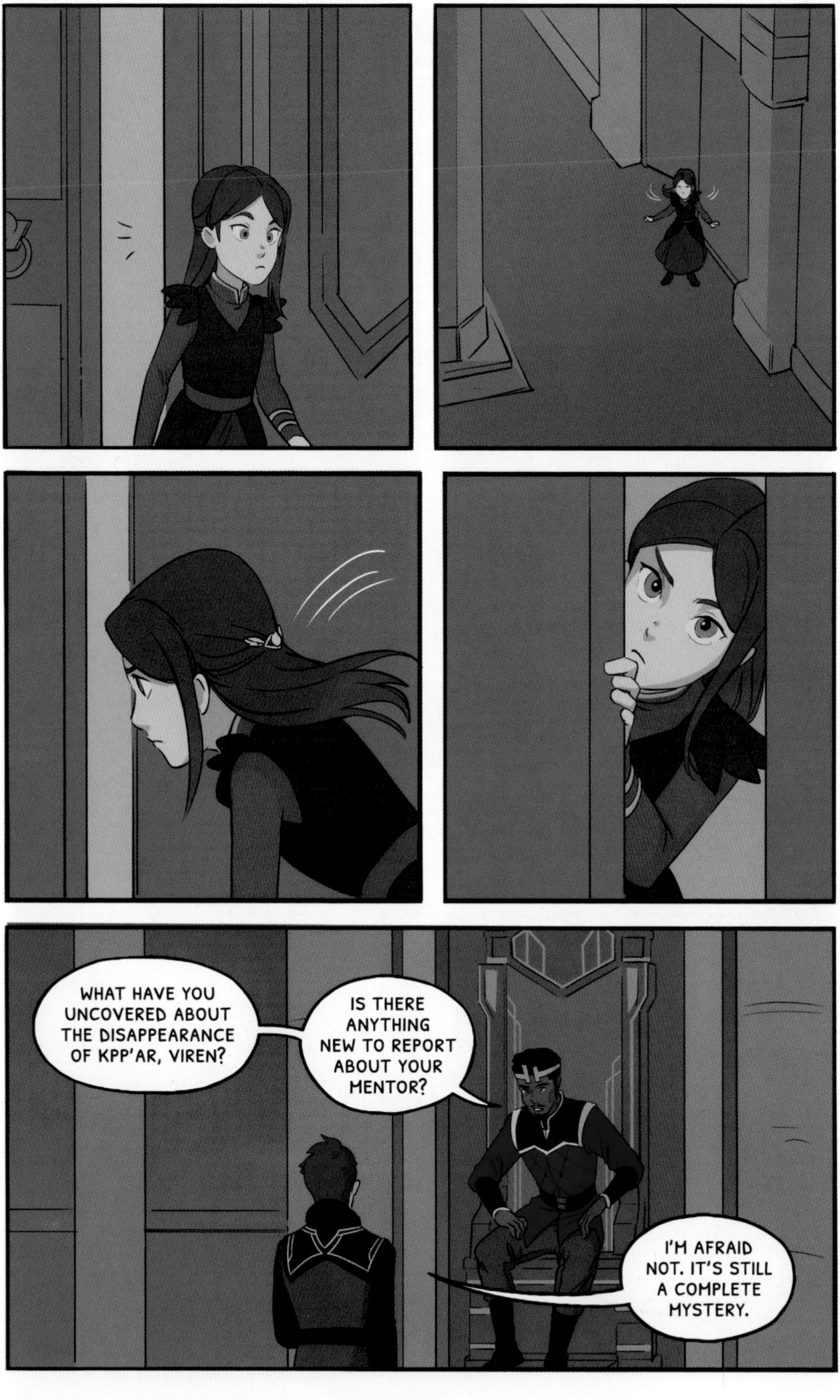
WHAT HAVE YOU UNCOVERED ABOUT THE DISAPPEARANCE OF KPP'AR, VIREN?
IS THERE ANYTHING NEW TO REPORT ABOUT YOUR MENTOR?
I'M AFRAID NOT. IT'S STILL A COMPLETE MYSTERY.

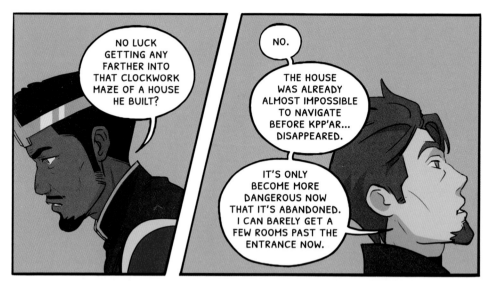

NO LUCK GETTING ANY FARTHER INTO THAT CLOCKWORK MAZE OF A HOUSE HE BUILT?

NO.

THE HOUSE WAS ALREADY ALMOST IMPOSSIBLE TO NAVIGATE BEFORE KPP'AR... DISAPPEARED.

IT'S ONLY BECOME MORE DANGEROUS NOW THAT IT'S ABANDONED. I CAN BARELY GET A FEW ROOMS PAST THE ENTRANCE NOW.

HE WAS MAKING SOMETHING, WASN'T HE?

SOME STRANGE AND POWERFUL MAGICAL CONTRAPTION?

NO, HE WAS BECOMING... WEARY OF MAGIC.

HE TOLD ME THE PROJECT WAS SOMETHING QUAINTER—A SURPRISE FOR CLAUDIA AND SOREN, UP IN THE TOWER.

A *SURPRISE*?

AND WHAT ABOUT YOU, VIREN?

HOW ARE YOU HOLDING UP?

SIR?

YOUR SON WAS DEATHLY ILL, YOUR MENTOR MYSTERIOUSLY DISAPPEARED, AND THEN YOUR WIFE LEFT.

ALL ONE AFTER THE OTHER.

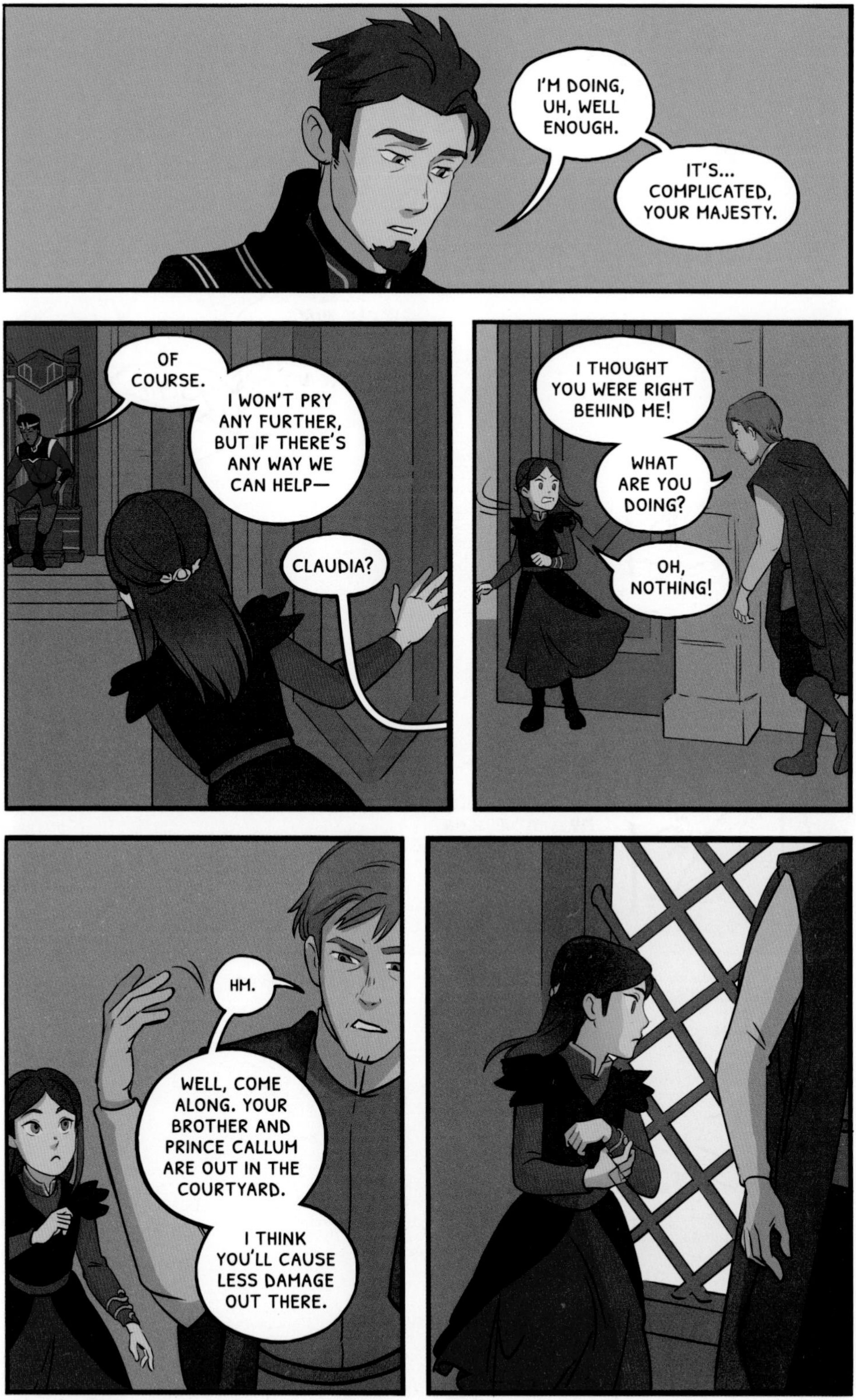
I'M DOING, UH, WELL ENOUGH.
IT'S... COMPLICATED, YOUR MAJESTY.
OF COURSE.
I WON'T PRY ANY FURTHER, BUT IF THERE'S ANY WAY WE CAN HELP—
CLAUDIA?
I THOUGHT YOU WERE RIGHT BEHIND ME!
WHAT ARE YOU DOING?
OH, NOTHING!
HM.
WELL, COME ALONG. YOUR BROTHER AND PRINCE CALLUM ARE OUT IN THE COURTYARD.
I THINK YOU'LL CAUSE LESS DAMAGE OUT THERE.

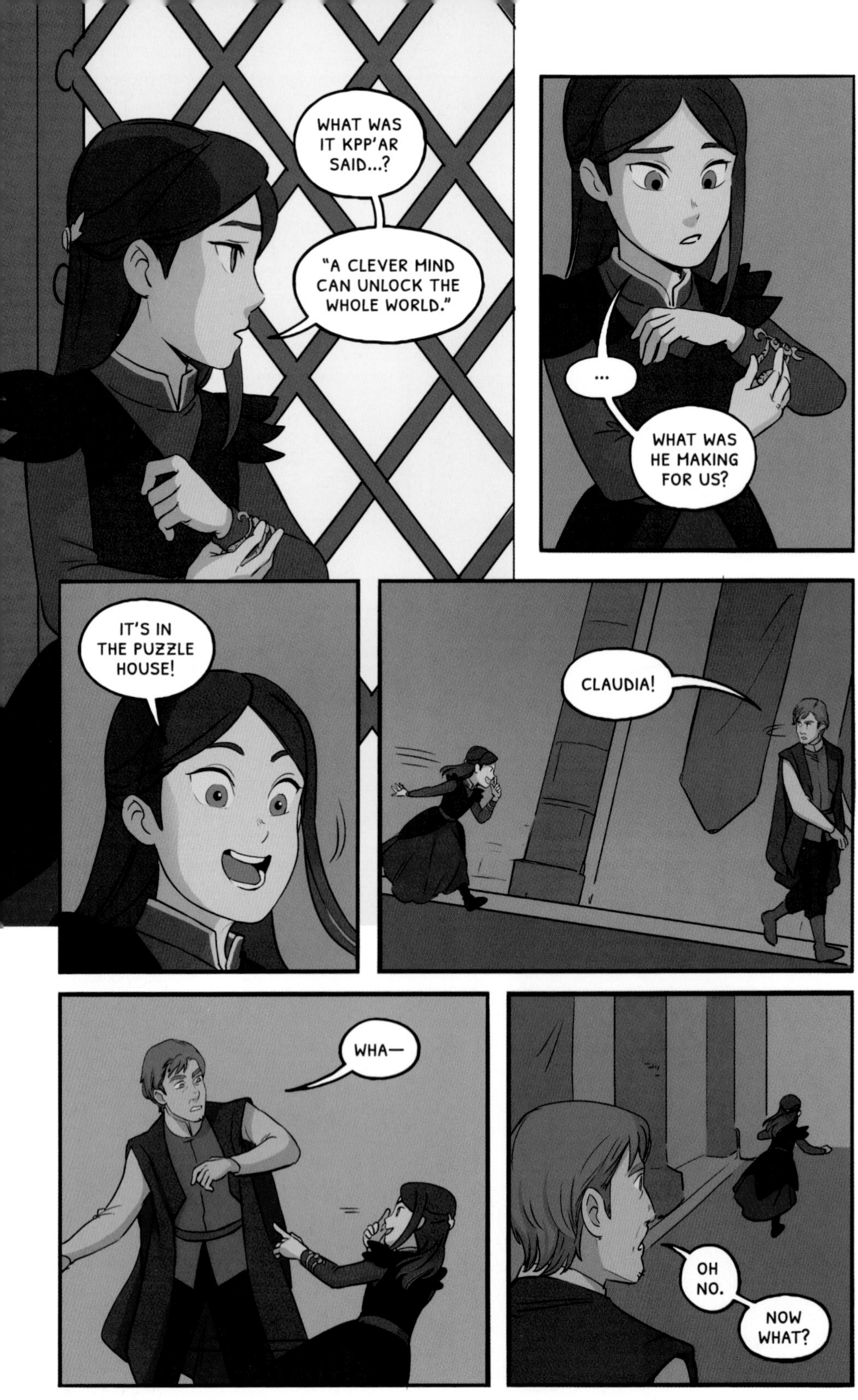
WHAT WAS IT KPP'AR SAID...?
"A CLEVER MIND CAN UNLOCK THE WHOLE WORLD."
...
WHAT WAS HE MAKING FOR US?
IT'S IN THE PUZZLE HOUSE!
CLAUDIA!
WHA—
OH NO.
NOW WHAT?

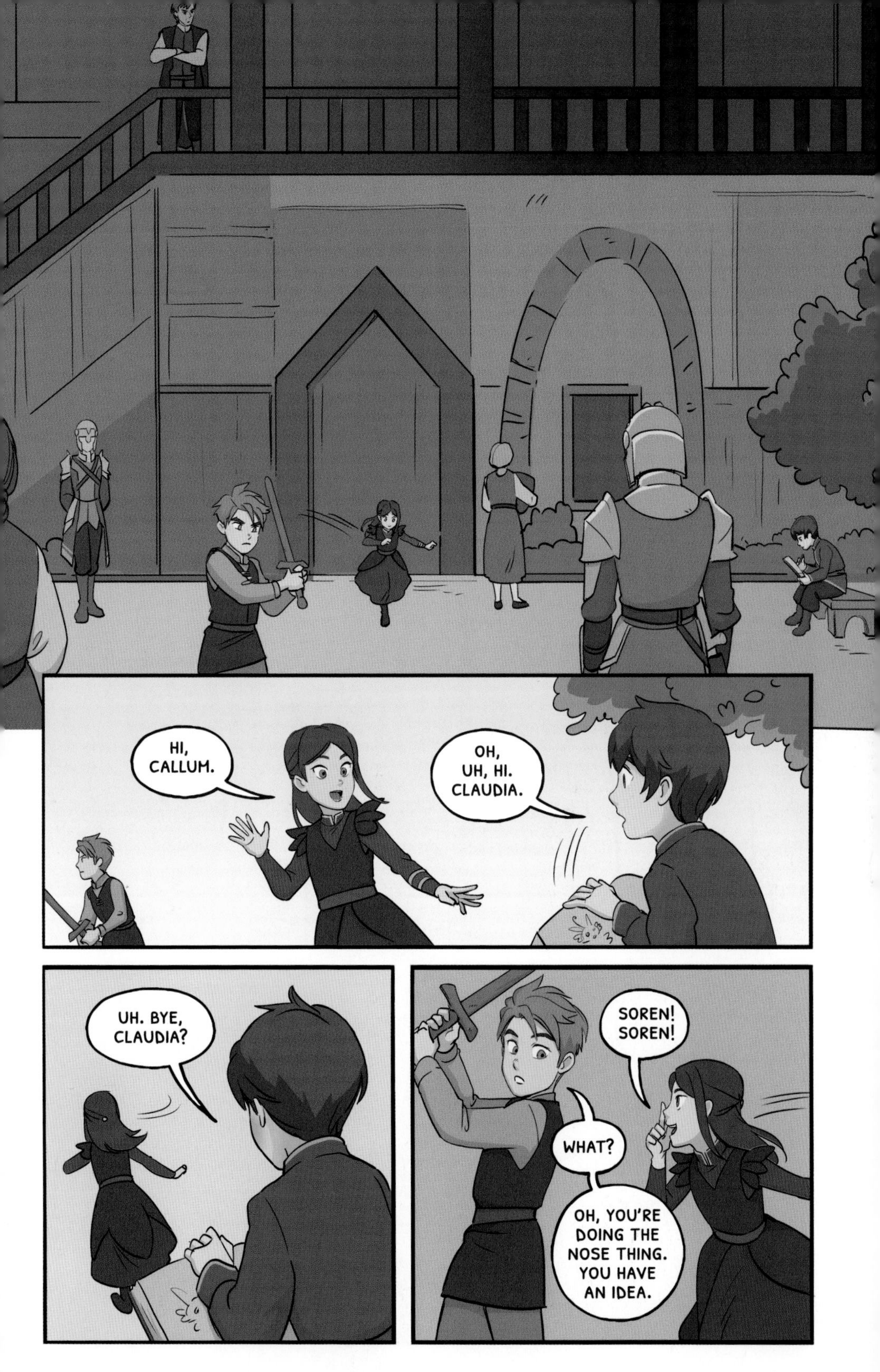
HI, CALLUM.
OH, UH, HI. CLAUDIA.
UH. BYE, CLAUDIA?
SOREN! SOREN!
WHAT?
OH, YOU'RE DOING THE NOSE THING. YOU HAVE AN IDEA.

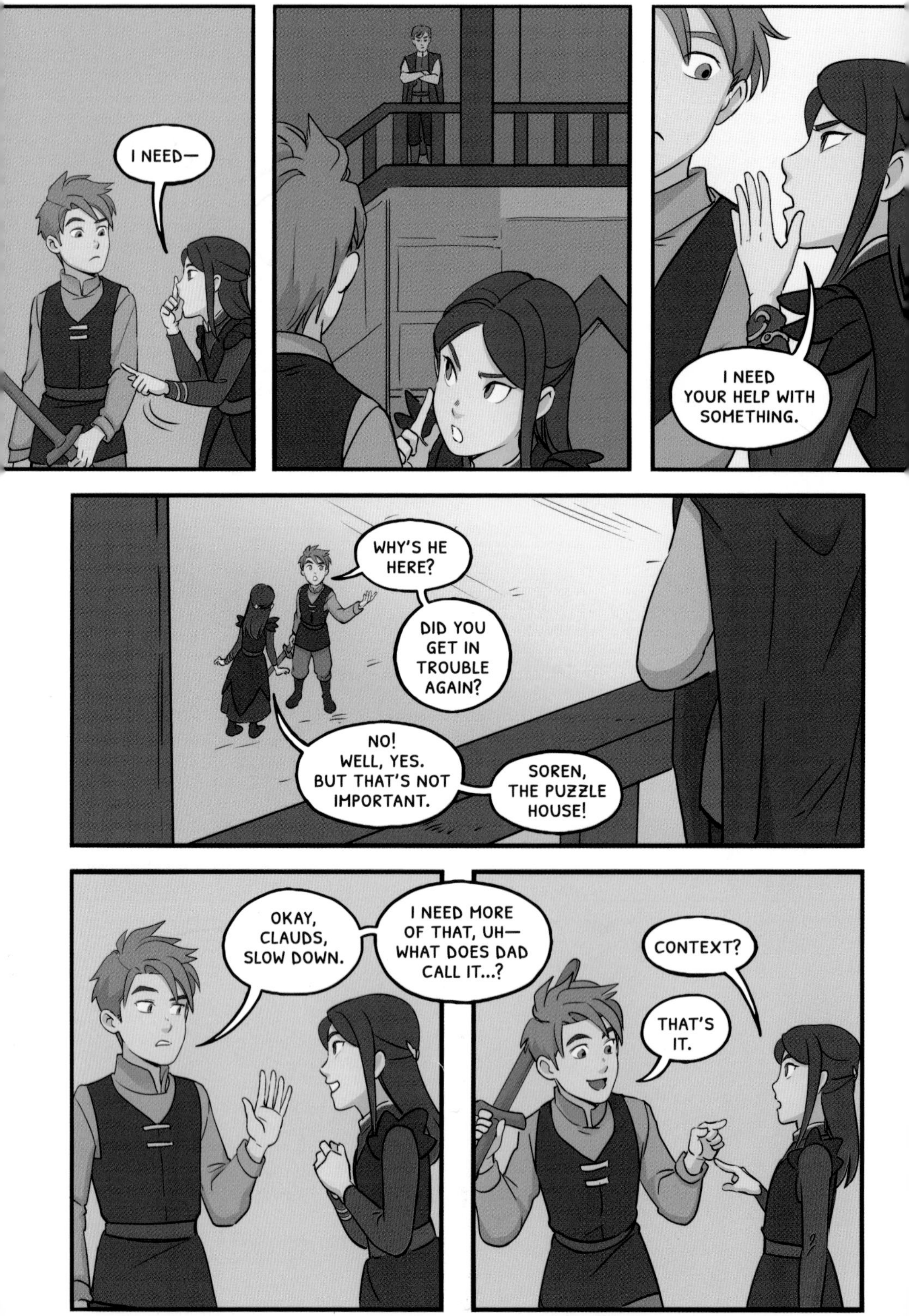
I NEED—
I NEED YOUR HELP WITH SOMETHING.
WHY'S HE HERE?
DID YOU GET IN TROUBLE AGAIN?
NO! WELL, YES. BUT THAT'S NOT IMPORTANT.
SOREN, THE PUZZLE HOUSE!
OKAY, CLAUDS, SLOW DOWN.
I NEED MORE OF THAT, UH— WHAT DOES DAD CALL IT...?
CONTEXT?
THAT'S IT.

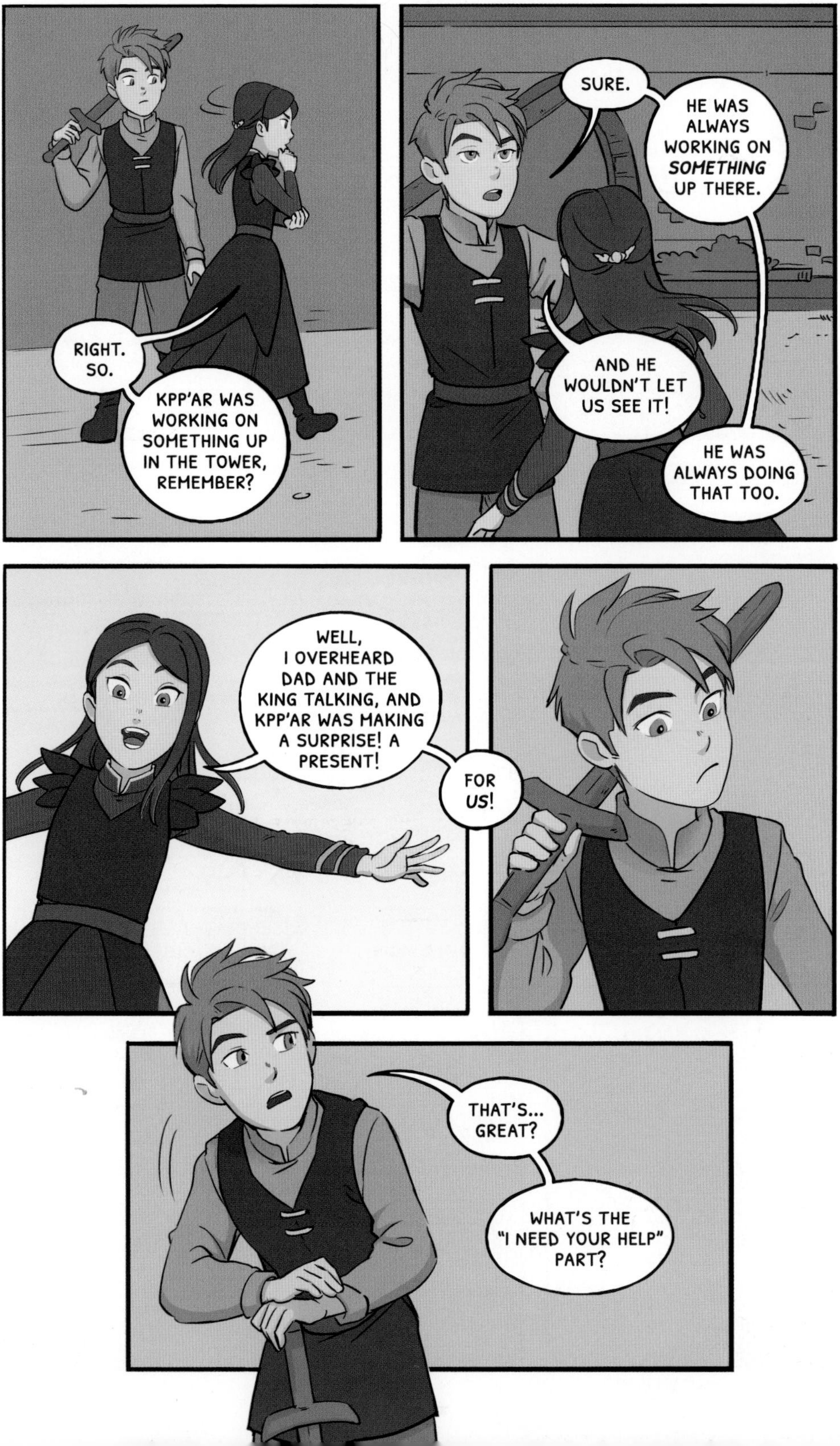
RIGHT. SO.
KPP'AR WAS WORKING ON SOMETHING UP IN THE TOWER, REMEMBER?
SURE.
HE WAS ALWAYS WORKING ON *SOMETHING* UP THERE.
AND HE WOULDN'T LET US SEE IT!
HE WAS ALWAYS DOING THAT TOO.
WELL, I OVERHEARD DAD AND THE KING TALKING, AND KPP'AR WAS MAKING A SURPRISE! A PRESENT!
FOR *US*!
THAT'S... GREAT?
WHAT'S THE "I NEED YOUR HELP" PART?

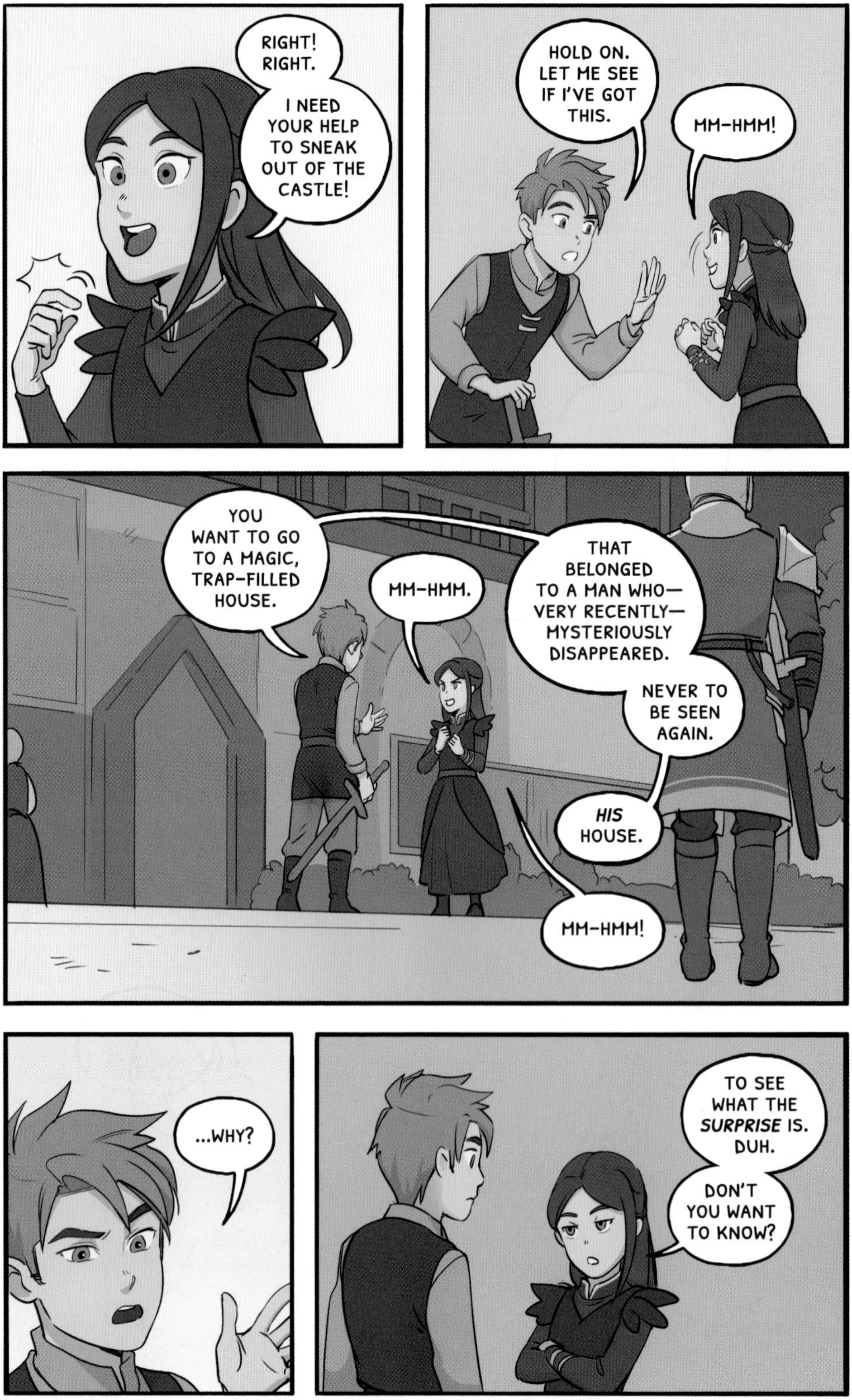
RIGHT! RIGHT.
I NEED YOUR HELP TO SNEAK OUT OF THE CASTLE!
HOLD ON. LET ME SEE IF I'VE GOT THIS.
MM-HMM!
YOU WANT TO GO TO A MAGIC, TRAP-FILLED HOUSE.
MM-HMM.
THAT BELONGED TO A MAN WHO—VERY RECENTLY—MYSTERIOUSLY DISAPPEARED.
NEVER TO BE SEEN AGAIN.
HIS HOUSE.
MM-HMM!
...WHY?
TO SEE WHAT THE *SURPRISE* IS. DUH.
DON'T YOU WANT TO KNOW?

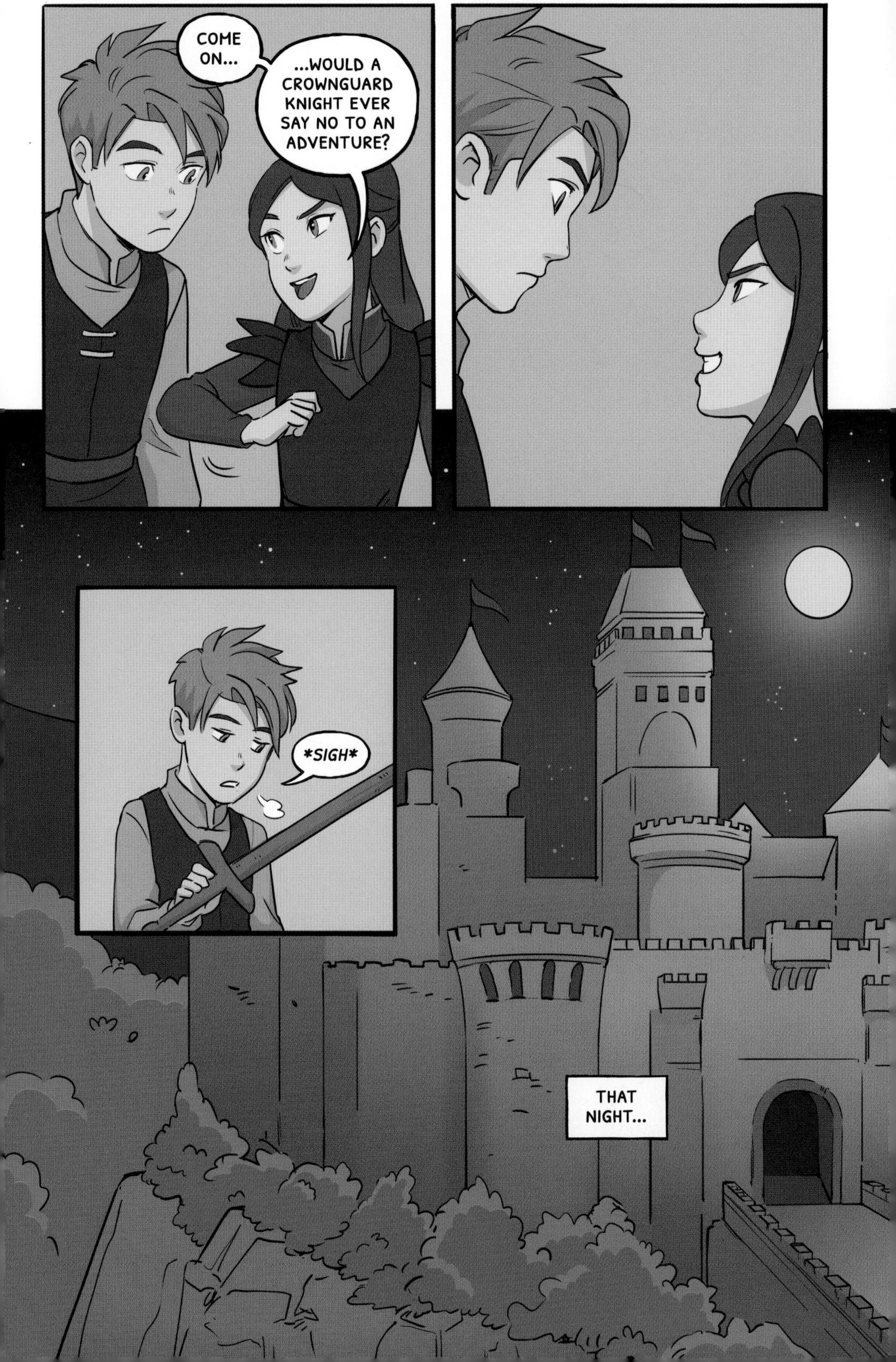
COME ON...
...WOULD A CROWNGUARD KNIGHT EVER SAY NO TO AN ADVENTURE?
SIGH
THAT NIGHT...

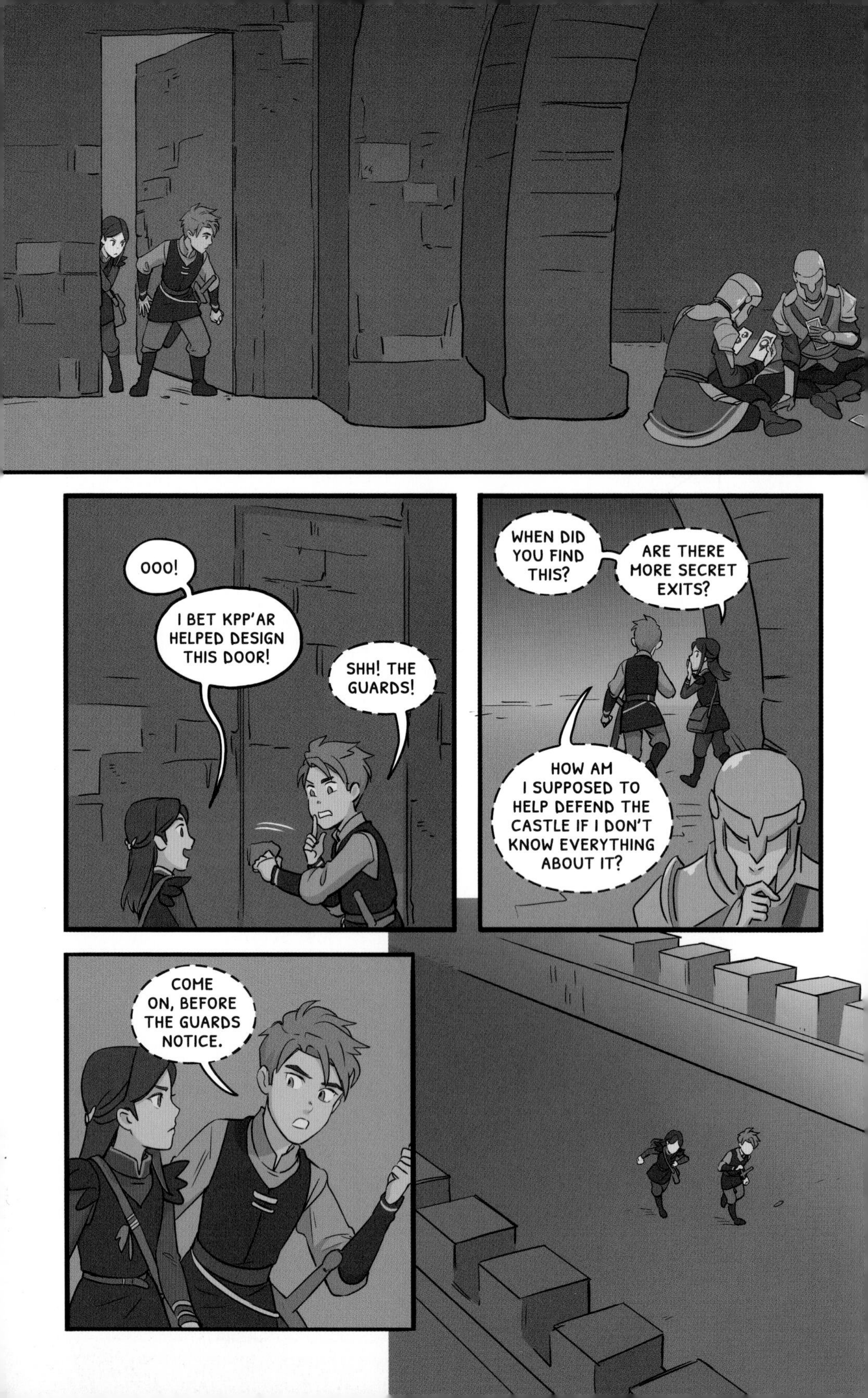
OOO!
I BET KPP'AR HELPED DESIGN THIS DOOR!
SHH! THE GUARDS!
WHEN DID YOU FIND THIS?
ARE THERE MORE SECRET EXITS?
HOW AM I SUPPOSED TO HELP DEFEND THE CASTLE IF I DON'T KNOW EVERYTHING ABOUT IT?
COME ON, BEFORE THE GUARDS NOTICE.

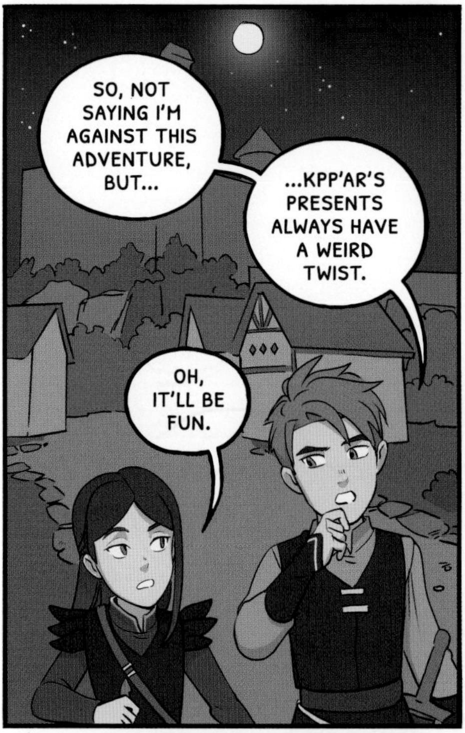
SO, NOT SAYING I'M AGAINST THIS ADVENTURE, BUT...
...KPP'AR'S PRESENTS ALWAYS HAVE A WEIRD TWIST.
OH, IT'LL BE FUN.

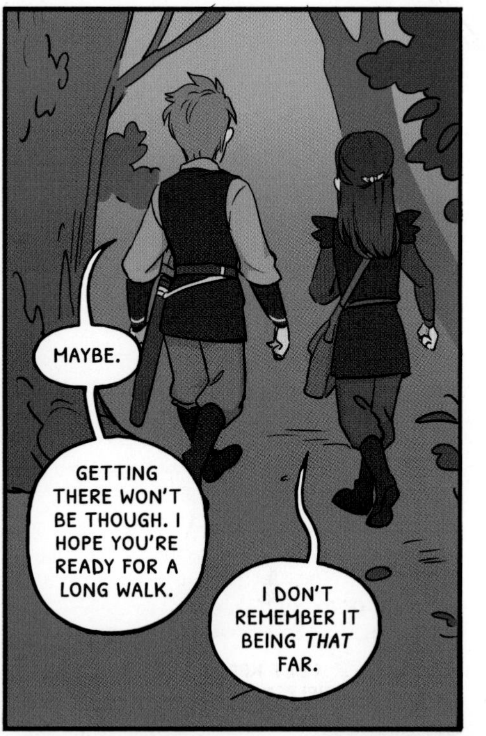
MAYBE.
GETTING THERE WON'T BE THOUGH. I HOPE YOU'RE READY FOR A LONG WALK.
I DON'T REMEMBER IT BEING *THAT* FAR.

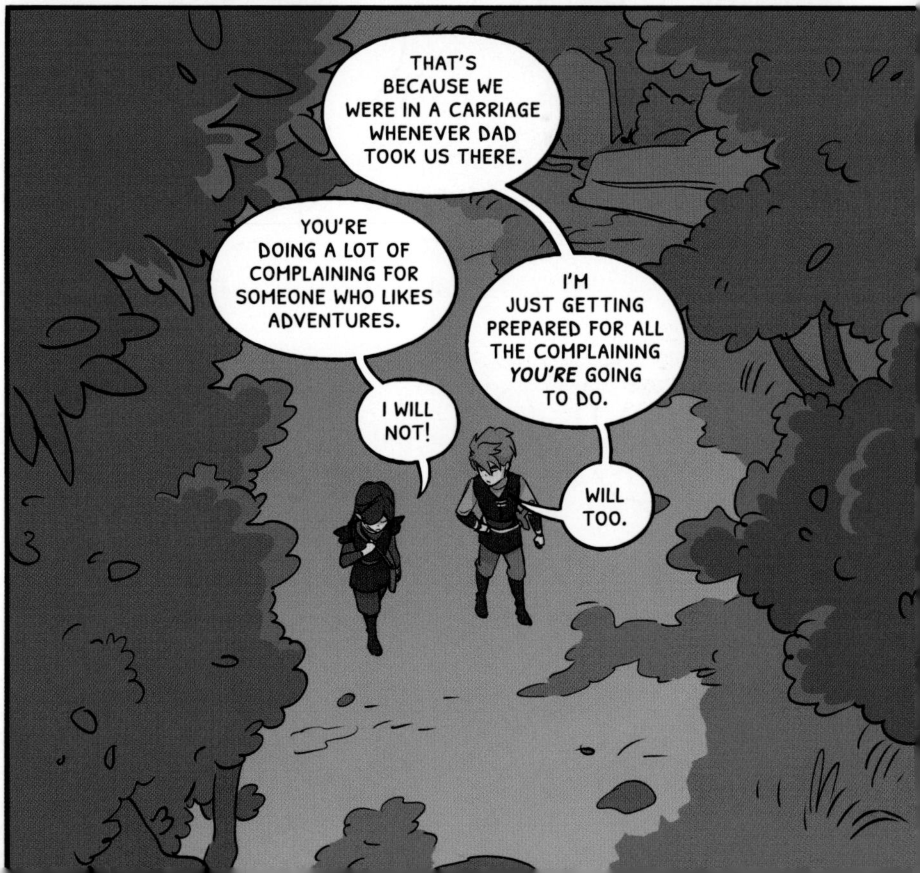
THAT'S BECAUSE WE WERE IN A CARRIAGE WHENEVER DAD TOOK US THERE.
YOU'RE DOING A LOT OF COMPLAINING FOR SOMEONE WHO LIKES ADVENTURES.
I'M JUST GETTING PREPARED FOR ALL THE COMPLAINING *YOU'RE* GOING TO DO.
I WILL NOT!
WILL TOO.

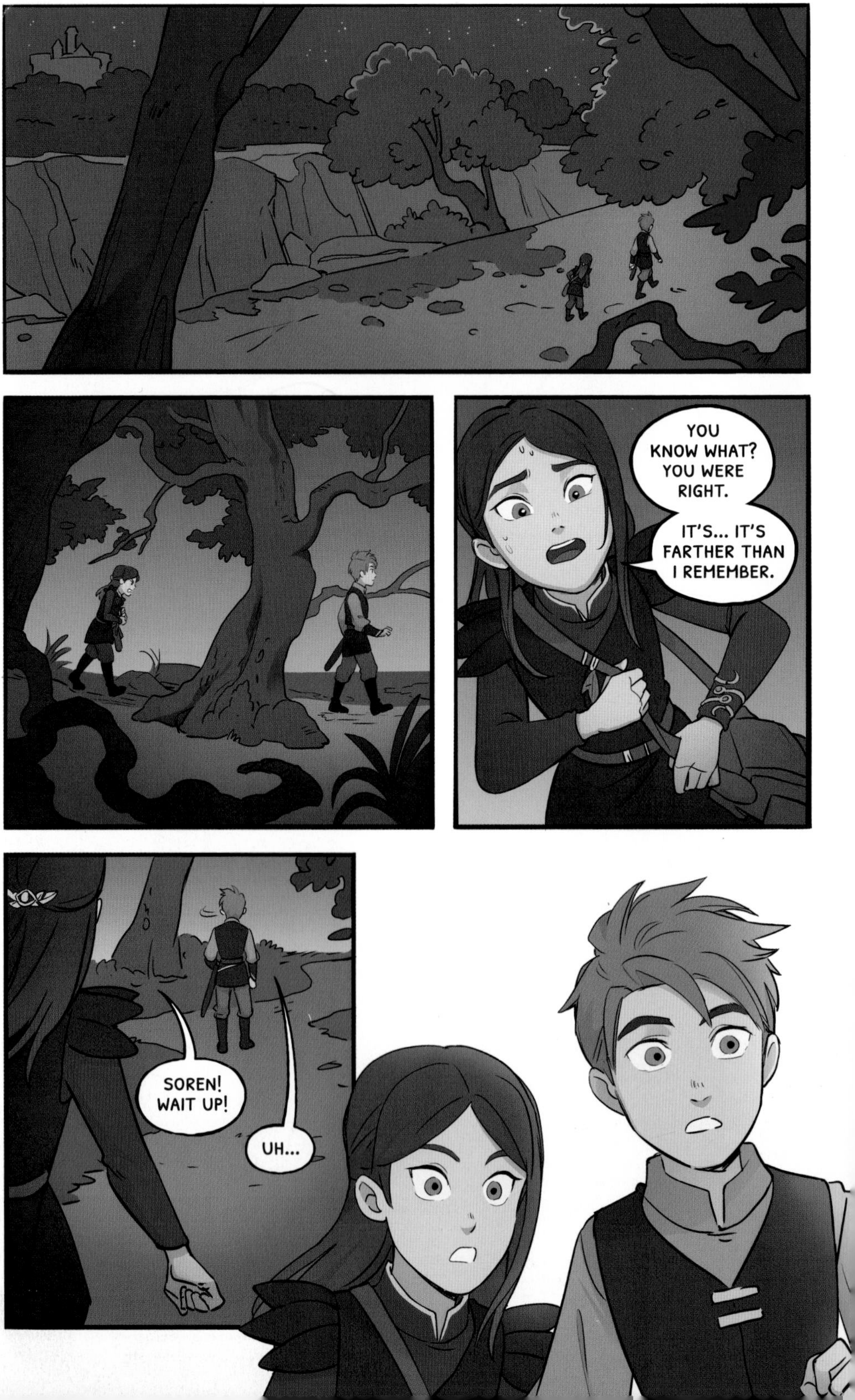
YOU KNOW WHAT? YOU WERE RIGHT.
IT'S... IT'S FARTHER THAN I REMEMBER.
SOREN! WAIT UP!
UH...

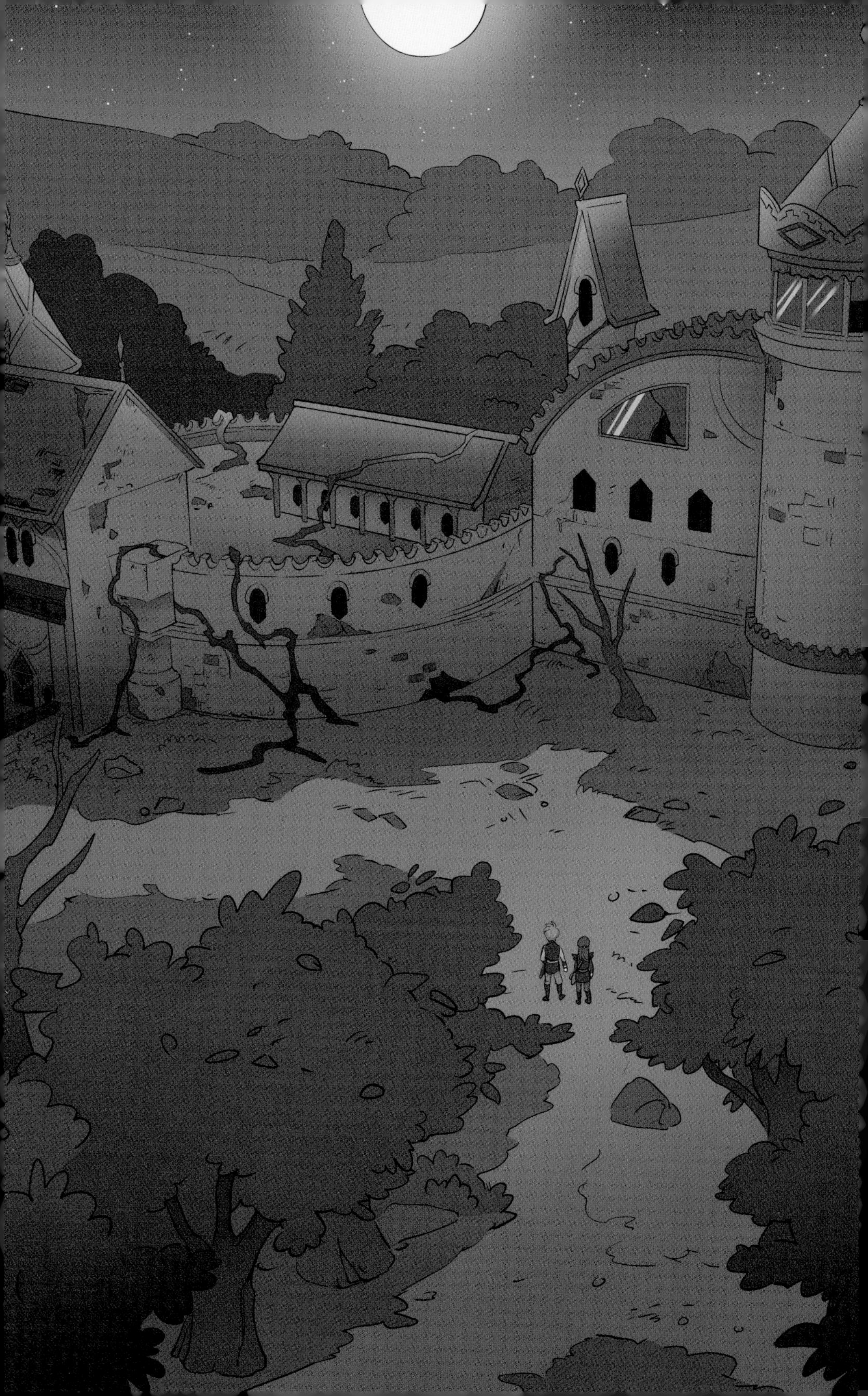

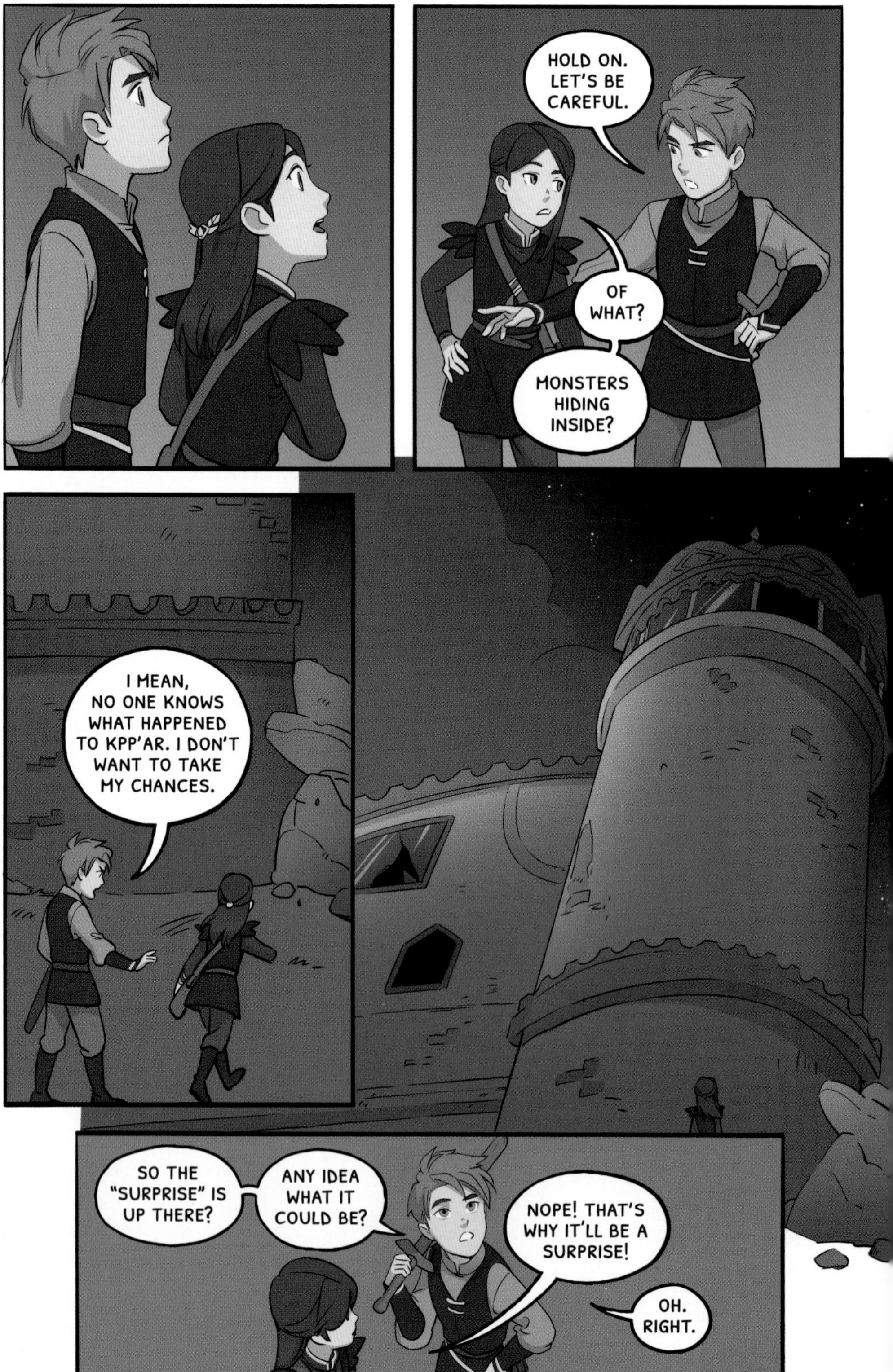
HOLD ON. LET'S BE CAREFUL.
OF WHAT?
MONSTERS HIDING INSIDE?
I MEAN, NO ONE KNOWS WHAT HAPPENED TO KPP'AR. I DON'T WANT TO TAKE MY CHANCES.
SO THE "SURPRISE" IS UP THERE?
ANY IDEA WHAT IT COULD BE?
NOPE! THAT'S WHY IT'LL BE A SURPRISE!
OH. RIGHT.

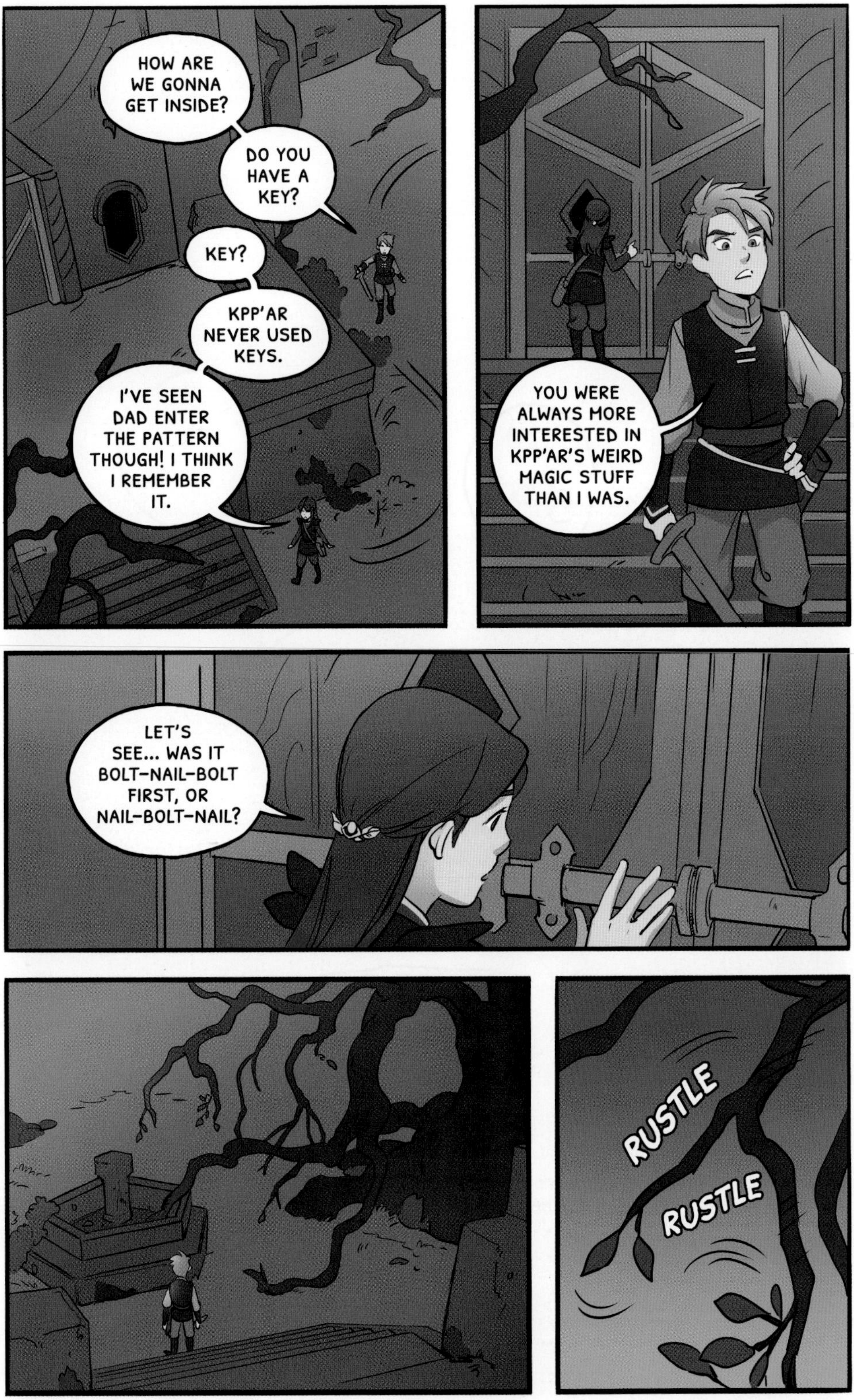
HOW ARE WE GONNA GET INSIDE?
DO YOU HAVE A KEY?
KEY?
KPP'AR NEVER USED KEYS.
I'VE SEEN DAD ENTER THE PATTERN THOUGH! I THINK I REMEMBER IT.
YOU WERE ALWAYS MORE INTERESTED IN KPP'AR'S WEIRD MAGIC STUFF THAN I WAS.
LET'S SEE... WAS IT BOLT-NAIL-BOLT FIRST, OR NAIL-BOLT-NAIL?
RUSTLE
RUSTLE

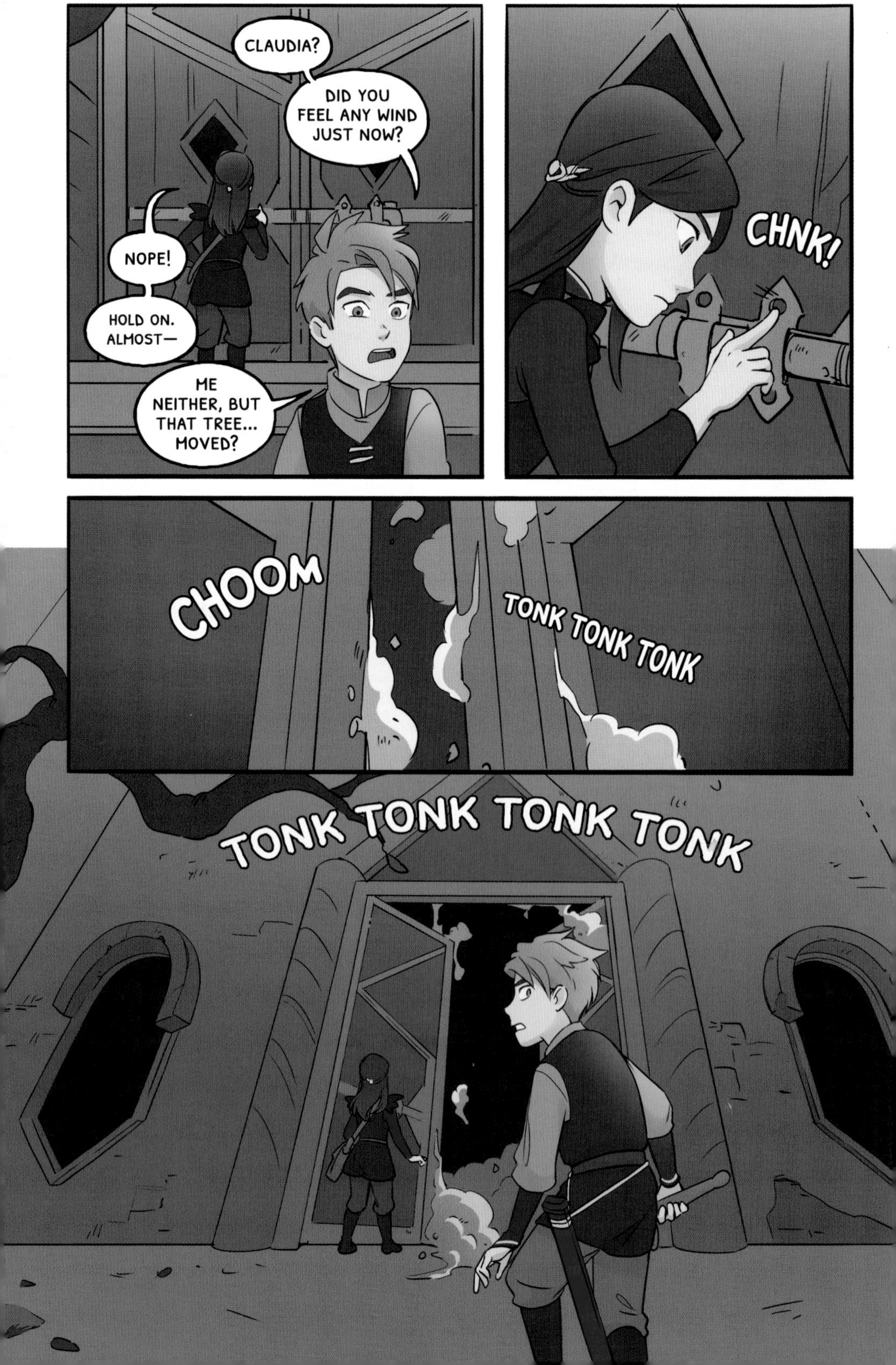
CLAUDIA?
DID YOU FEEL ANY WIND JUST NOW?
NOPE!
HOLD ON. ALMOST—
ME NEITHER, BUT THAT TREE... MOVED?
CHNK!
CHOOM
TONK TONK TONK
TONK TONK TONK TONK

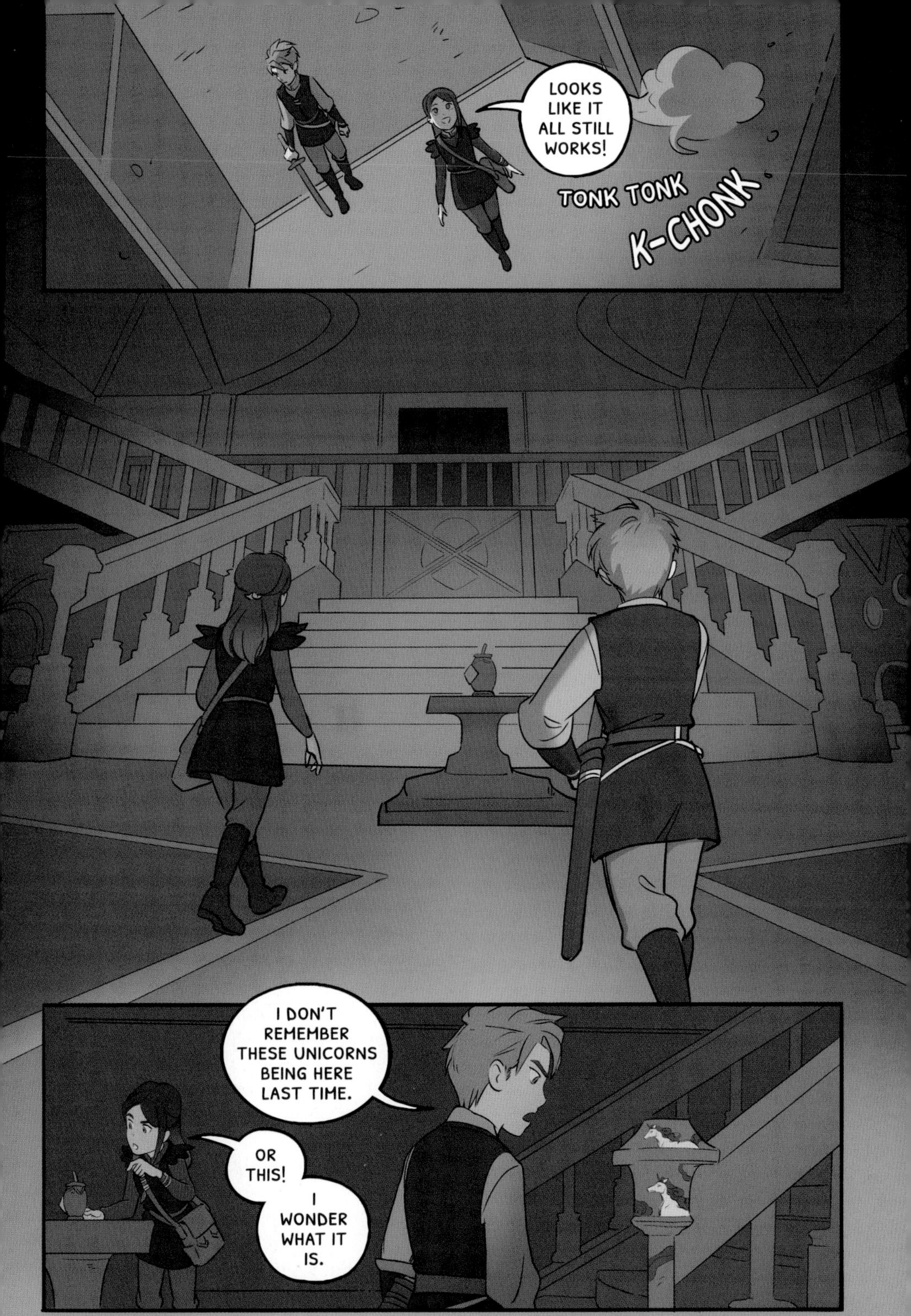
LOOKS LIKE IT ALL STILL WORKS!
TONK TONK
K-CHONK
I DON'T REMEMBER THESE UNICORNS BEING HERE LAST TIME.
OR THIS!
I WONDER WHAT IT IS.

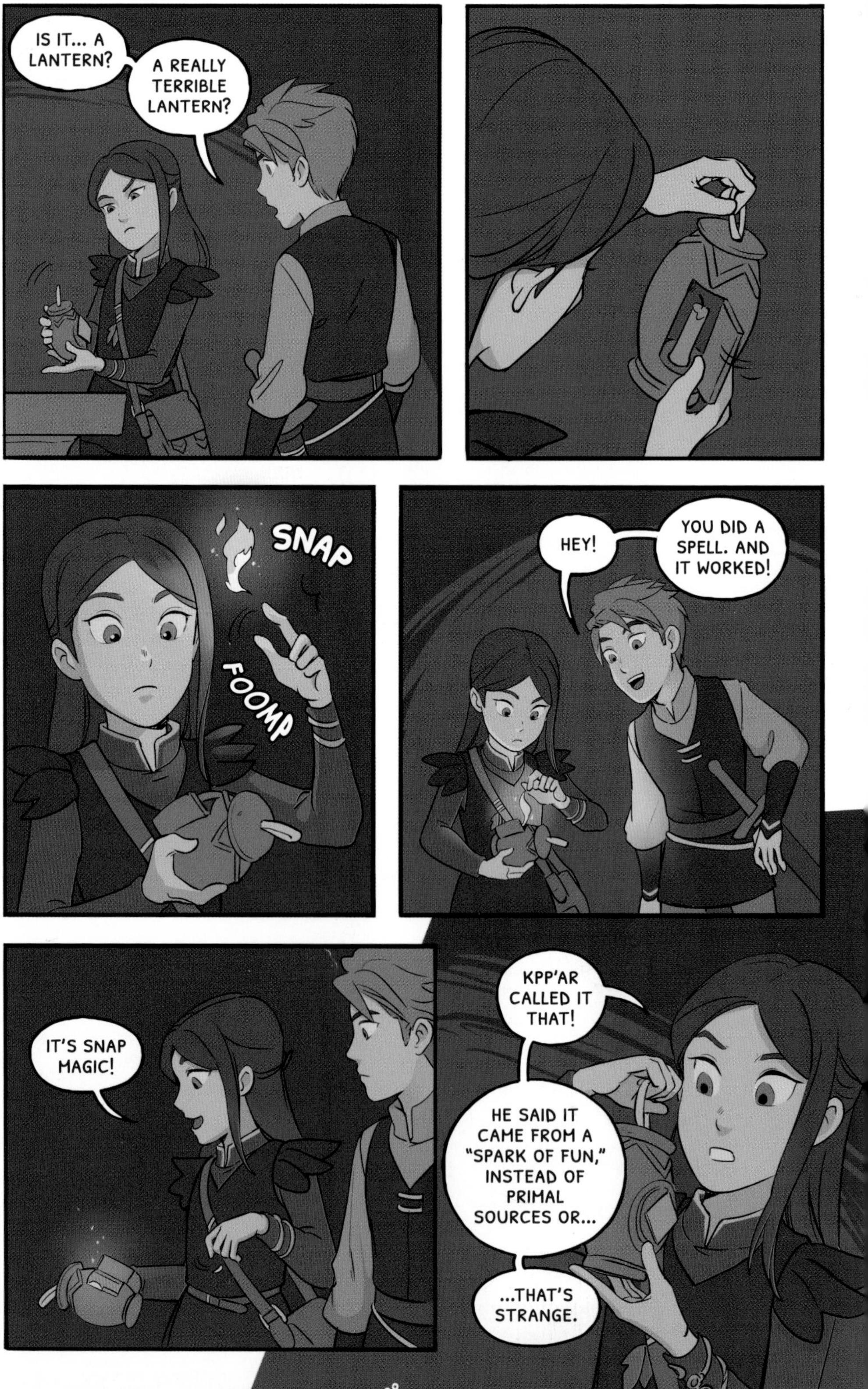
IS IT... A LANTERN?
A REALLY TERRIBLE LANTERN?
SNAP
FOOMP
HEY!
YOU DID A SPELL. AND IT WORKED!
IT'S SNAP MAGIC!
KPP'AR CALLED IT THAT!
HE SAID IT CAME FROM A "SPARK OF FUN," INSTEAD OF PRIMAL SOURCES OR...
...THAT'S STRANGE.

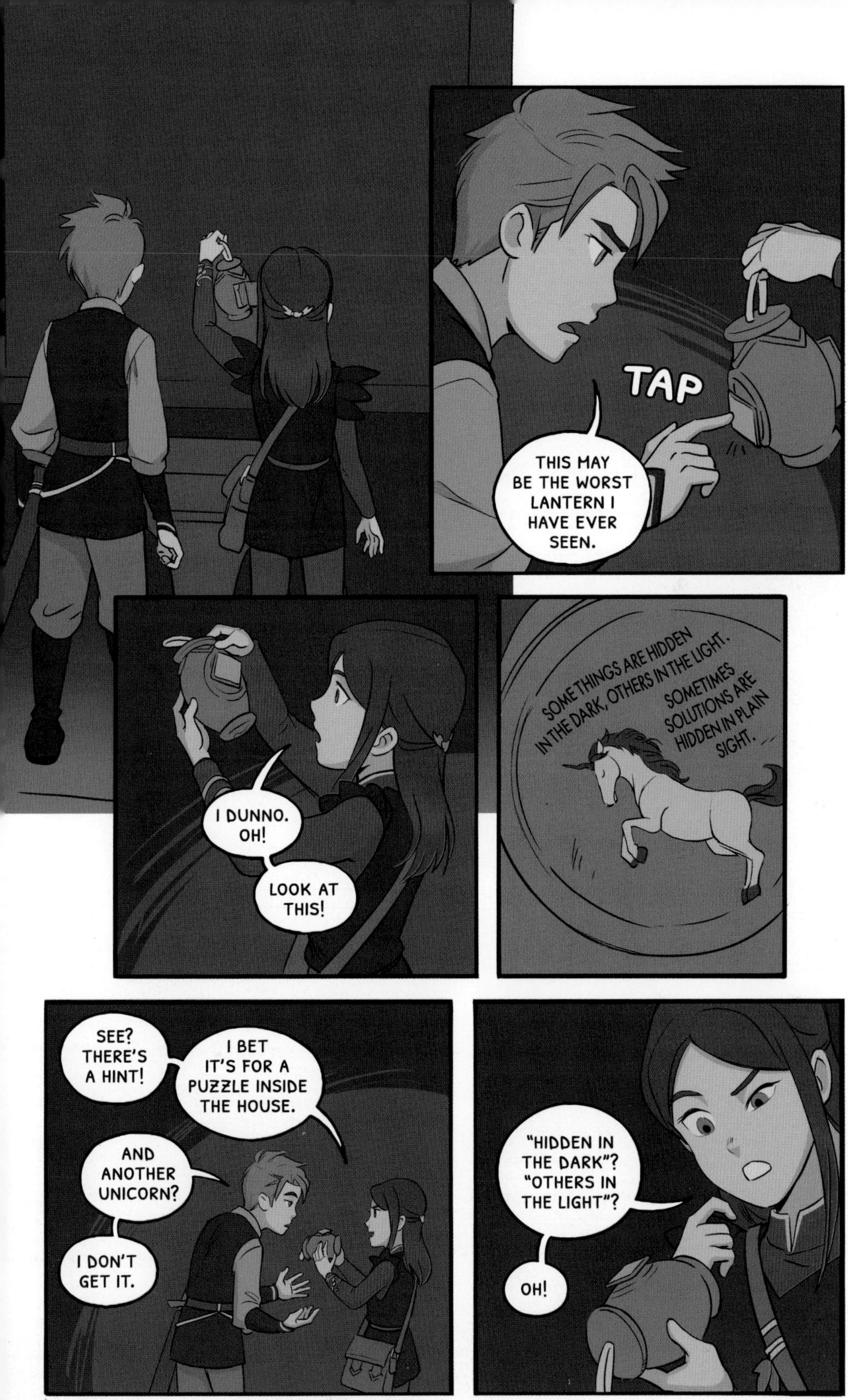
TAP
THIS MAY BE THE WORST LANTERN I HAVE EVER SEEN.
I DUNNO. OH!
LOOK AT THIS!
SOME THINGS ARE HIDDEN IN THE DARK, OTHERS IN THE LIGHT.
SOMETIMES SOLUTIONS ARE HIDDEN IN PLAIN SIGHT.
SEE? THERE'S A HINT!
I BET IT'S FOR A PUZZLE INSIDE THE HOUSE.
AND ANOTHER UNICORN?
I DON'T GET IT.
"HIDDEN IN THE DARK"? "OTHERS IN THE LIGHT"?
OH!

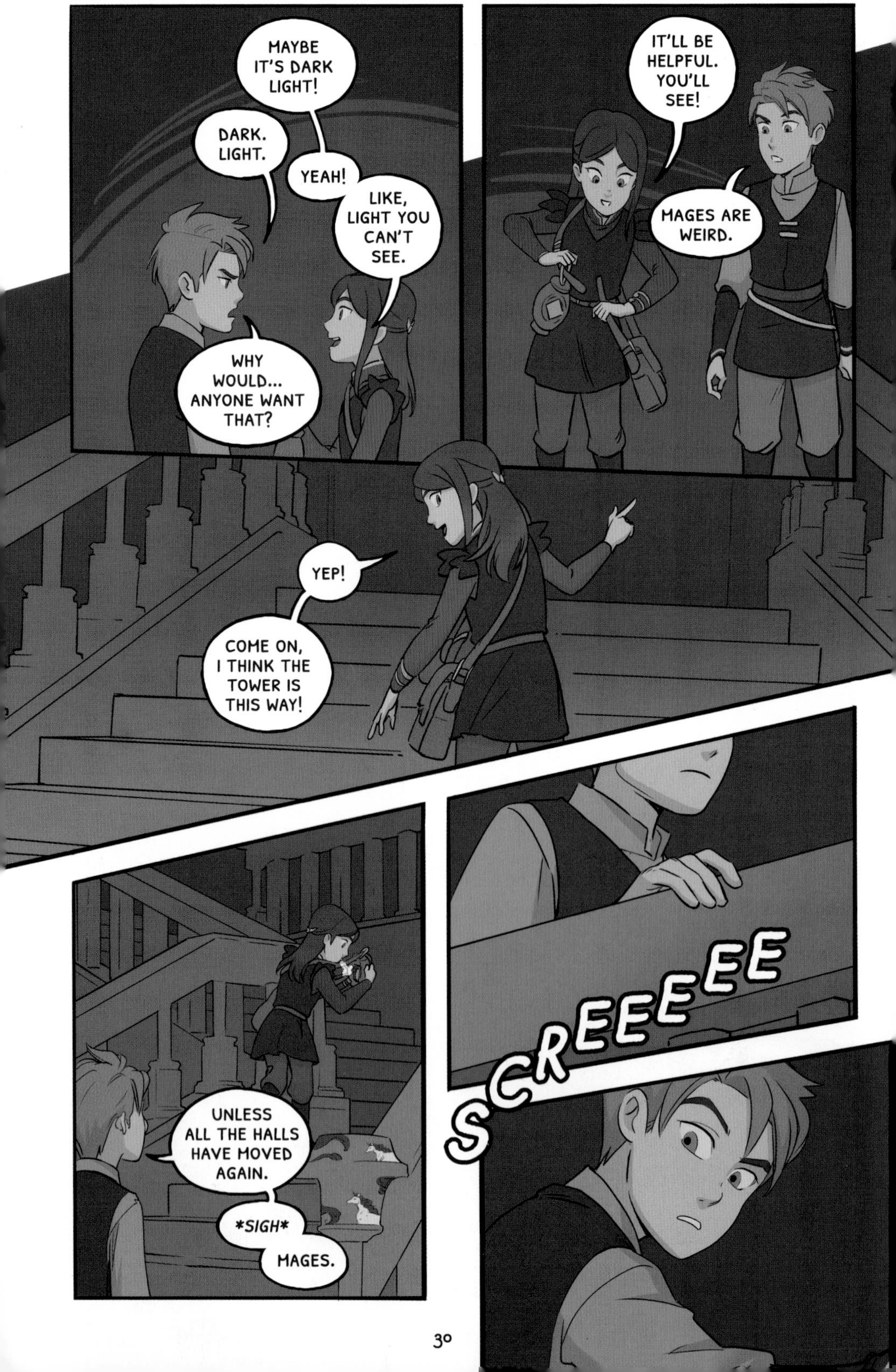
MAYBE IT'S DARK LIGHT!
DARK. LIGHT.
YEAH!
LIKE, LIGHT YOU CAN'T SEE.
WHY WOULD... ANYONE WANT THAT?
IT'LL BE HELPFUL. YOU'LL SEE!
MAGES ARE WEIRD.
YEP!
COME ON, I THINK THE TOWER IS THIS WAY!
UNLESS ALL THE HALLS HAVE MOVED AGAIN.
SIGH
MAGES.
SCREEEEEE

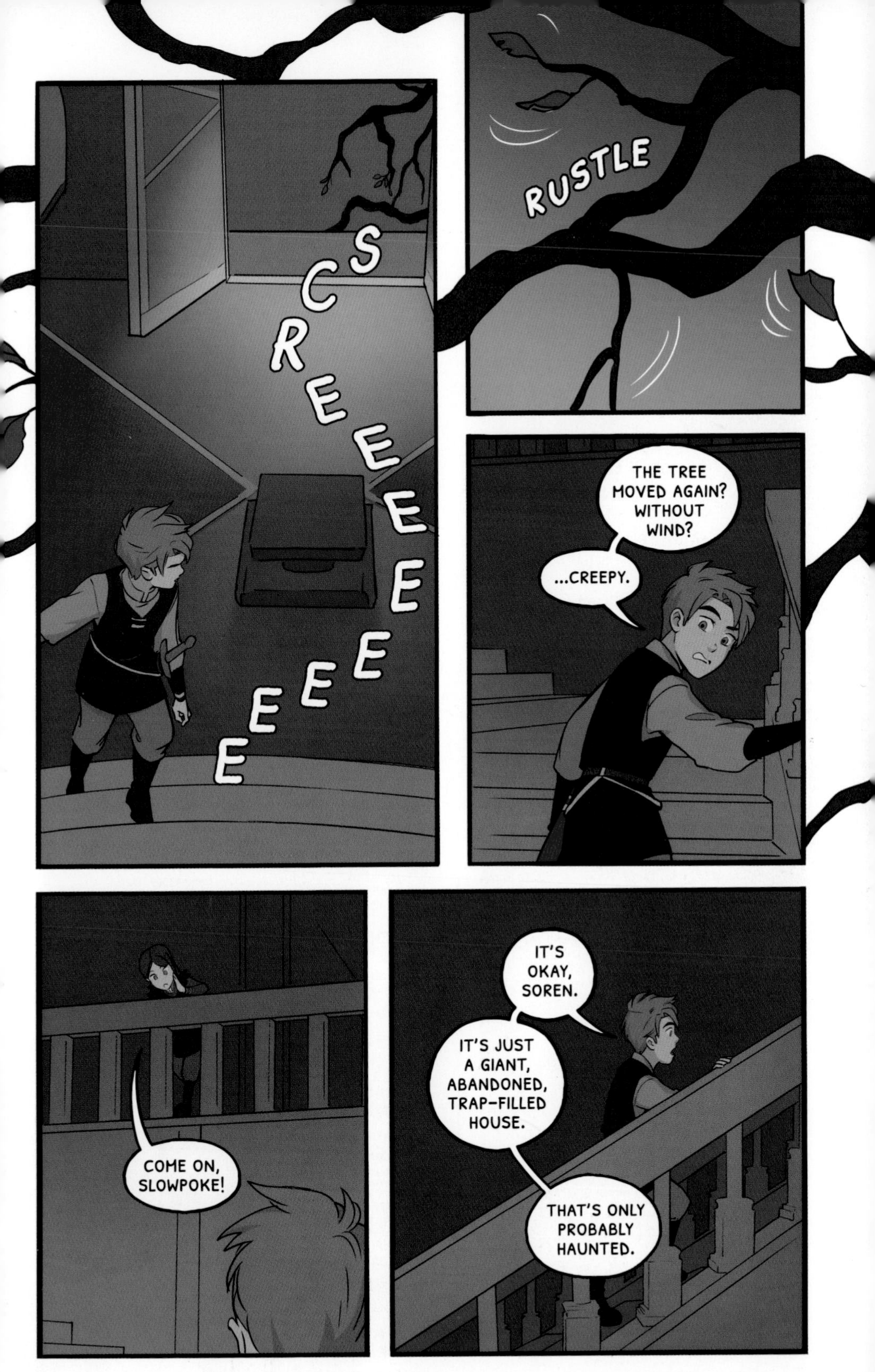
SCREEEEEEEE
RUSTLE
THE TREE MOVED AGAIN? WITHOUT WIND?
...CREEPY.
COME ON, SLOWPOKE!
IT'S OKAY, SOREN.
IT'S JUST A GIANT, ABANDONED, TRAP-FILLED HOUSE.
THAT'S ONLY PROBABLY HAUNTED.

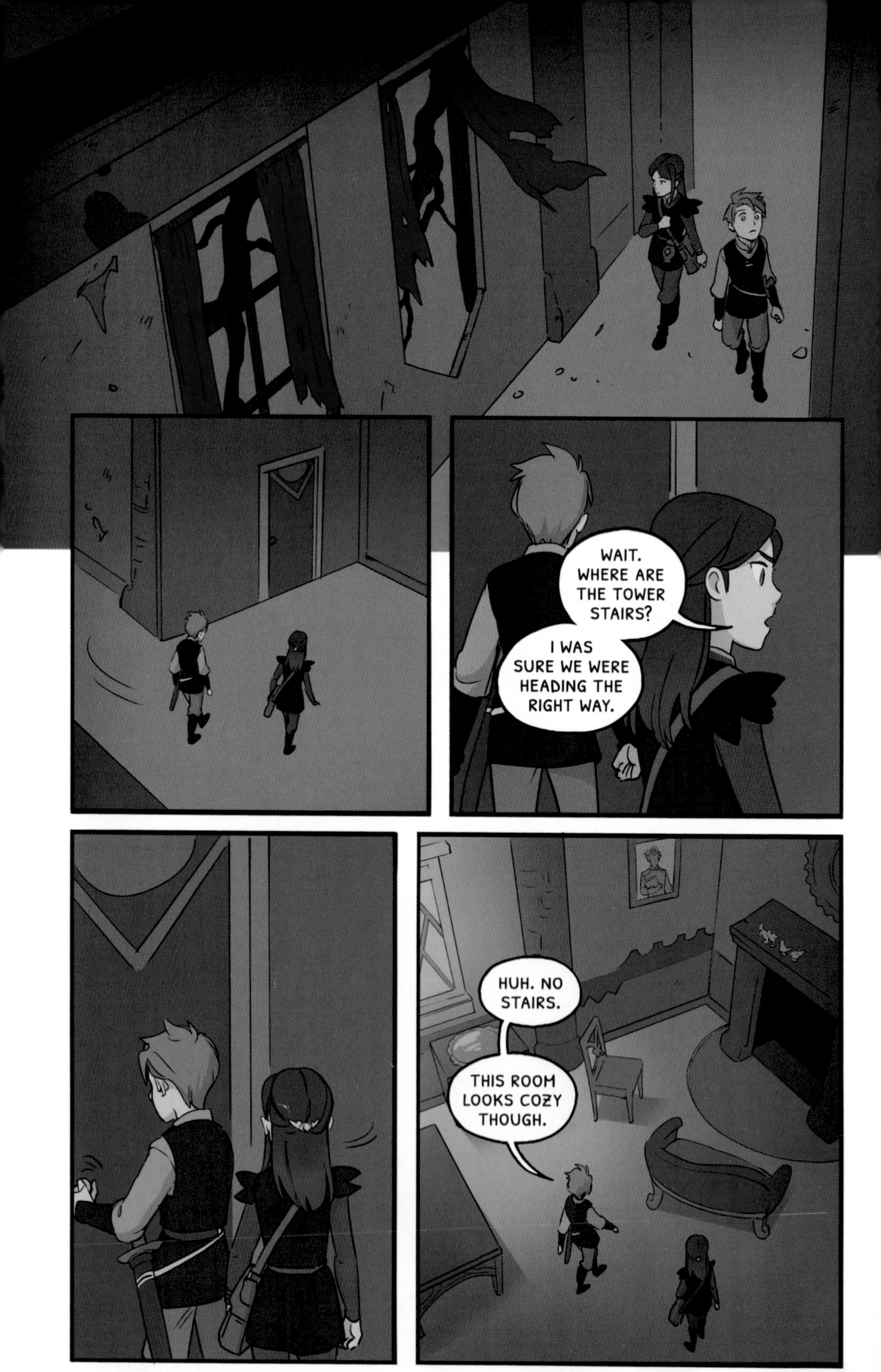
WAIT. WHERE ARE THE TOWER STAIRS?
I WAS SURE WE WERE HEADING THE RIGHT WAY.
HUH. NO STAIRS.
THIS ROOM LOOKS COZY THOUGH.

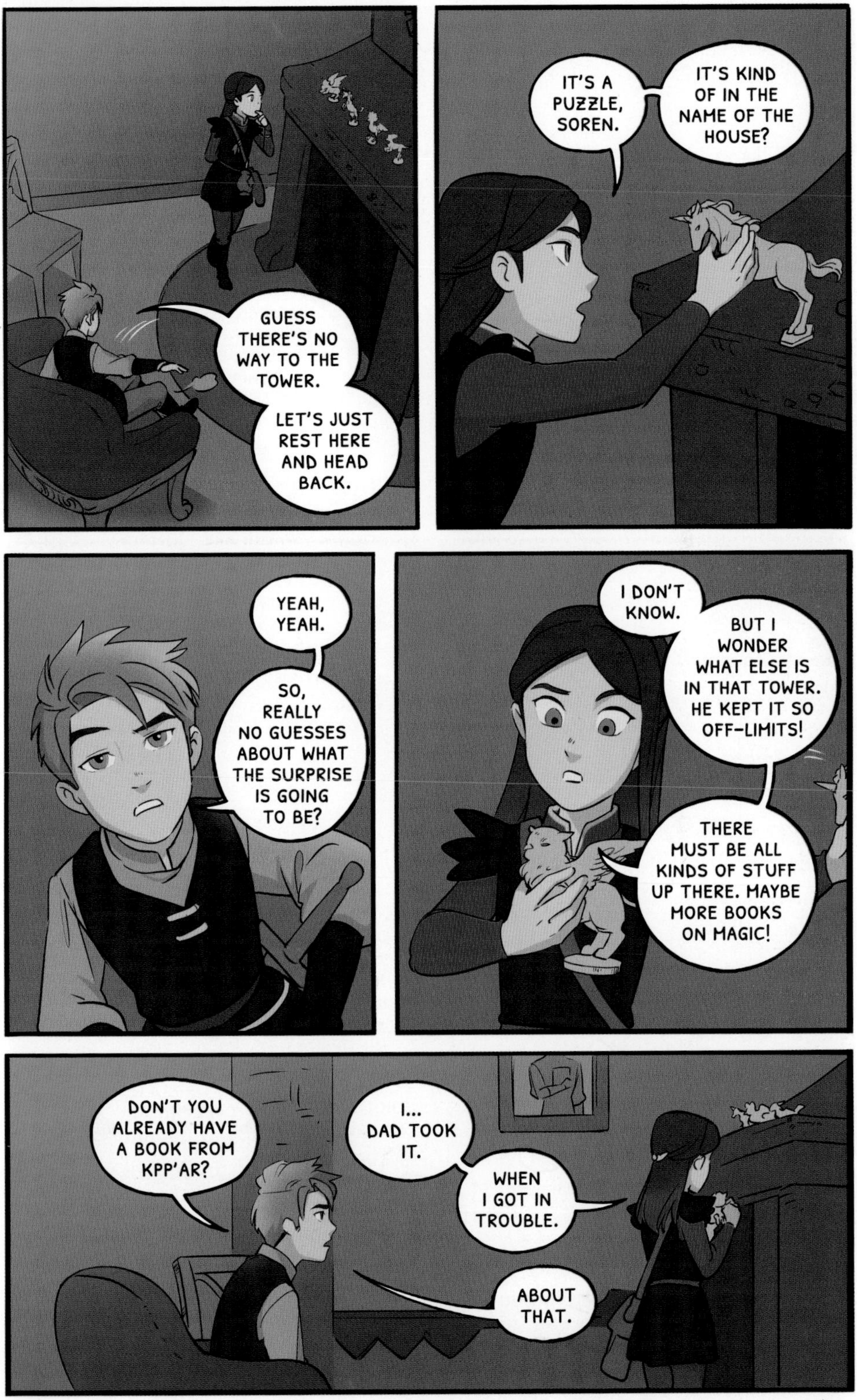
GUESS THERE'S NO WAY TO THE TOWER.
LET'S JUST REST HERE AND HEAD BACK.
IT'S A PUZZLE, SOREN.
IT'S KIND OF IN THE NAME OF THE HOUSE?
YEAH, YEAH.
SO, REALLY NO GUESSES ABOUT WHAT THE SURPRISE IS GOING TO BE?
I DON'T KNOW.
BUT I WONDER WHAT ELSE IS IN THAT TOWER. HE KEPT IT SO OFF-LIMITS!
THERE MUST BE ALL KINDS OF STUFF UP THERE. MAYBE MORE BOOKS ON MAGIC!
DON'T YOU ALREADY HAVE A BOOK FROM KPP'AR?
I... DAD TOOK IT.
WHEN I GOT IN TROUBLE.
ABOUT THAT.

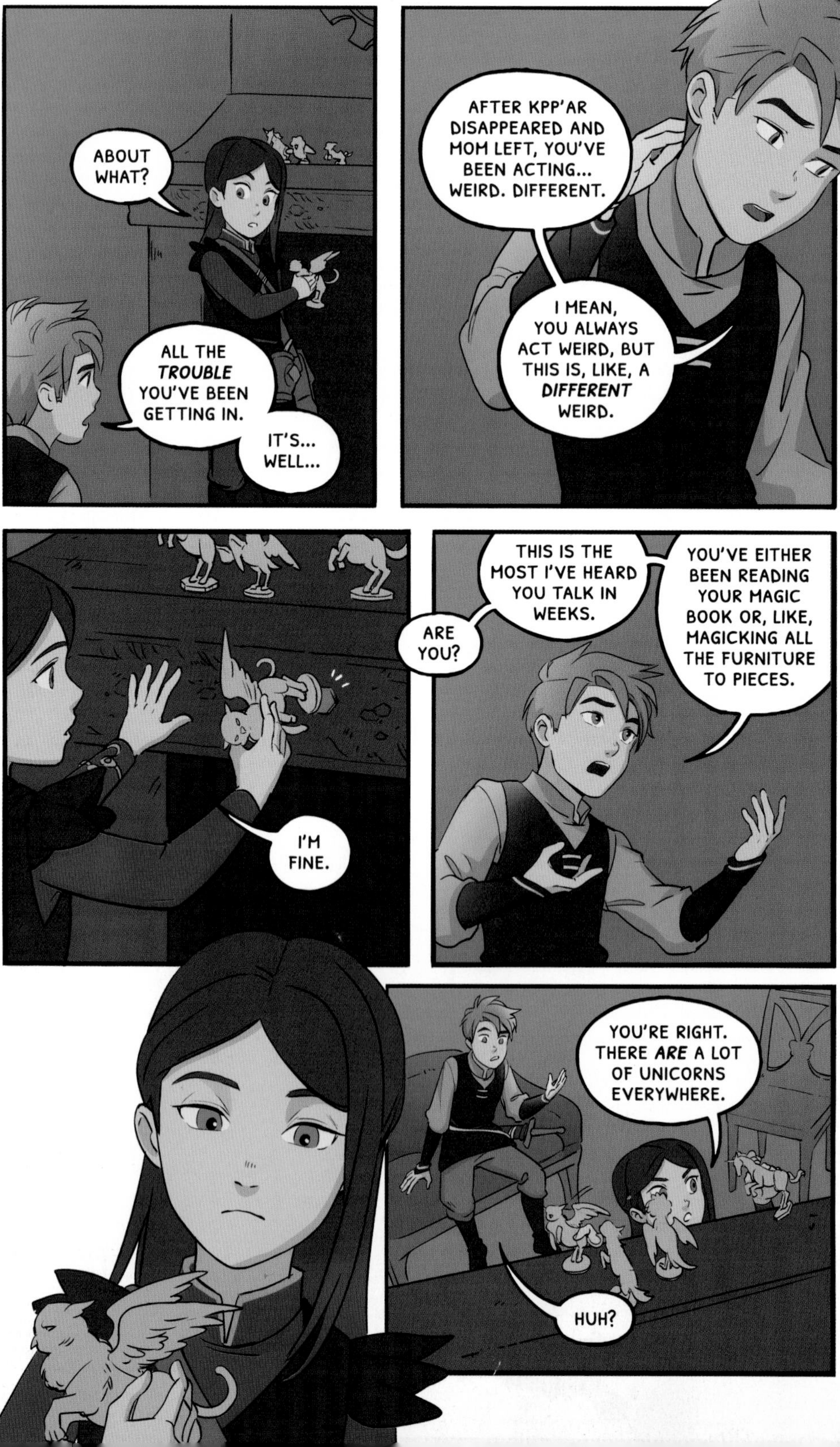
ABOUT WHAT?
ALL THE *TROUBLE* YOU'VE BEEN GETTING IN.
IT'S... WELL...
AFTER KPP'AR DISAPPEARED AND MOM LEFT, YOU'VE BEEN ACTING... WEIRD. DIFFERENT.
I MEAN, YOU ALWAYS ACT WEIRD, BUT THIS IS, LIKE, A *DIFFERENT* WEIRD.
I'M FINE.
ARE YOU?
THIS IS THE MOST I'VE HEARD YOU TALK IN WEEKS.
YOU'VE EITHER BEEN READING YOUR MAGIC BOOK OR, LIKE, MAGICKING ALL THE FURNITURE TO PIECES.
YOU'RE RIGHT. THERE *ARE* A LOT OF UNICORNS EVERYWHERE.
HUH?

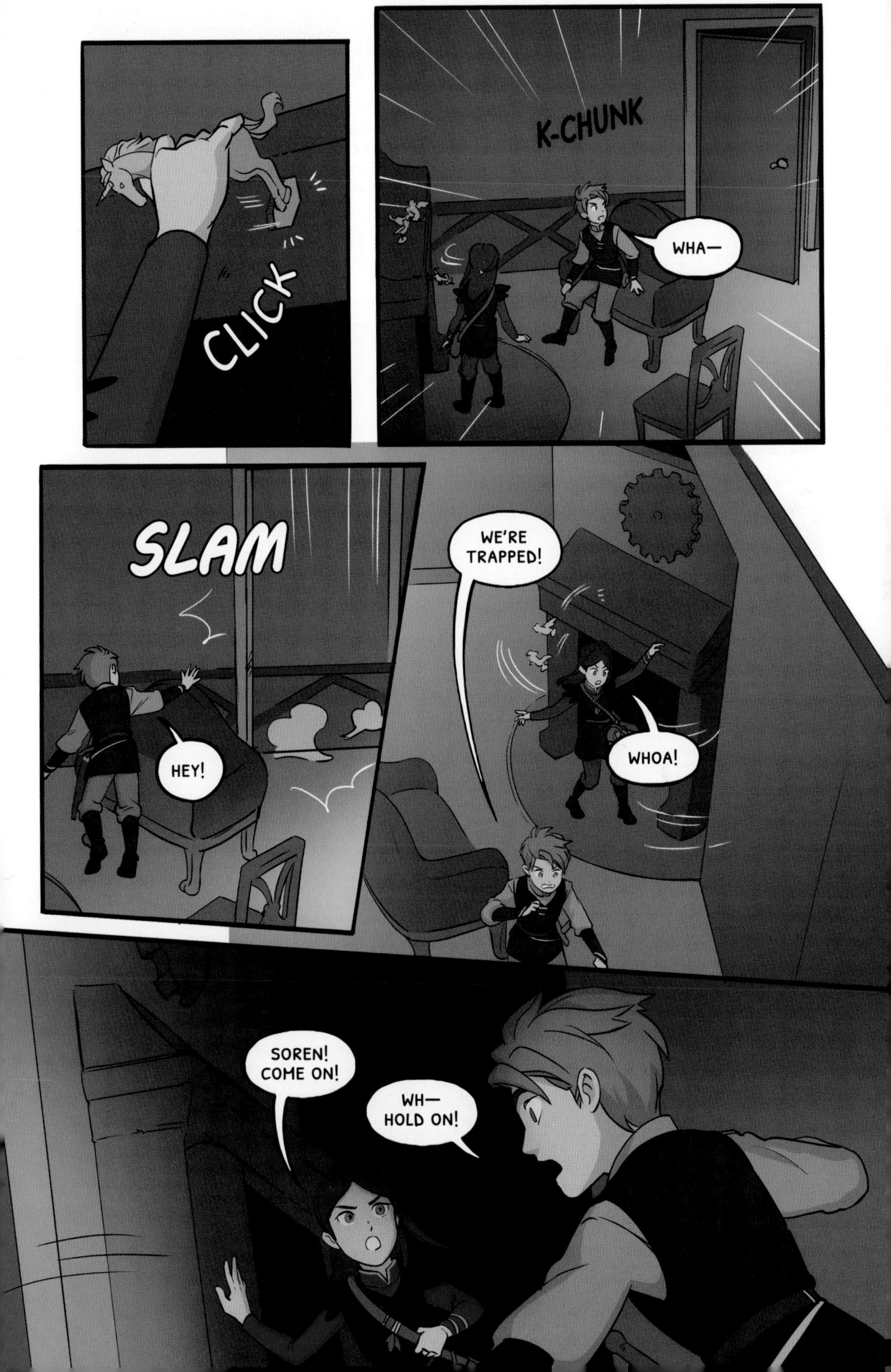
CLICK
K-CHUNK
WHA—
SLAM
HEY!
WE'RE TRAPPED!
WHOA!
SOREN! COME ON!
WH— HOLD ON!

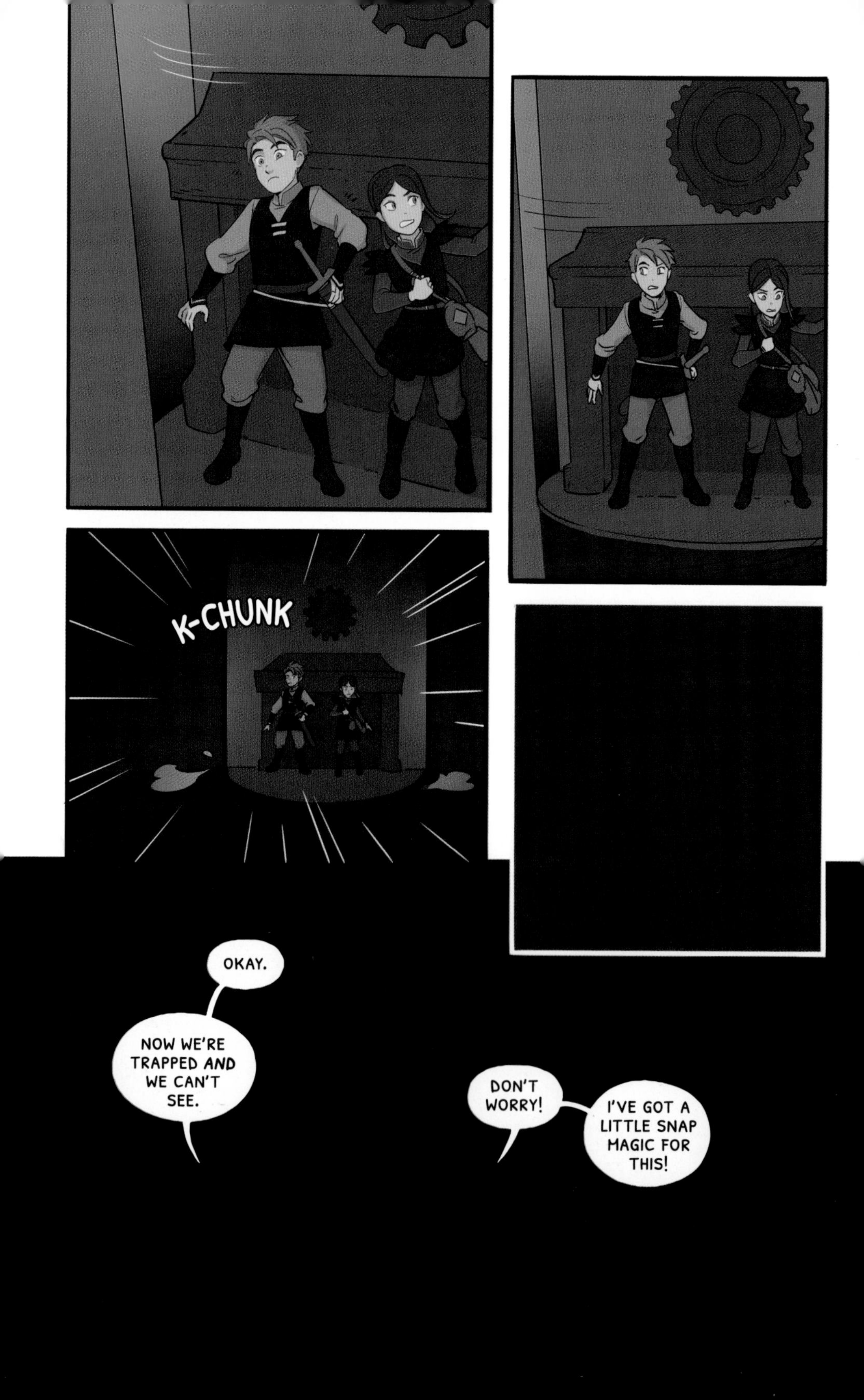
K-CHUNK
OKAY.
NOW WE'RE TRAPPED AND WE CAN'T SEE.
DON'T WORRY!
I'VE GOT A LITTLE SNAP MAGIC FOR THIS!

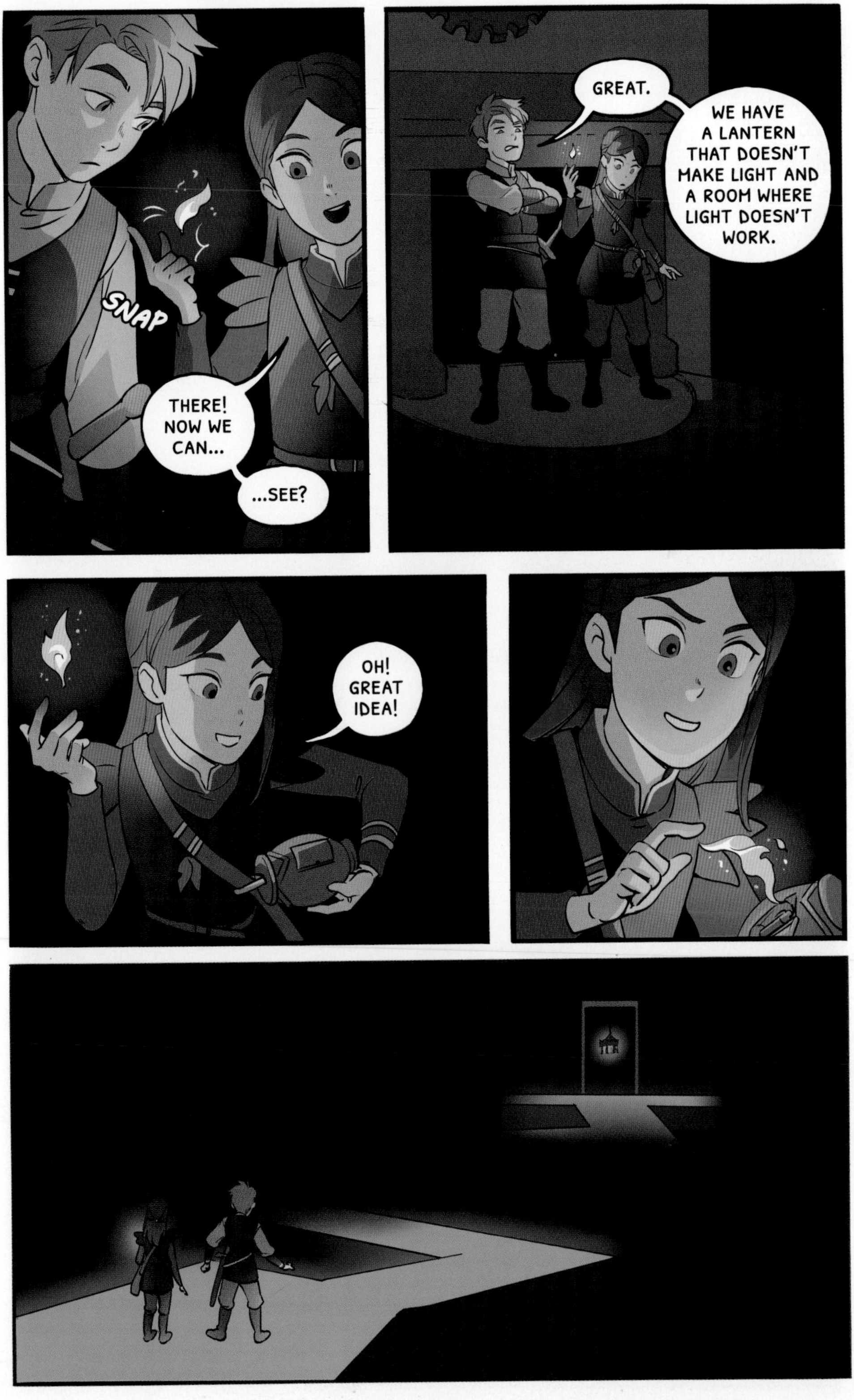
SNAP
THERE! NOW WE CAN...
...SEE?
GREAT.
WE HAVE A LANTERN THAT DOESN'T MAKE LIGHT AND A ROOM WHERE LIGHT DOESN'T WORK.
OH! GREAT IDEA!

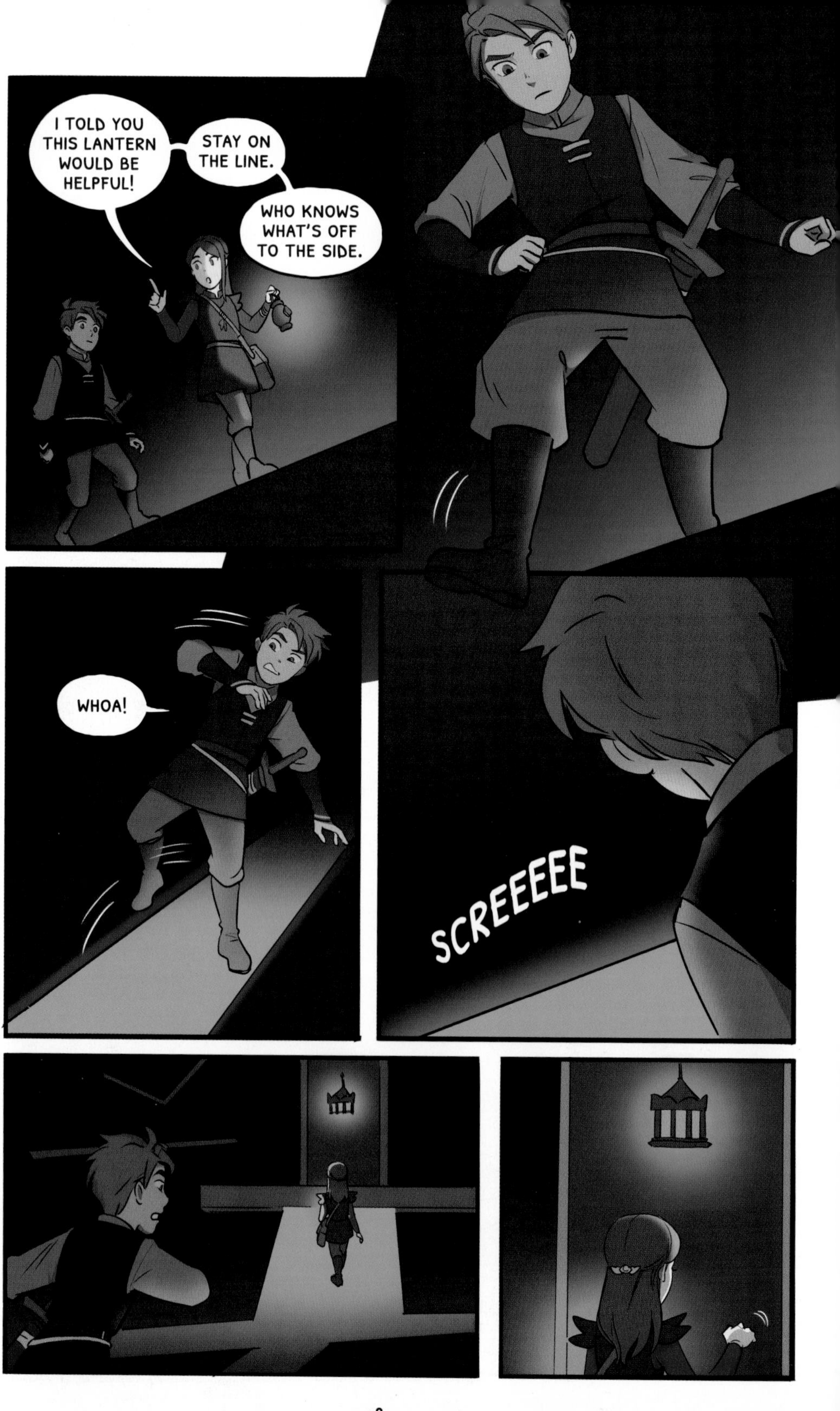
I TOLD YOU THIS LANTERN WOULD BE HELPFUL!
STAY ON THE LINE.
WHO KNOWS WHAT'S OFF TO THE SIDE.
WHOA!
SCREEEEEE

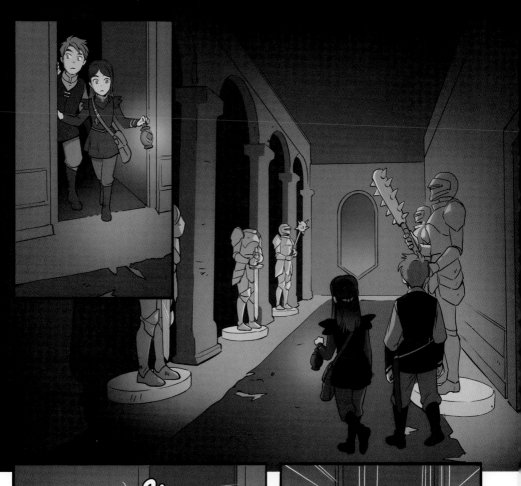

SLAM

K-CHUNK

IT *STILL* FEELS LIKE WE'RE GETTING TRAPPED.

IT'S JUST A PUZZLE, SOREN!

KPP'AR WOULDN'T MAKE A PUZZLE WITHOUT A SOLUTION.

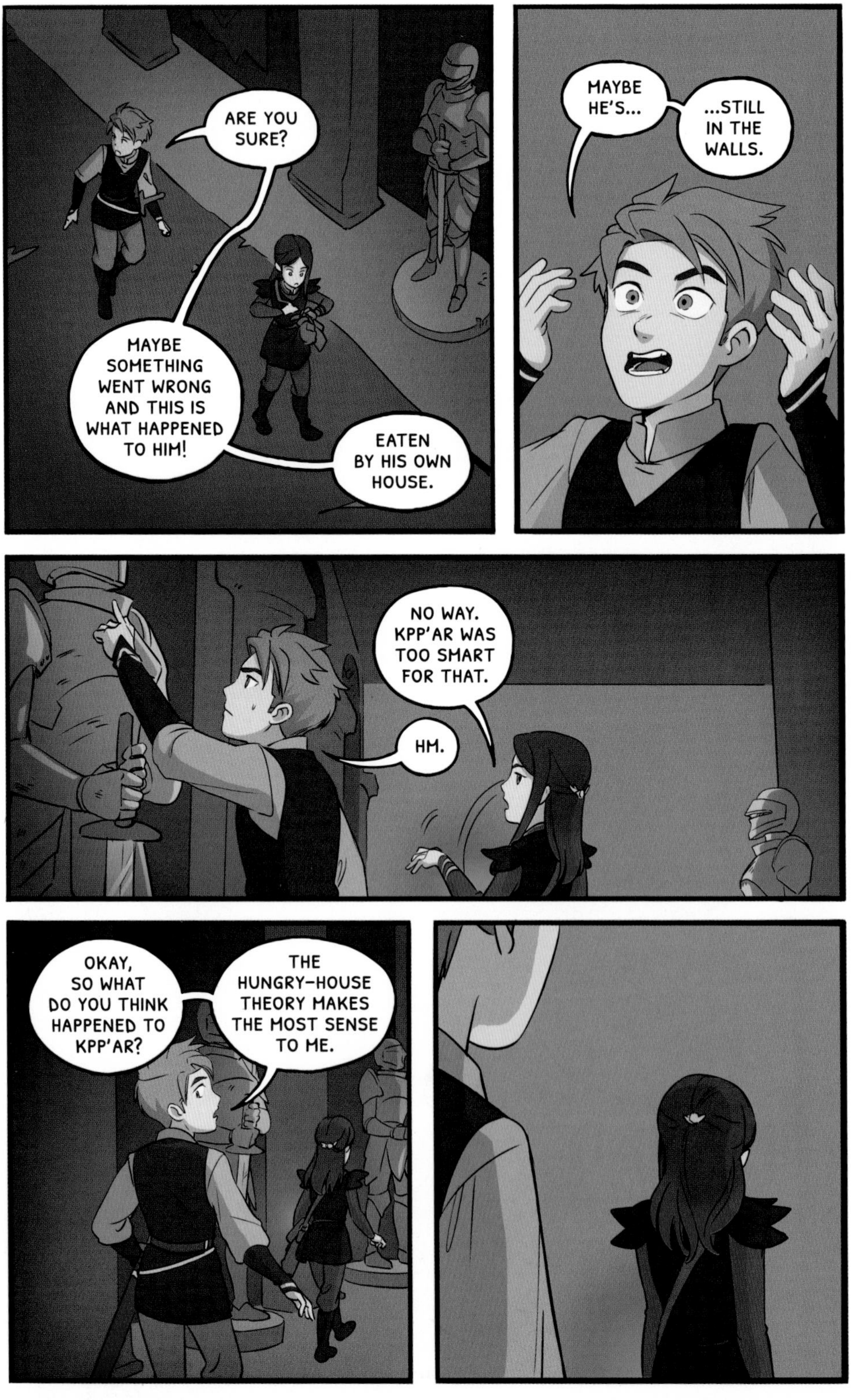

ARE YOU SURE?
MAYBE SOMETHING WENT WRONG AND THIS IS WHAT HAPPENED TO HIM!
EATEN BY HIS OWN HOUSE.
MAYBE HE'S...
...STILL IN THE WALLS.
NO WAY. KPP'AR WAS TOO SMART FOR THAT.
HM.
OKAY, SO WHAT DO YOU THINK HAPPENED TO KPP'AR?
THE HUNGRY-HOUSE THEORY MAKES THE MOST SENSE TO ME.

I DON'T KNOW.

BUT...

IF HE LEFT A SURPRISE FOR US, MAYBE HE LEFT A... LETTER TOO. OR A NOTE.

OKAY.

SO WE'RE LOOKING FOR SOME KIND OF PRESENT, A NEW SPELL BOOK, AND A... NOTE?

CLAUDS, I FEEL LIKE YOU KEEP ADDING THINGS FOR US TO DO HERE.

WHA— NO, I DON'T!

WE'RE HERE TO SEE KPP'AR'S SURPRISE! THAT'S ALL.

I JUST... HAVE LOTS OF QUESTIONS.

LIKE, I DUNNO, WHAT THE RIGHT MATERIALS ARE FOR A SPELL OR THE RIGHT WORDS TO CAST IT OR...

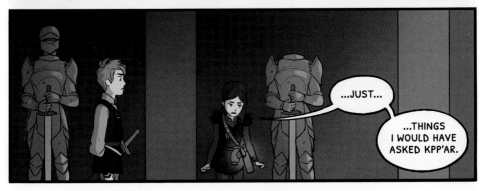

...JUST...

...THINGS I WOULD HAVE ASKED KPP'AR.

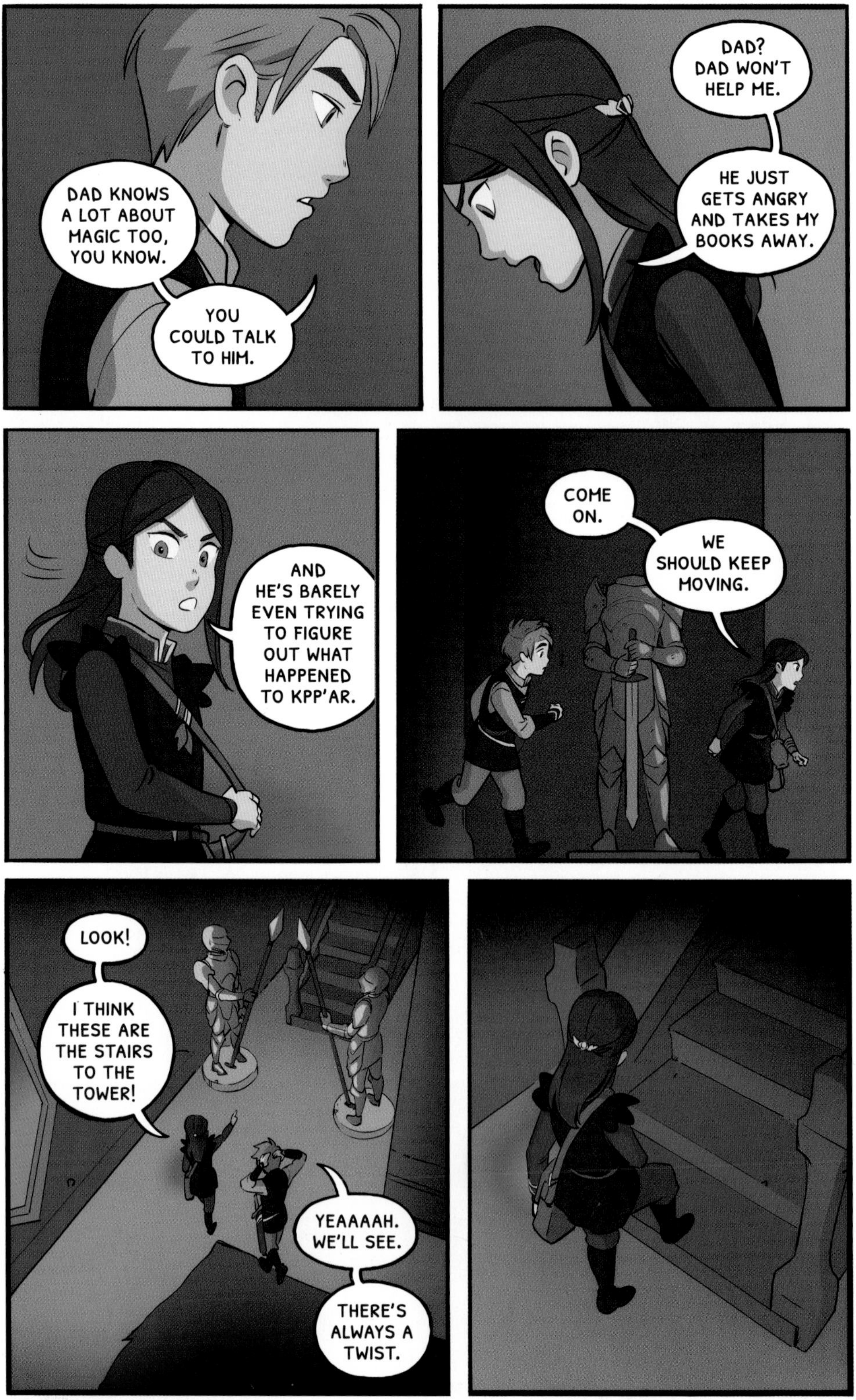
DAD KNOWS A LOT ABOUT MAGIC TOO, YOU KNOW.
YOU COULD TALK TO HIM.
DAD? DAD WON'T HELP ME.
HE JUST GETS ANGRY AND TAKES MY BOOKS AWAY.
AND HE'S BARELY EVEN TRYING TO FIGURE OUT WHAT HAPPENED TO KPP'AR.
COME ON.
WE SHOULD KEEP MOVING.
LOOK!
I THINK THESE ARE THE STAIRS TO THE TOWER!
YEAAAAH. WE'LL SEE.
THERE'S ALWAYS A TWIST.

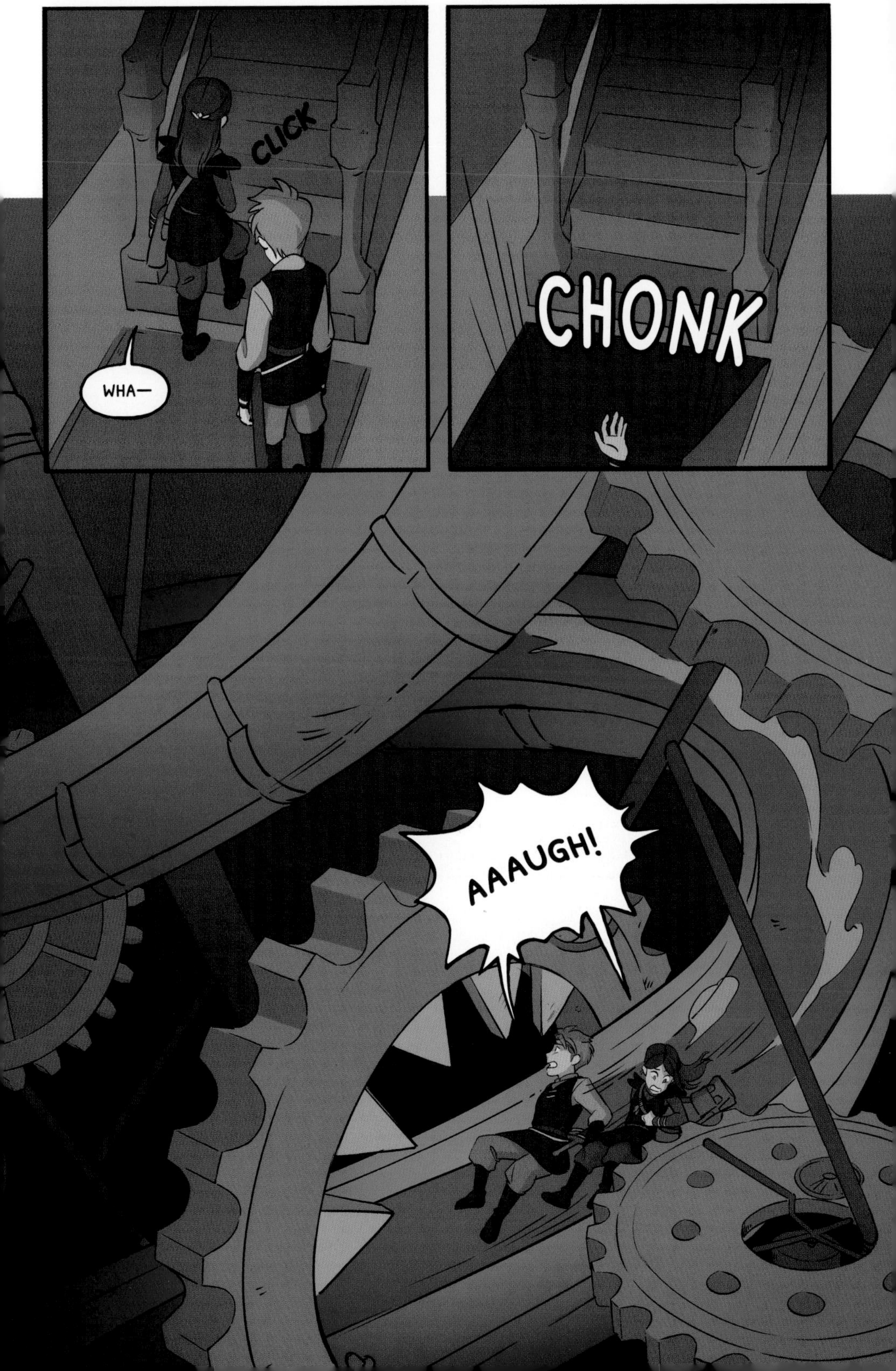
CLICK
WHA—
CHONK
AAAUGH!

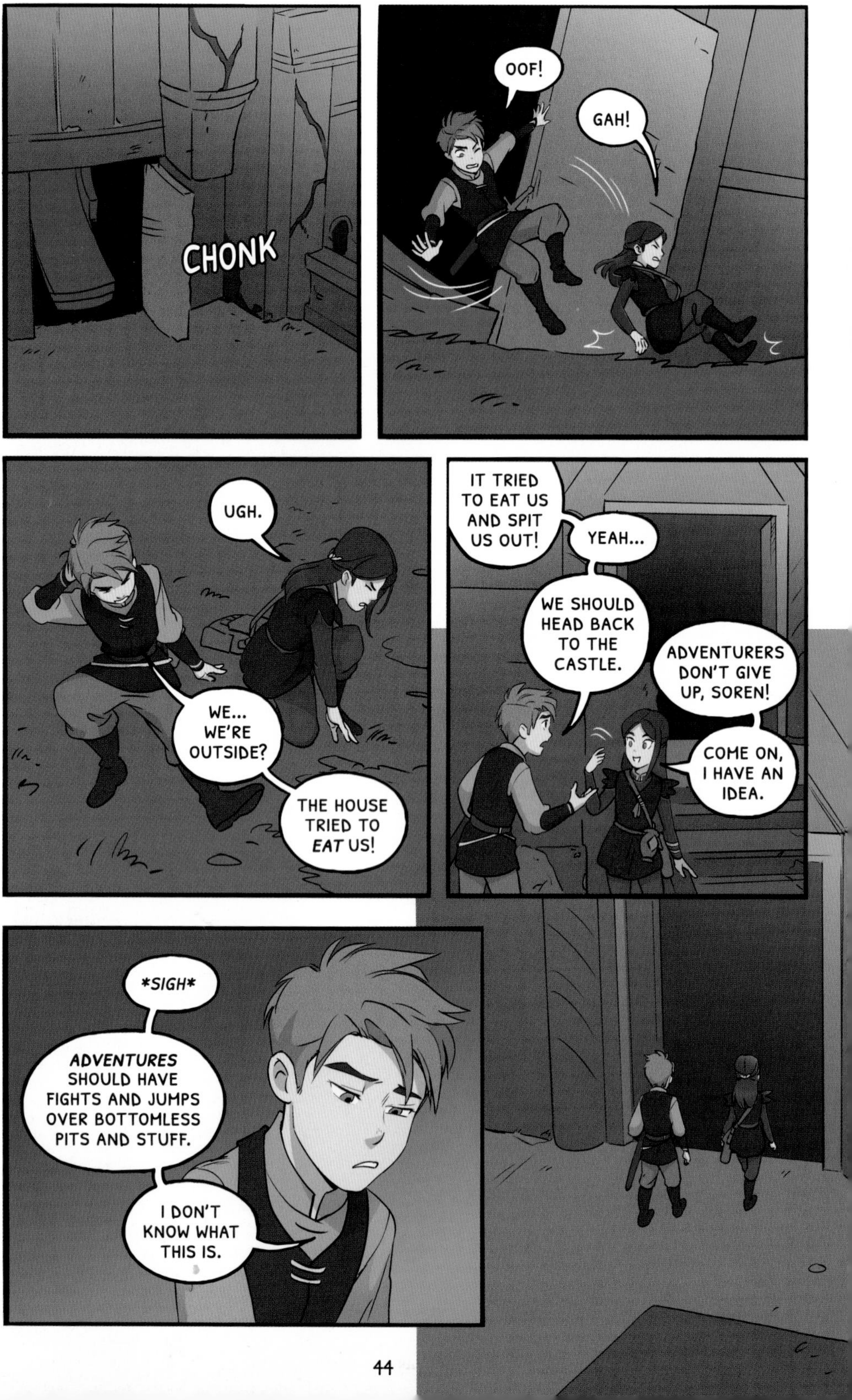
CHONK
OOF!
GAH!
UGH.
WE... WE'RE OUTSIDE?
THE HOUSE TRIED TO *EAT* US!
IT TRIED TO EAT US AND SPIT US OUT!
YEAH...
WE SHOULD HEAD BACK TO THE CASTLE.
ADVENTURERS DON'T GIVE UP, SOREN!
COME ON, I HAVE AN IDEA.
SIGH
ADVENTURES SHOULD HAVE FIGHTS AND JUMPS OVER BOTTOMLESS PITS AND STUFF.
I DON'T KNOW WHAT THIS IS.

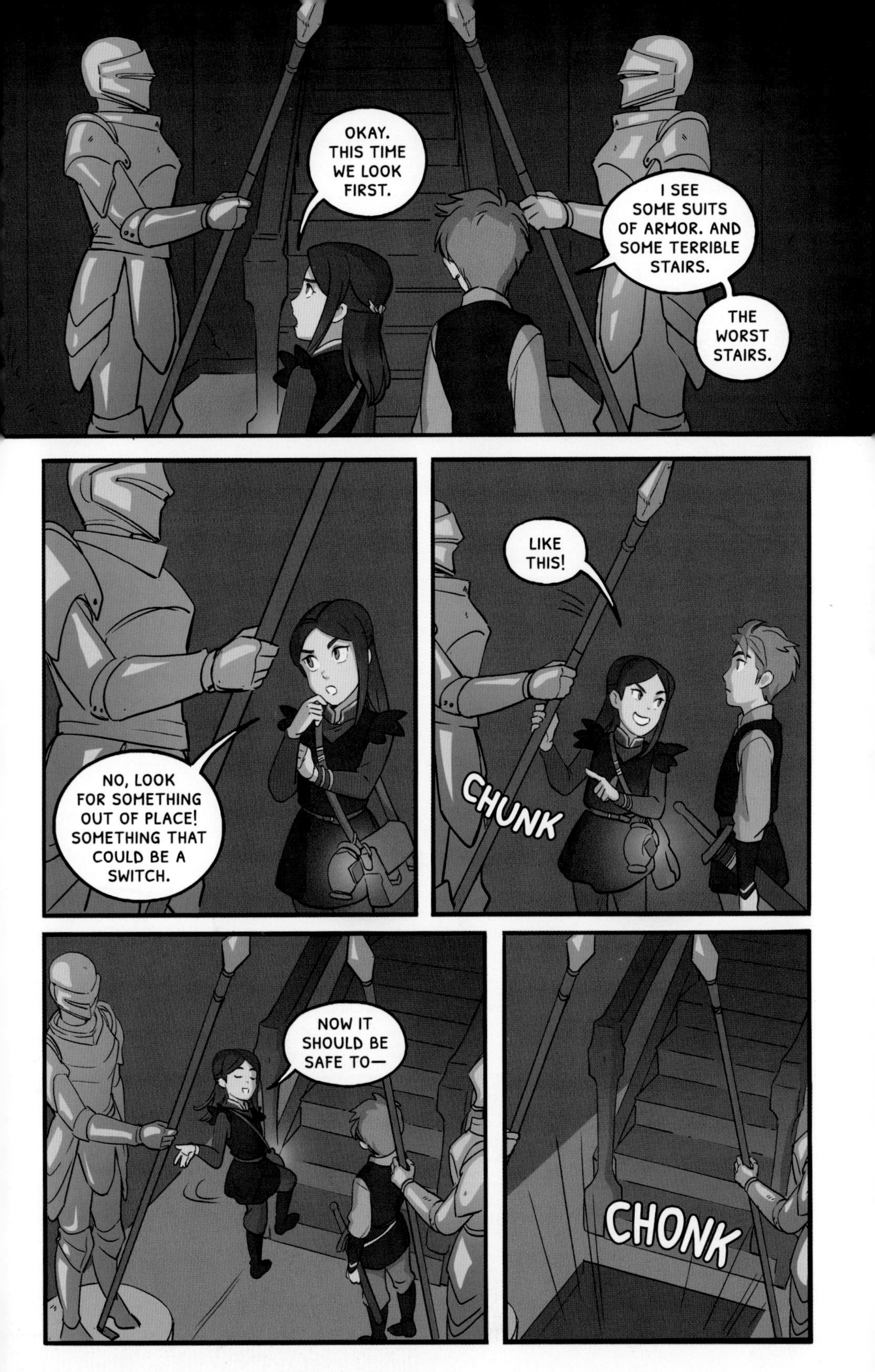
OKAY. THIS TIME WE LOOK FIRST.
I SEE SOME SUITS OF ARMOR. AND SOME TERRIBLE STAIRS.
THE WORST STAIRS.
NO, LOOK FOR SOMETHING OUT OF PLACE! SOMETHING THAT COULD BE A SWITCH.
LIKE THIS!
CHUNK
NOW IT SHOULD BE SAFE TO—
CHONK

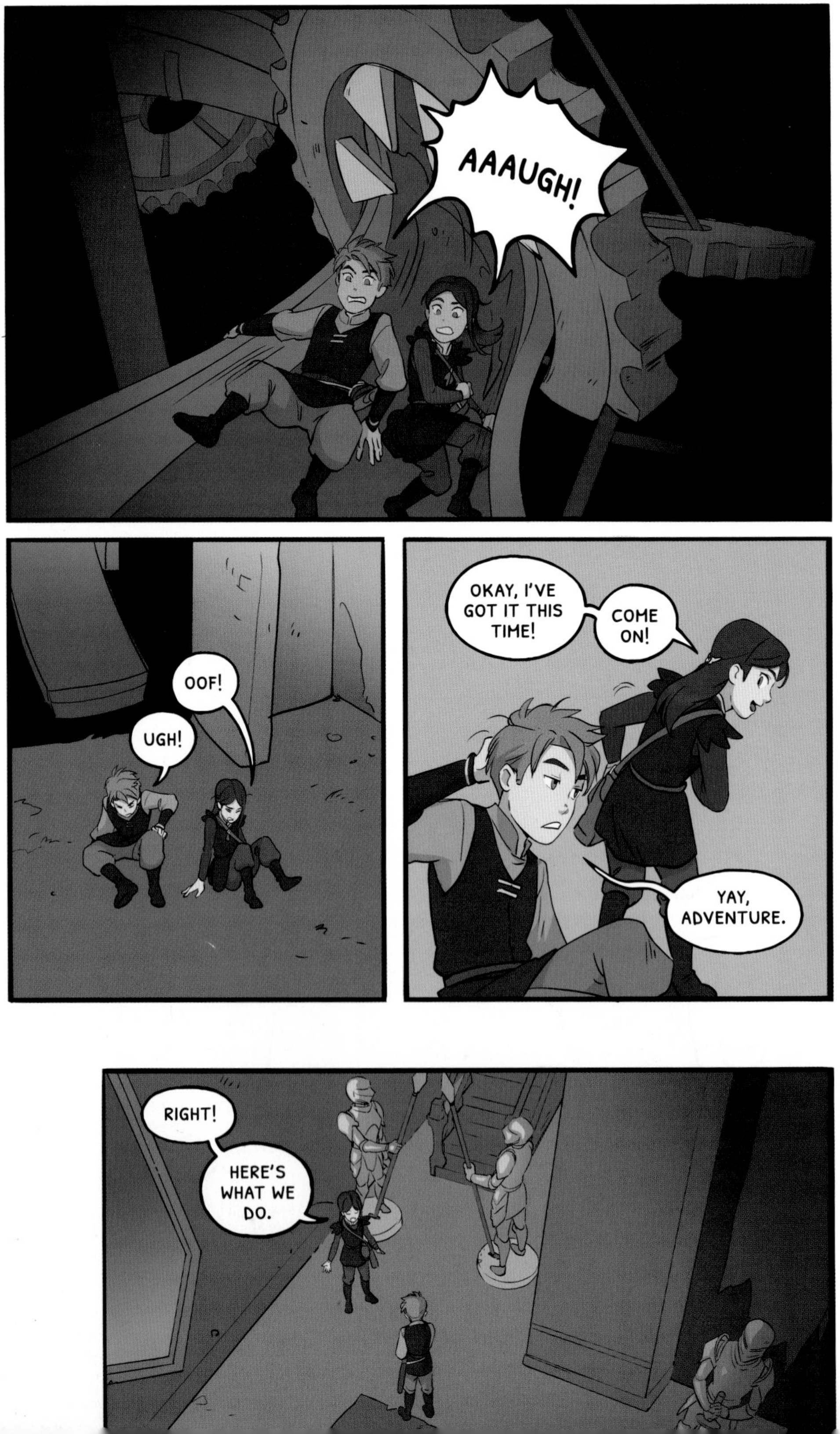
AAAUGH!
OOF!
UGH!
OKAY, I'VE GOT IT THIS TIME!
COME ON!
YAY, ADVENTURE.
RIGHT!
HERE'S WHAT WE DO.

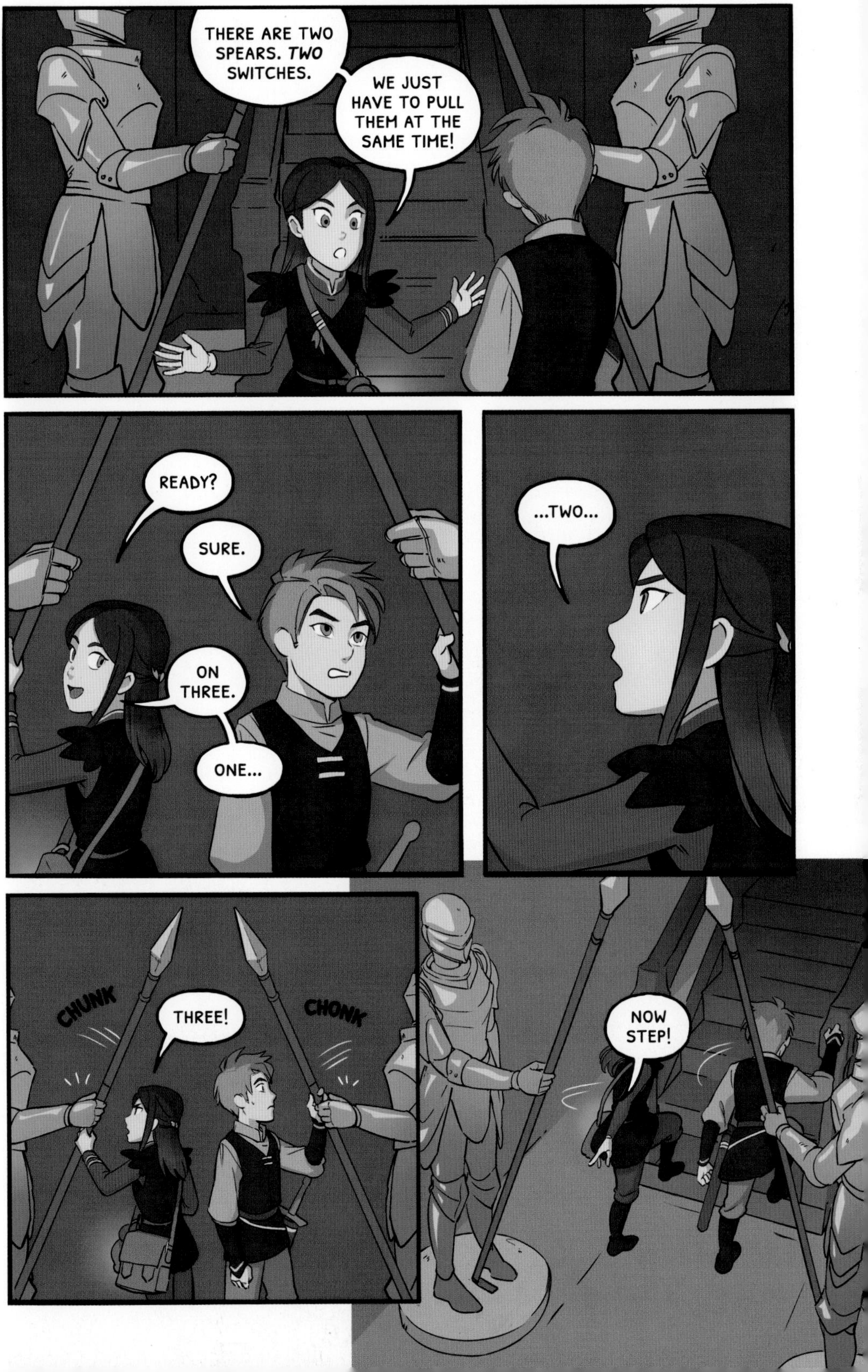
THERE ARE TWO SPEARS. *TWO* SWITCHES.
WE JUST HAVE TO PULL THEM AT THE SAME TIME!
READY?
SURE.
ON THREE.
ONE...
...TWO...
CHUNK
THREE!
CHONK
NOW STEP!

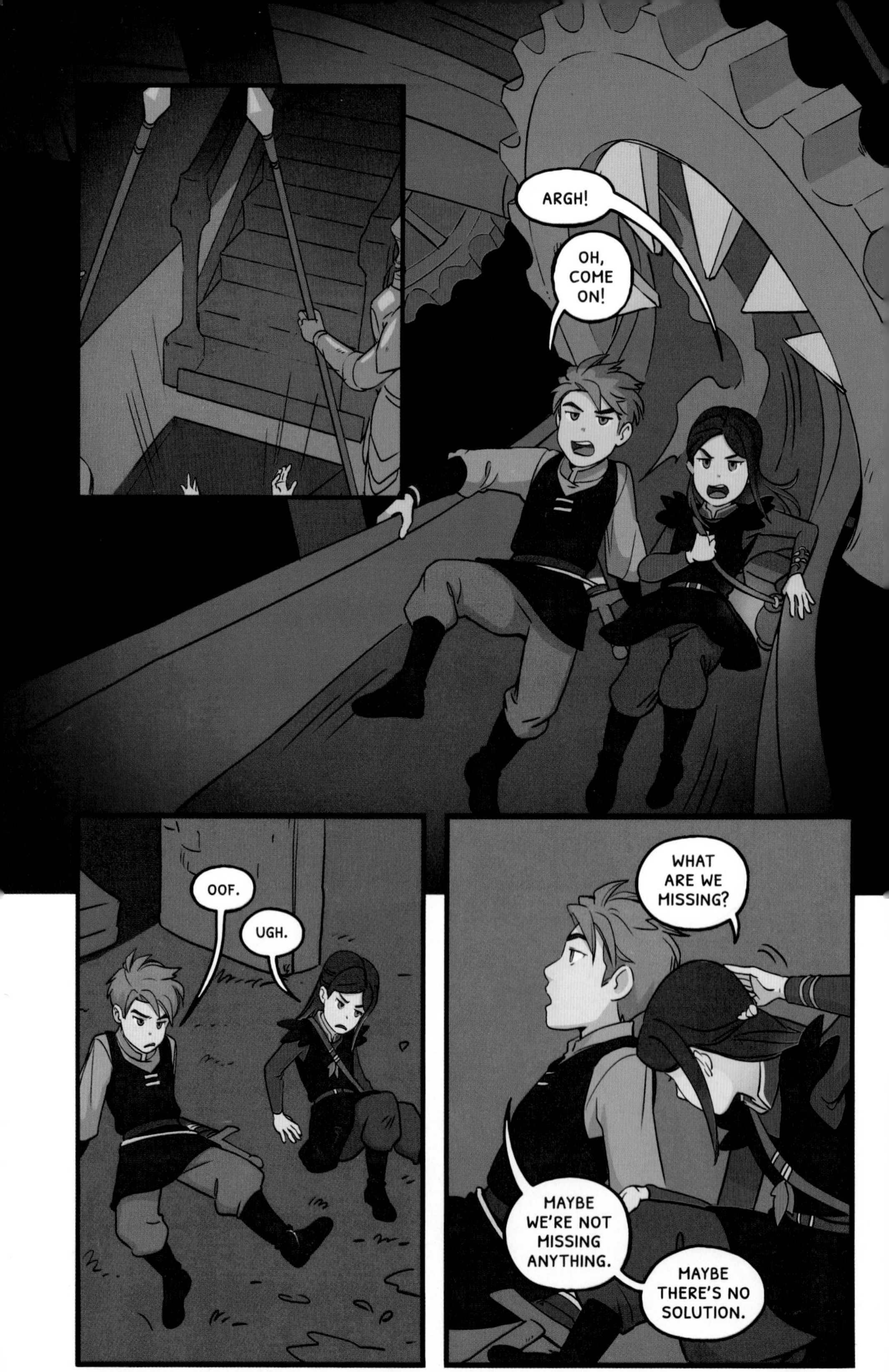
ARGH!
OH, COME ON!
OOF.
UGH.
WHAT ARE WE MISSING?
MAYBE WE'RE NOT MISSING ANYTHING.
MAYBE THERE'S NO SOLUTION.

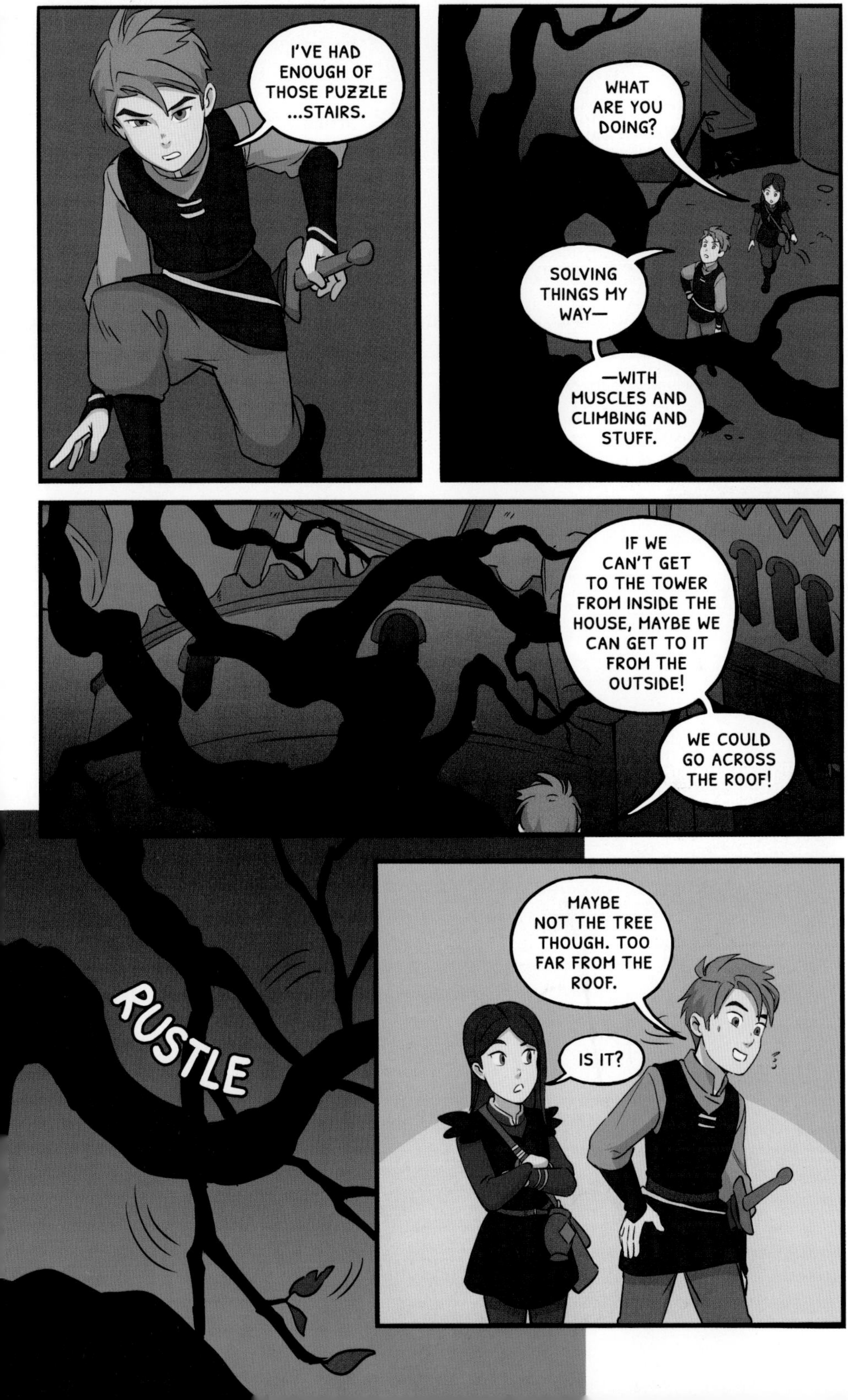
I'VE HAD ENOUGH OF THOSE PUZZLE ...STAIRS.
WHAT ARE YOU DOING?
SOLVING THINGS MY WAY—
—WITH MUSCLES AND CLIMBING AND STUFF.
IF WE CAN'T GET TO THE TOWER FROM INSIDE THE HOUSE, MAYBE WE CAN GET TO IT FROM THE OUTSIDE!
WE COULD GO ACROSS THE ROOF!
RUSTLE
MAYBE NOT THE TREE THOUGH. TOO FAR FROM THE ROOF.
IS IT?

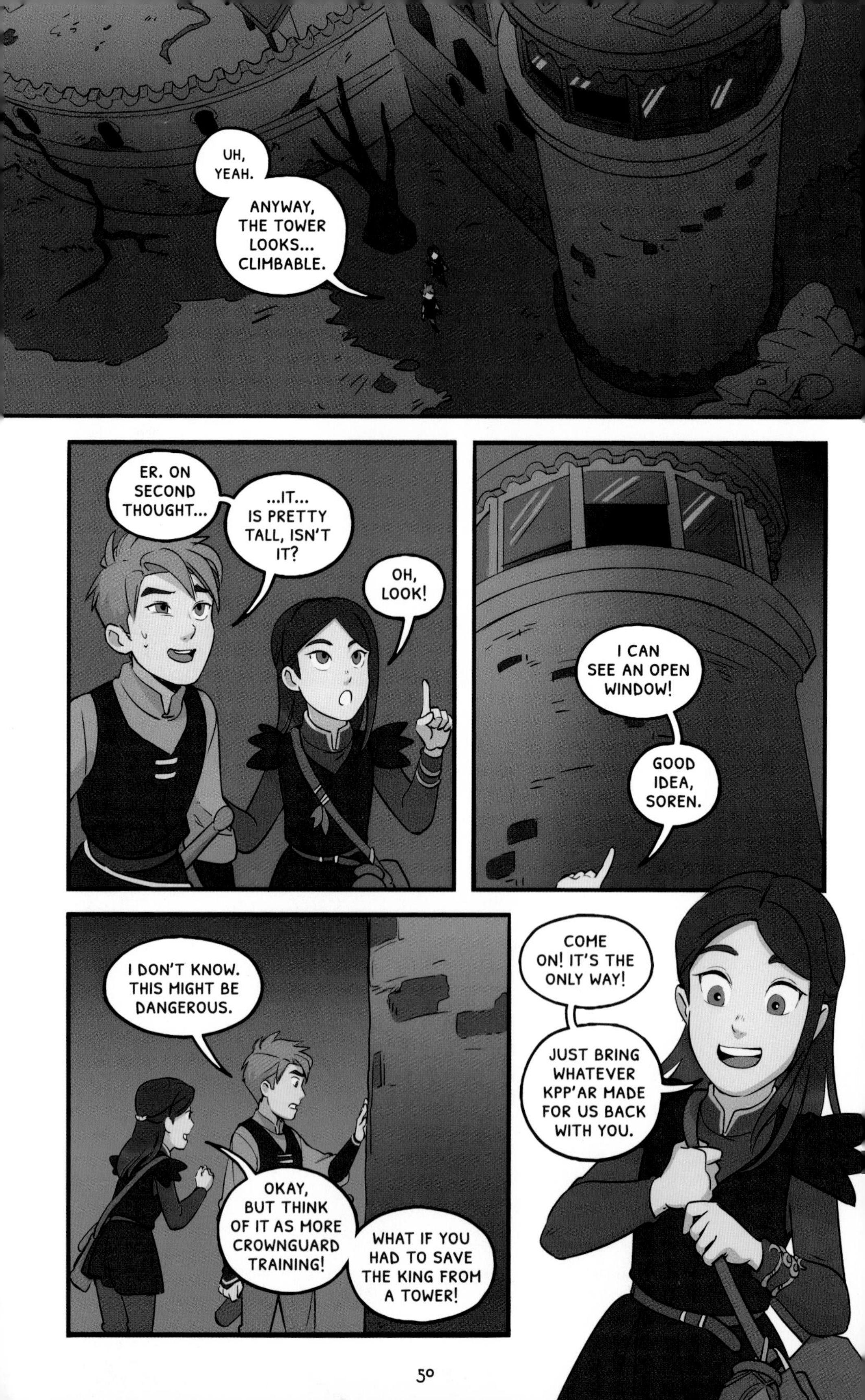
UH, YEAH.
ANYWAY, THE TOWER LOOKS... CLIMBABLE.
ER. ON SECOND THOUGHT...
...IT... IS PRETTY TALL, ISN'T IT?
OH, LOOK!
I CAN SEE AN OPEN WINDOW!
GOOD IDEA, SOREN.
I DON'T KNOW. THIS MIGHT BE DANGEROUS.
OKAY, BUT THINK OF IT AS MORE CROWNGUARD TRAINING!
WHAT IF YOU HAD TO SAVE THE KING FROM A TOWER!
COME ON! IT'S THE ONLY WAY!
JUST BRING WHATEVER KPP'AR MADE FOR US BACK WITH YOU.

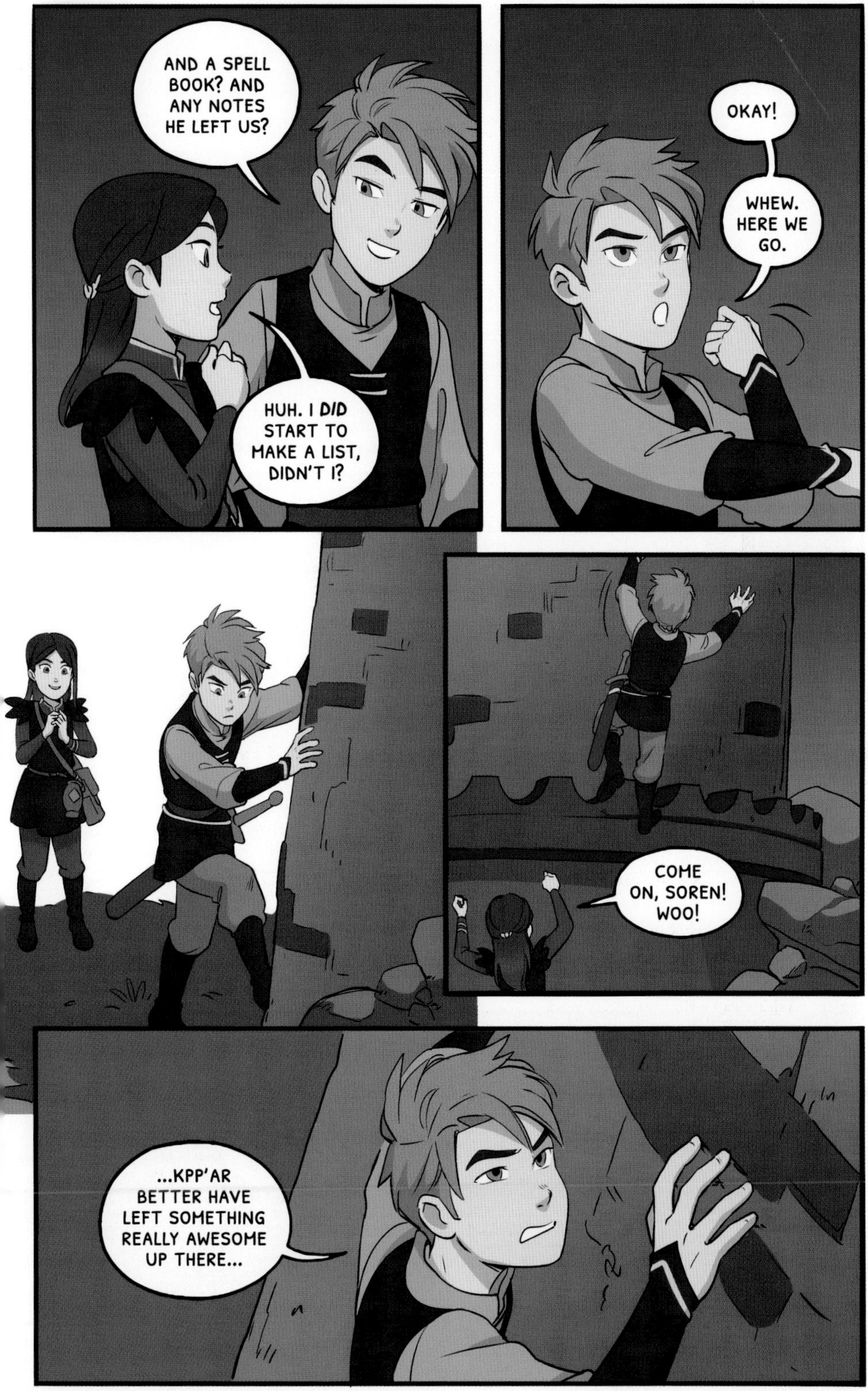
AND A SPELL BOOK? AND ANY NOTES HE LEFT US?
HUH. I DID START TO MAKE A LIST, DIDN'T I?
OKAY!
WHEW. HERE WE GO.
COME ON, SOREN! WOO!
...KPP'AR BETTER HAVE LEFT SOMETHING REALLY AWESOME UP THERE...

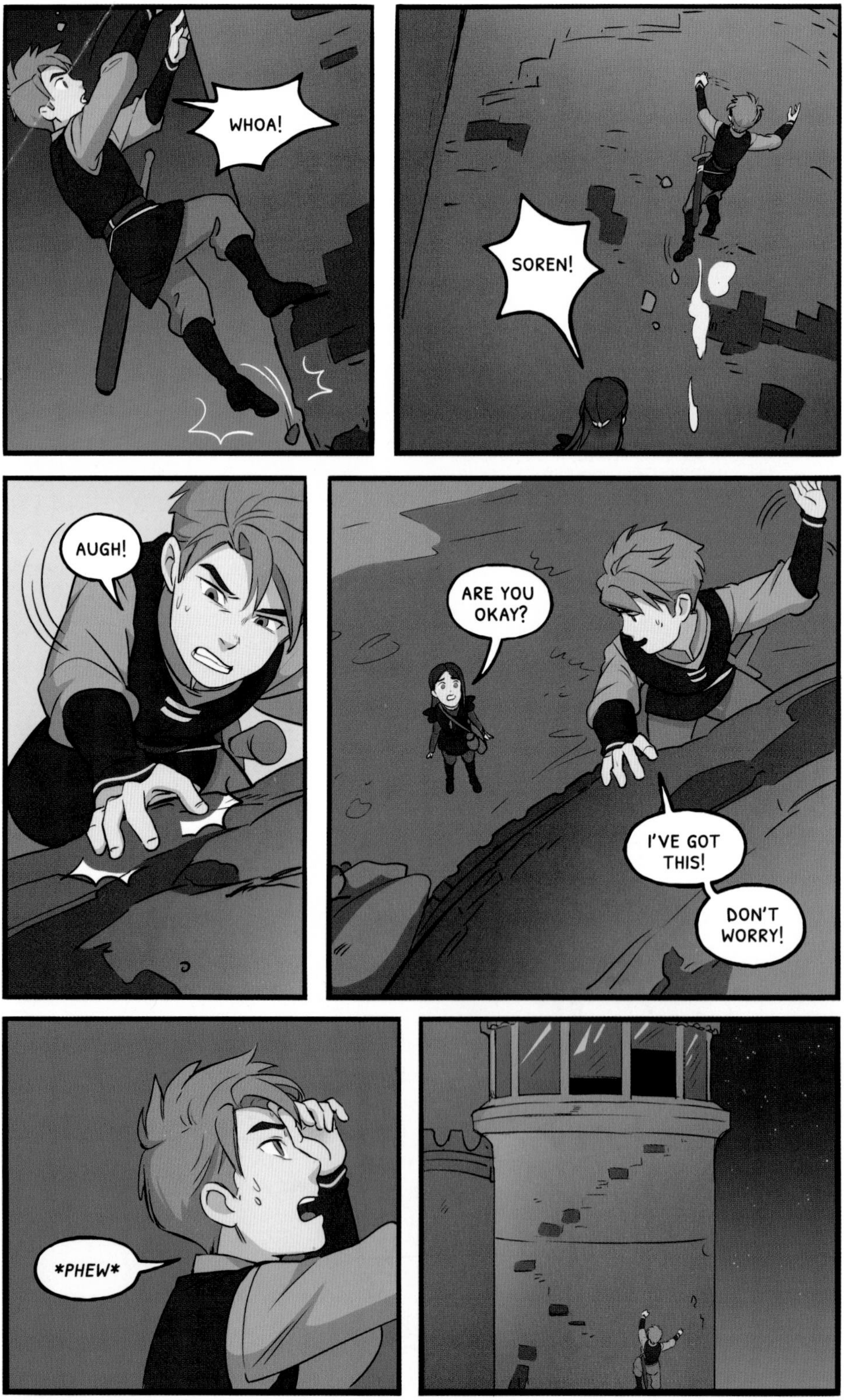
WHOA!
SOREN!
AUGH!
ARE YOU OKAY?
I'VE GOT THIS!
DON'T WORRY!
PHEW

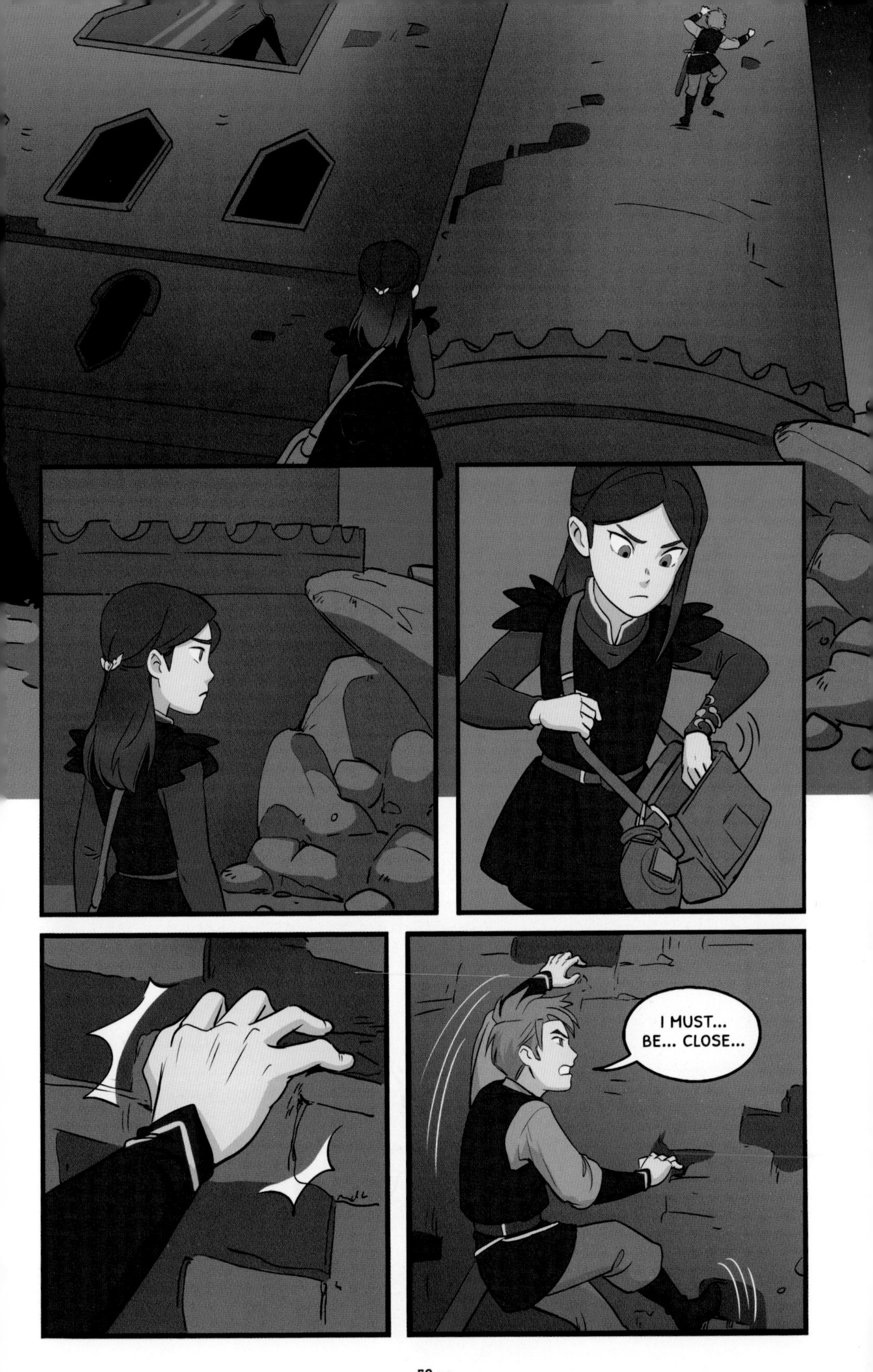
I MUST... BE... CLOSE...

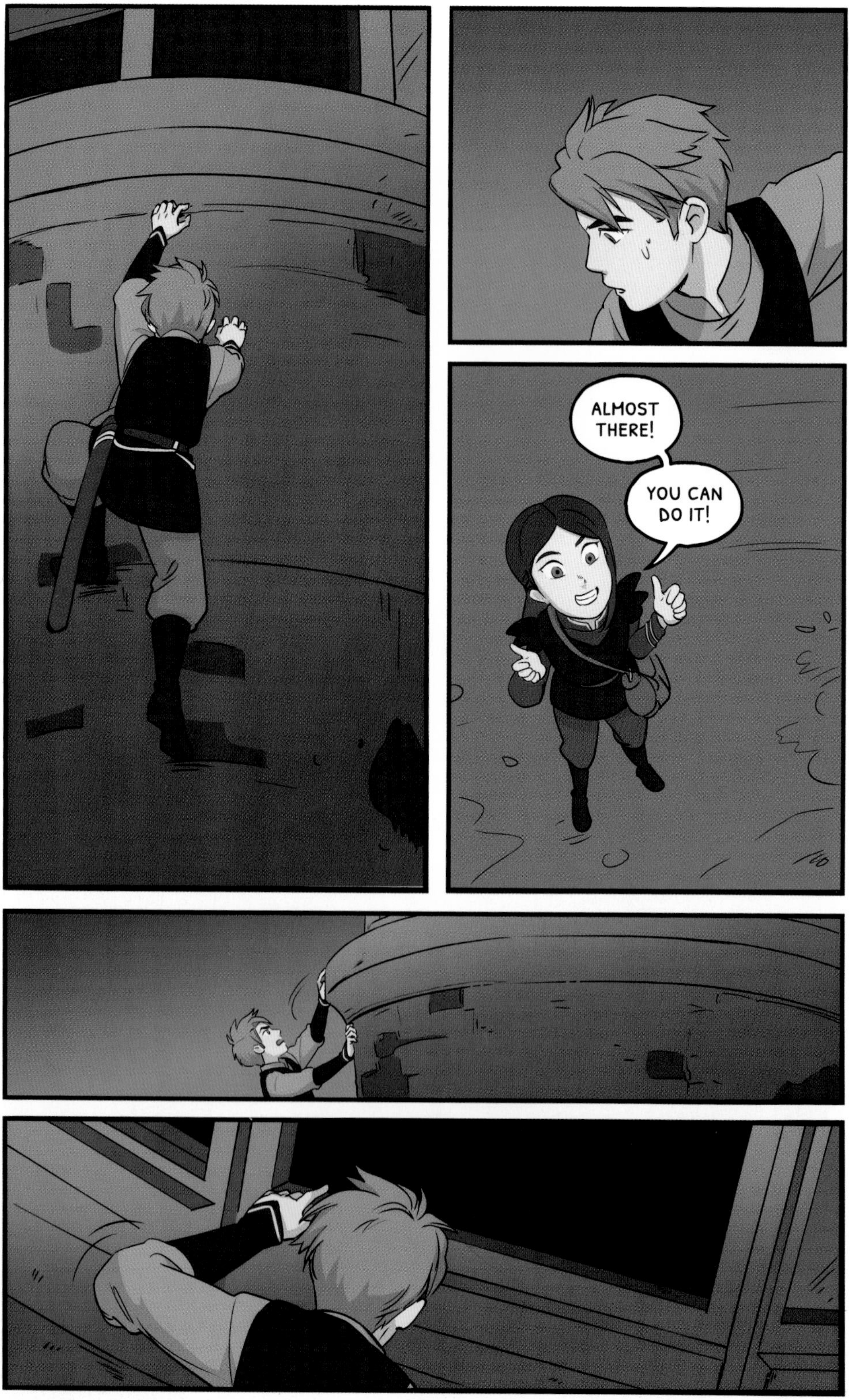
ALMOST THERE!
YOU CAN DO IT!

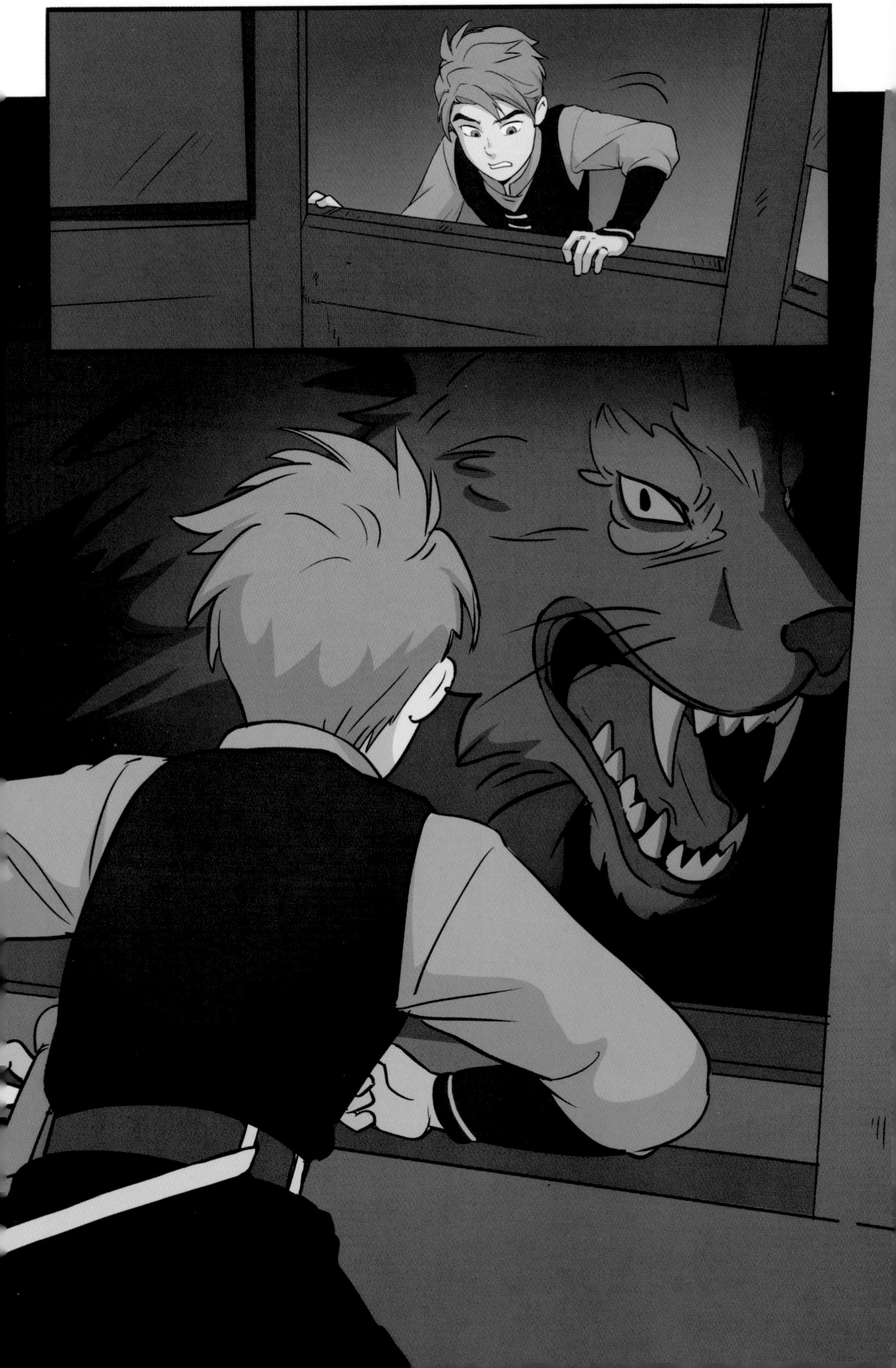

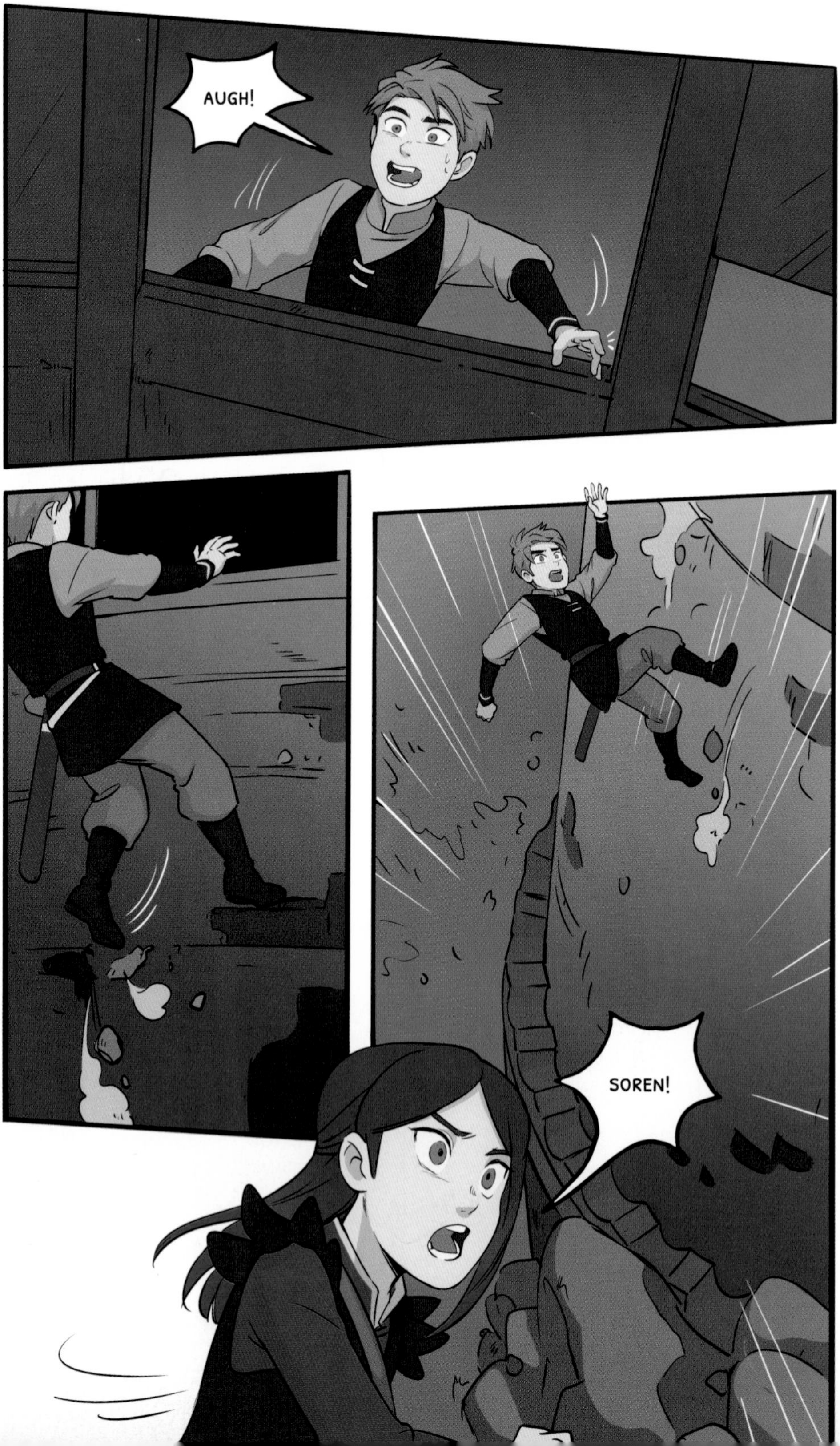
AUGH!
SOREN!

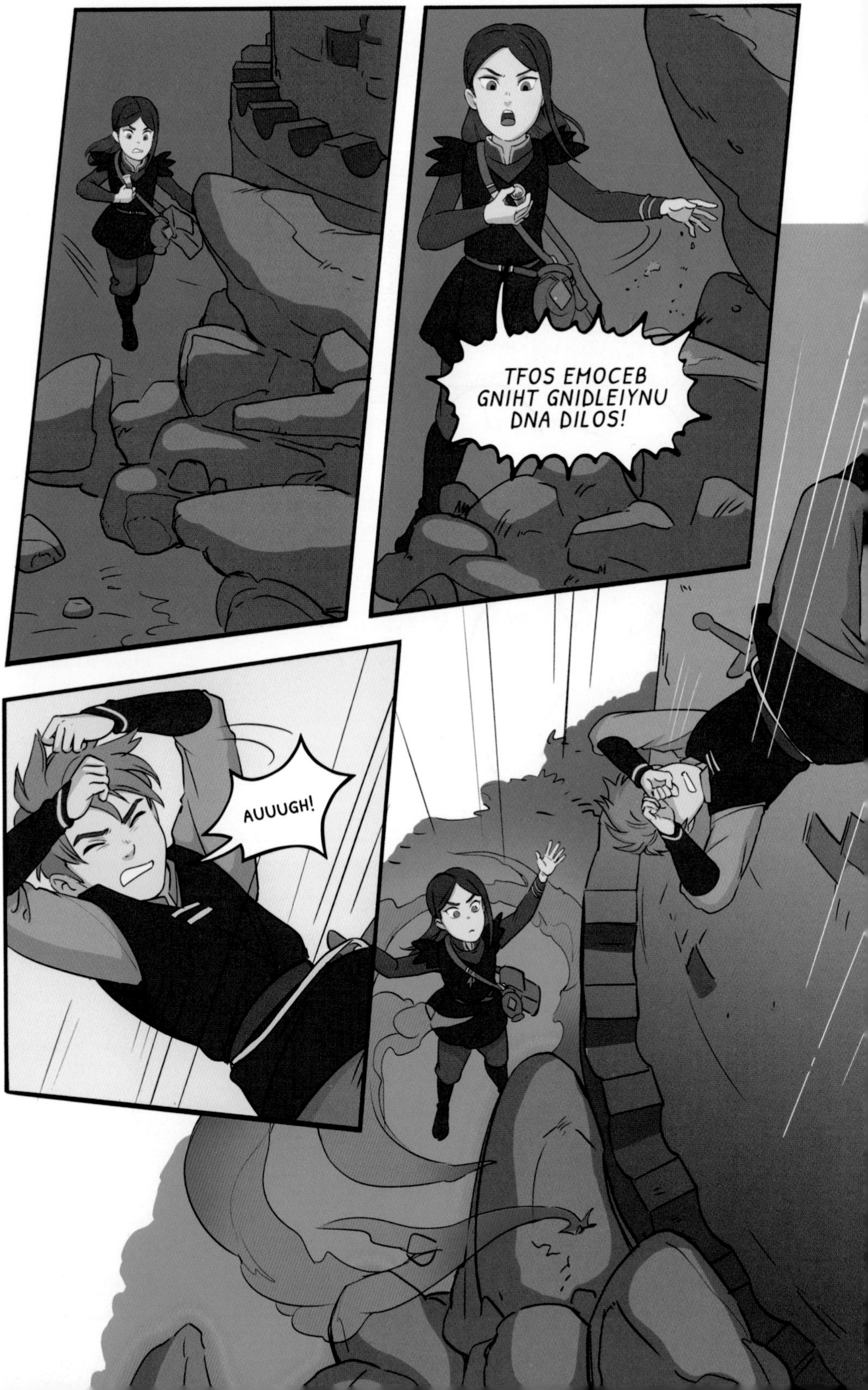
TFOS EMOCEB GNIHT GNIDLEIYNU DNA DILOS!
AUUUGH!

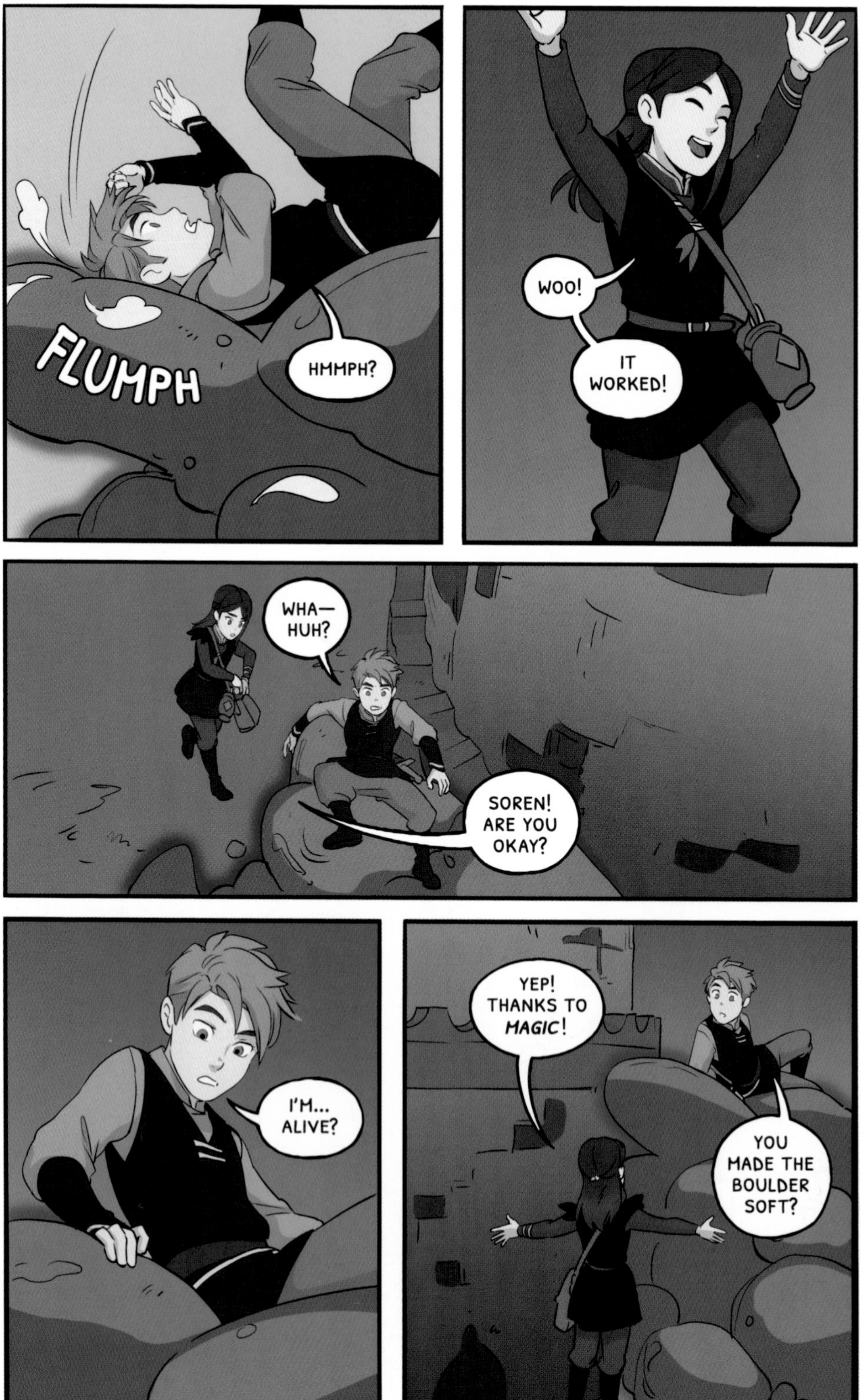
FLUMPH
HMMPH?
WOO!
IT WORKED!
WHA—HUH?
SOREN! ARE YOU OKAY?
I'M... ALIVE?
YEP! THANKS TO *MAGIC*!
YOU MADE THE BOULDER SOFT?

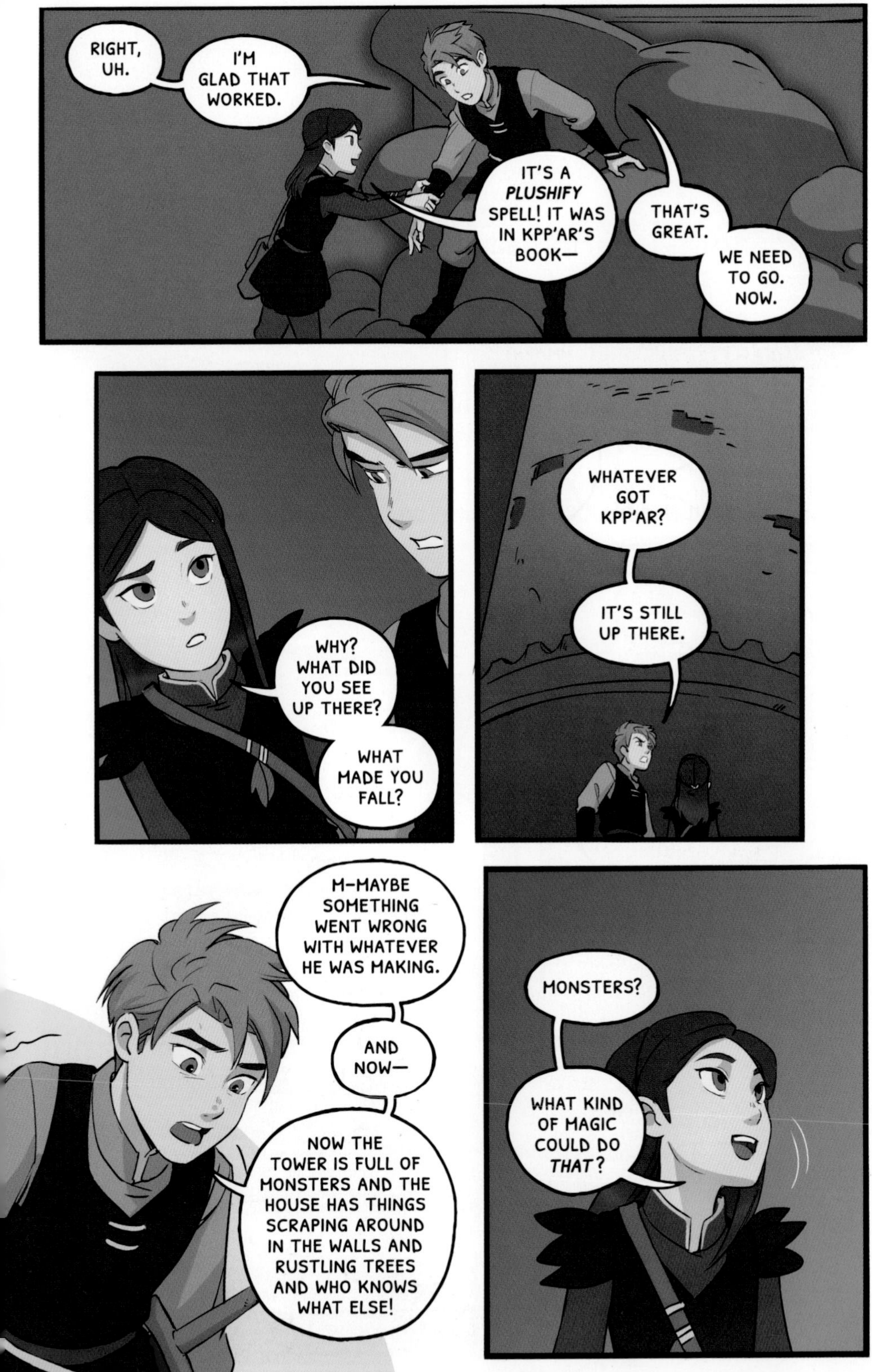
RIGHT, UH.
I'M GLAD THAT WORKED.
IT'S A *PLUSHIFY* SPELL! IT WAS IN KPP'AR'S BOOK—
THAT'S GREAT.
WE NEED TO GO. NOW.
WHY? WHAT DID YOU SEE UP THERE?
WHAT MADE YOU FALL?
WHATEVER GOT KPP'AR?
IT'S STILL UP THERE.
M-MAYBE SOMETHING WENT WRONG WITH WHATEVER HE WAS MAKING.
AND NOW—
NOW THE TOWER IS FULL OF MONSTERS AND THE HOUSE HAS THINGS SCRAPING AROUND IN THE WALLS AND RUSTLING TREES AND WHO KNOWS WHAT ELSE!
MONSTERS?
WHAT KIND OF MAGIC COULD DO *THAT*?

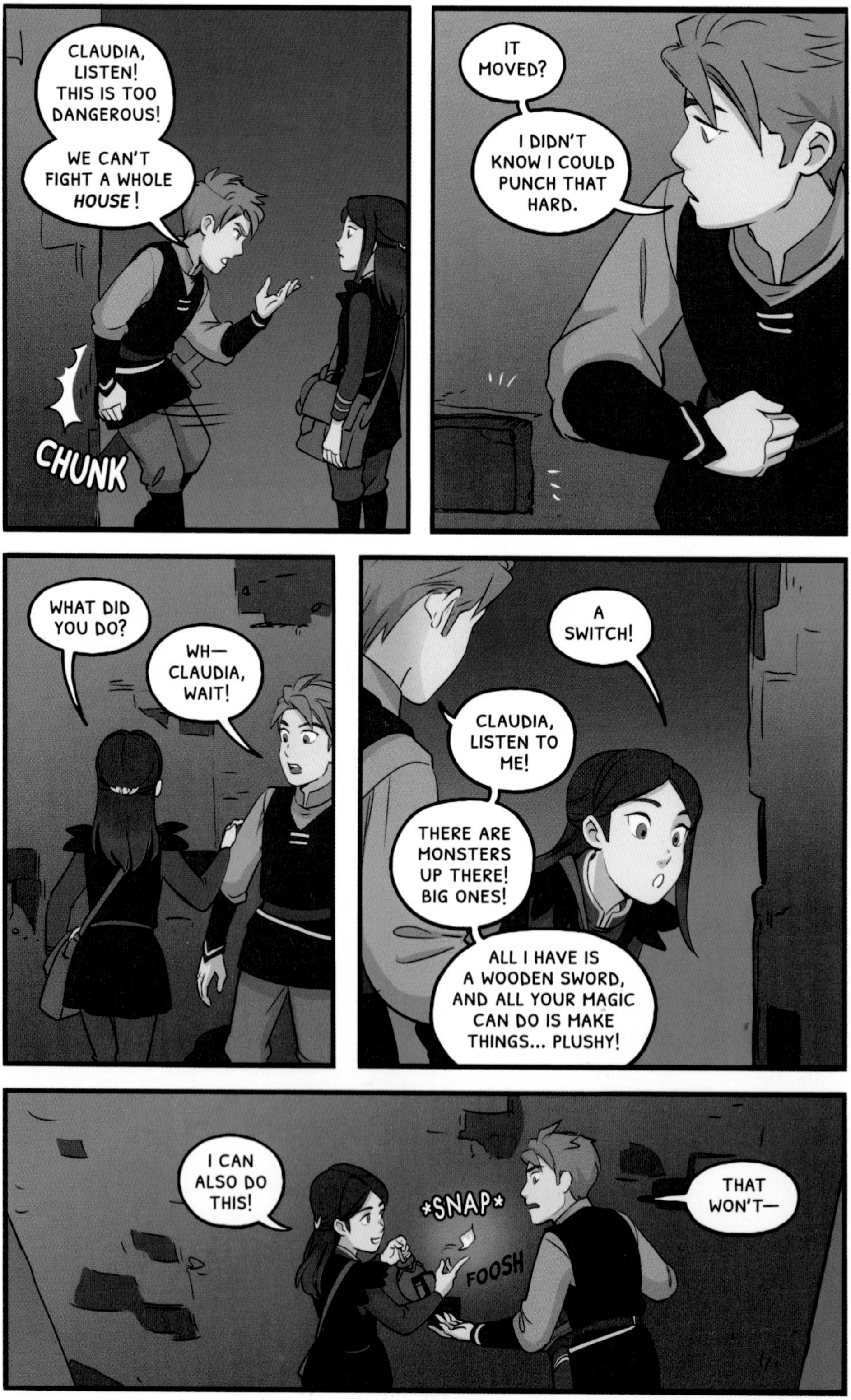
CLAUDIA, LISTEN! THIS IS TOO DANGEROUS!
WE CAN'T FIGHT A WHOLE *HOUSE*!
CHUNK
IT MOVED?
I DIDN'T KNOW I COULD PUNCH THAT HARD.
WHAT DID YOU DO?
WH— CLAUDIA, WAIT!
A SWITCH!
CLAUDIA, LISTEN TO ME!
THERE ARE MONSTERS UP THERE! BIG ONES!
ALL I HAVE IS A WOODEN SWORD, AND ALL YOUR MAGIC CAN DO IS MAKE THINGS... PLUSHY!
I CAN ALSO DO THIS!
SNAP
FOOSH
THAT WON'T—

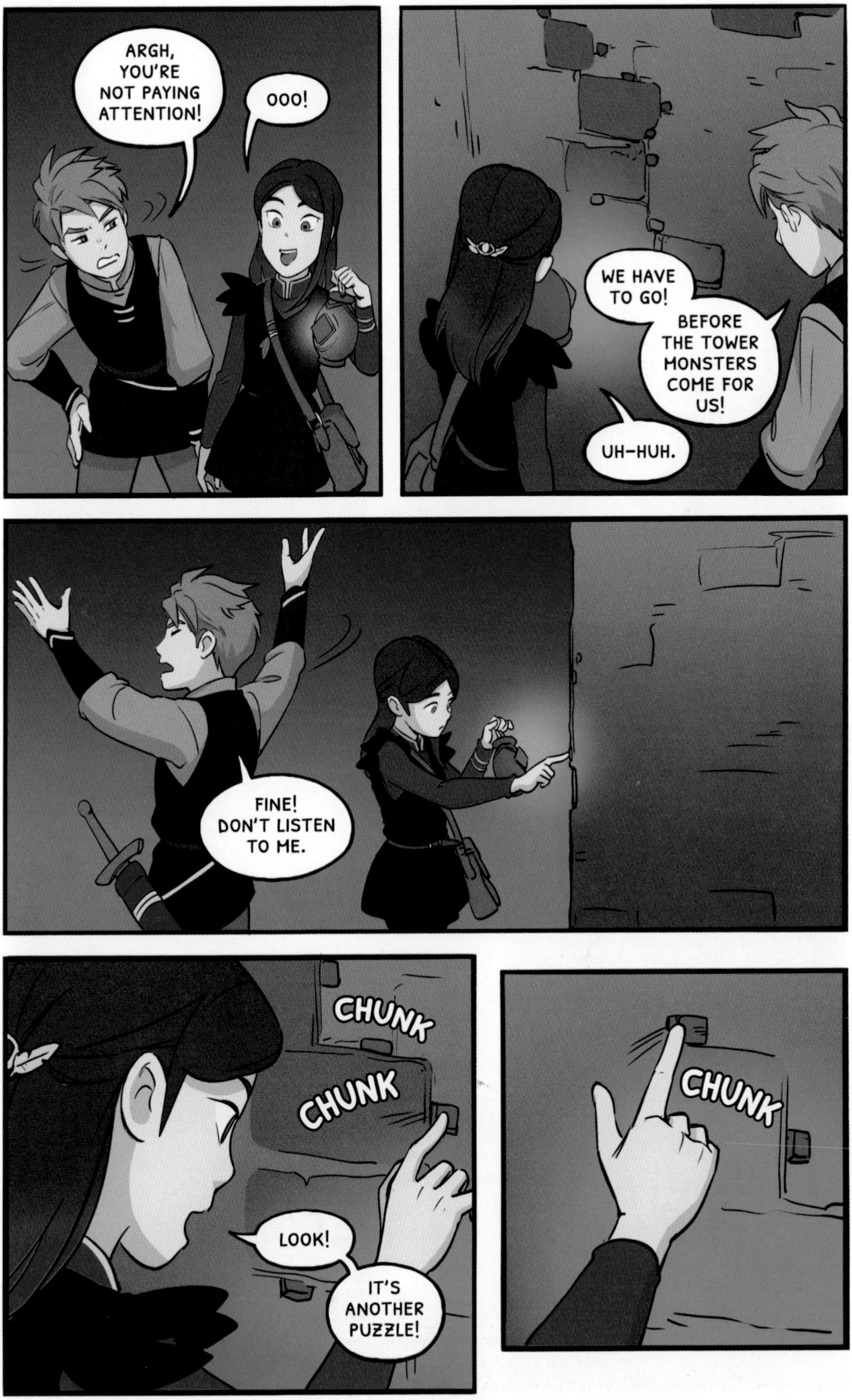
ARGH, YOU'RE NOT PAYING ATTENTION!
OOO!
WE HAVE TO GO!
BEFORE THE TOWER MONSTERS COME FOR US!
UH-HUH.
FINE! DON'T LISTEN TO ME.
CHUNK
CHUNK
LOOK!
IT'S ANOTHER PUZZLE!
CHUNK

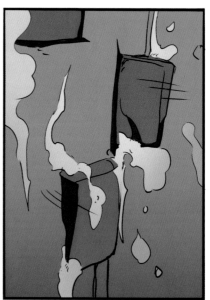

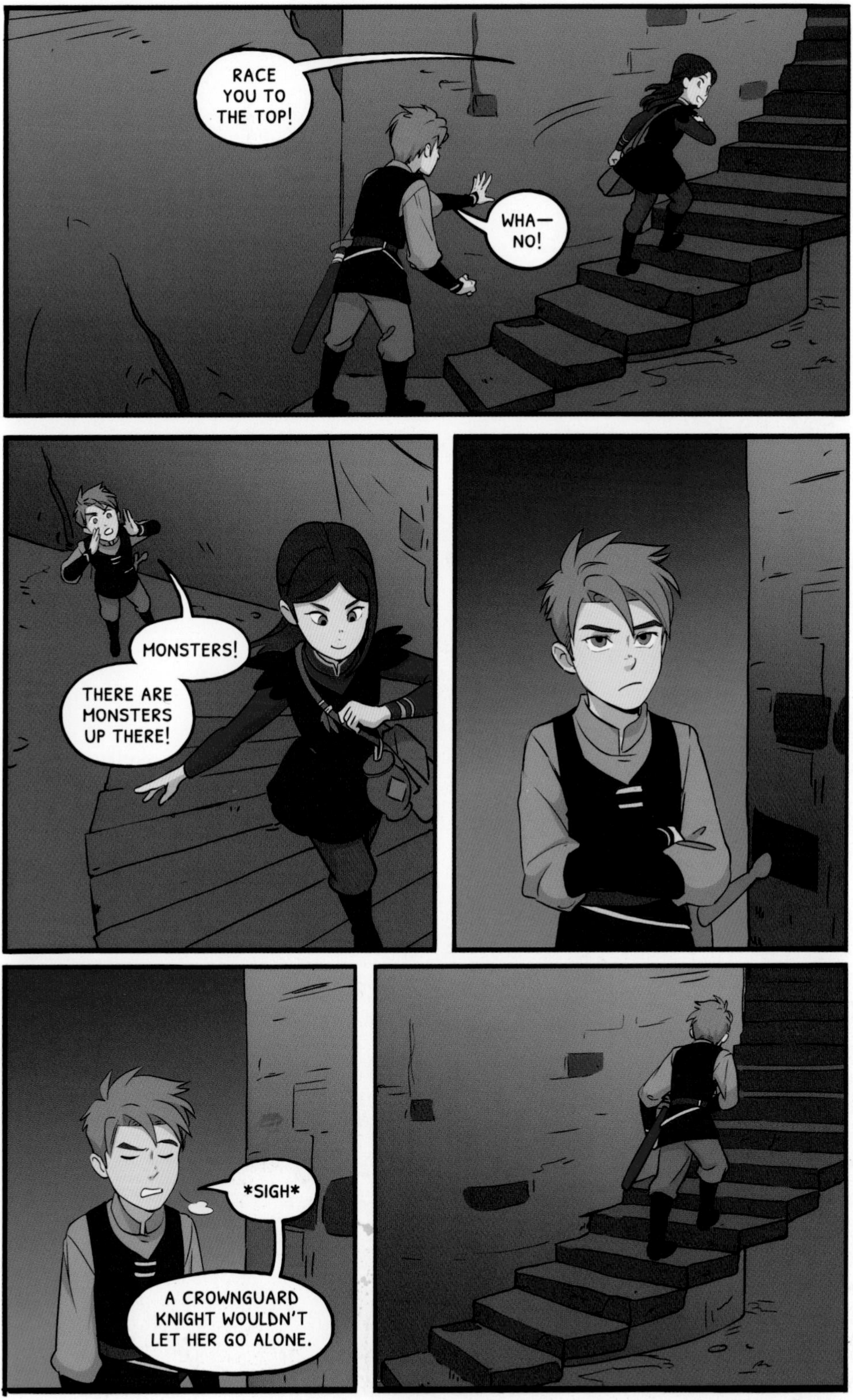
RACE YOU TO THE TOP!
WHA— NO!
MONSTERS!
THERE ARE MONSTERS UP THERE!
SIGH
A CROWNGUARD KNIGHT WOULDN'T LET HER GO ALONE.

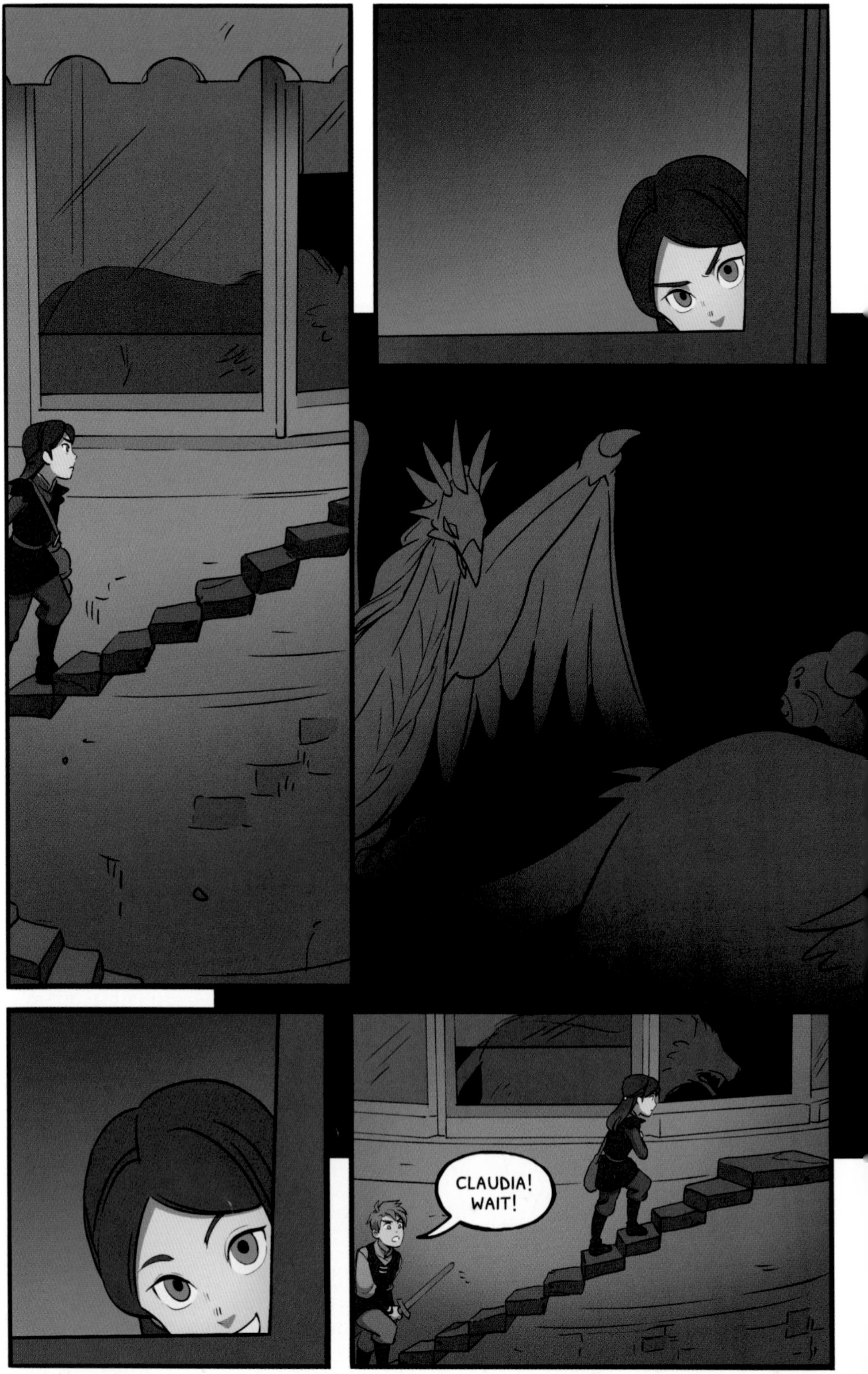
CLAUDIA! WAIT!

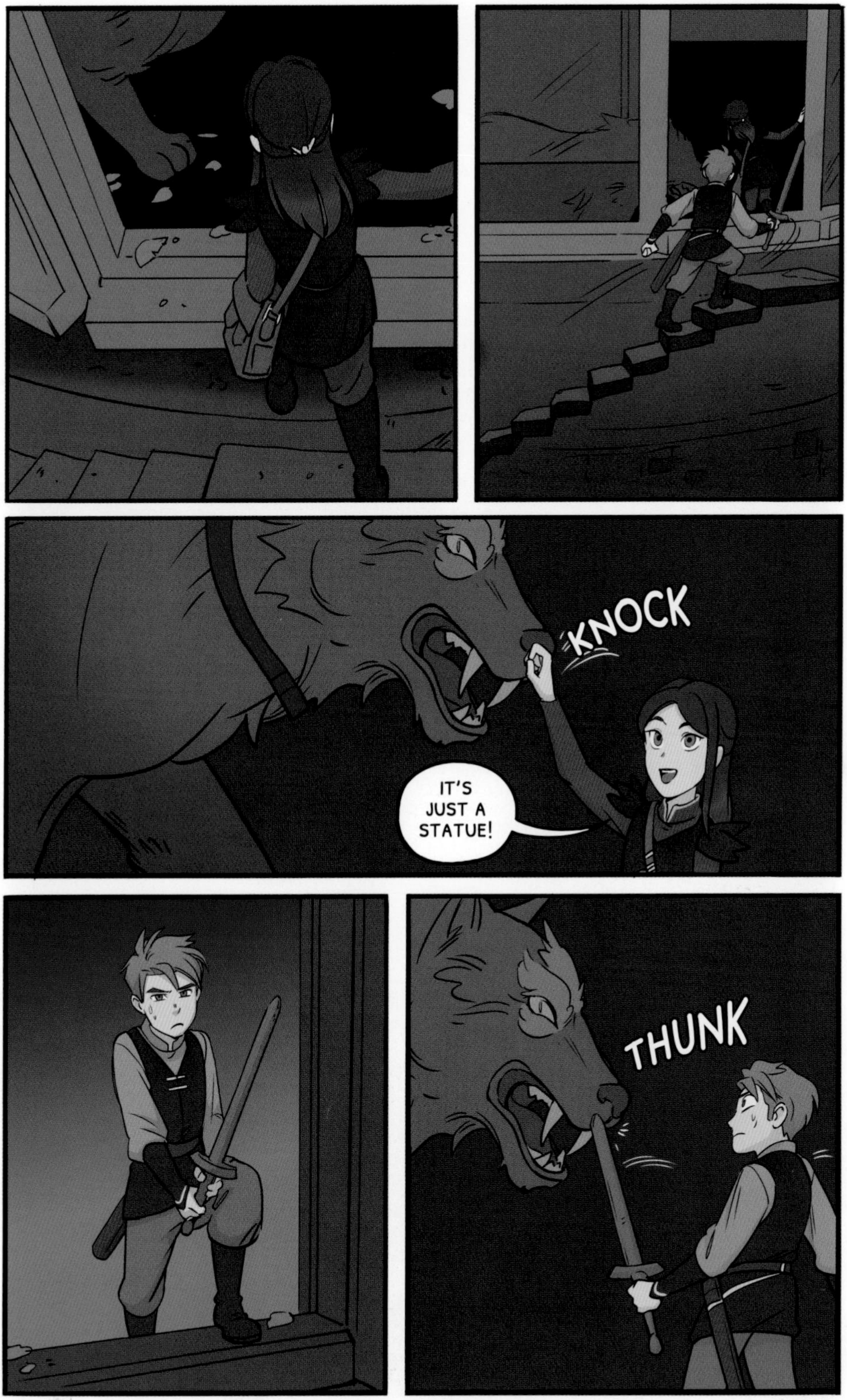
KNOCK
IT'S JUST A STATUE!
THUNK

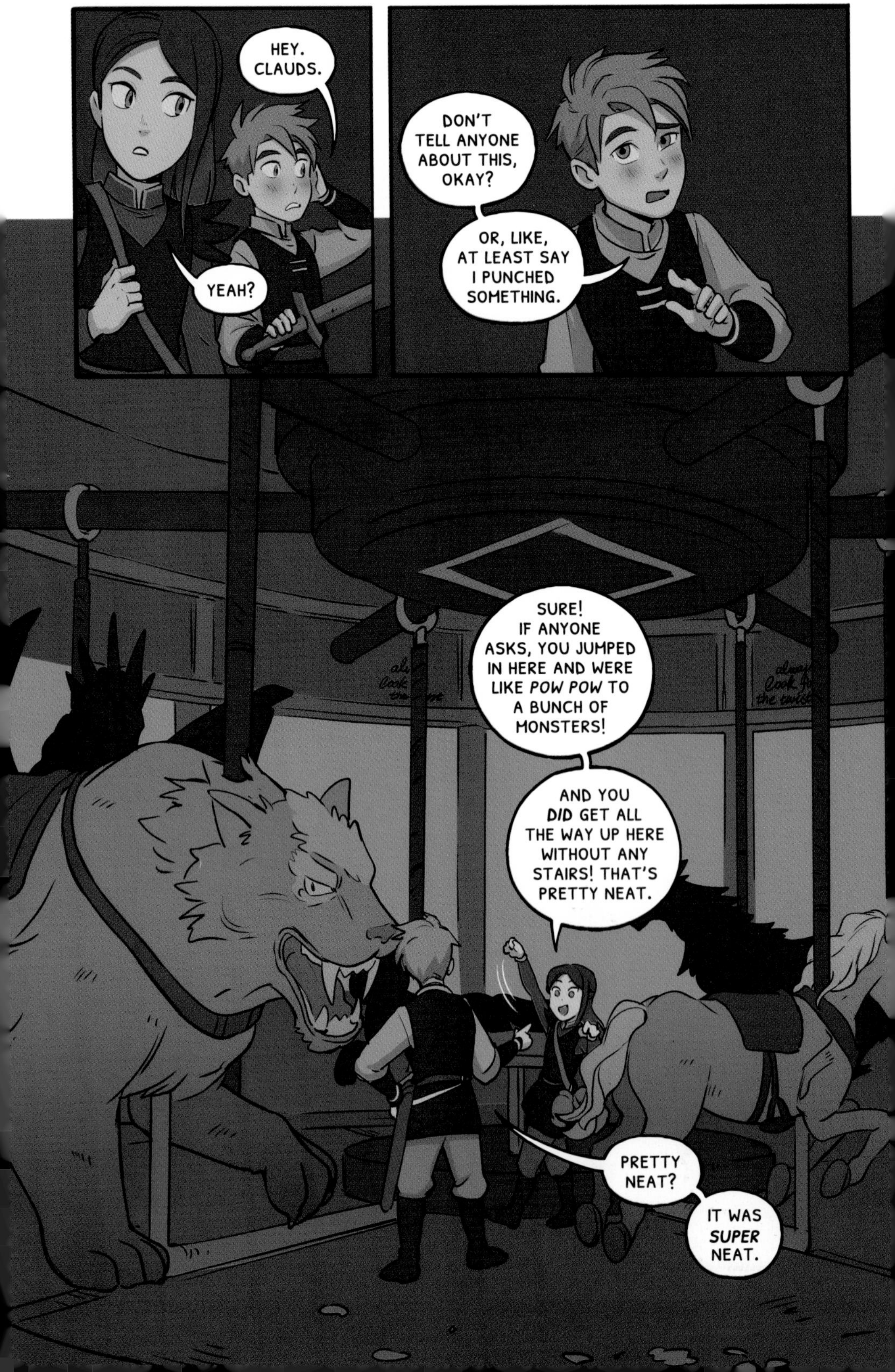
HEY.
CLAUDS.
YEAH?
DON'T TELL ANYONE ABOUT THIS, OKAY?
OR, LIKE, AT LEAST SAY I PUNCHED SOMETHING.
SURE! IF ANYONE ASKS, YOU JUMPED IN HERE AND WERE LIKE *POW POW* TO A BUNCH OF MONSTERS!
AND YOU ***DID*** GET ALL THE WAY UP HERE WITHOUT ANY STAIRS! THAT'S PRETTY NEAT.
PRETTY NEAT?
IT WAS ***SUPER*** NEAT.

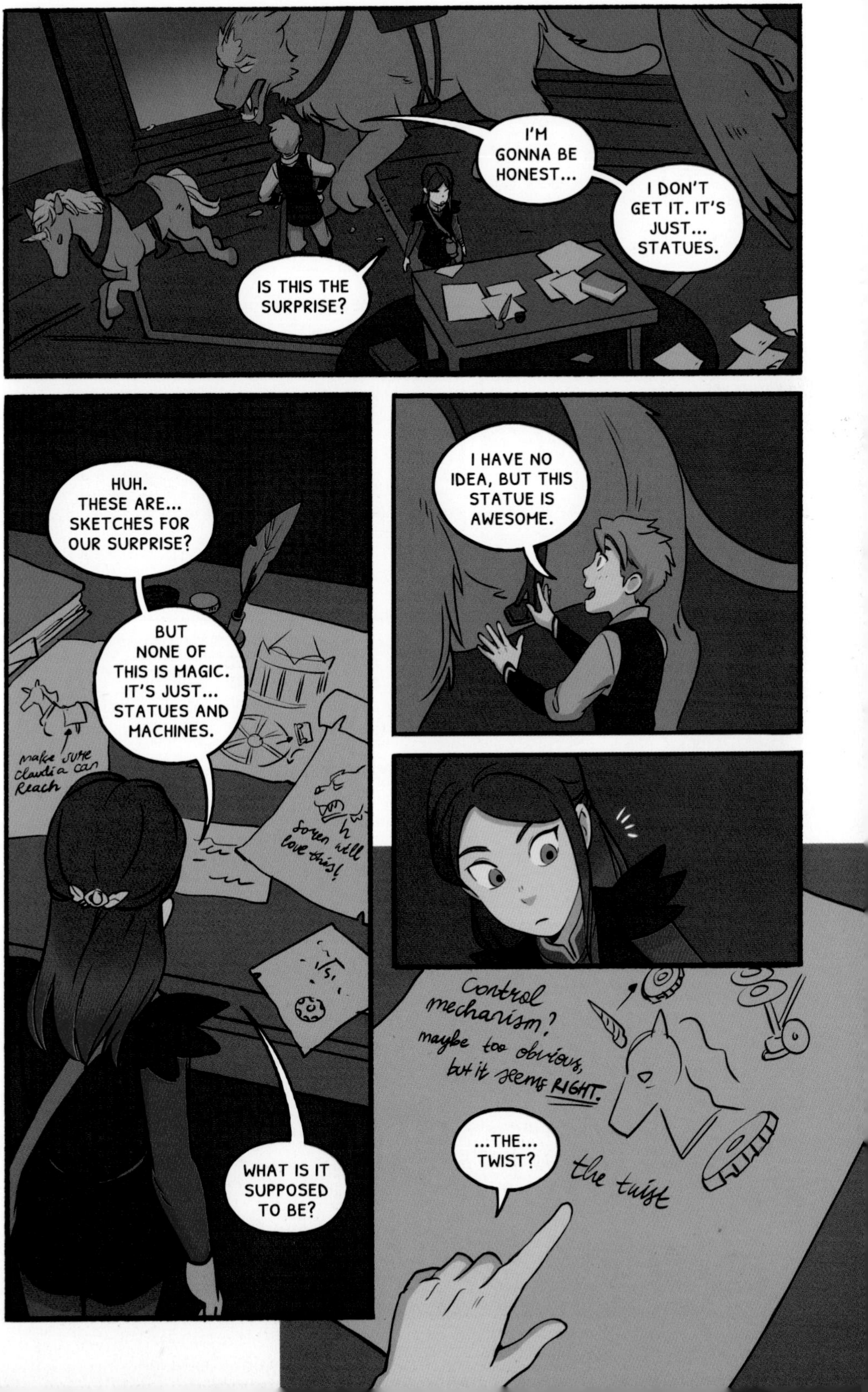

I'M GONNA BE HONEST...
I DON'T GET IT. IT'S JUST... STATUES.
IS THIS THE SURPRISE?
HUH. THESE ARE... SKETCHES FOR OUR SURPRISE?
BUT NONE OF THIS IS MAGIC. IT'S JUST... STATUES AND MACHINES.
make sure Claudia can Reach
Soren will love this!
WHAT IS IT SUPPOSED TO BE?
I HAVE NO IDEA, BUT THIS STATUE IS AWESOME.
Control mechanism? maybe too obvious, but it seems RIGHT.
...THE... TWIST?
the twist

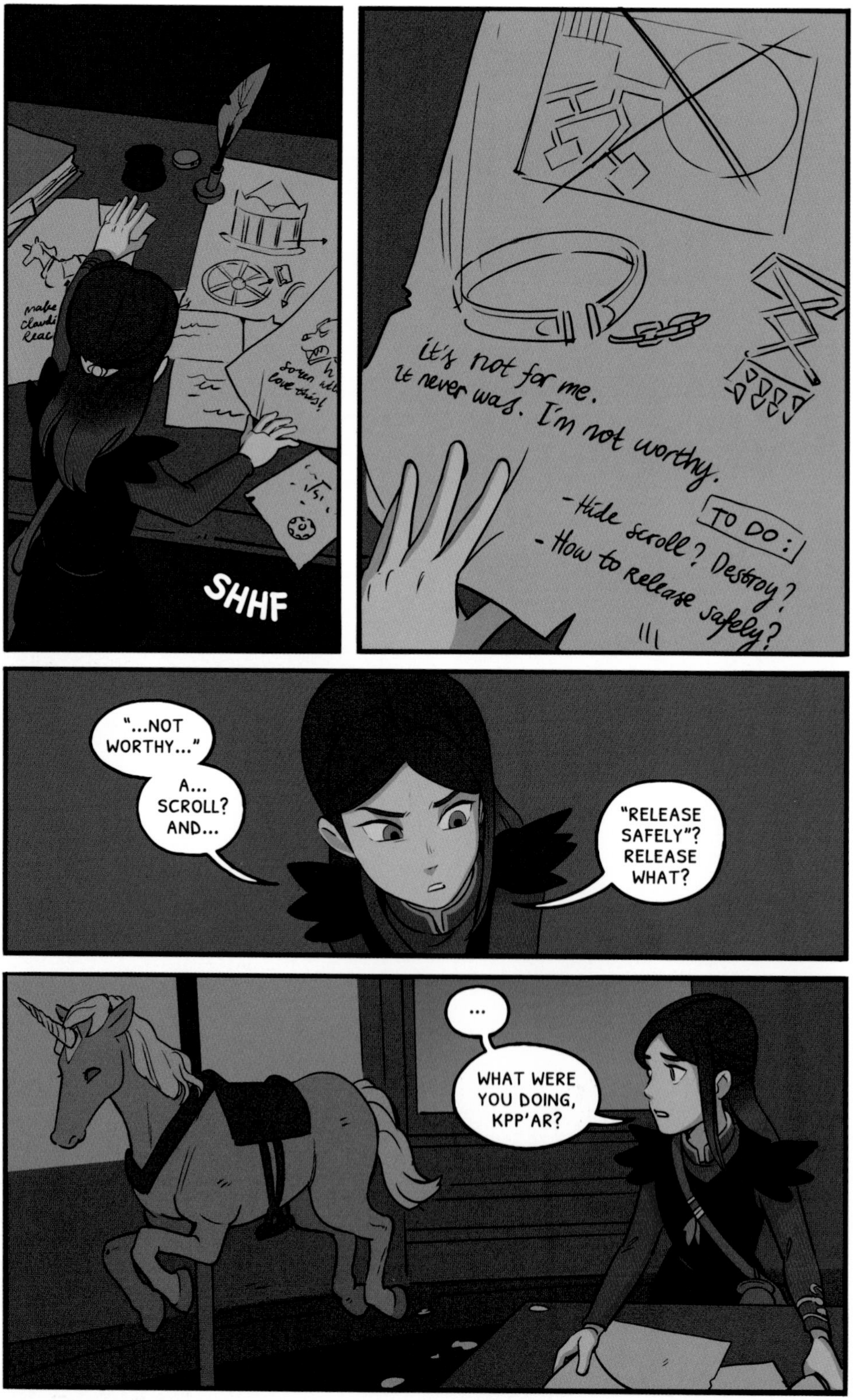
SHHF
It's not for me.
It never was. I'm not worthy.
TO DO:
- Hide scroll? Destroy?
- How to Release safely?
"...NOT WORTHY..."
A... SCROLL? AND...
"RELEASE SAFELY"? RELEASE WHAT?
...
WHAT WERE YOU DOING, KPP'AR?

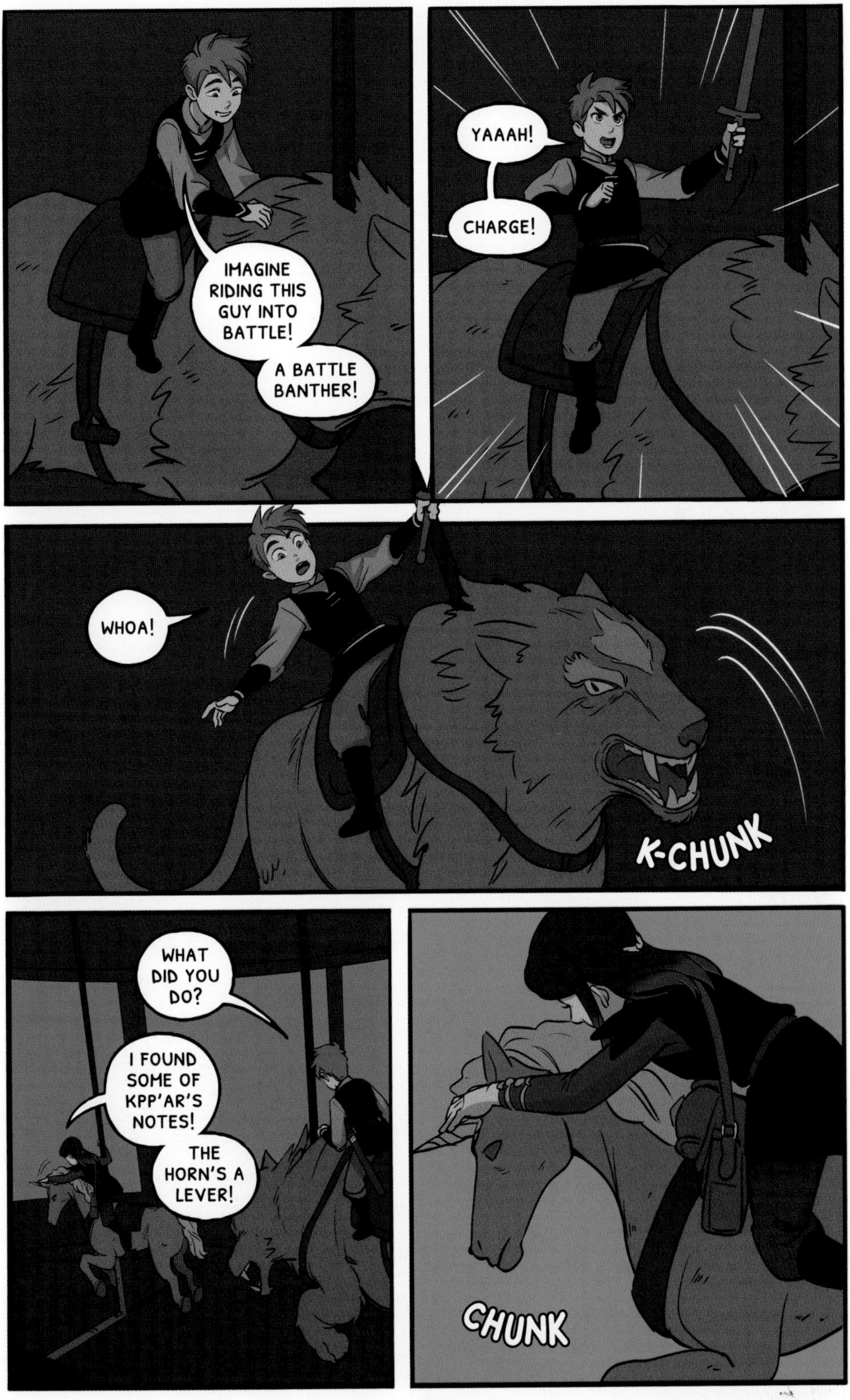
IMAGINE RIDING THIS GUY INTO BATTLE!
A BATTLE BANTHER!
YAAAH!
CHARGE!
WHOA!
K-CHUNK
WHAT DID YOU DO?
I FOUND SOME OF KPP'AR'S NOTES!
THE HORN'S A LEVER!
CHUNK

WOO-HOO! HA HA!

THIS IS GREAT!

always look for the twist

A TWIST?

I THINK THERE'S SOMETHING ELSE HIDDEN HERE!

HUH? WHAT?

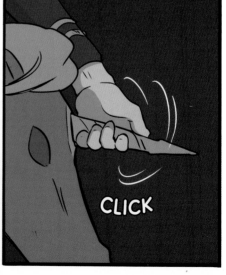

CLICK

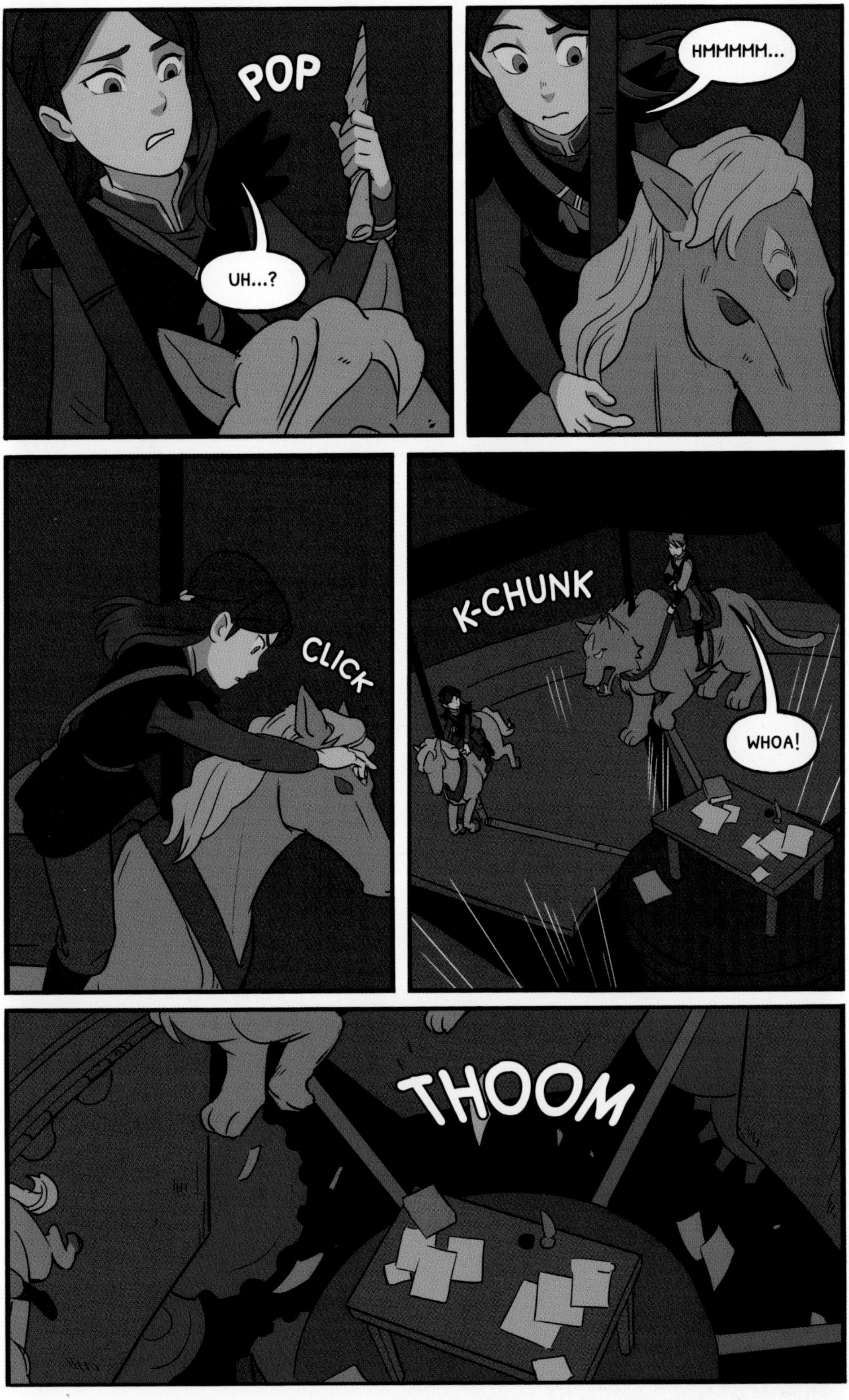
POP
UH...?
HMMMMM...
CLICK
K-CHUNK
WHOA!
THOOM

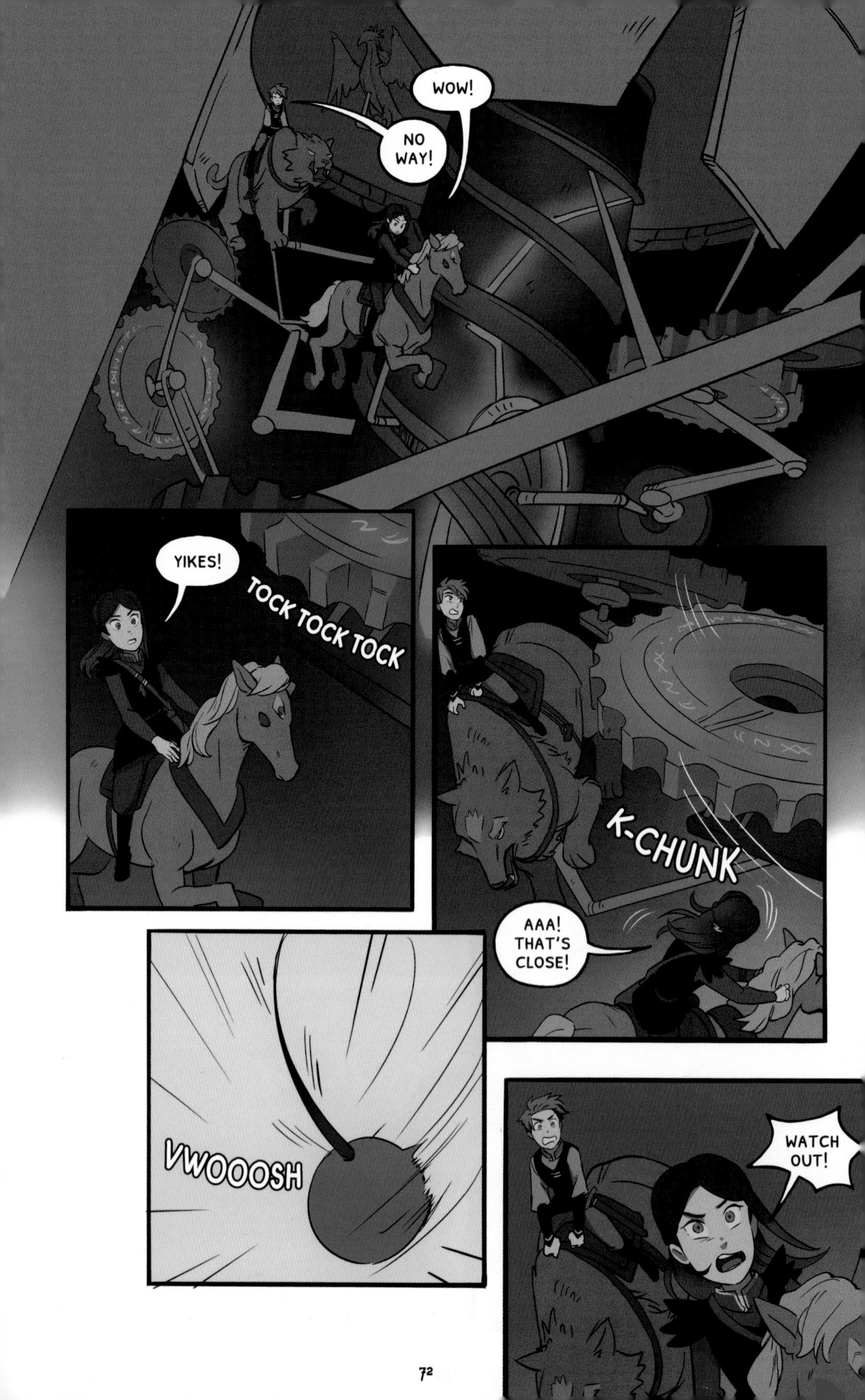

WOW!
NO WAY!
YIKES!
TOCK TOCK TOCK
K-CHUNK
AAA! THAT'S CLOSE!
VWOOOSH
WATCH OUT!

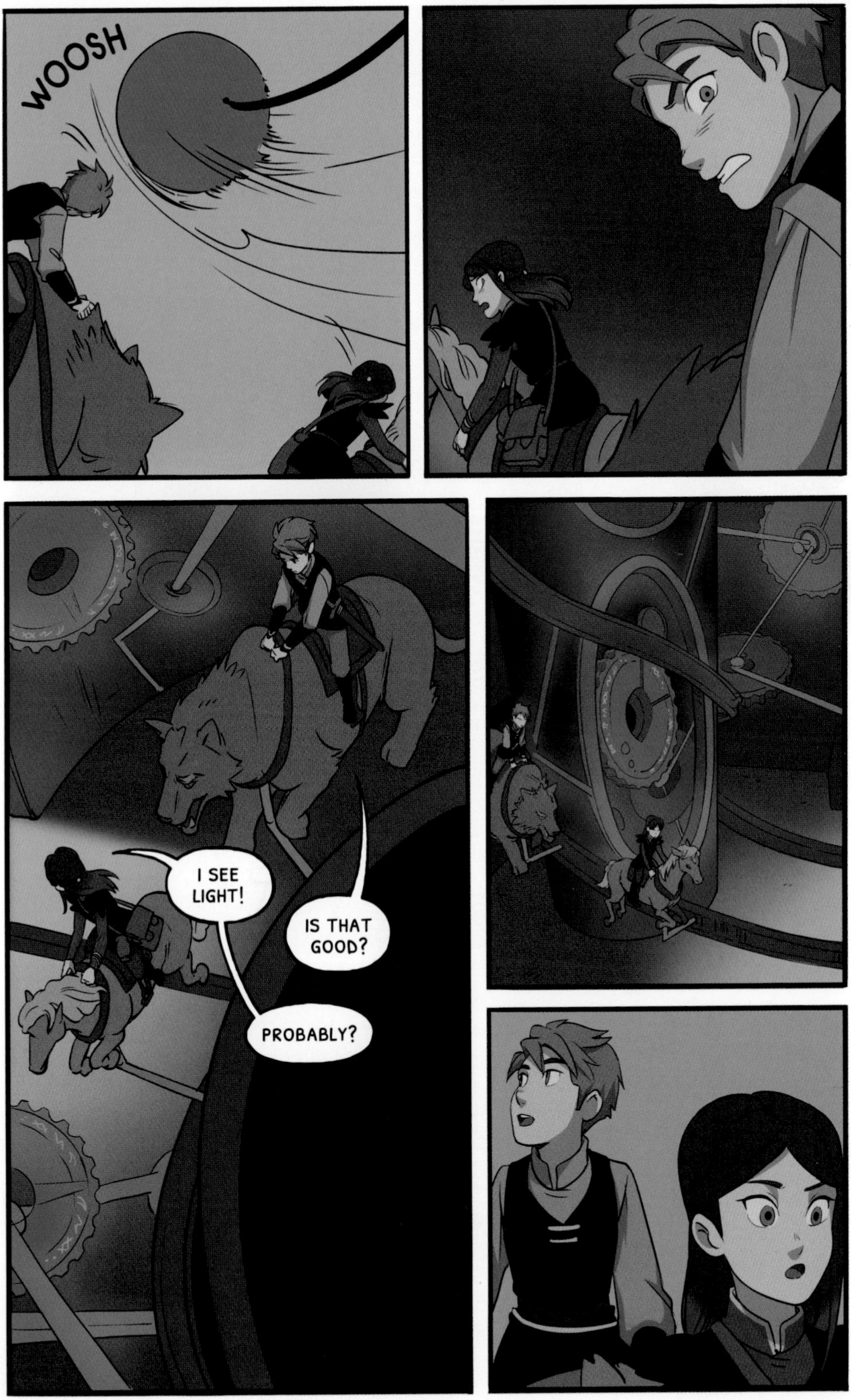
WOOSH
I SEE LIGHT!
IS THAT GOOD?
PROBABLY?

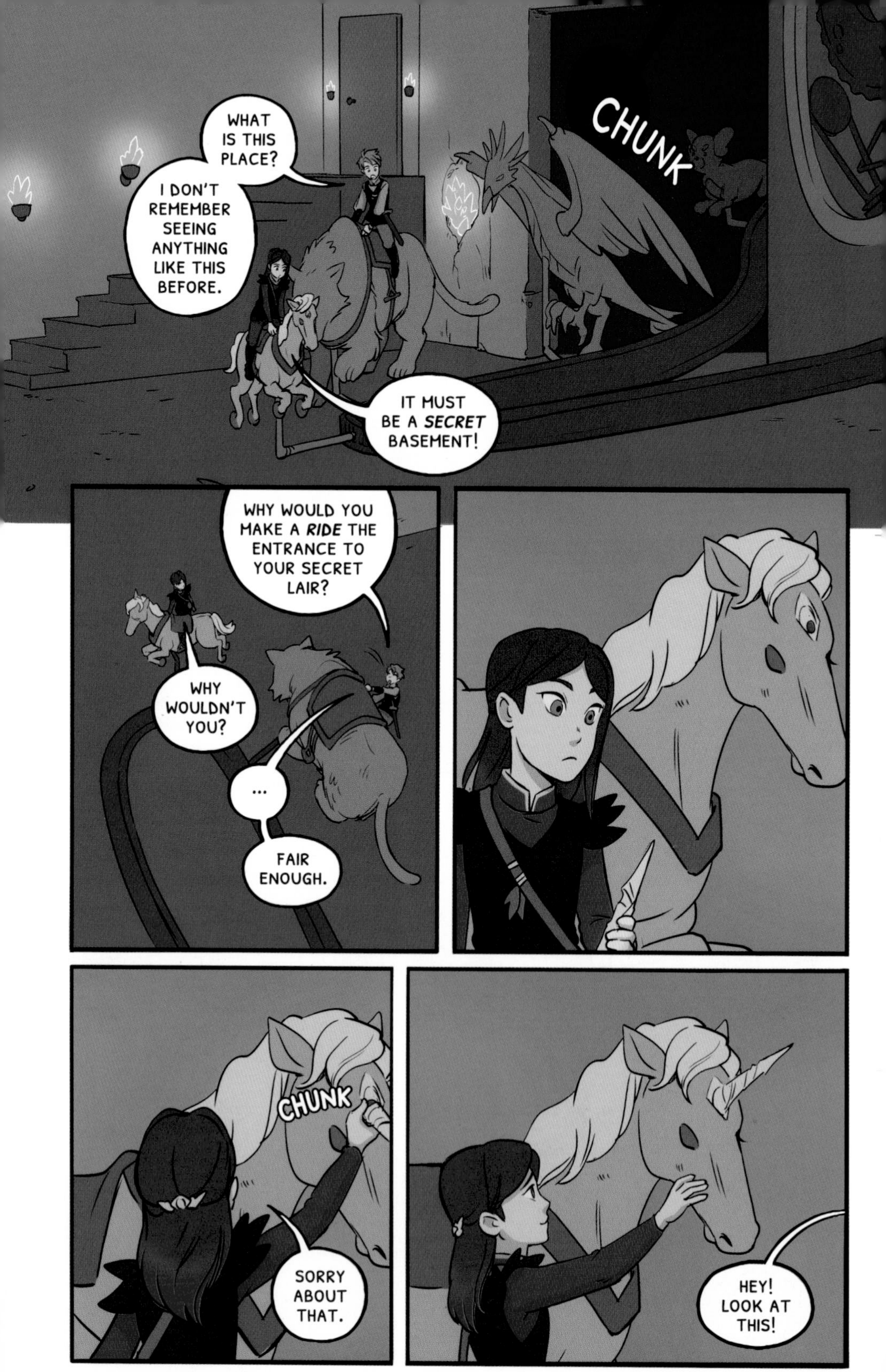
CHUNK
WHAT IS THIS PLACE?
I DON'T REMEMBER SEEING ANYTHING LIKE THIS BEFORE.
IT MUST BE A SECRET BASEMENT!
WHY WOULD YOU MAKE A RIDE THE ENTRANCE TO YOUR SECRET LAIR?
WHY WOULDN'T YOU?
...
FAIR ENOUGH.
CHUNK
SORRY ABOUT THAT.
HEY! LOOK AT THIS!

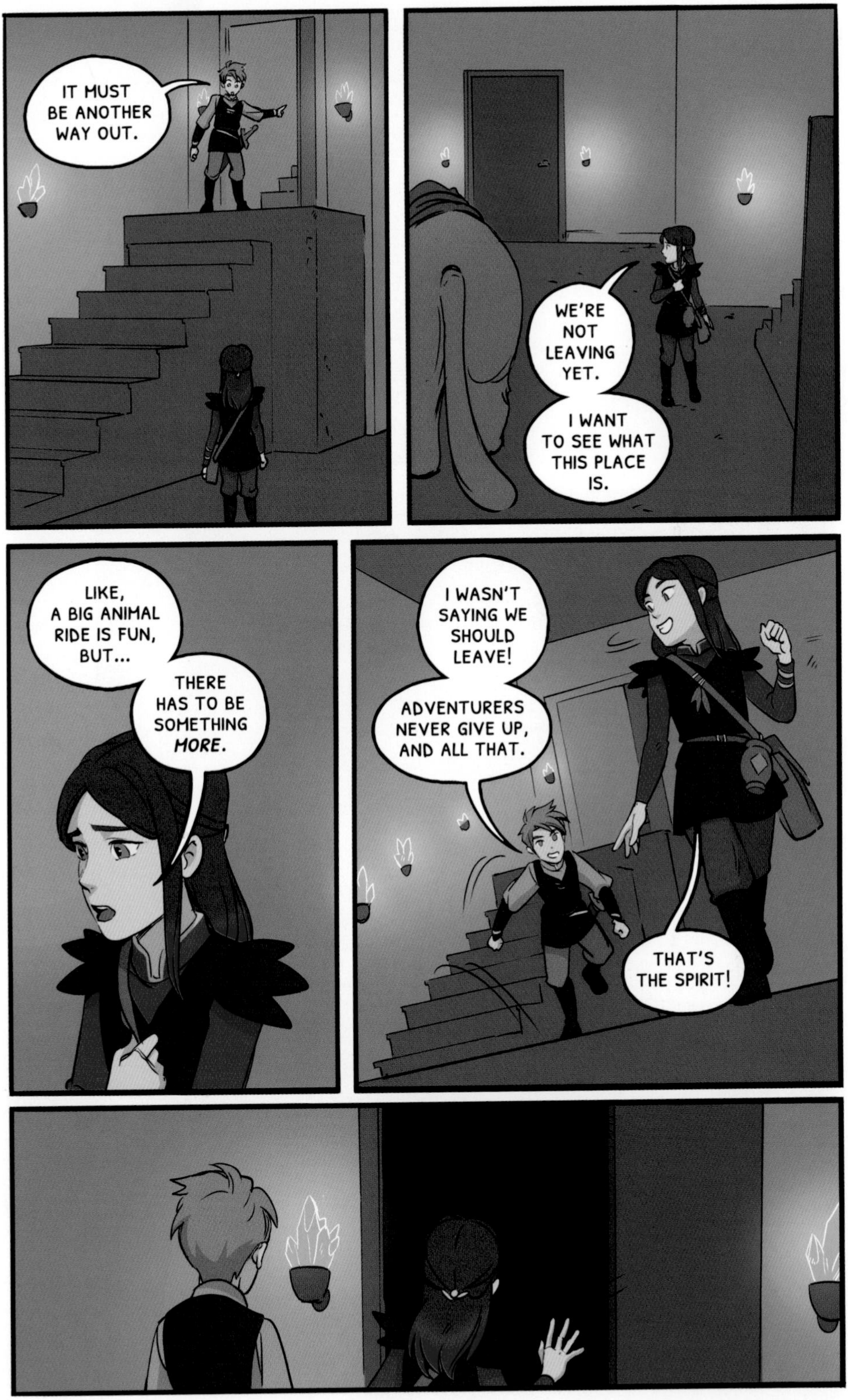
IT MUST BE ANOTHER WAY OUT.
WE'RE NOT LEAVING YET.
I WANT TO SEE WHAT THIS PLACE IS.
LIKE, A BIG ANIMAL RIDE IS FUN, BUT...
THERE HAS TO BE SOMETHING *MORE*.
I WASN'T SAYING WE SHOULD LEAVE!
ADVENTURERS NEVER GIVE UP, AND ALL THAT.
THAT'S THE SPIRIT!

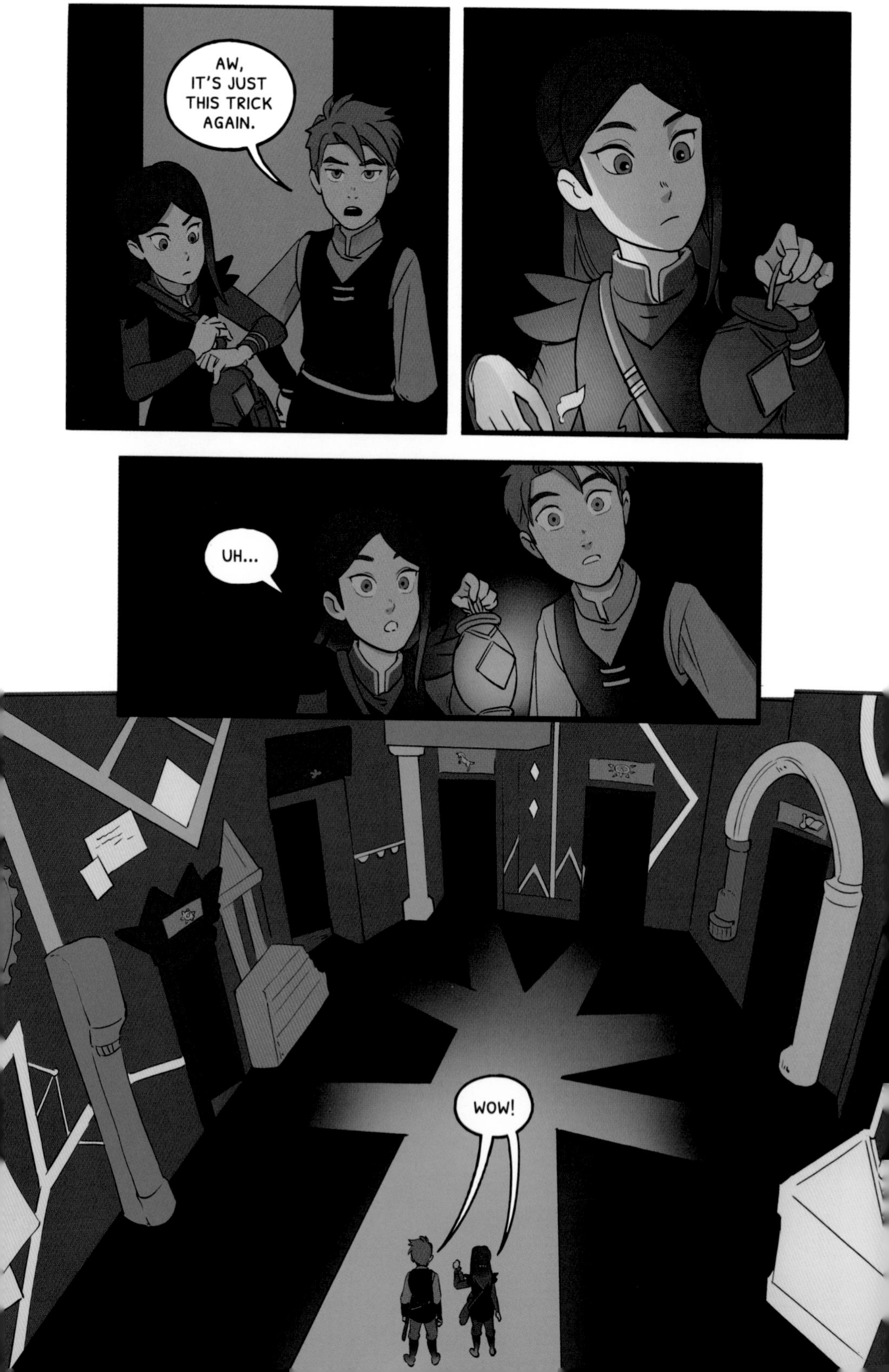
AW, IT'S JUST THIS TRICK AGAIN.
UH...
WOW!

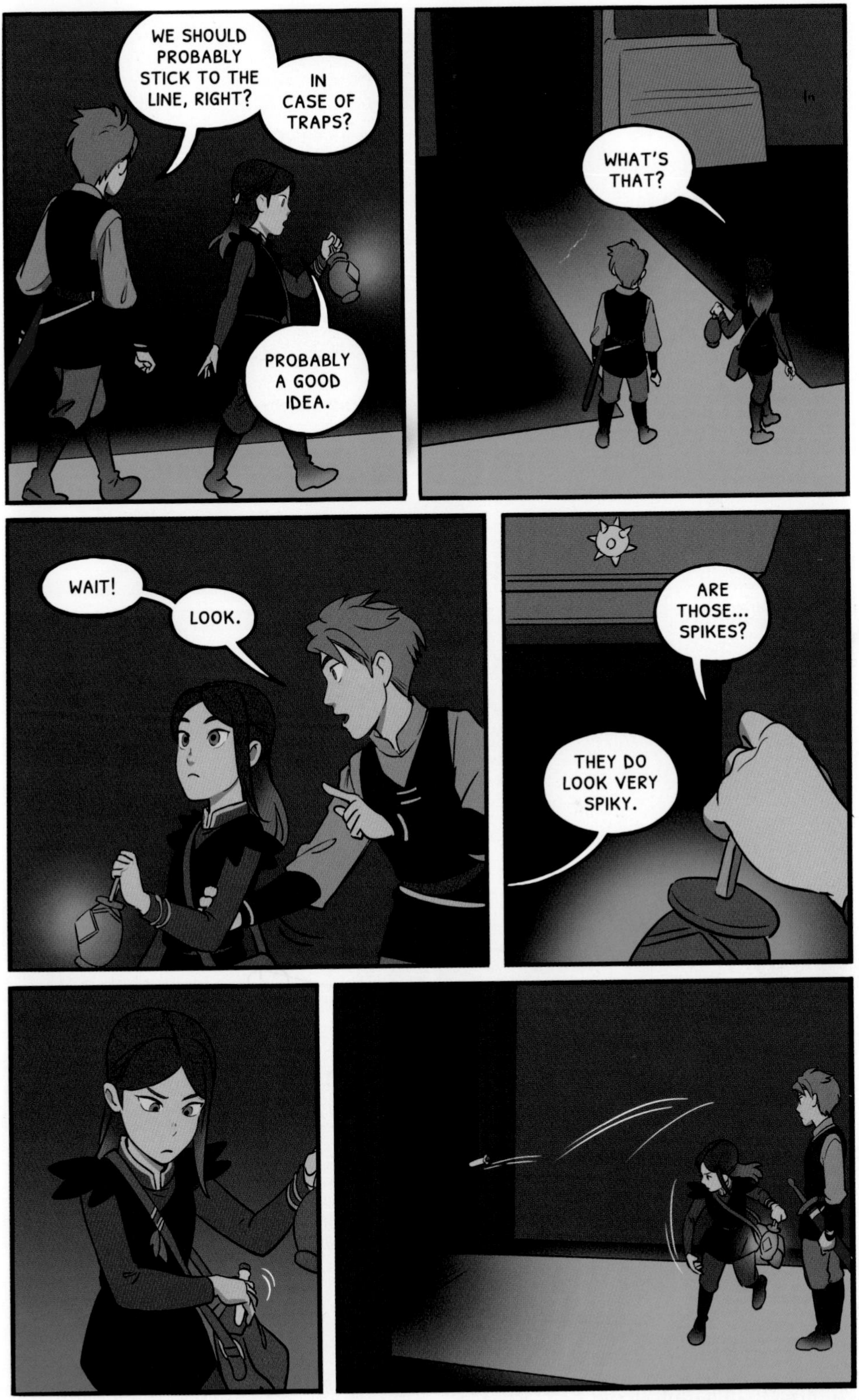
WE SHOULD PROBABLY STICK TO THE LINE, RIGHT?
IN CASE OF TRAPS?
PROBABLY A GOOD IDEA.
WHAT'S THAT?
WAIT!
LOOK.
ARE THOSE... SPIKES?
THEY DO LOOK VERY SPIKY.

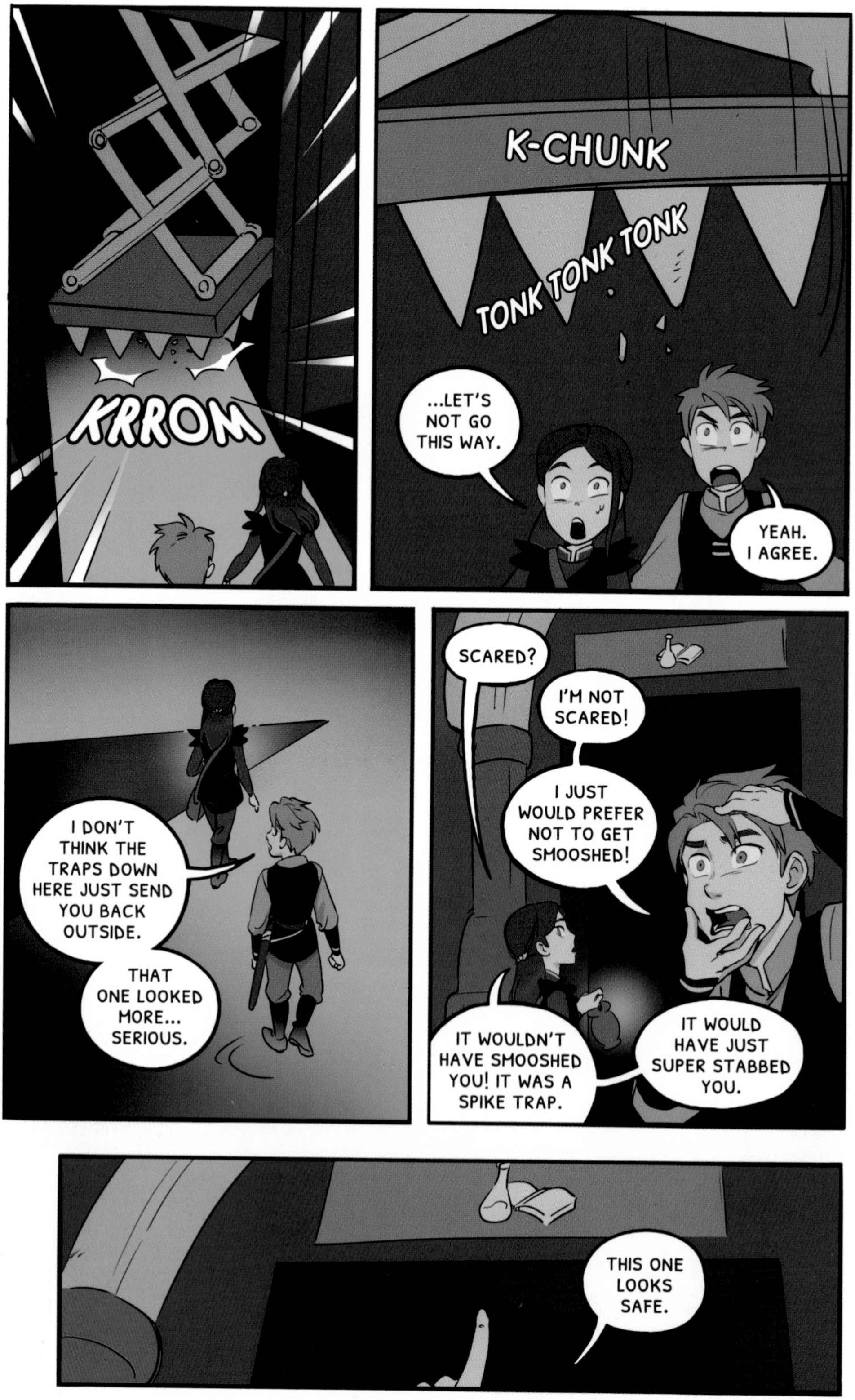
KRROM
K-CHUNK
TONK TONK TONK
...LET'S NOT GO THIS WAY.
YEAH. I AGREE.
I DON'T THINK THE TRAPS DOWN HERE JUST SEND YOU BACK OUTSIDE.
THAT ONE LOOKED MORE... SERIOUS.
SCARED?
I'M NOT SCARED!
I JUST WOULD PREFER NOT TO GET SMOOSHED!
IT WOULDN'T HAVE SMOOSHED YOU! IT WAS A SPIKE TRAP.
IT WOULD HAVE JUST SUPER STABBED YOU.
THIS ONE LOOKS SAFE.

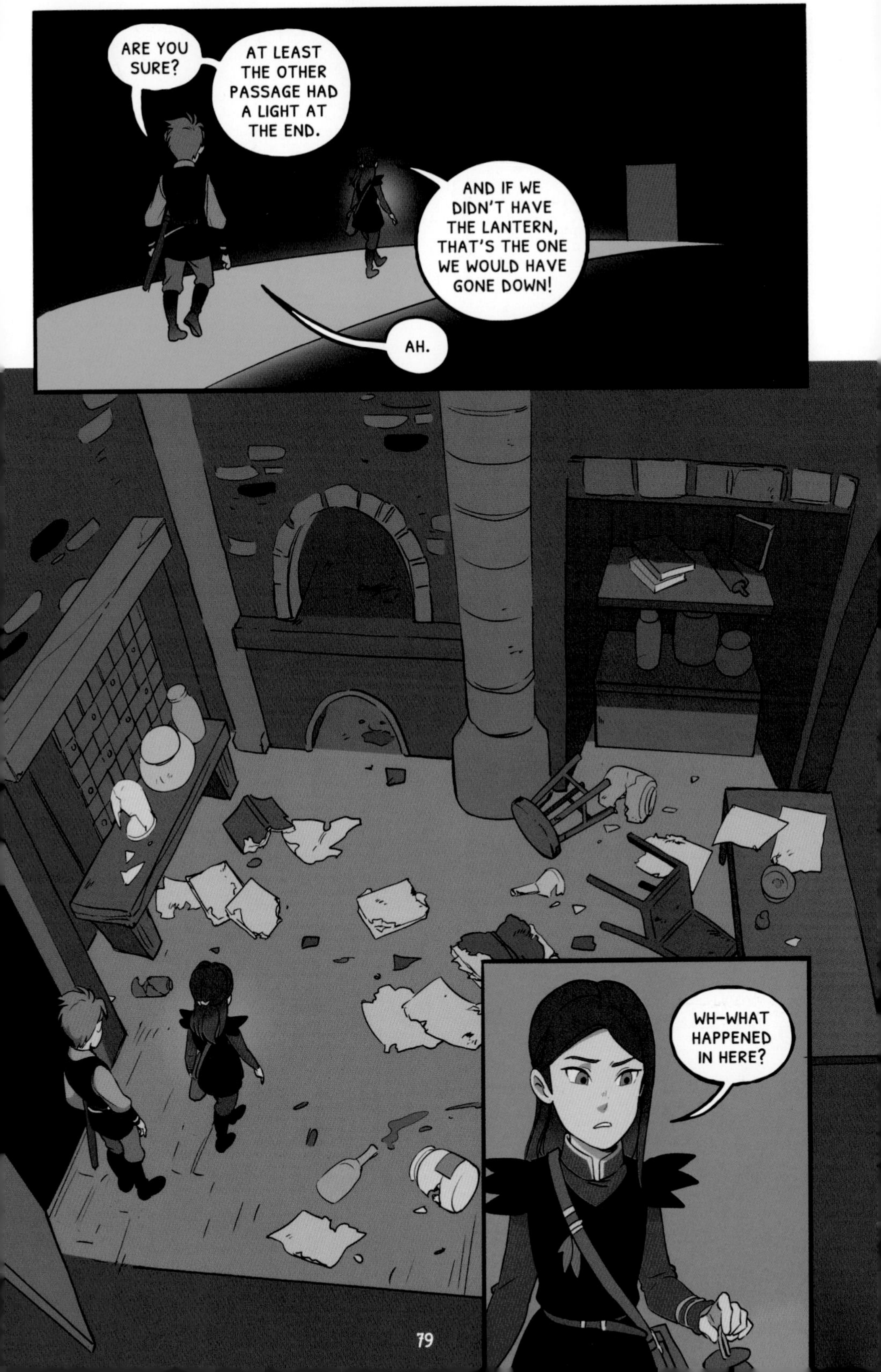
ARE YOU SURE?
AT LEAST THE OTHER PASSAGE HAD A LIGHT AT THE END.
AND IF WE DIDN'T HAVE THE LANTERN, THAT'S THE ONE WE WOULD HAVE GONE DOWN!
AH.
WH-WHAT HAPPENED IN HERE?

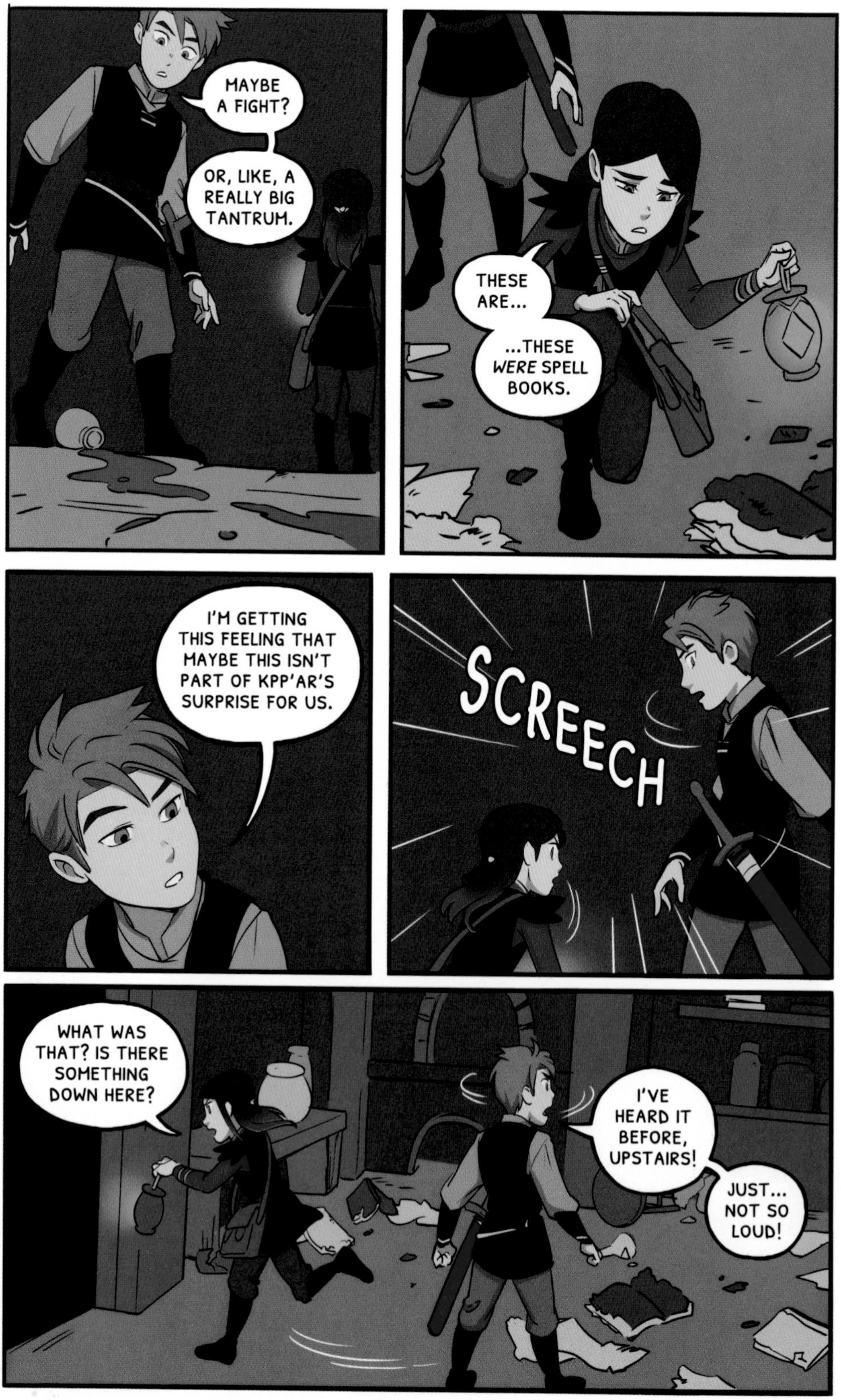
MAYBE A FIGHT?
OR, LIKE, A REALLY BIG TANTRUM.
THESE ARE...
...THESE *WERE* SPELL BOOKS.
I'M GETTING THIS FEELING THAT MAYBE THIS ISN'T PART OF KPP'AR'S SURPRISE FOR US.
SCREECH
WHAT WAS THAT? IS THERE SOMETHING DOWN HERE?
I'VE HEARD IT BEFORE, UPSTAIRS!
JUST... NOT SO LOUD!

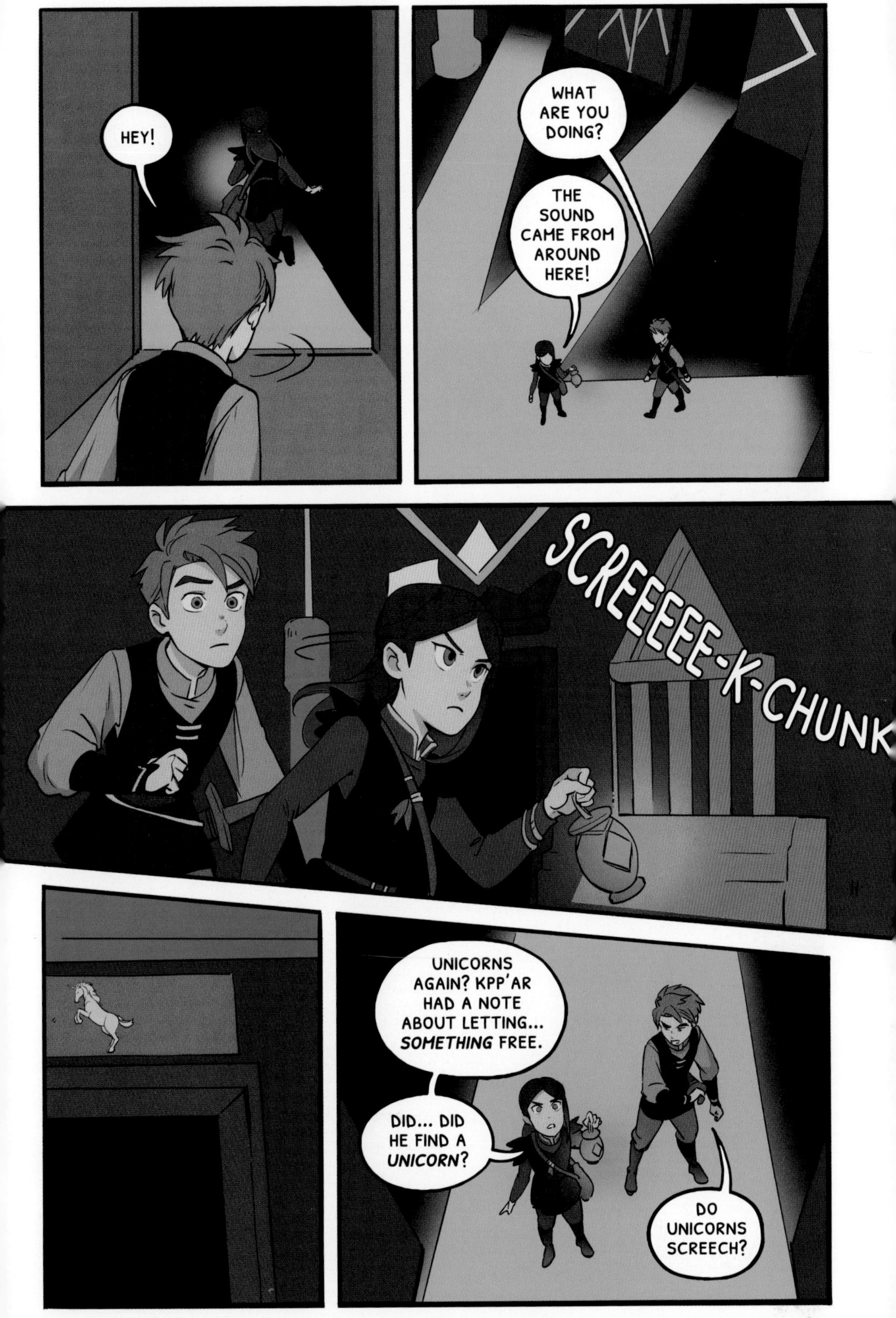
HEY!
WHAT ARE YOU DOING?
THE SOUND CAME FROM AROUND HERE!
SCREEEEE-K-CHUNK
UNICORNS AGAIN? KPP'AR HAD A NOTE ABOUT LETTING... *SOMETHING* FREE.
DID... DID HE FIND A *UNICORN*?
DO UNICORNS SCREECH?

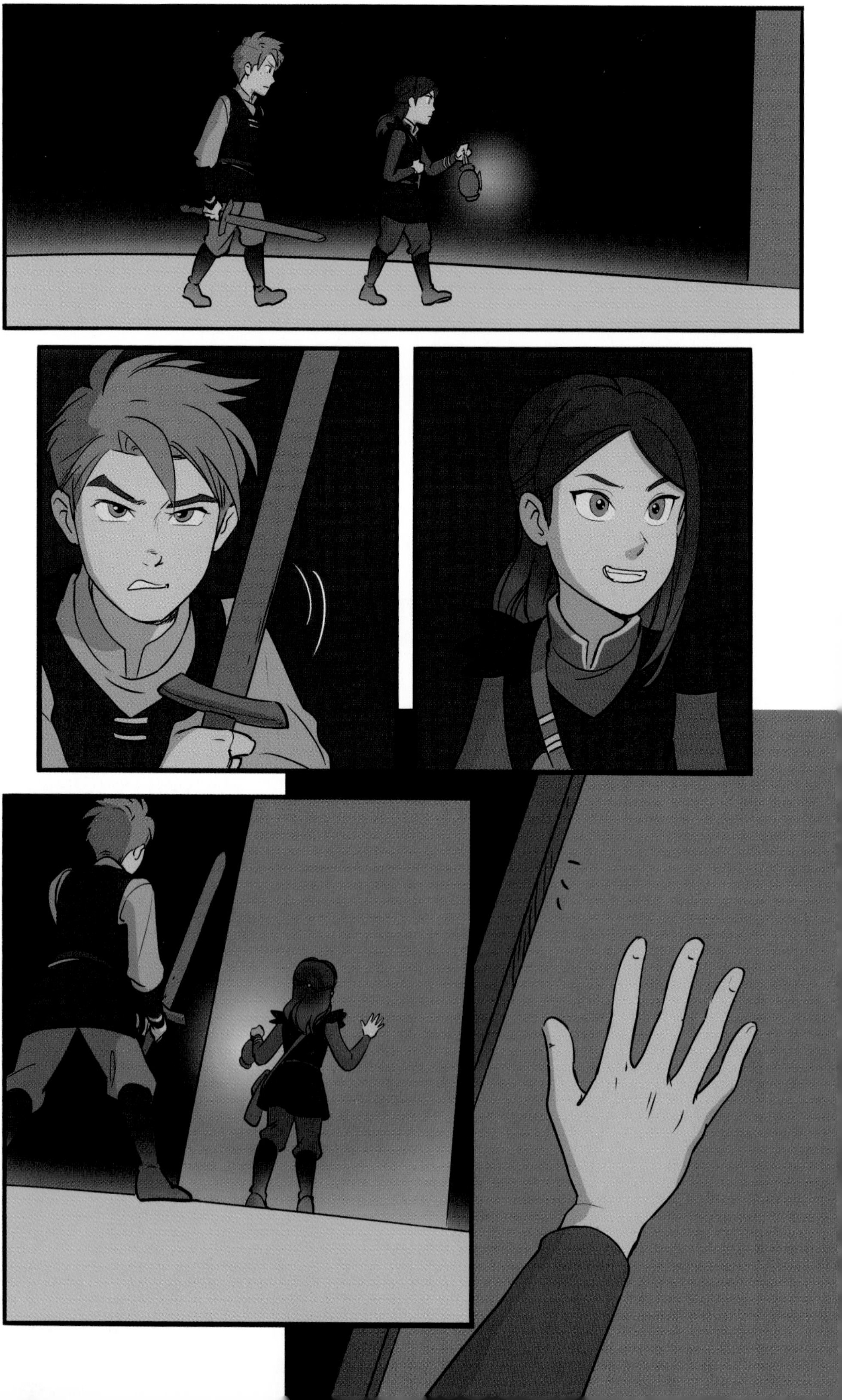

... UNICORN?

UGH. WHAT'S THAT SMELL?

RATTLE

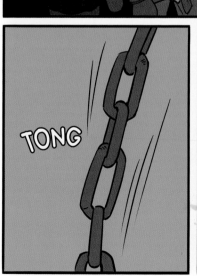

TONG

SCREEEEEEE

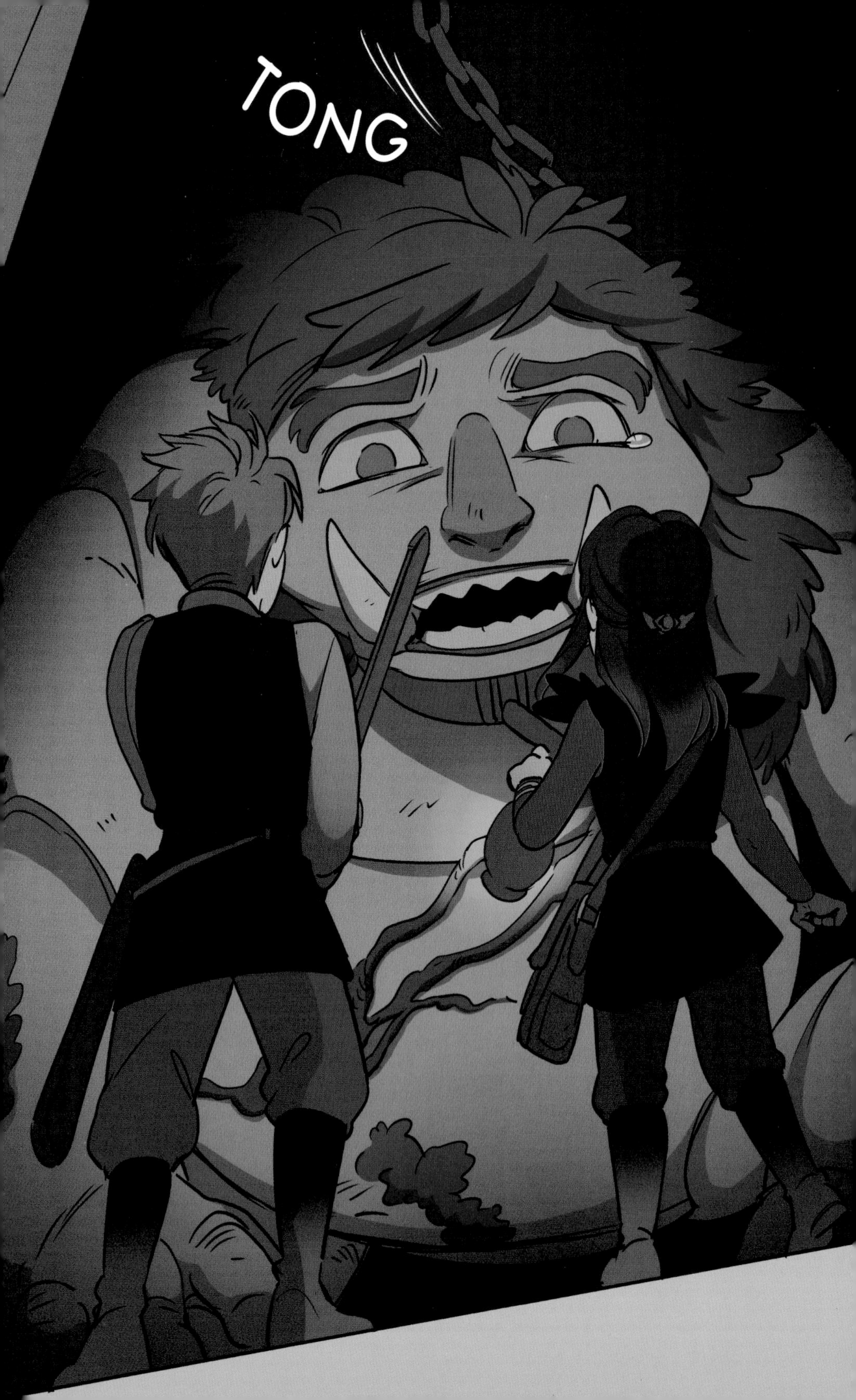
TONG

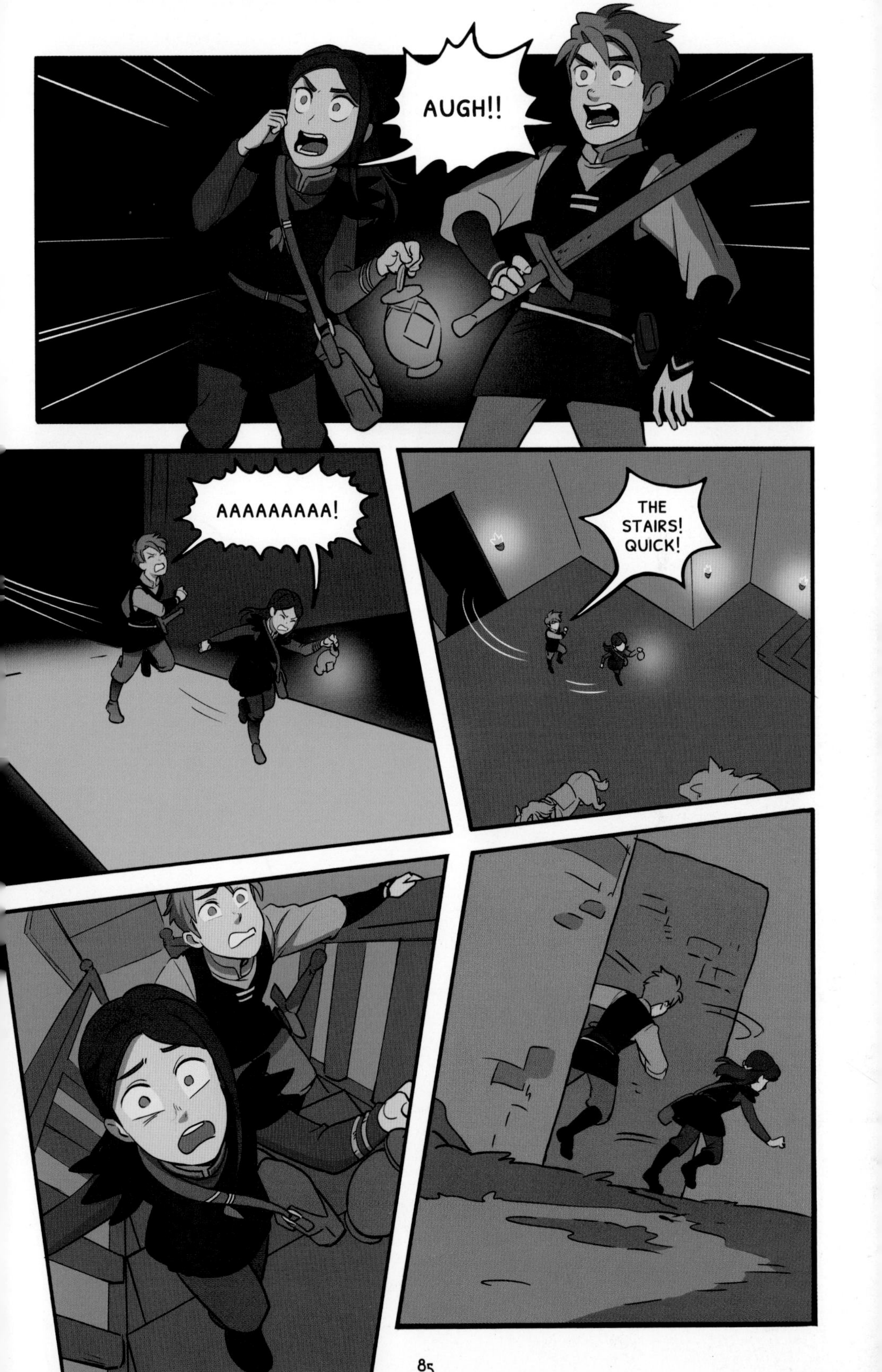
AUGH!!
AAAAAAAAA!
THE STAIRS! QUICK!

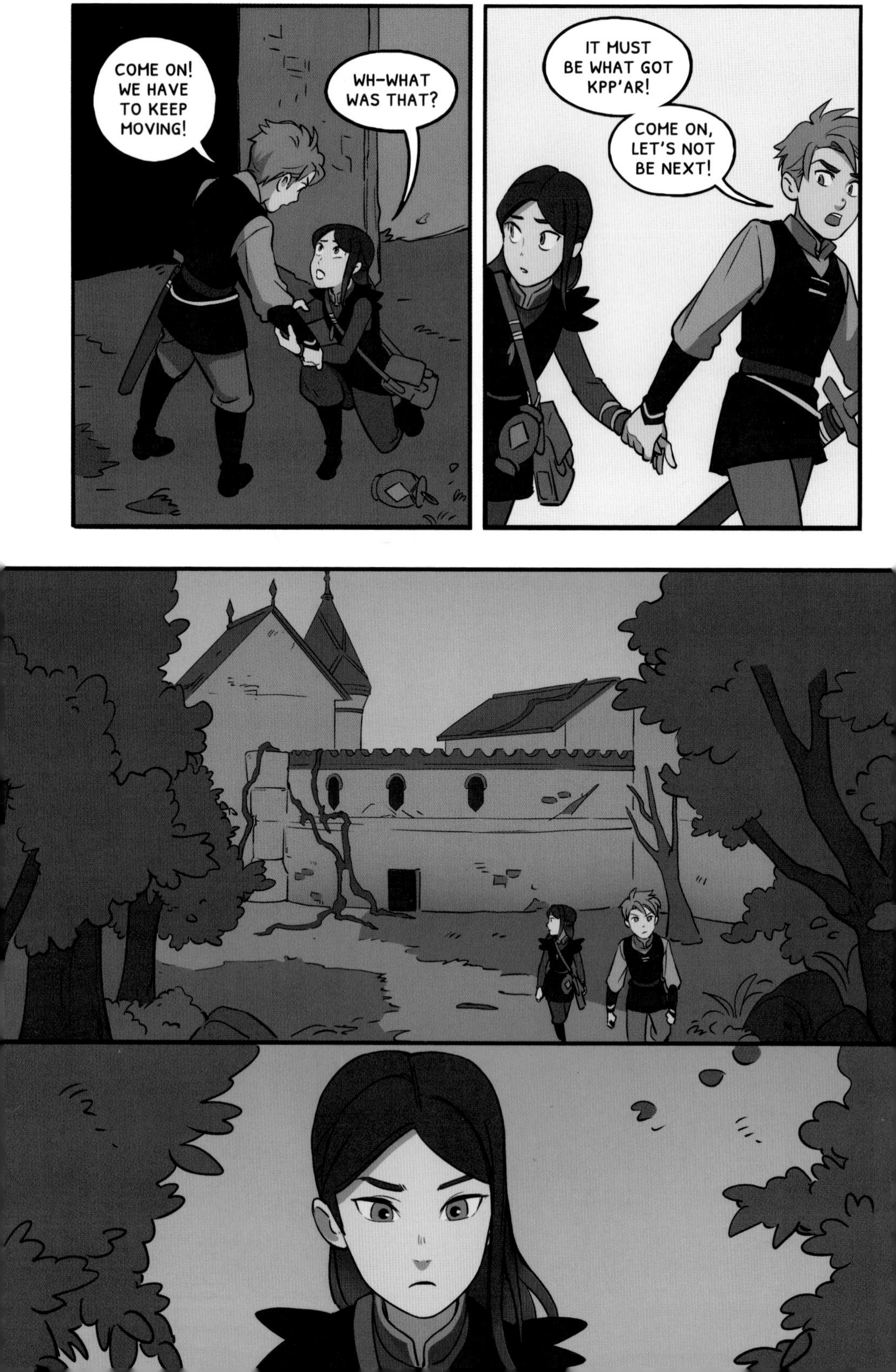
COME ON! WE HAVE TO KEEP MOVING!
WH-WHAT WAS THAT?
IT MUST BE WHAT GOT KPP'AR!
COME ON, LET'S NOT BE NEXT!

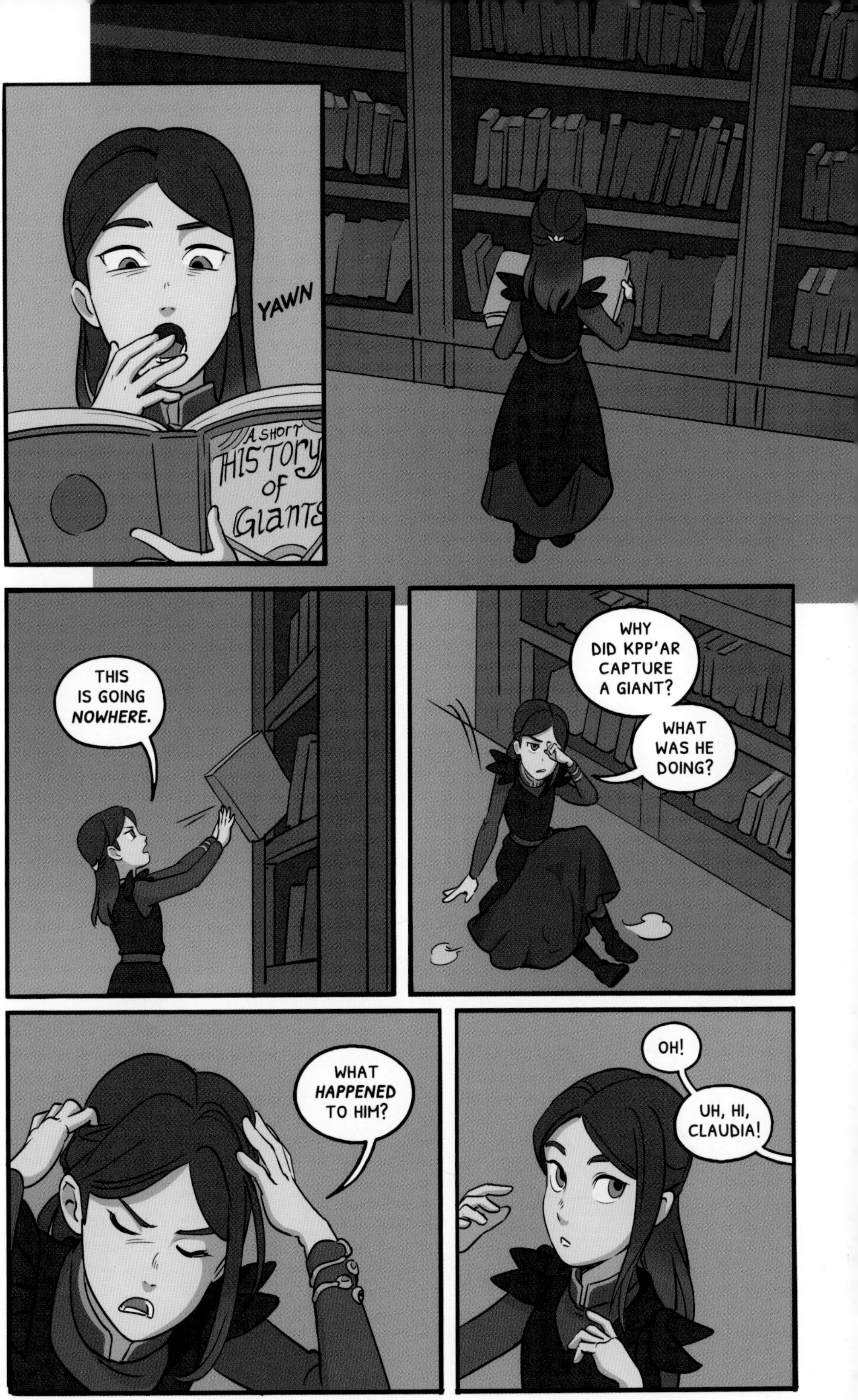
YAWN
A SHORT HISTORY of GIANTS
THIS IS GOING NOWHERE.
WHY DID KPP'AR CAPTURE A GIANT?
WHAT WAS HE DOING?
WHAT HAPPENED TO HIM?
OH!
UH, HI, CLAUDIA!

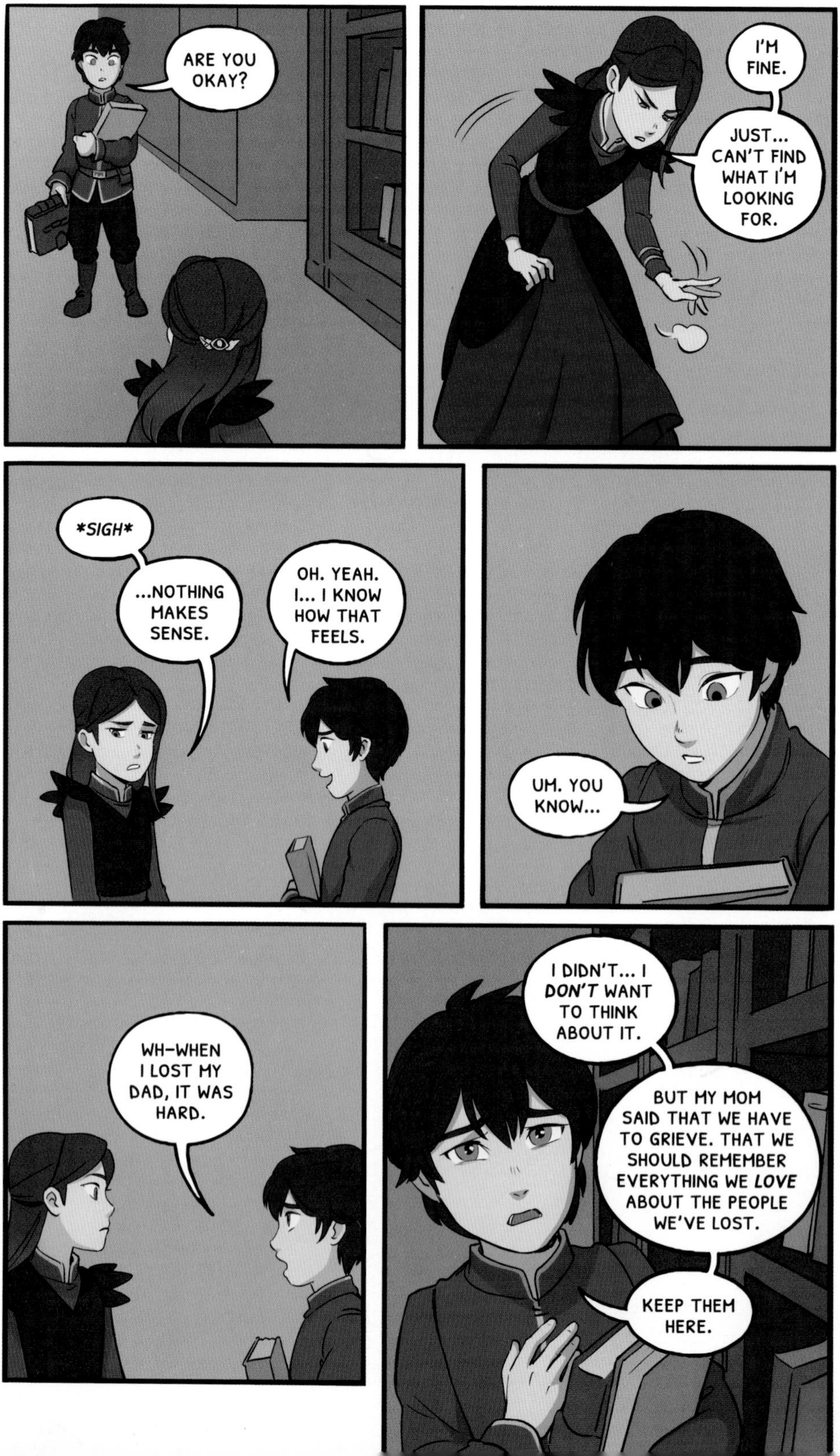
ARE YOU OKAY?
I'M FINE.
JUST... CAN'T FIND WHAT I'M LOOKING FOR.
SIGH
...NOTHING MAKES SENSE.
OH. YEAH. I... I KNOW HOW THAT FEELS.
UM. YOU KNOW...
WH-WHEN I LOST MY DAD, IT WAS HARD.
I DIDN'T... I *DON'T* WANT TO THINK ABOUT IT.
BUT MY MOM SAID THAT WE HAVE TO GRIEVE. THAT WE SHOULD REMEMBER EVERYTHING WE *LOVE* ABOUT THE PEOPLE WE'VE LOST.
KEEP THEM HERE.

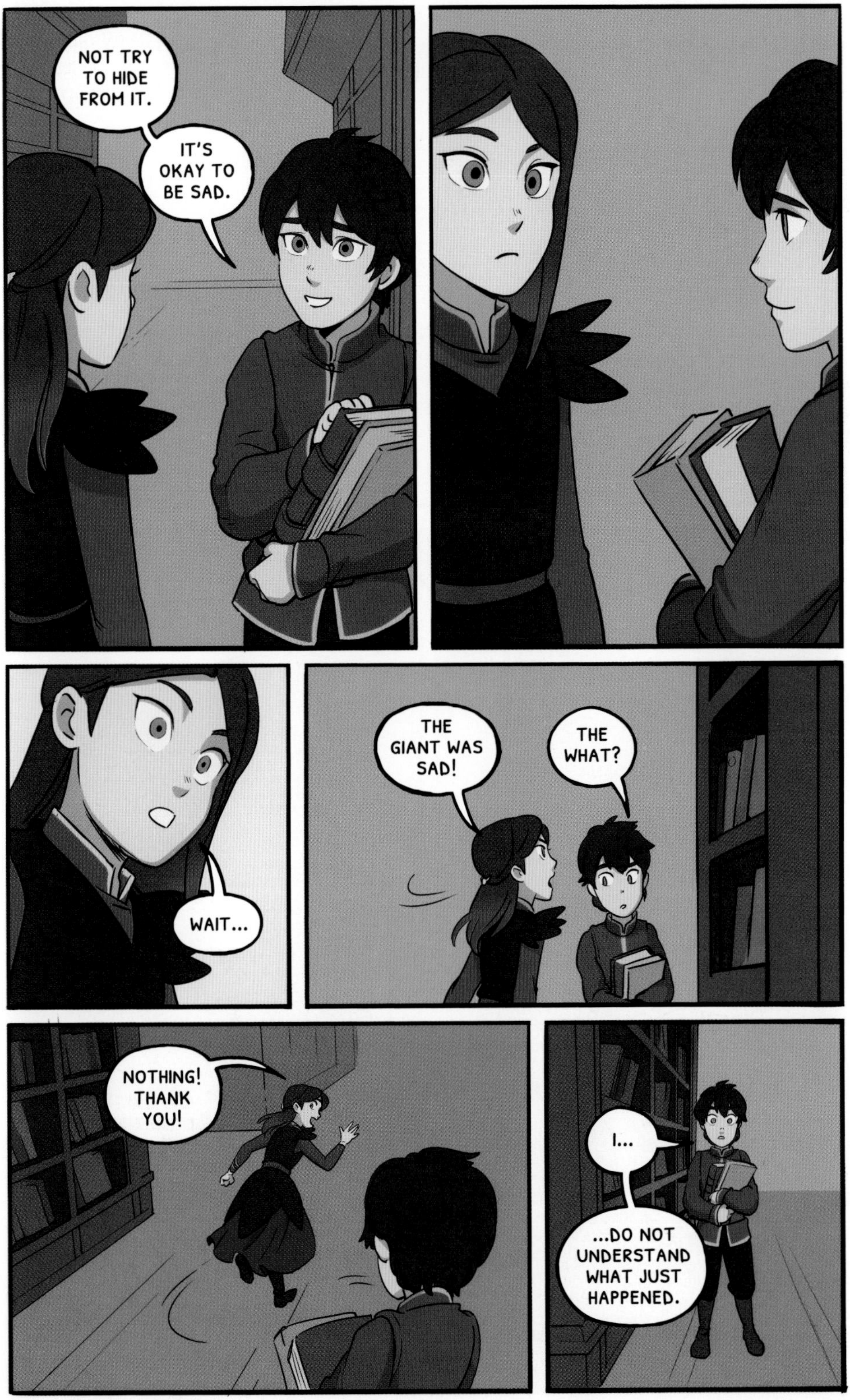
NOT TRY TO HIDE FROM IT.
IT'S OKAY TO BE SAD.
WAIT...
THE GIANT WAS SAD!
THE WHAT?
NOTHING! THANK YOU!
I...
...DO NOT UNDERSTAND WHAT JUST HAPPENED.

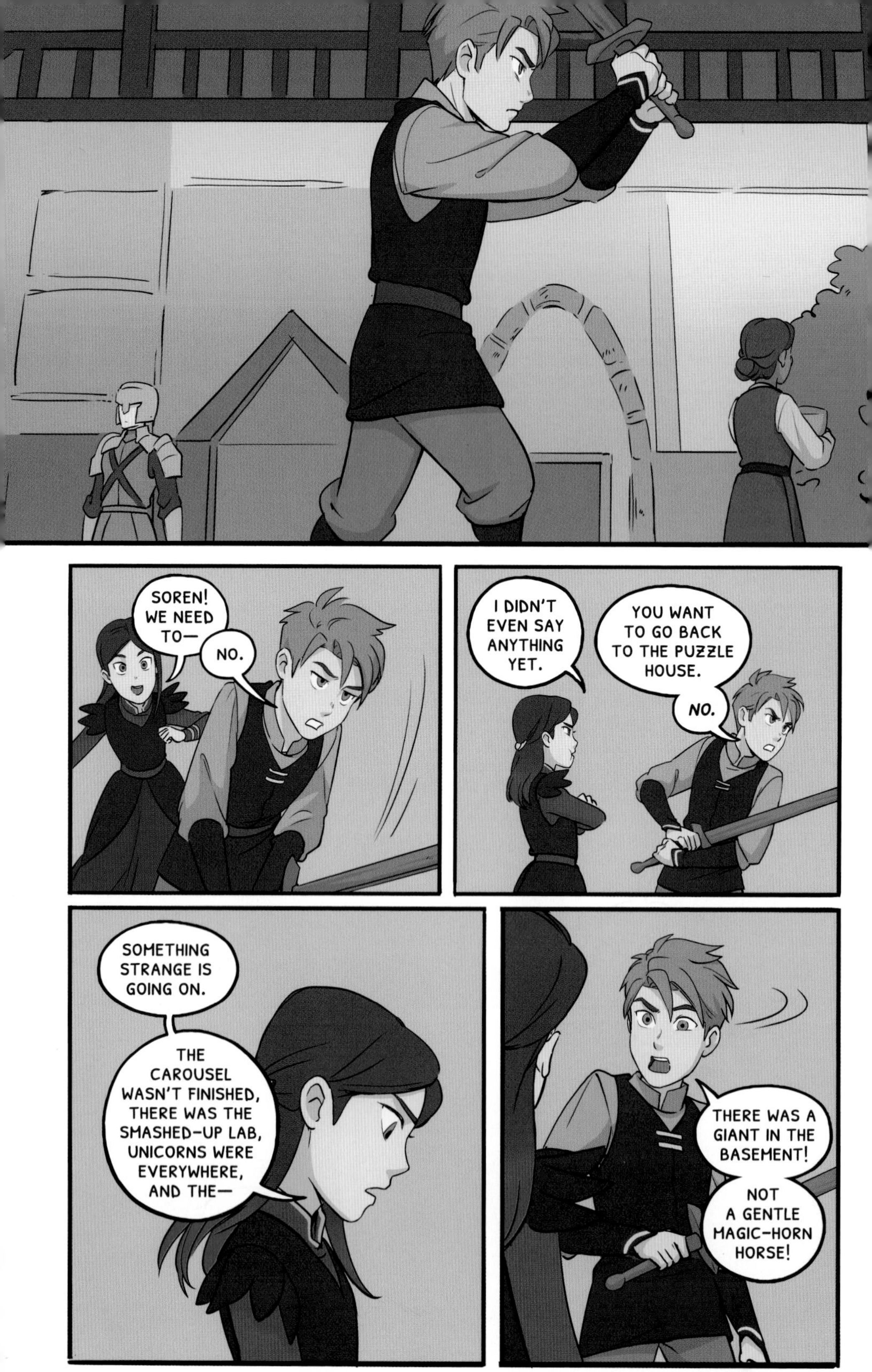
SOREN! WE NEED TO—
NO.
I DIDN'T EVEN SAY ANYTHING YET.
YOU WANT TO GO BACK TO THE PUZZLE HOUSE.
NO.
SOMETHING STRANGE IS GOING ON.
THE CAROUSEL WASN'T FINISHED, THERE WAS THE SMASHED-UP LAB, UNICORNS WERE EVERYWHERE, AND THE—
THERE WAS A GIANT IN THE BASEMENT!
NOT A GENTLE MAGIC-HORN HORSE!

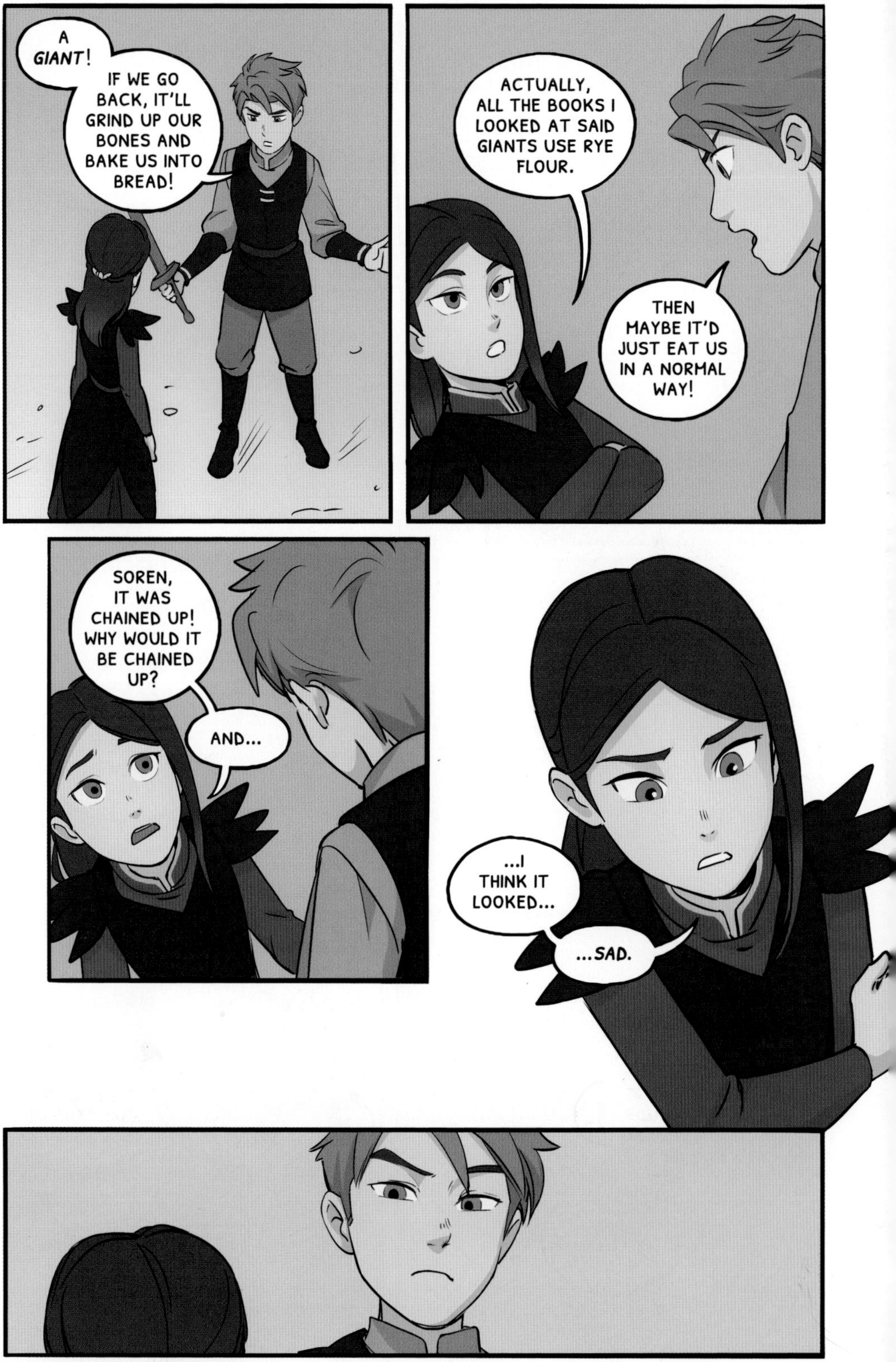
A GIANT!
IF WE GO BACK, IT'LL GRIND UP OUR BONES AND BAKE US INTO BREAD!
ACTUALLY, ALL THE BOOKS I LOOKED AT SAID GIANTS USE RYE FLOUR.
THEN MAYBE IT'D JUST EAT US IN A NORMAL WAY!
SOREN, IT WAS CHAINED UP! WHY WOULD IT BE CHAINED UP?
AND...
...I THINK IT LOOKED...
...SAD.

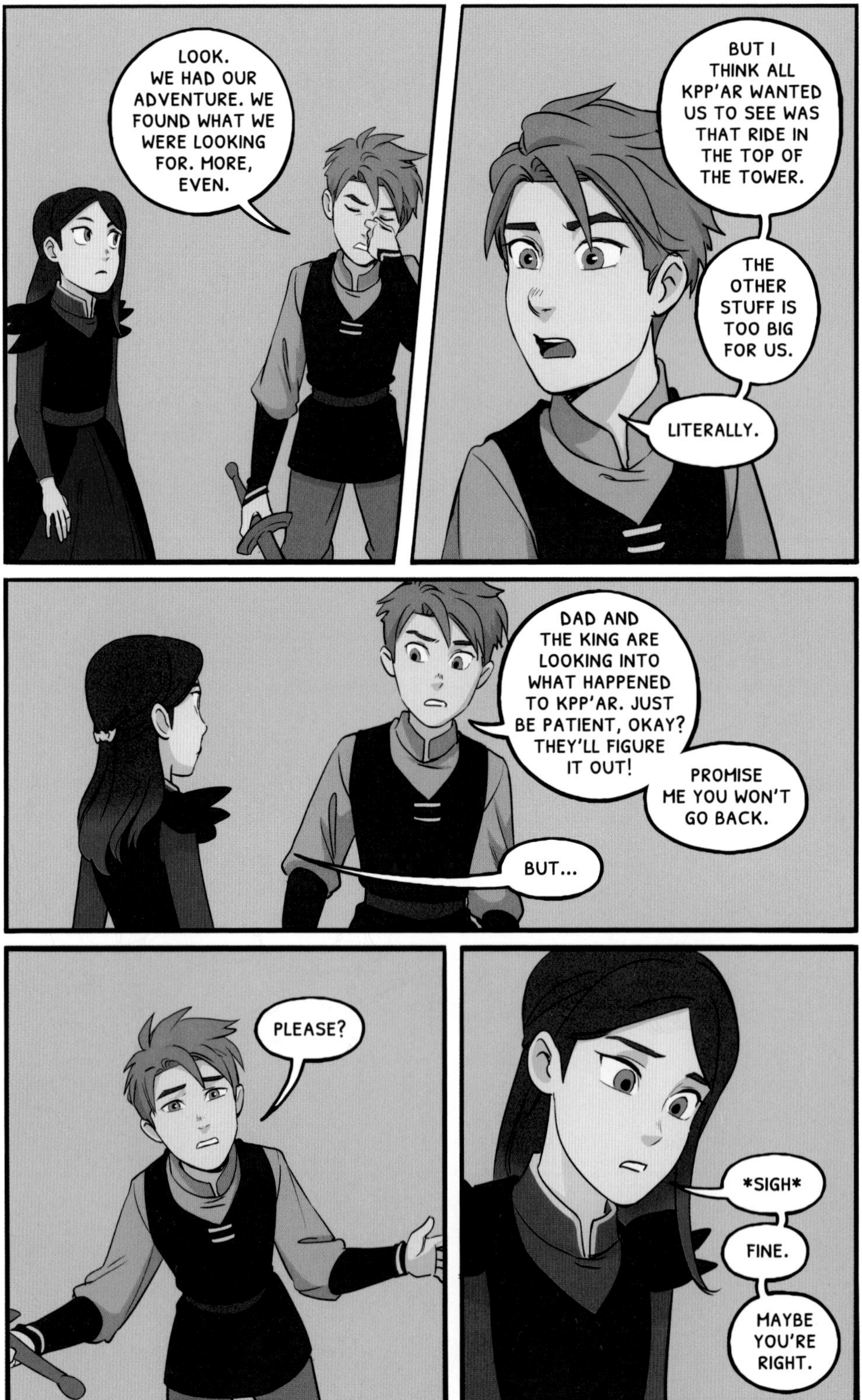
LOOK. WE HAD OUR ADVENTURE. WE FOUND WHAT WE WERE LOOKING FOR. MORE, EVEN.
BUT I THINK ALL KPP'AR WANTED US TO SEE WAS THAT RIDE IN THE TOP OF THE TOWER.
THE OTHER STUFF IS TOO BIG FOR US.
LITERALLY.
DAD AND THE KING ARE LOOKING INTO WHAT HAPPENED TO KPP'AR. JUST BE PATIENT, OKAY? THEY'LL FIGURE IT OUT!
PROMISE ME YOU WON'T GO BACK.
BUT...
PLEASE?
SIGH
FINE.
MAYBE YOU'RE RIGHT.

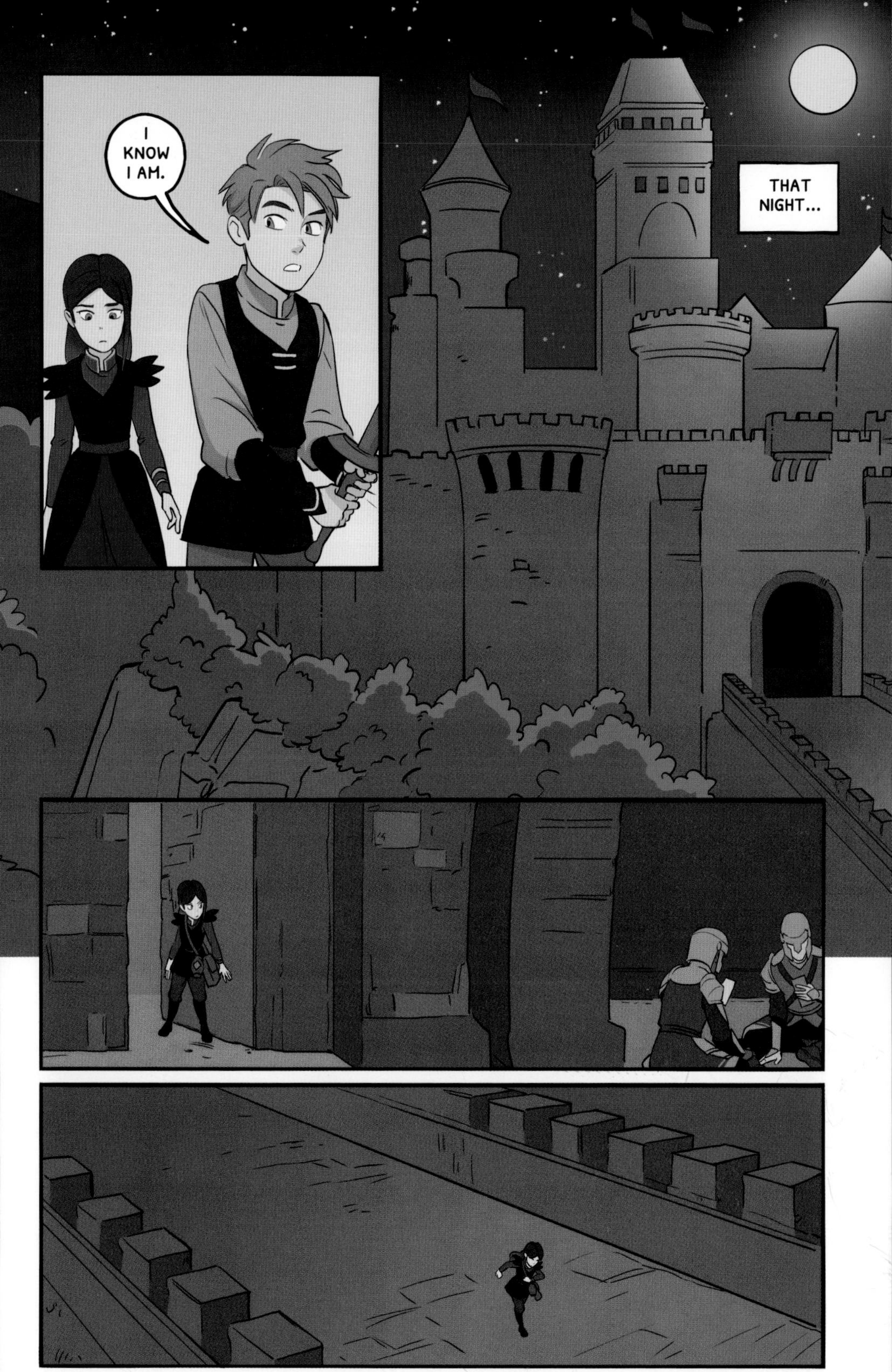
I KNOW I AM.
THAT NIGHT...

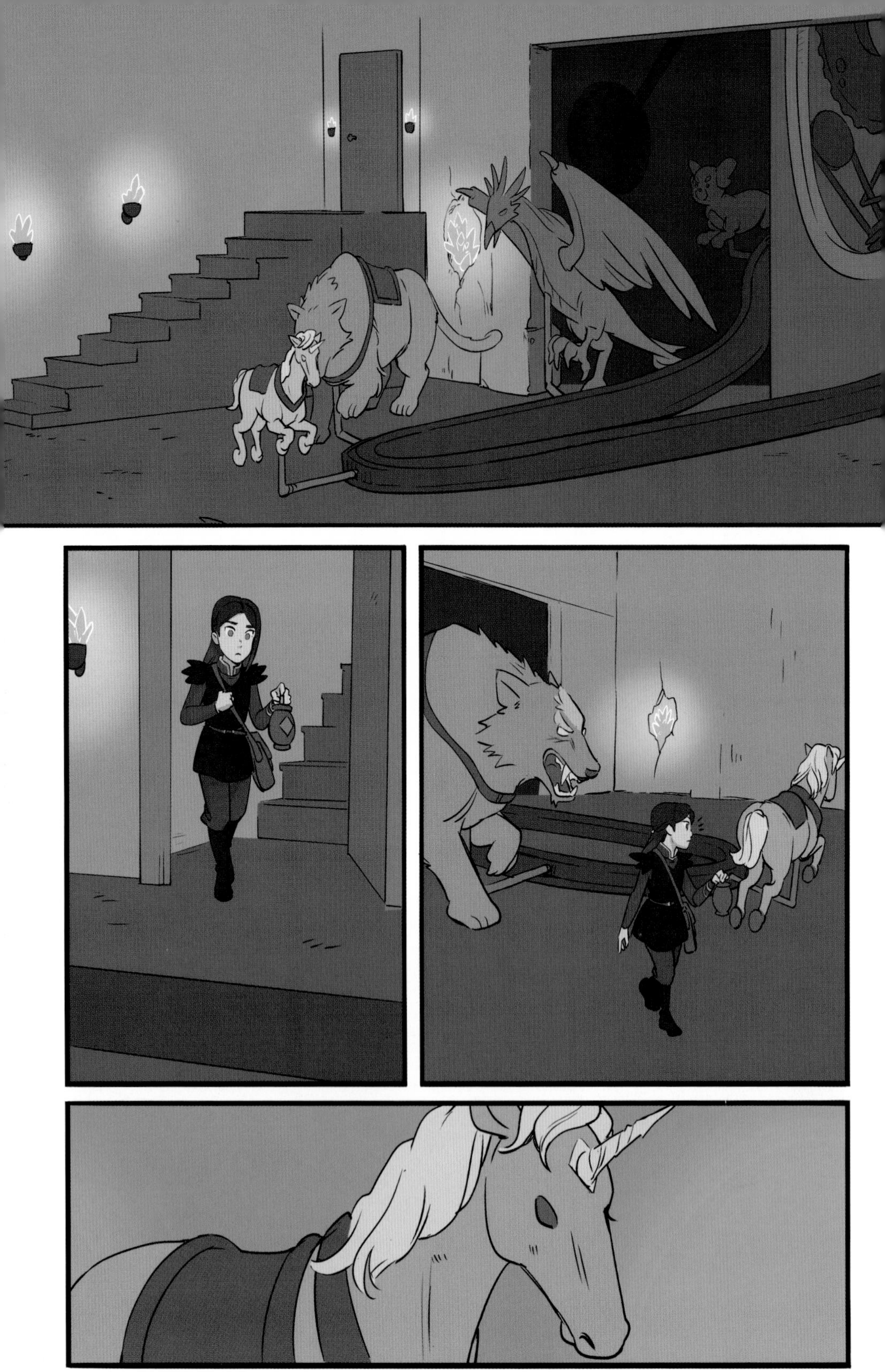

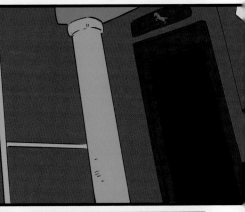

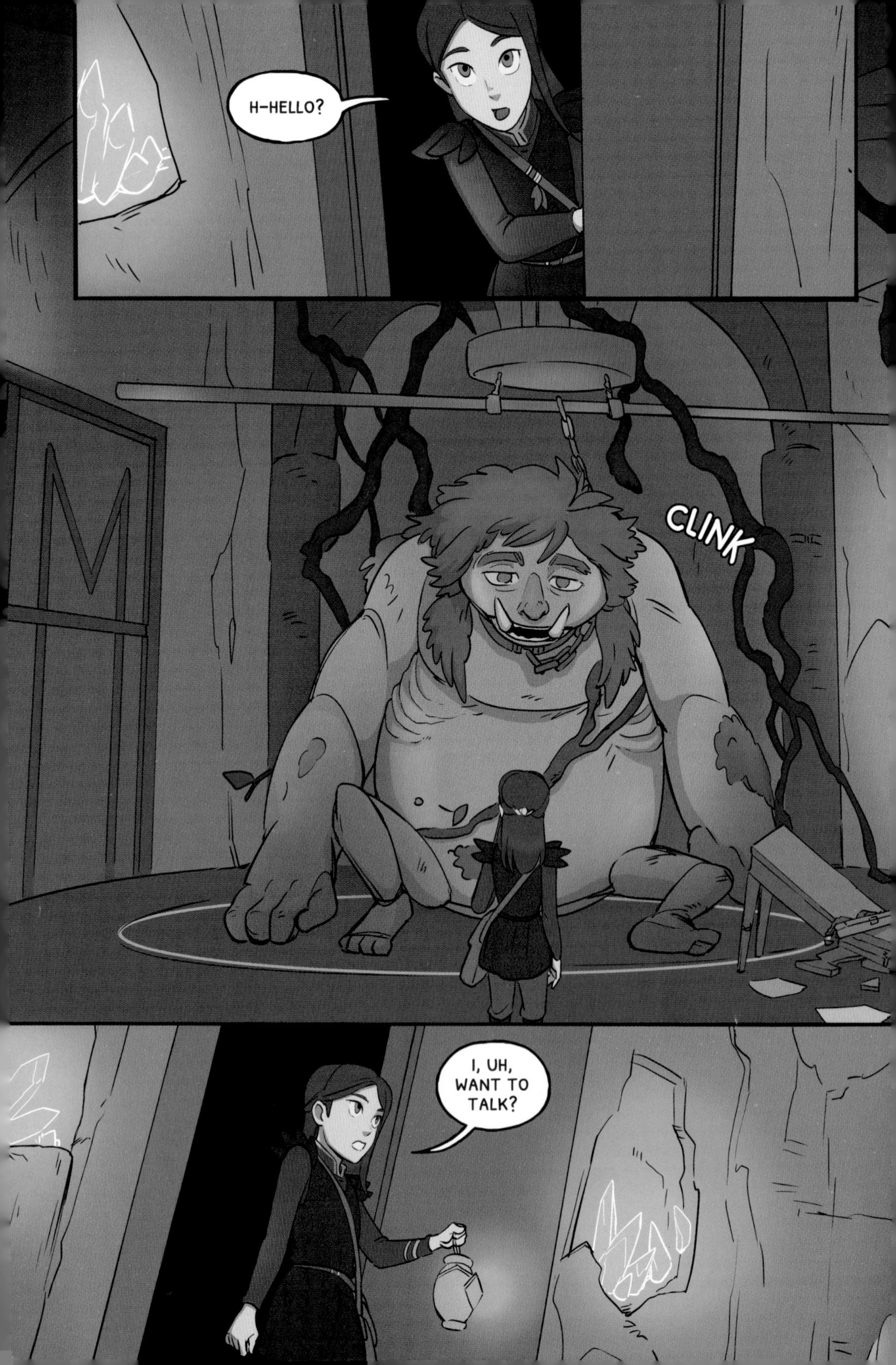
H-HELLO?
CLINK
I, UH, WANT TO TALK?

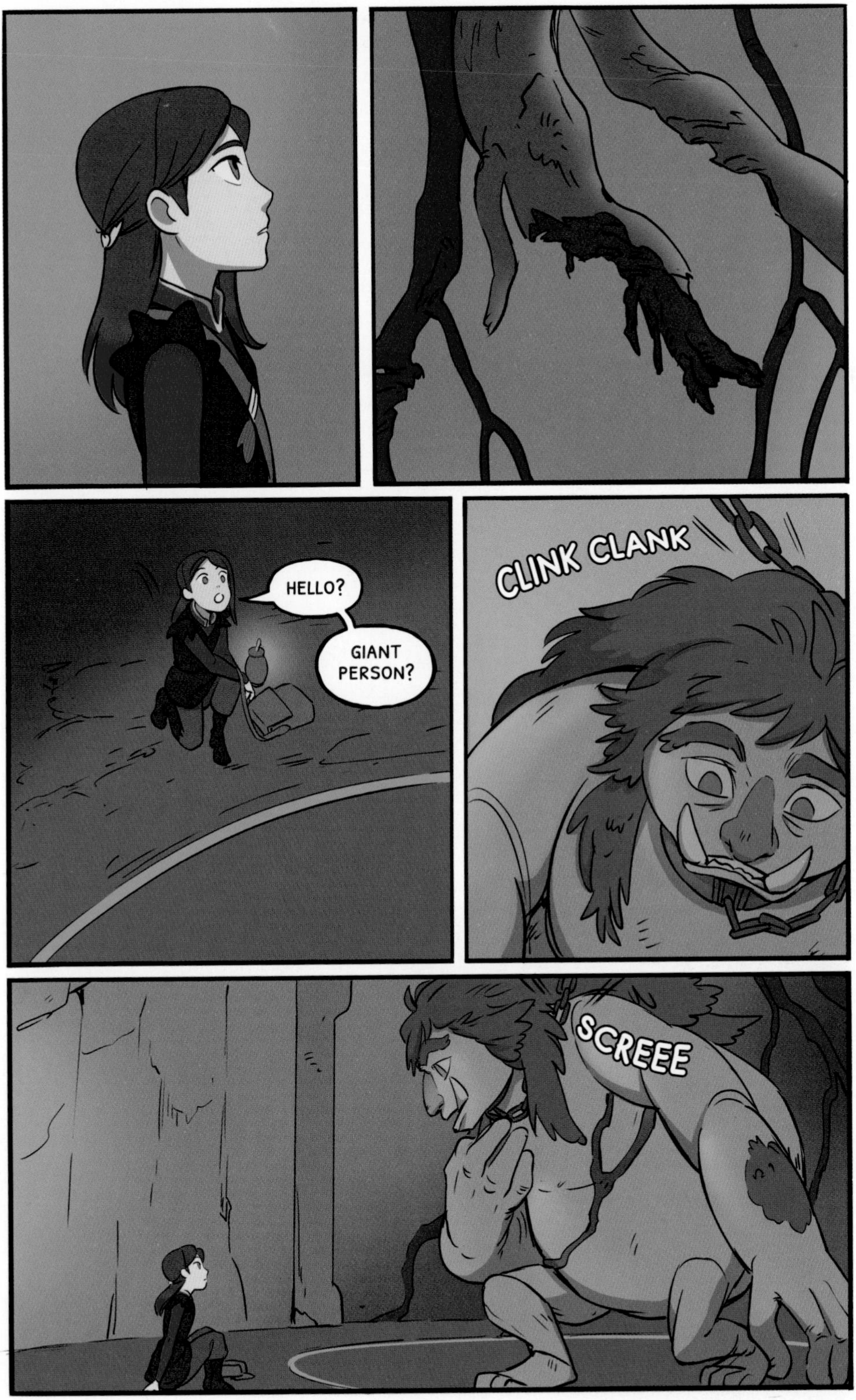
HELLO?
GIANT PERSON?
CLINK CLANK
SCREEE

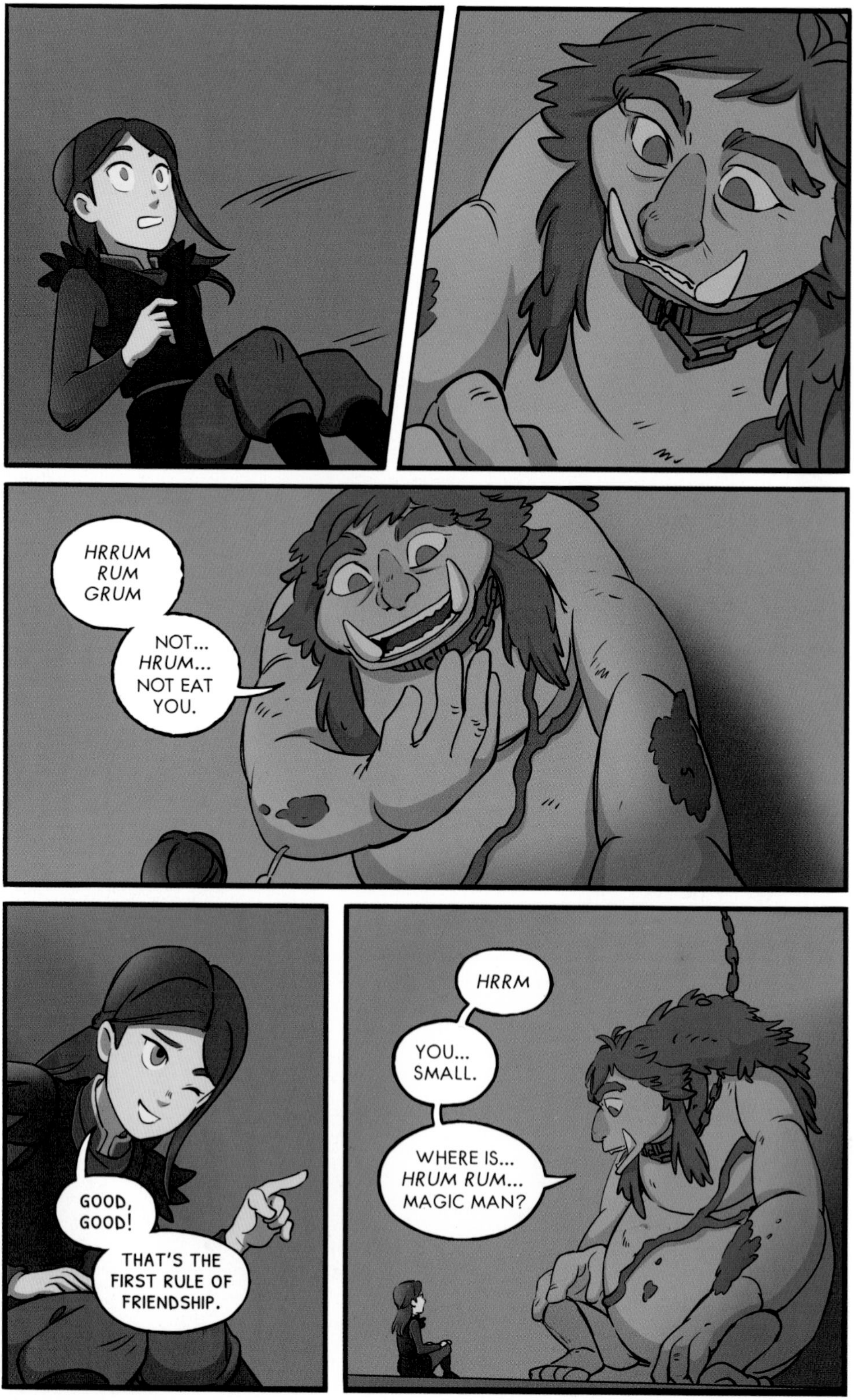
HRRUM RUM GRUM
NOT... HRUM... NOT EAT YOU.
GOOD, GOOD!
THAT'S THE FIRST RULE OF FRIENDSHIP.
HRRM
YOU... SMALL.
WHERE IS... HRUM RUM... MAGIC MAN?

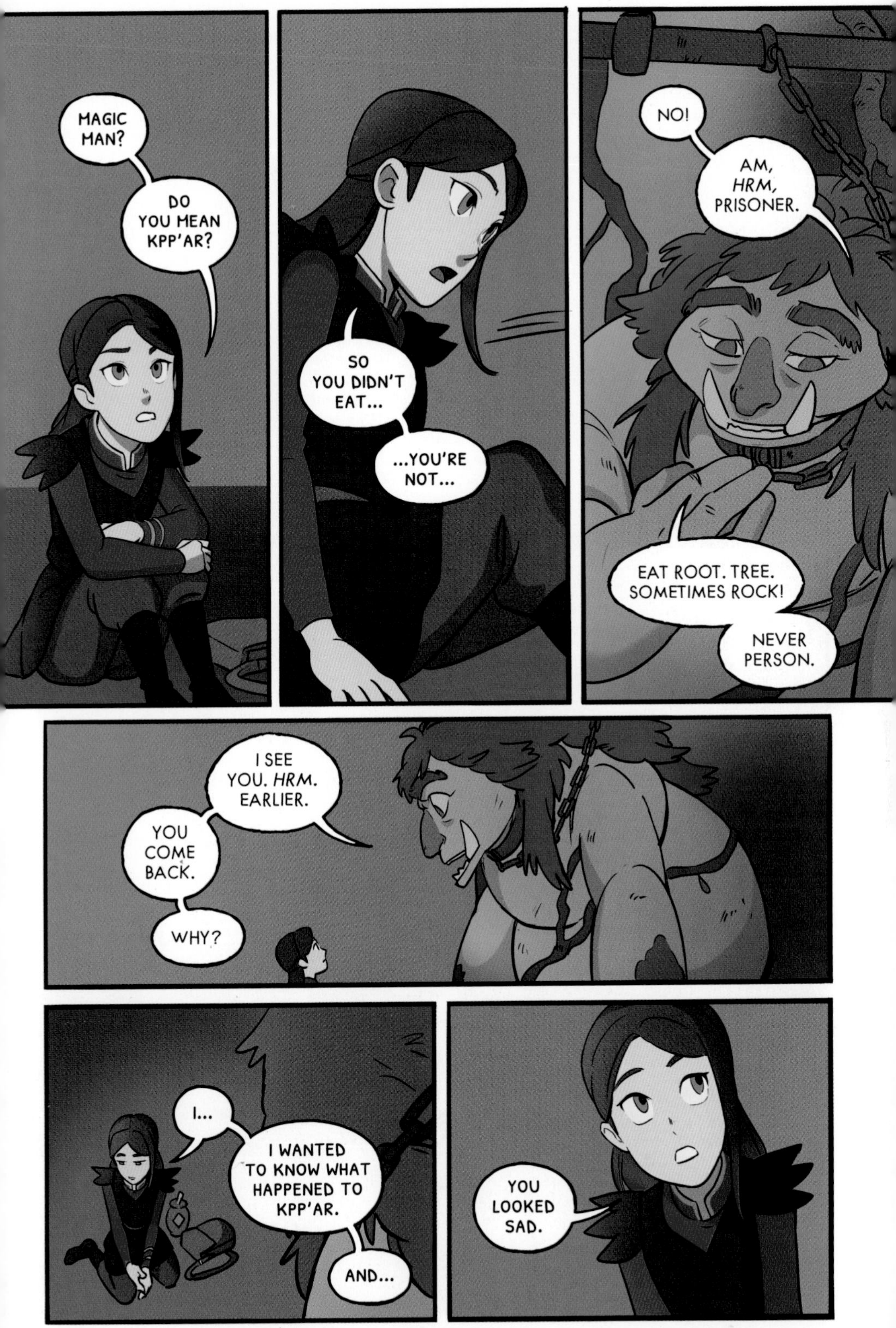
MAGIC MAN?
DO YOU MEAN KPP'AR?
SO YOU DIDN'T EAT...
...YOU'RE NOT...
NO!
AM, *HRM*, PRISONER.
EAT ROOT. TREE. SOMETIMES ROCK!
NEVER PERSON.
I SEE YOU. *HRM*. EARLIER.
YOU COME BACK.
WHY?
I...
I WANTED TO KNOW WHAT HAPPENED TO KPP'AR.
AND...
YOU LOOKED SAD.

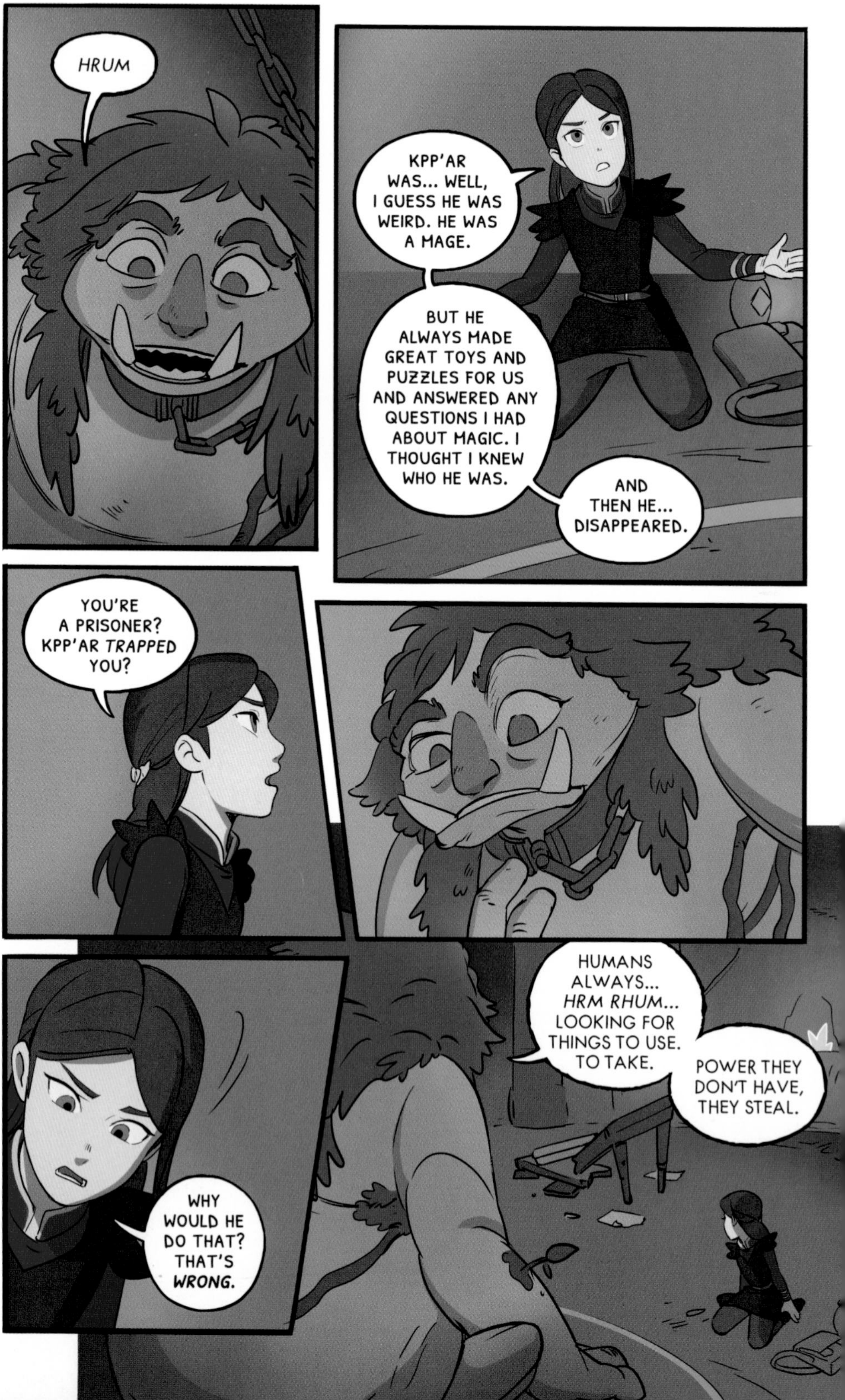
HRUM
KPP'AR WAS... WELL, I GUESS HE WAS WEIRD. HE WAS A MAGE.
BUT HE ALWAYS MADE GREAT TOYS AND PUZZLES FOR US AND ANSWERED ANY QUESTIONS I HAD ABOUT MAGIC. I THOUGHT I KNEW WHO HE WAS.
AND THEN HE... DISAPPEARED.
YOU'RE A PRISONER? KPP'AR TRAPPED YOU?
HUMANS ALWAYS... HRM RHUM... LOOKING FOR THINGS TO USE. TO TAKE.
POWER THEY DON'T HAVE, THEY STEAL.
WHY WOULD HE DO THAT? THAT'S WRONG.

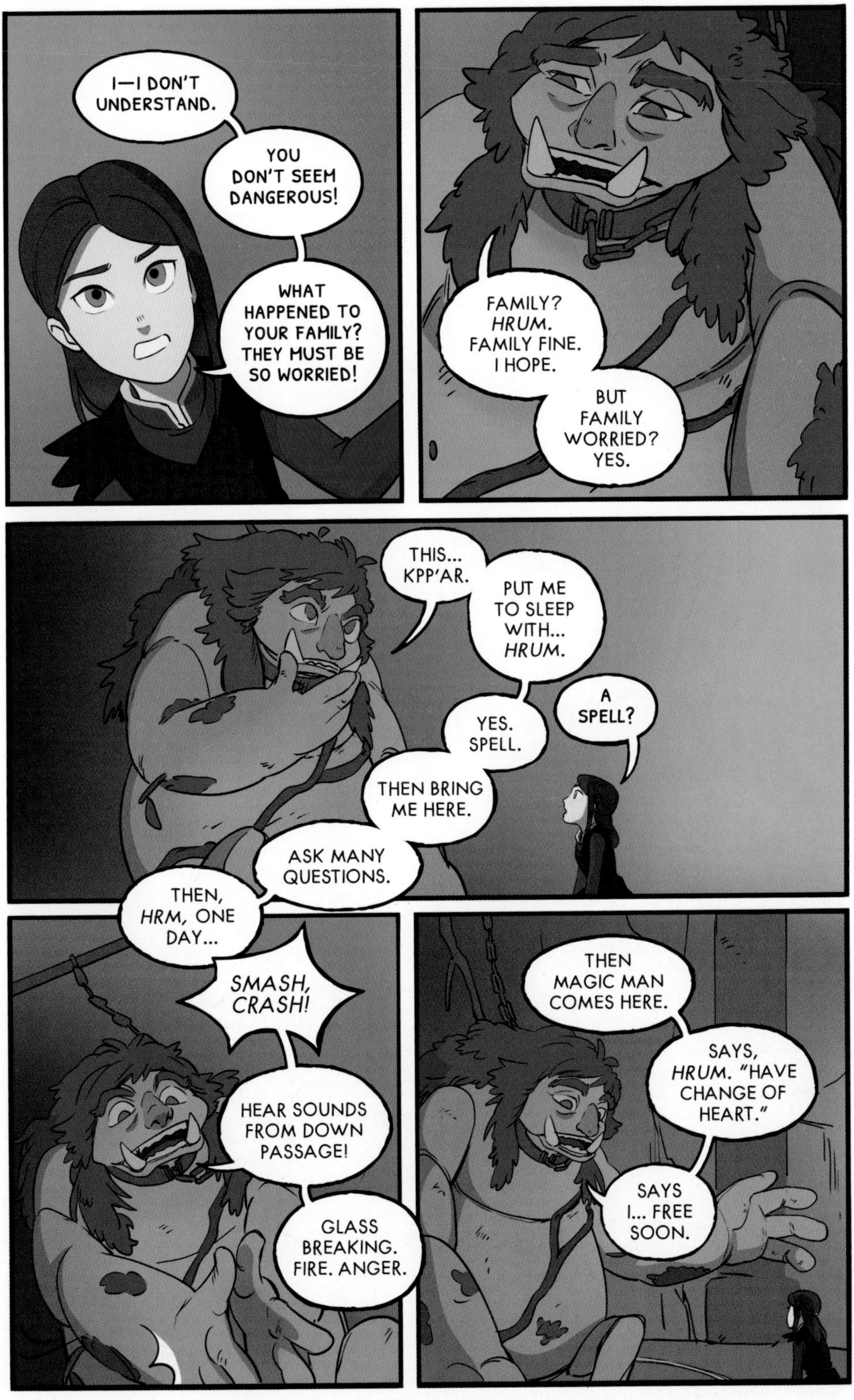
I—I DON'T UNDERSTAND.
YOU DON'T SEEM DANGEROUS!
WHAT HAPPENED TO YOUR FAMILY? THEY MUST BE SO WORRIED!
FAMILY? *HRUM.* FAMILY FINE. I HOPE.
BUT FAMILY WORRIED? YES.
THIS... KPP'AR.
PUT ME TO SLEEP WITH... *HRUM.*
A SPELL?
YES. SPELL.
THEN BRING ME HERE.
ASK MANY QUESTIONS.
THEN, *HRM,* ONE DAY...
SMASH, CRASH!
HEAR SOUNDS FROM DOWN PASSAGE!
GLASS BREAKING. FIRE. ANGER.
THEN MAGIC MAN COMES HERE.
SAYS, *HRUM.* "HAVE CHANGE OF HEART."
SAYS I... FREE SOON.

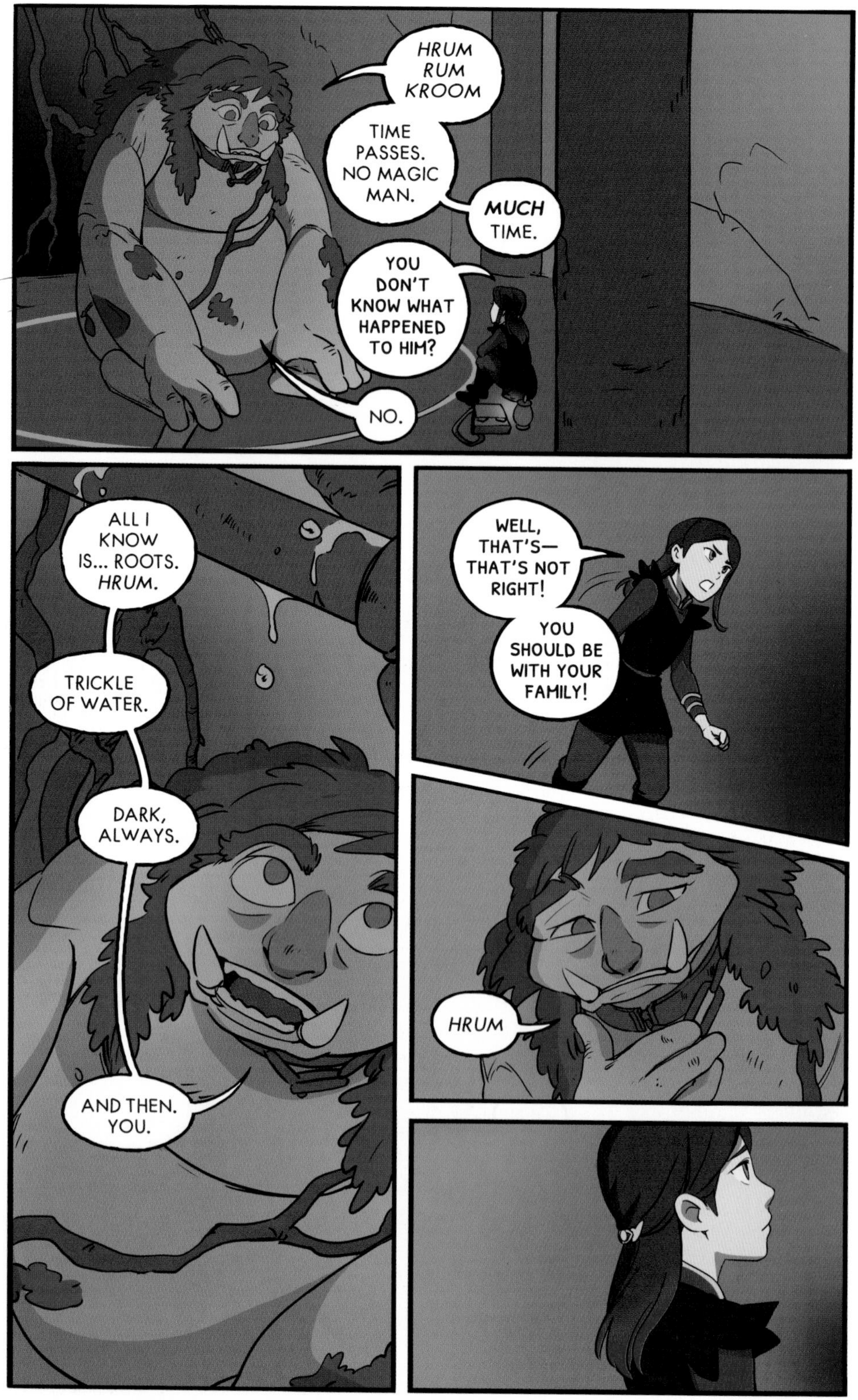

HRUM RUM KROOM
TIME PASSES. NO MAGIC MAN.
MUCH TIME.
YOU DON'T KNOW WHAT HAPPENED TO HIM?
NO.
ALL I KNOW IS... ROOTS. *HRUM.*
TRICKLE OF WATER.
DARK, ALWAYS.
AND THEN. YOU.
WELL, THAT'S— THAT'S NOT RIGHT!
YOU SHOULD BE WITH YOUR FAMILY!
HRUM

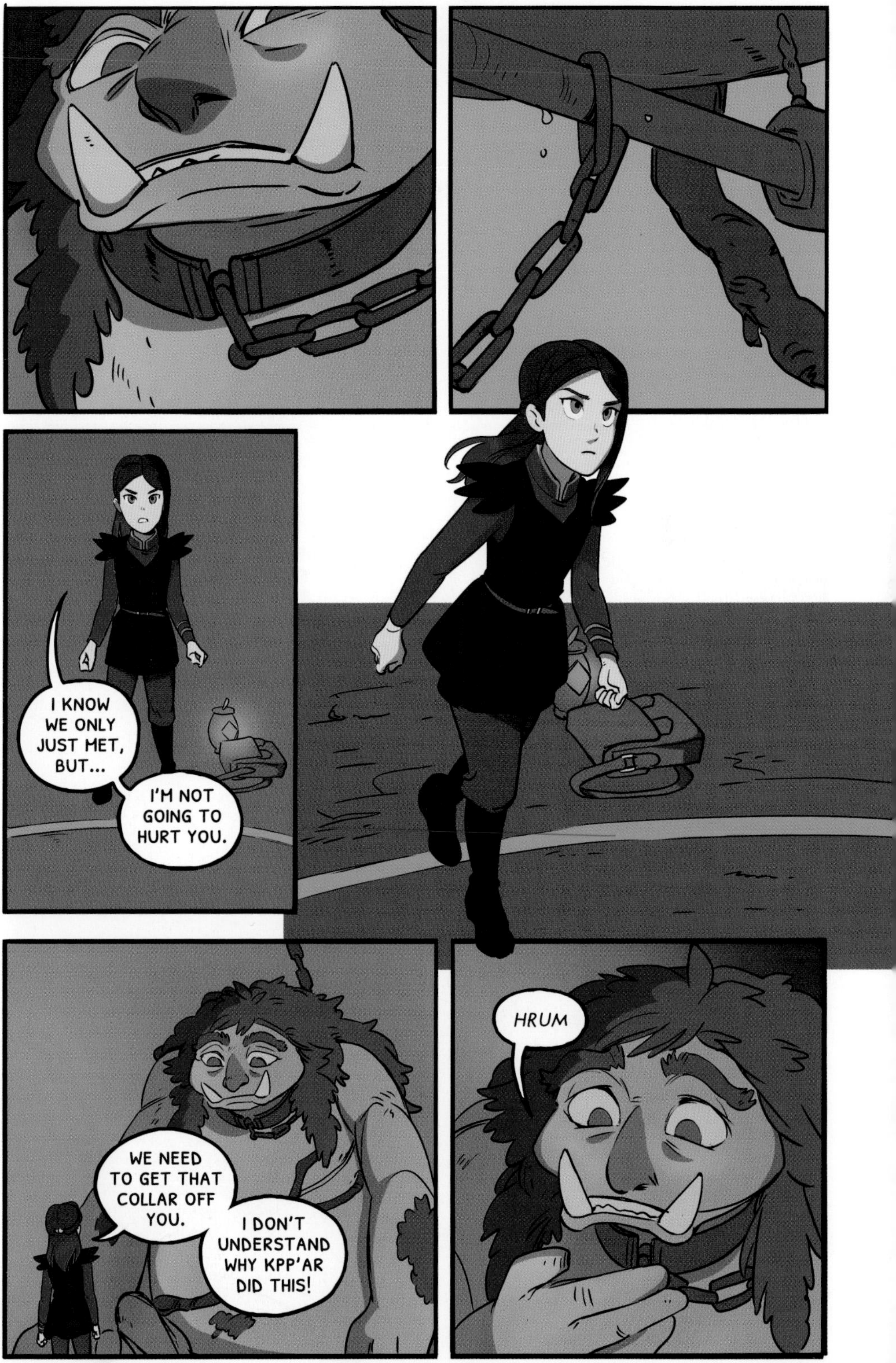
I KNOW WE ONLY JUST MET, BUT...
I'M NOT GOING TO HURT YOU.
WE NEED TO GET THAT COLLAR OFF YOU.
I DON'T UNDERSTAND WHY KPP'AR DID THIS!
HRUM

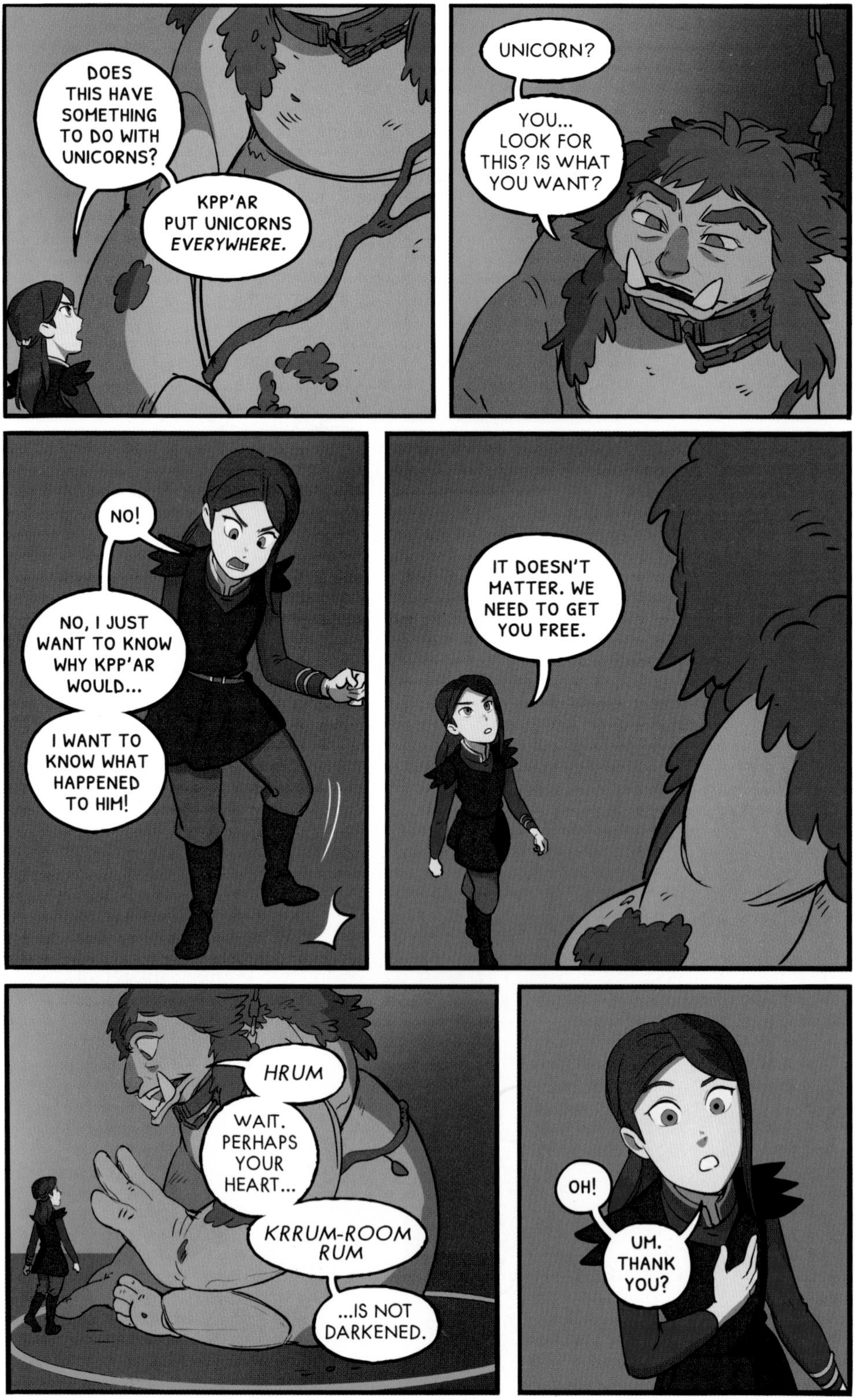
DOES THIS HAVE SOMETHING TO DO WITH UNICORNS?
KPP'AR PUT UNICORNS *EVERYWHERE.*
UNICORN?
YOU... LOOK FOR THIS? IS WHAT YOU WANT?
NO!
NO, I JUST WANT TO KNOW WHY KPP'AR WOULD...
I WANT TO KNOW WHAT HAPPENED TO HIM!
IT DOESN'T MATTER. WE NEED TO GET YOU FREE.
HRUM
WAIT. PERHAPS YOUR HEART...
KRRUM-ROOM RUM
...IS NOT DARKENED.
OH!
UM. THANK YOU?

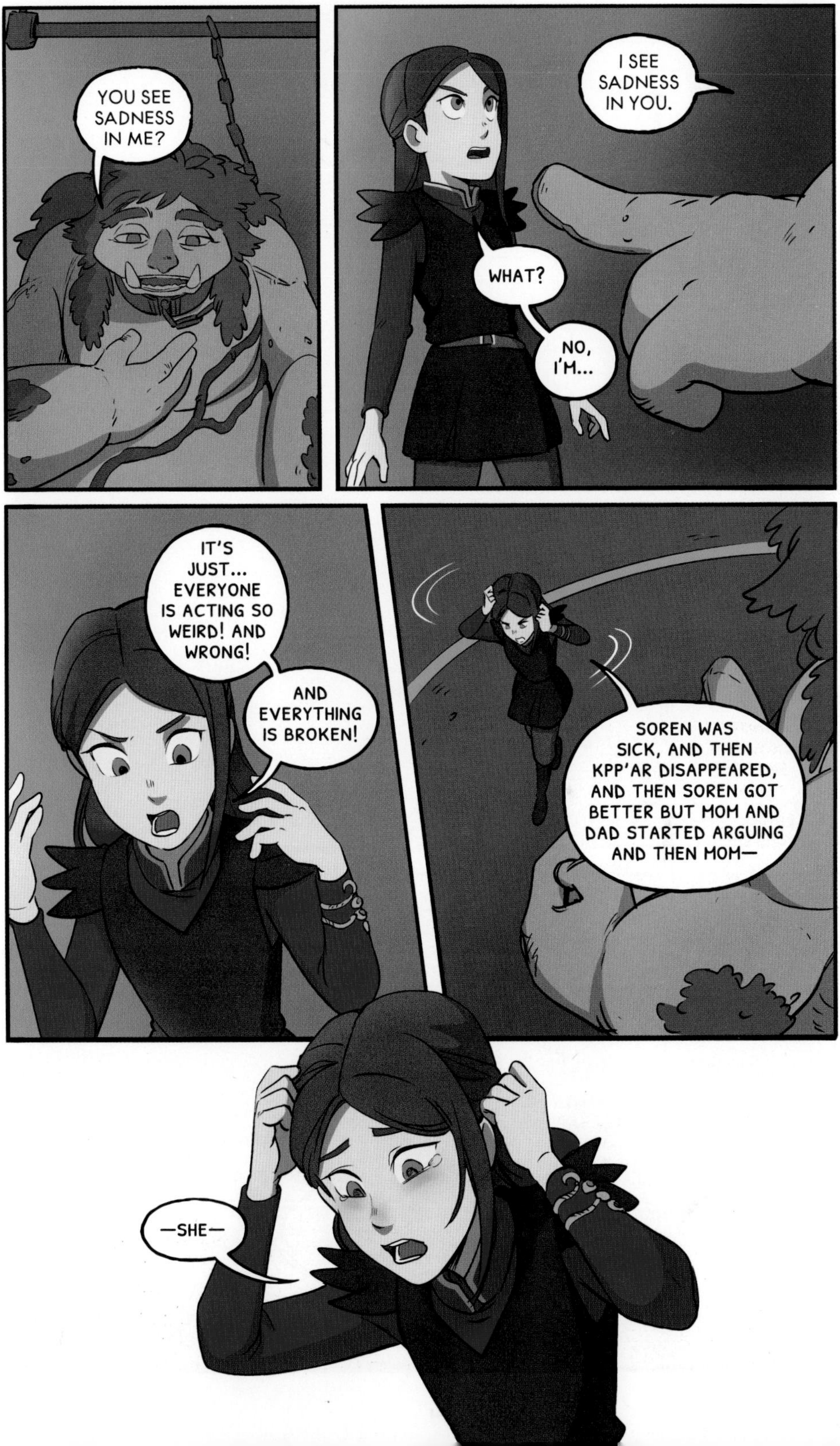
YOU SEE SADNESS IN ME?
I SEE SADNESS IN YOU.
WHAT?
NO, I'M...
IT'S JUST... EVERYONE IS ACTING SO WEIRD! AND WRONG!
AND EVERYTHING IS BROKEN!
SOREN WAS SICK, AND THEN KPP'AR DISAPPEARED, AND THEN SOREN GOT BETTER BUT MOM AND DAD STARTED ARGUING AND THEN MOM—
—SHE—

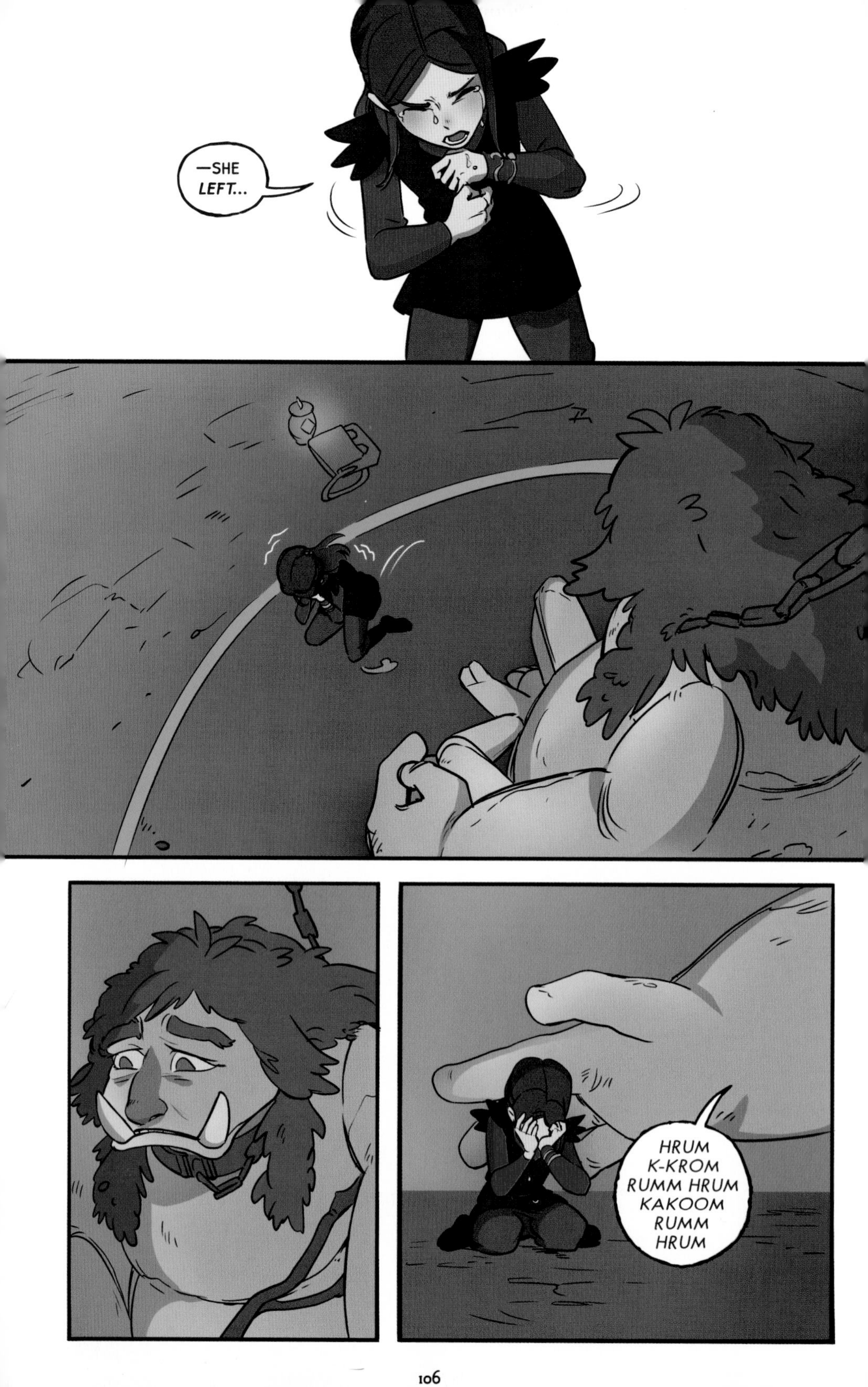
—SHE LEFT...
HRUM K-KROM RUMM HRUM KAKOOM RUMM HRUM

WH—WHAT?

HRUM

WORDS OF... COMFORT.

FOR LOSS.

"YOU WILL FIND A WAY. LIKE RIVER THROUGH ROCK."

S-SORRY. *SNIFF*

I DON'T KNOW WHAT HAPPENED TO ME.

SORRY.

I WAS GOING TO HELP WITH YOUR COLLAR.

CAN YOU LEAN DOWN?

HRUM. DO NOT KNOW WHAT YOU CAN DO.

I TRY EVERYTHING.

MAYBE, BUT I KNOW KPP'AR.

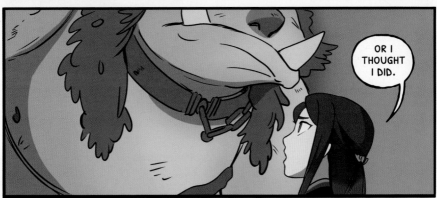

OR I THOUGHT I DID.

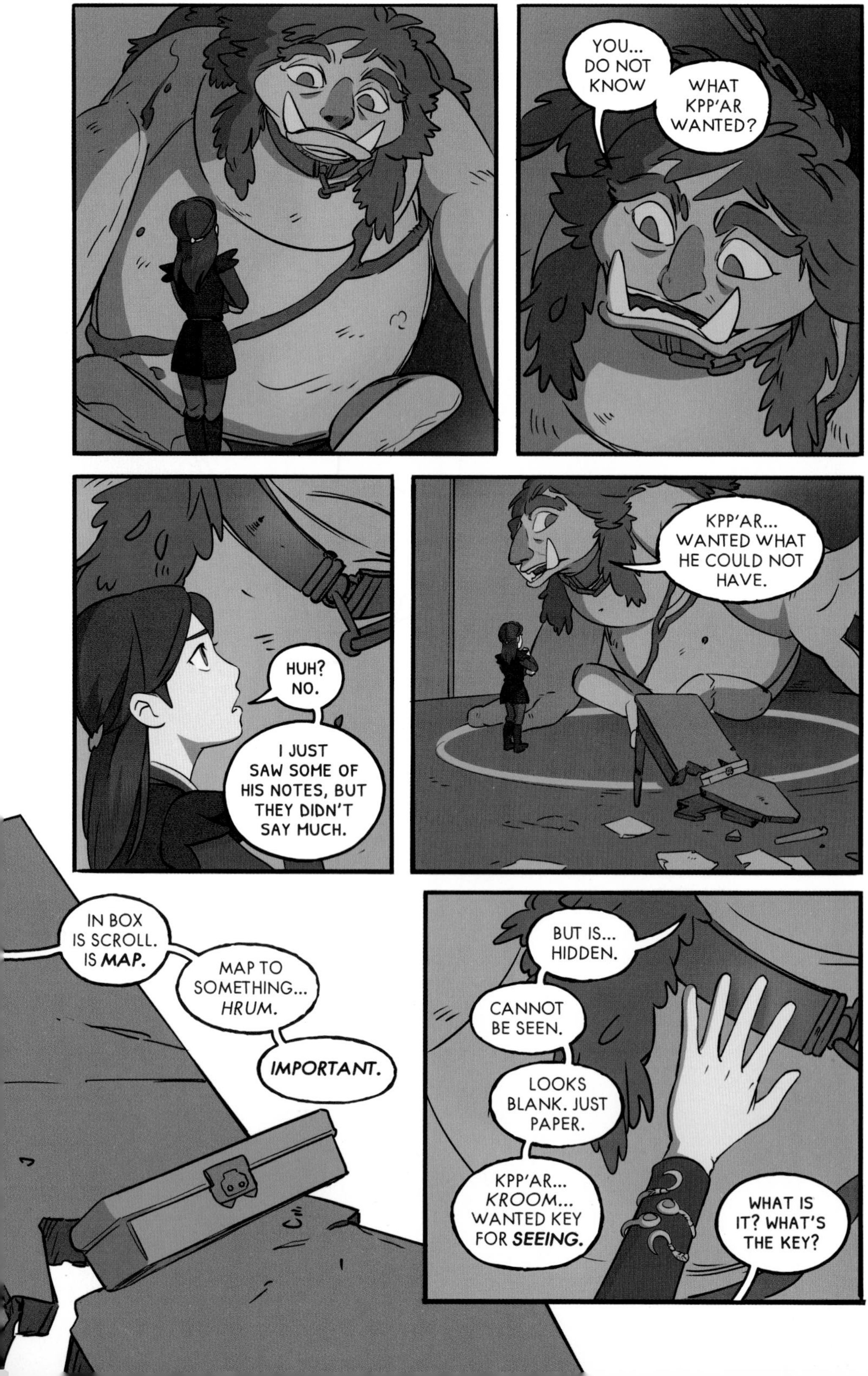
YOU... DO NOT KNOW
WHAT KPP'AR WANTED?
HUH? NO.
I JUST SAW SOME OF HIS NOTES, BUT THEY DIDN'T SAY MUCH.
KPP'AR... WANTED WHAT HE COULD NOT HAVE.
IN BOX IS SCROLL. IS **MAP.**
MAP TO SOMETHING... *HRUM.*
IMPORTANT.
BUT IS... HIDDEN.
CANNOT BE SEEN.
LOOKS BLANK. JUST PAPER.
KPP'AR... *KROOM*... WANTED KEY FOR **SEEING.**
WHAT IS IT? WHAT'S THE KEY?

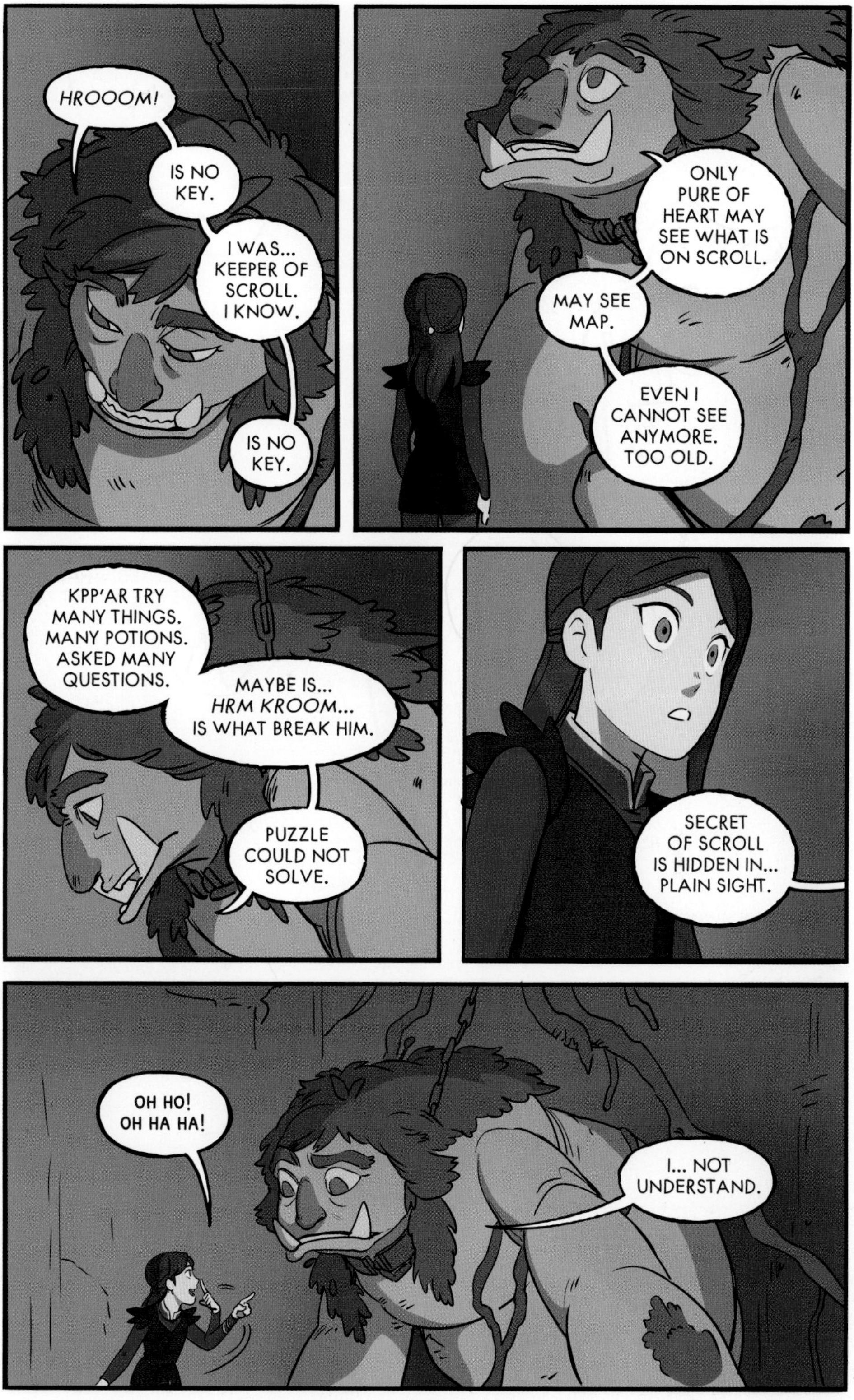
HROOOM!
IS NO KEY.
I WAS... KEEPER OF SCROLL. I KNOW.
IS NO KEY.
ONLY PURE OF HEART MAY SEE WHAT IS ON SCROLL.
MAY SEE MAP.
EVEN I CANNOT SEE ANYMORE. TOO OLD.
KPP'AR TRY MANY THINGS. MANY POTIONS. ASKED MANY QUESTIONS.
MAYBE IS... *HRM KROOM*... IS WHAT BREAK HIM.
PUZZLE COULD NOT SOLVE.
SECRET OF SCROLL IS HIDDEN IN... PLAIN SIGHT.
OH HO! OH HA HA!
I... NOT UNDERSTAND.

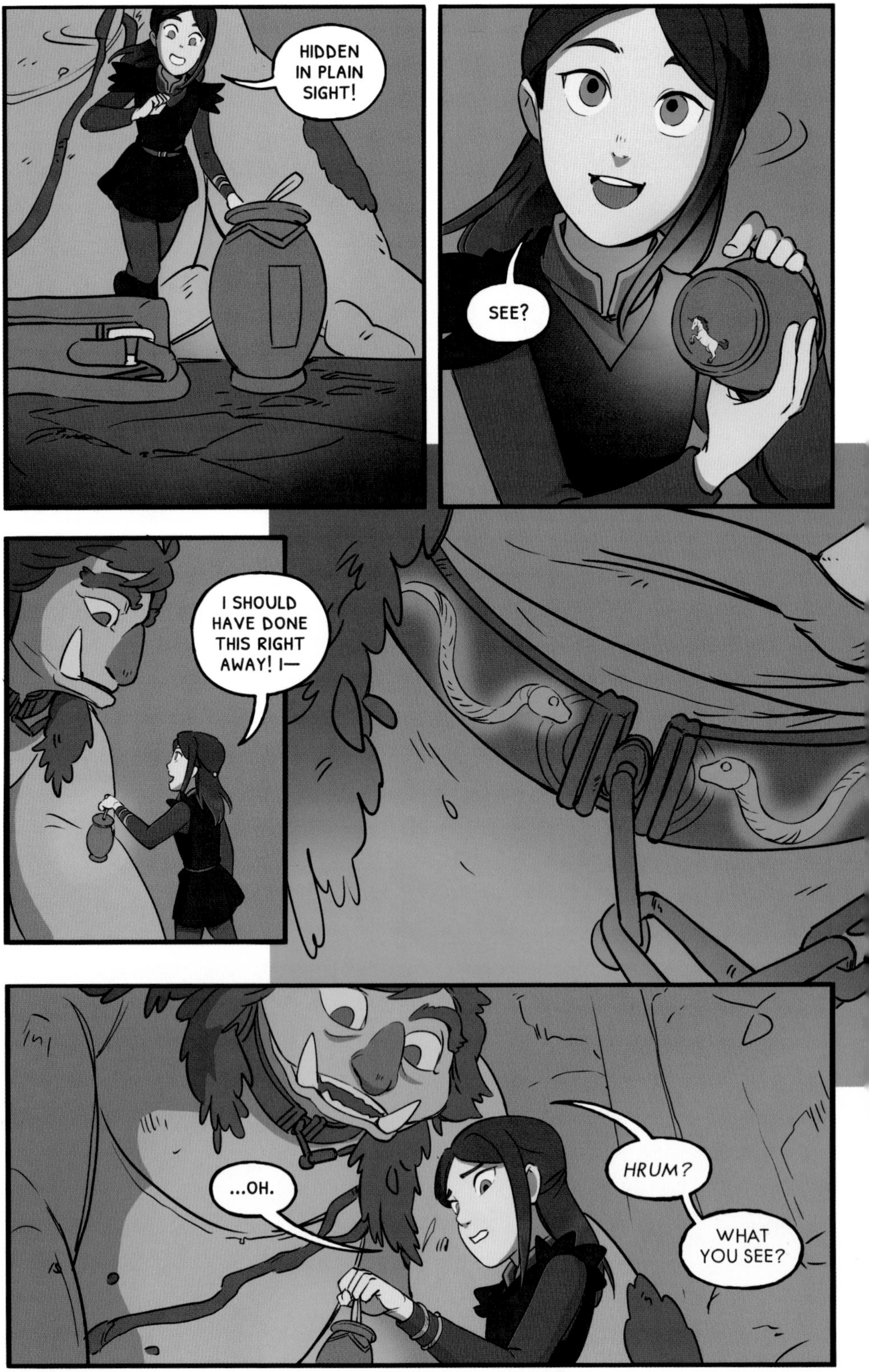
HIDDEN IN PLAIN SIGHT!
SEE?
I SHOULD HAVE DONE THIS RIGHT AWAY! I—
HRUM?
WHAT YOU SEE?
...OH.

IT'S... SOMETHING KPP'AR GAVE ME. NOT LONG BEFORE HE DISAPPEARED.

I WONDER IF HE KNEW SOMETHING...

AND MAYBE...

DLROW ELOHW EHT KCOLNU NAC DNIM REVELC A.

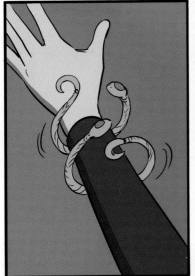

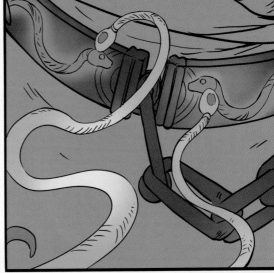

CLICK

DOFF

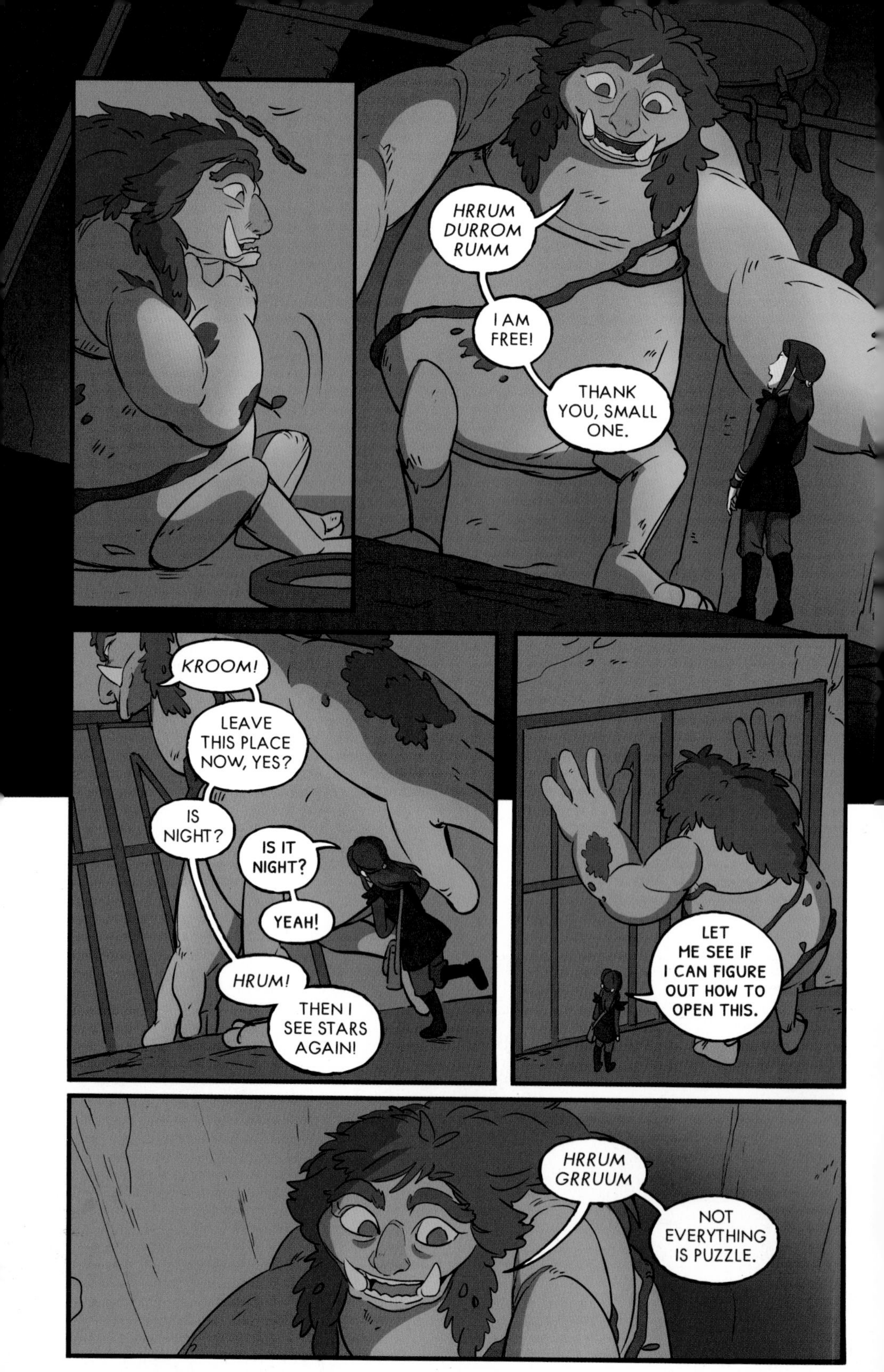
HRRUM DURROM RUMM
I AM FREE!
THANK YOU, SMALL ONE.
KROOM!
LEAVE THIS PLACE NOW, YES?
IS NIGHT?
IS IT NIGHT?
YEAH!
HRUM!
THEN I SEE STARS AGAIN!
LET ME SEE IF I CAN FIGURE OUT HOW TO OPEN THIS.
HRRUM GRRUUM
NOT EVERYTHING IS PUZZLE.

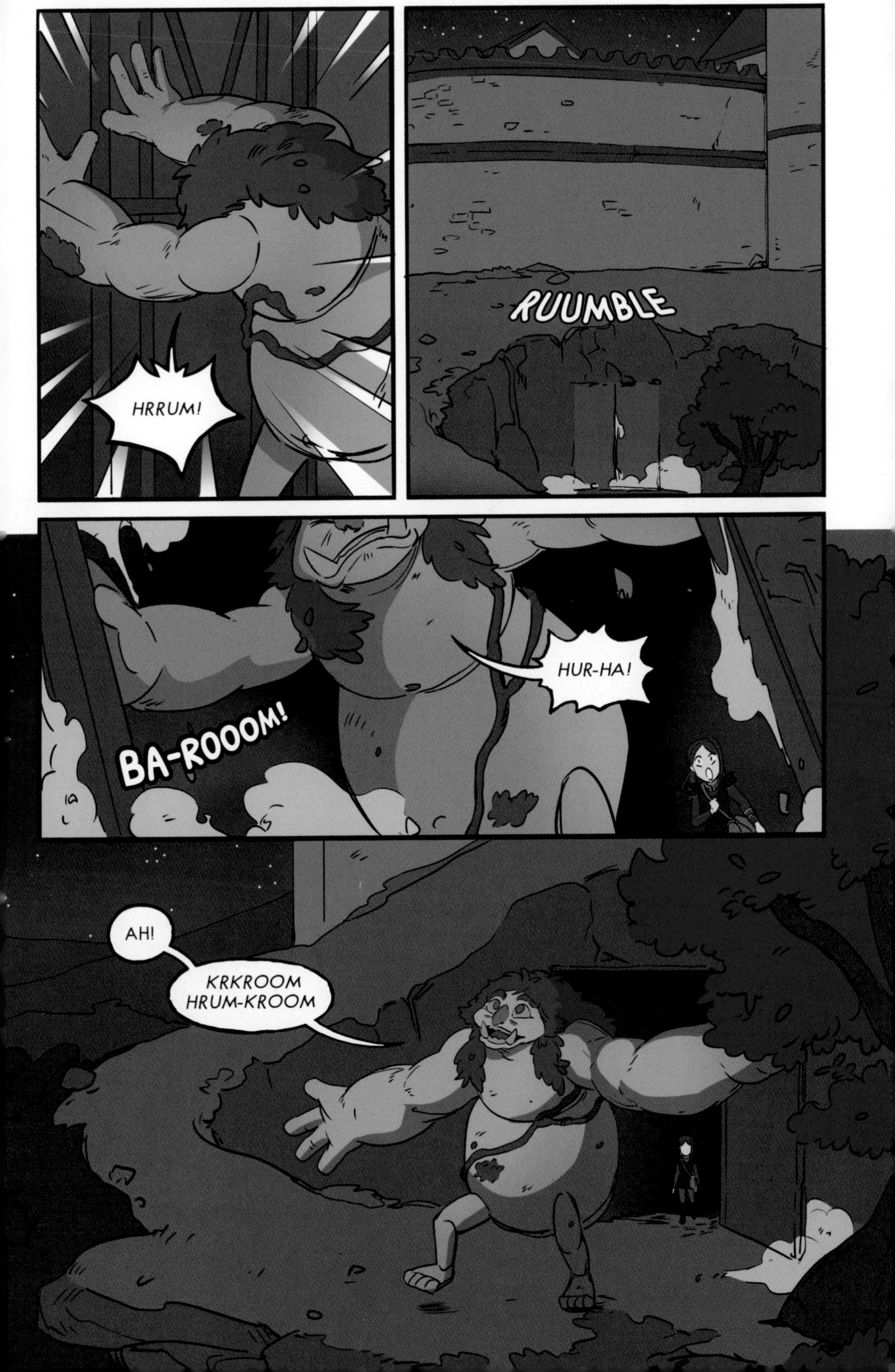
HRRUM!
RUUMBLE
HUR-HA!
BA-ROOOM!
AH!
KRKROOM
HRUM-KROOM

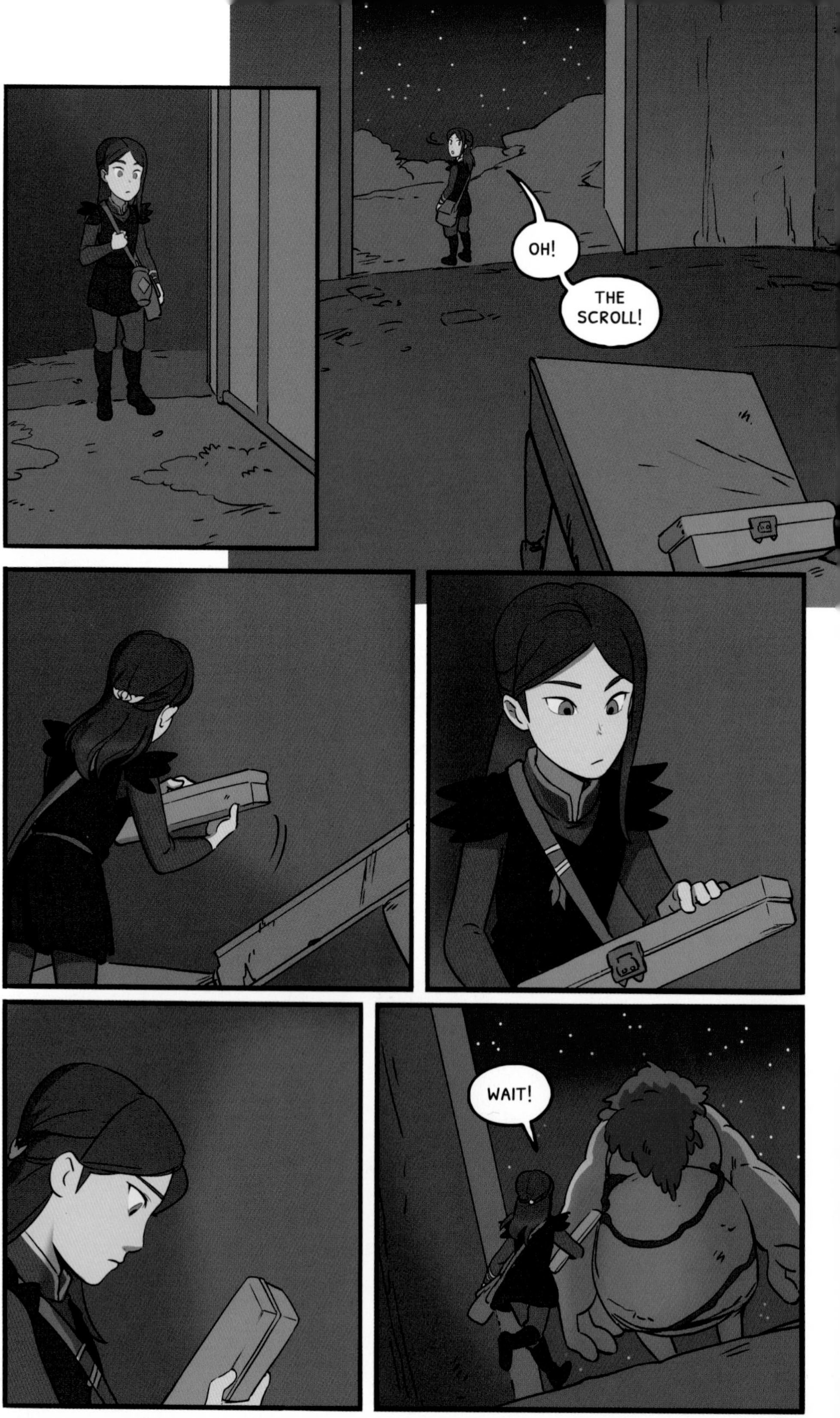
OH!
THE SCROLL!
WAIT!

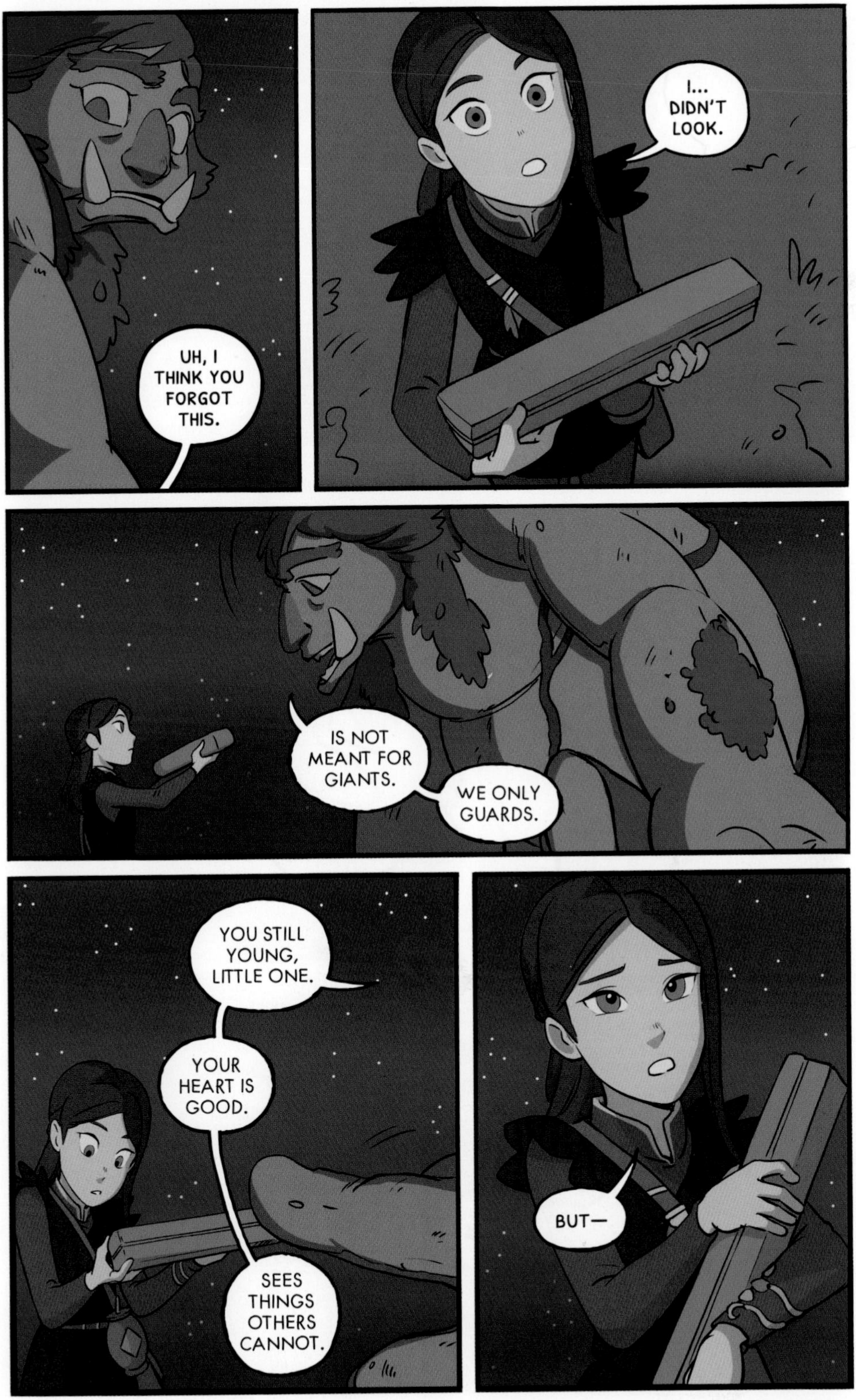
UH, I THINK YOU FORGOT THIS.
I... DIDN'T LOOK.
IS NOT MEANT FOR GIANTS.
WE ONLY GUARDS.
YOU STILL YOUNG, LITTLE ONE.
YOUR HEART IS GOOD.
SEES THINGS OTHERS CANNOT.
BUT—

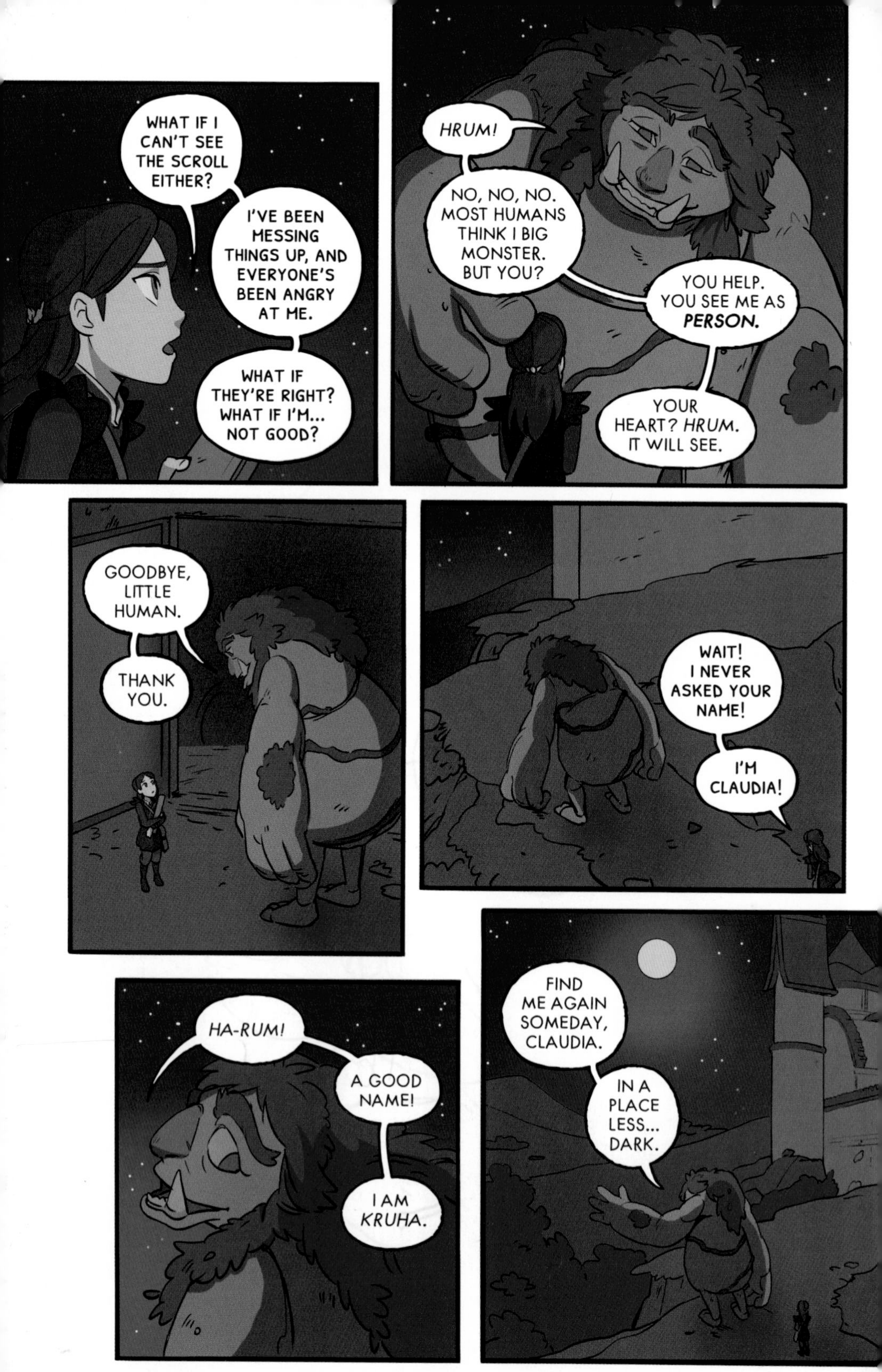
WHAT IF I CAN'T SEE THE SCROLL EITHER?
I'VE BEEN MESSING THINGS UP, AND EVERYONE'S BEEN ANGRY AT ME.
WHAT IF THEY'RE RIGHT? WHAT IF I'M... NOT GOOD?
HRUM!
NO, NO, NO. MOST HUMANS THINK I BIG MONSTER. BUT YOU?
YOU HELP. YOU SEE ME AS PERSON.
YOUR HEART? HRUM. IT WILL SEE.
GOODBYE, LITTLE HUMAN.
THANK YOU.
WAIT! I NEVER ASKED YOUR NAME!
I'M CLAUDIA!
HA-RUM!
A GOOD NAME!
I AM KRUHA.
FIND ME AGAIN SOMEDAY, CLAUDIA.
IN A PLACE LESS... DARK.

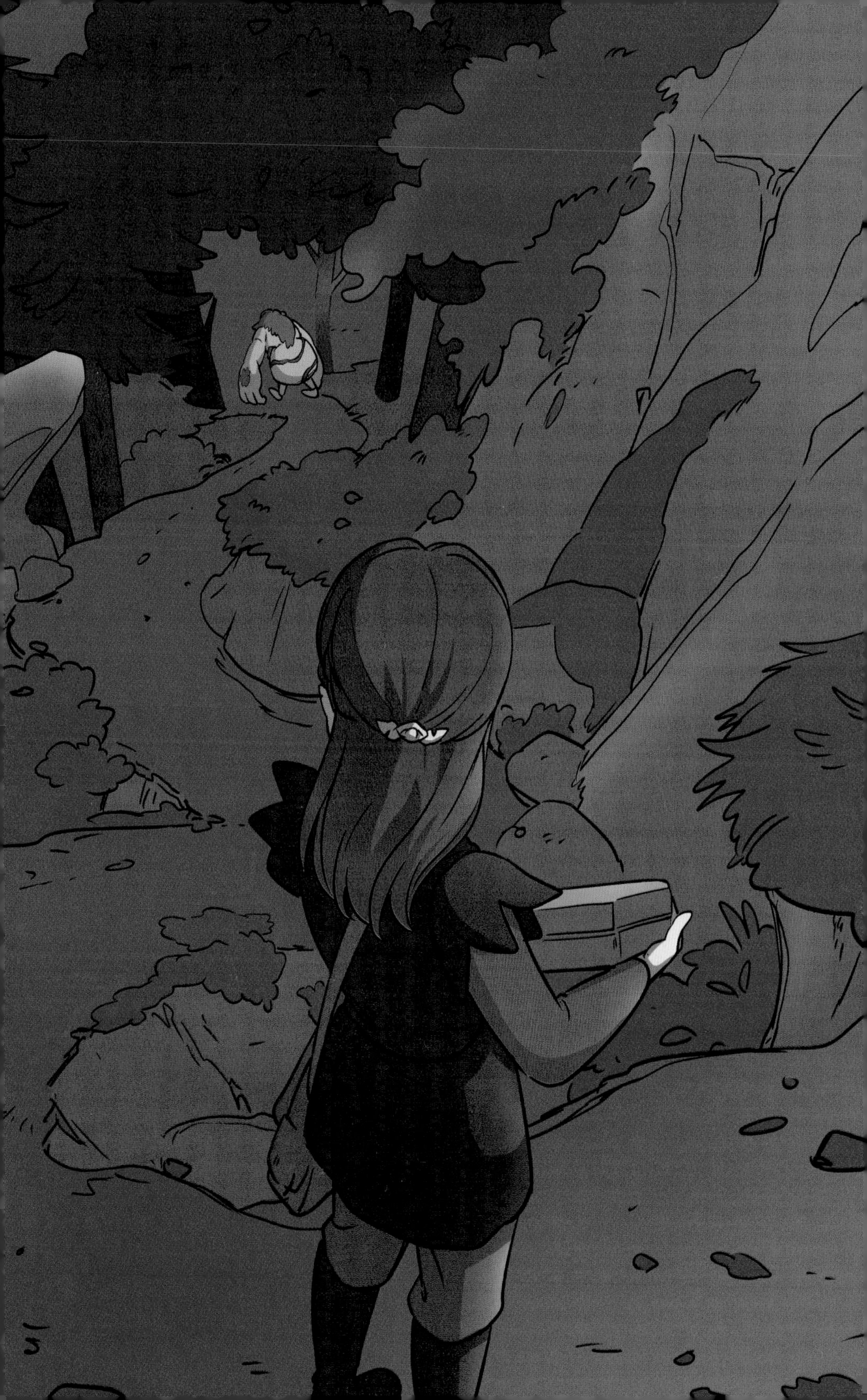

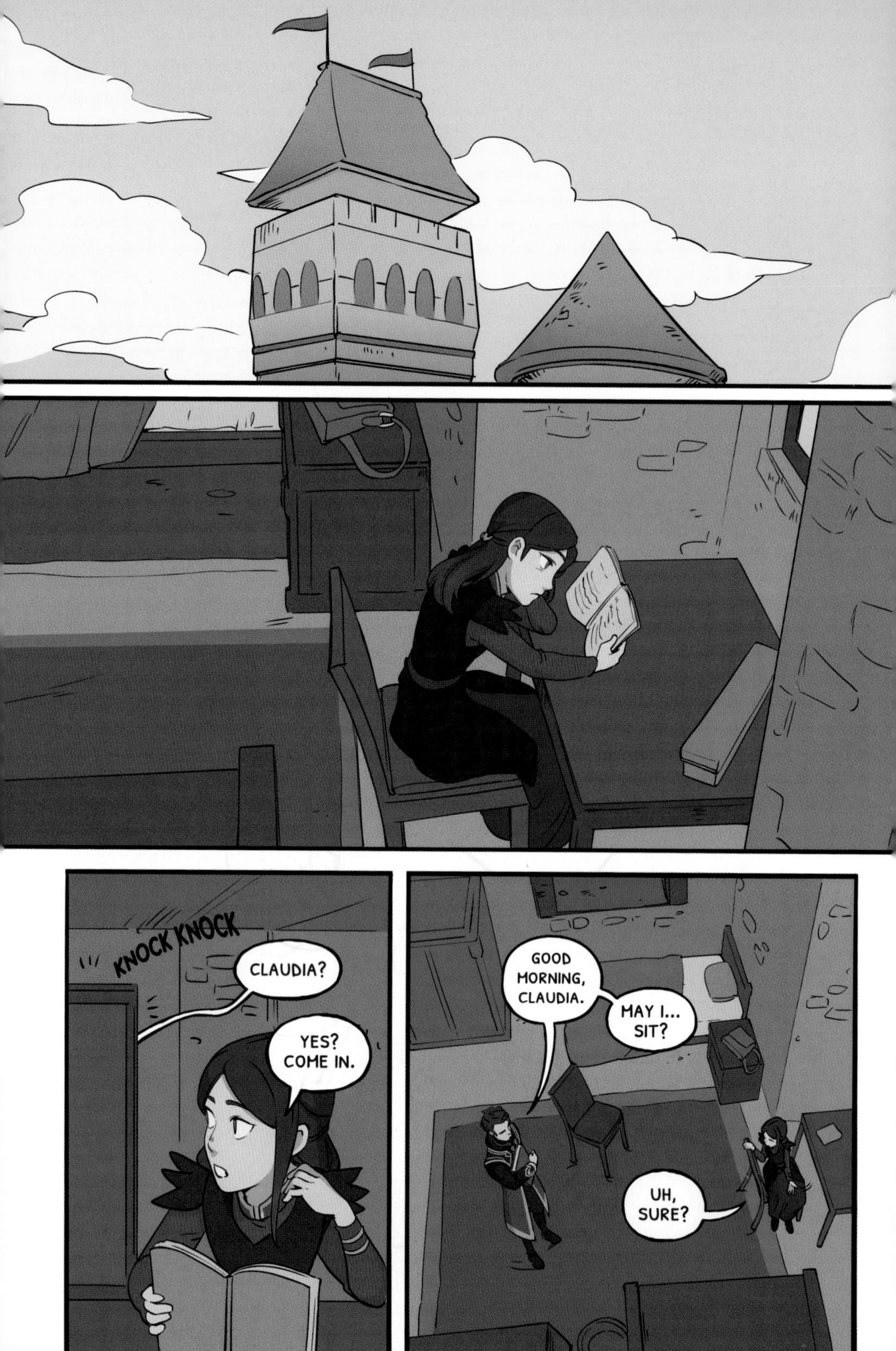
KNOCK KNOCK
CLAUDIA?
YES? COME IN.
GOOD MORNING, CLAUDIA.
MAY I... SIT?
UH, SURE?

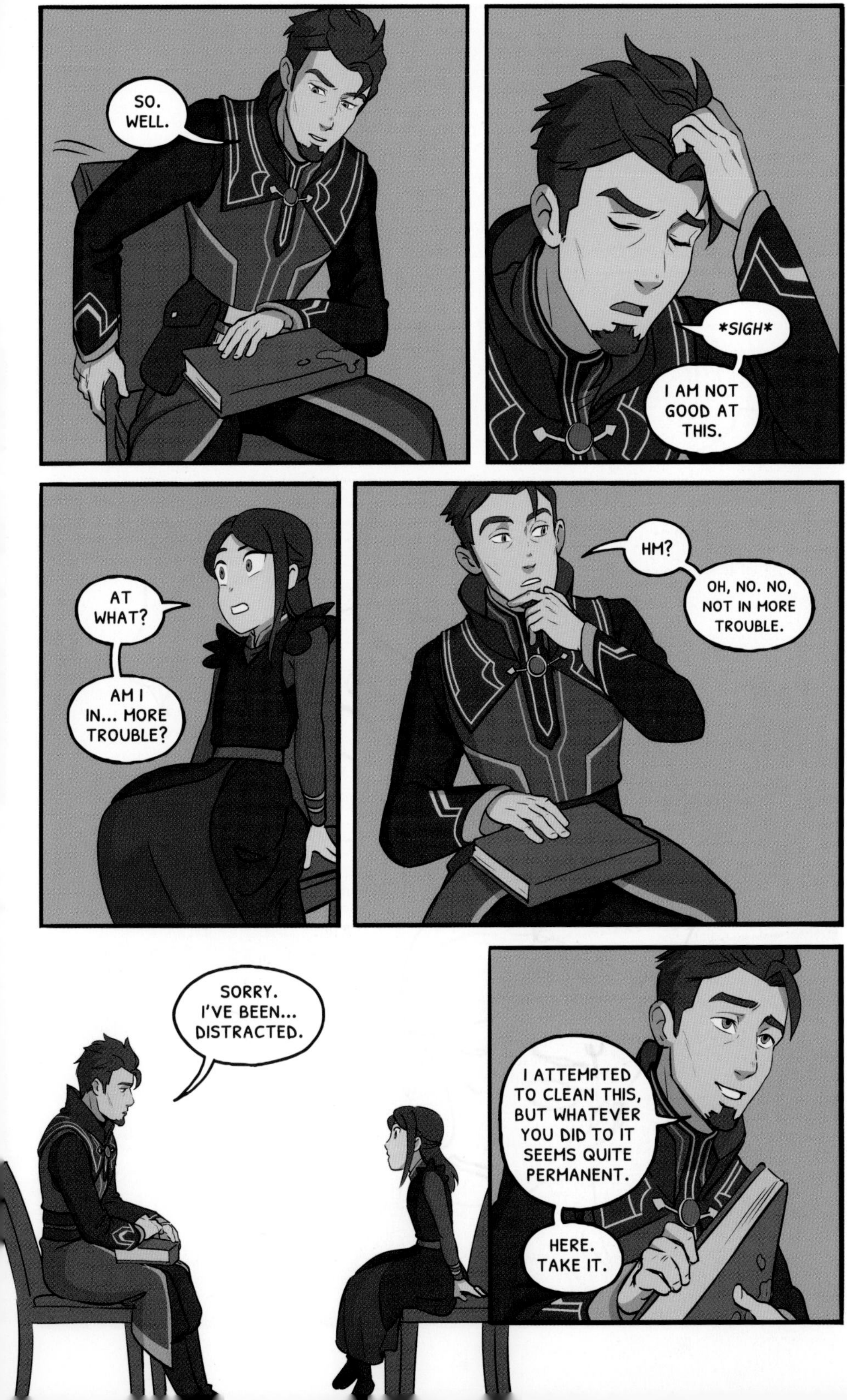
SO.
WELL.
SIGH
I AM NOT GOOD AT THIS.
AT WHAT?
AM I IN... MORE TROUBLE?
HM?
OH, NO. NO, NOT IN MORE TROUBLE.
SORRY. I'VE BEEN... DISTRACTED.
I ATTEMPTED TO CLEAN THIS, BUT WHATEVER YOU DID TO IT SEEMS QUITE PERMANENT.
HERE. TAKE IT.

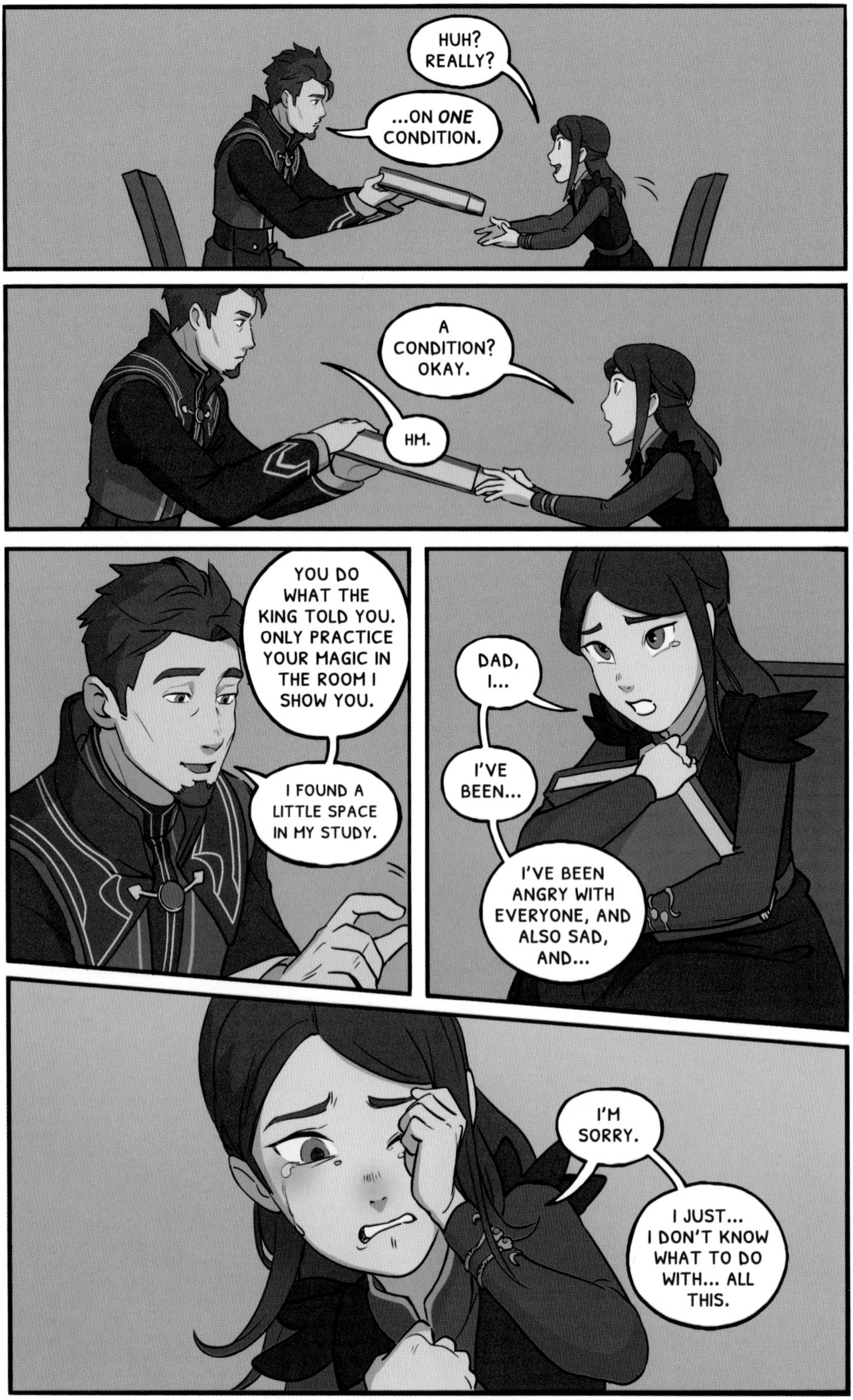
HUH? REALLY?
...ON *ONE* CONDITION.
A CONDITION? OKAY.
HM.
YOU DO WHAT THE KING TOLD YOU. ONLY PRACTICE YOUR MAGIC IN THE ROOM I SHOW YOU.
I FOUND A LITTLE SPACE IN MY STUDY.
DAD, I...
I'VE BEEN...
I'VE BEEN ANGRY WITH EVERYONE, AND ALSO SAD, AND...
I'M SORRY.
I JUST... I DON'T KNOW WHAT TO DO WITH... ALL THIS.

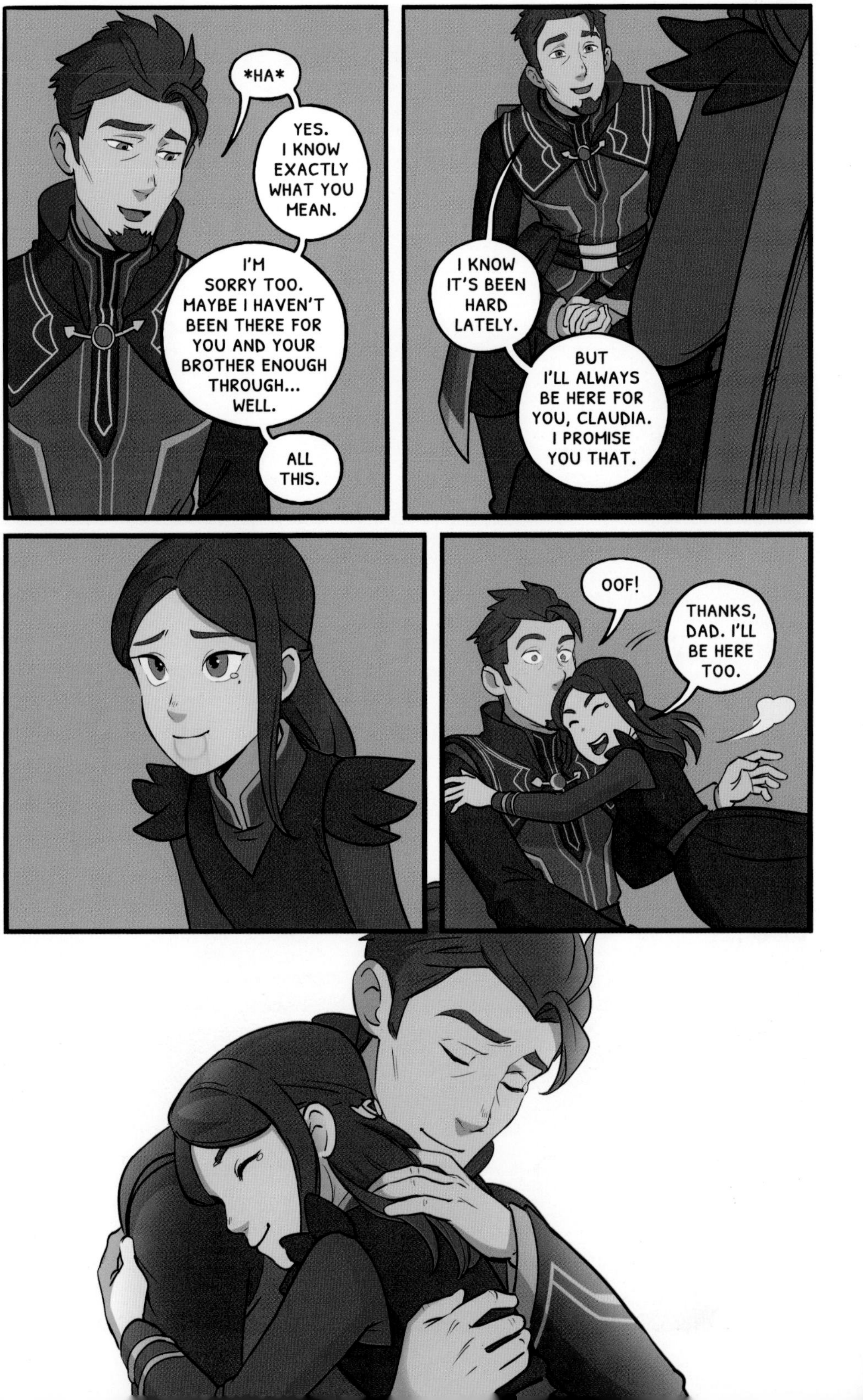
HA
YES. I KNOW EXACTLY WHAT YOU MEAN.
I'M SORRY TOO. MAYBE I HAVEN'T BEEN THERE FOR YOU AND YOUR BROTHER ENOUGH THROUGH... WELL.
ALL THIS.
I KNOW IT'S BEEN HARD LATELY.
BUT I'LL ALWAYS BE HERE FOR YOU, CLAUDIA. I PROMISE YOU THAT.
OOF!
THANKS, DAD. I'LL BE HERE TOO.

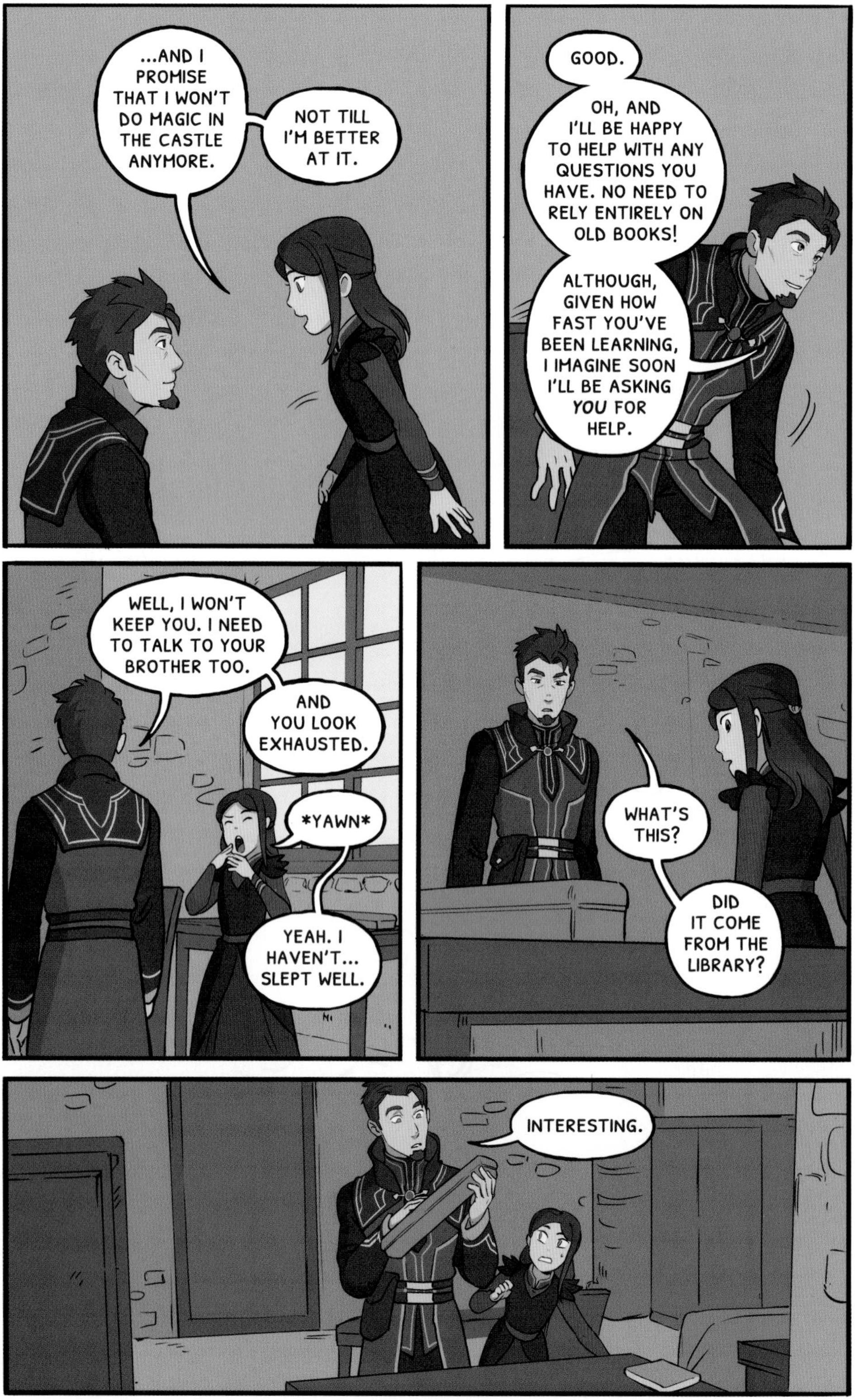
...AND I PROMISE THAT I WON'T DO MAGIC IN THE CASTLE ANYMORE.
NOT TILL I'M BETTER AT IT.
GOOD.
OH, AND I'LL BE HAPPY TO HELP WITH ANY QUESTIONS YOU HAVE. NO NEED TO RELY ENTIRELY ON OLD BOOKS!
ALTHOUGH, GIVEN HOW FAST YOU'VE BEEN LEARNING, I IMAGINE SOON I'LL BE ASKING *YOU* FOR HELP.
WELL, I WON'T KEEP YOU. I NEED TO TALK TO YOUR BROTHER TOO.
AND YOU LOOK EXHAUSTED.
YAWN
YEAH. I HAVEN'T... SLEPT WELL.
WHAT'S THIS?
DID IT COME FROM THE LIBRARY?
INTERESTING.

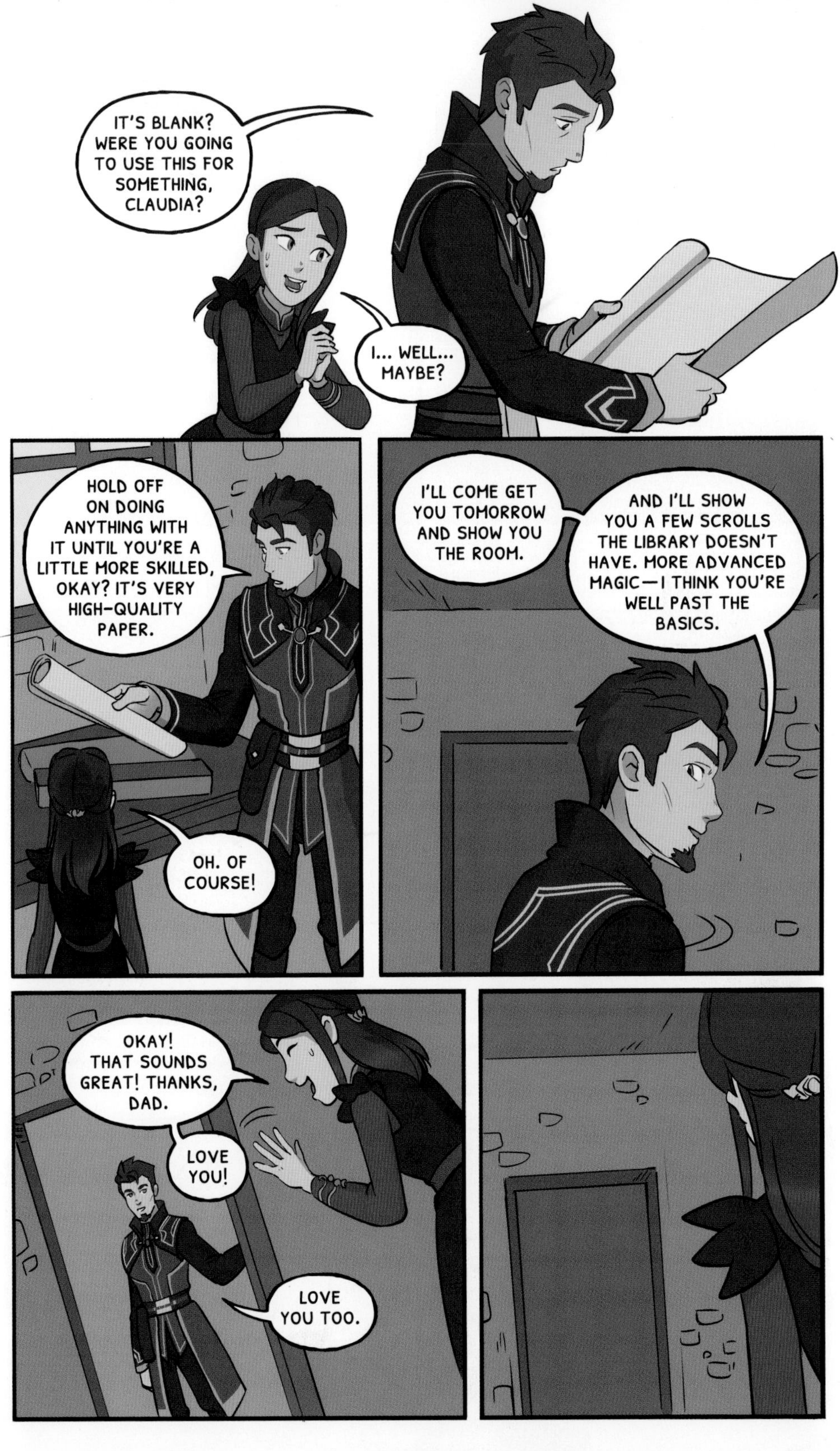
IT'S BLANK? WERE YOU GOING TO USE THIS FOR SOMETHING, CLAUDIA?
I... WELL... MAYBE?
HOLD OFF ON DOING ANYTHING WITH IT UNTIL YOU'RE A LITTLE MORE SKILLED, OKAY? IT'S VERY HIGH-QUALITY PAPER.
OH. OF COURSE!
I'LL COME GET YOU TOMORROW AND SHOW YOU THE ROOM.
AND I'LL SHOW YOU A FEW SCROLLS THE LIBRARY DOESN'T HAVE. MORE ADVANCED MAGIC—I THINK YOU'RE WELL PAST THE BASICS.
OKAY! THAT SOUNDS GREAT! THANKS, DAD.
LOVE YOU!
LOVE YOU TOO.

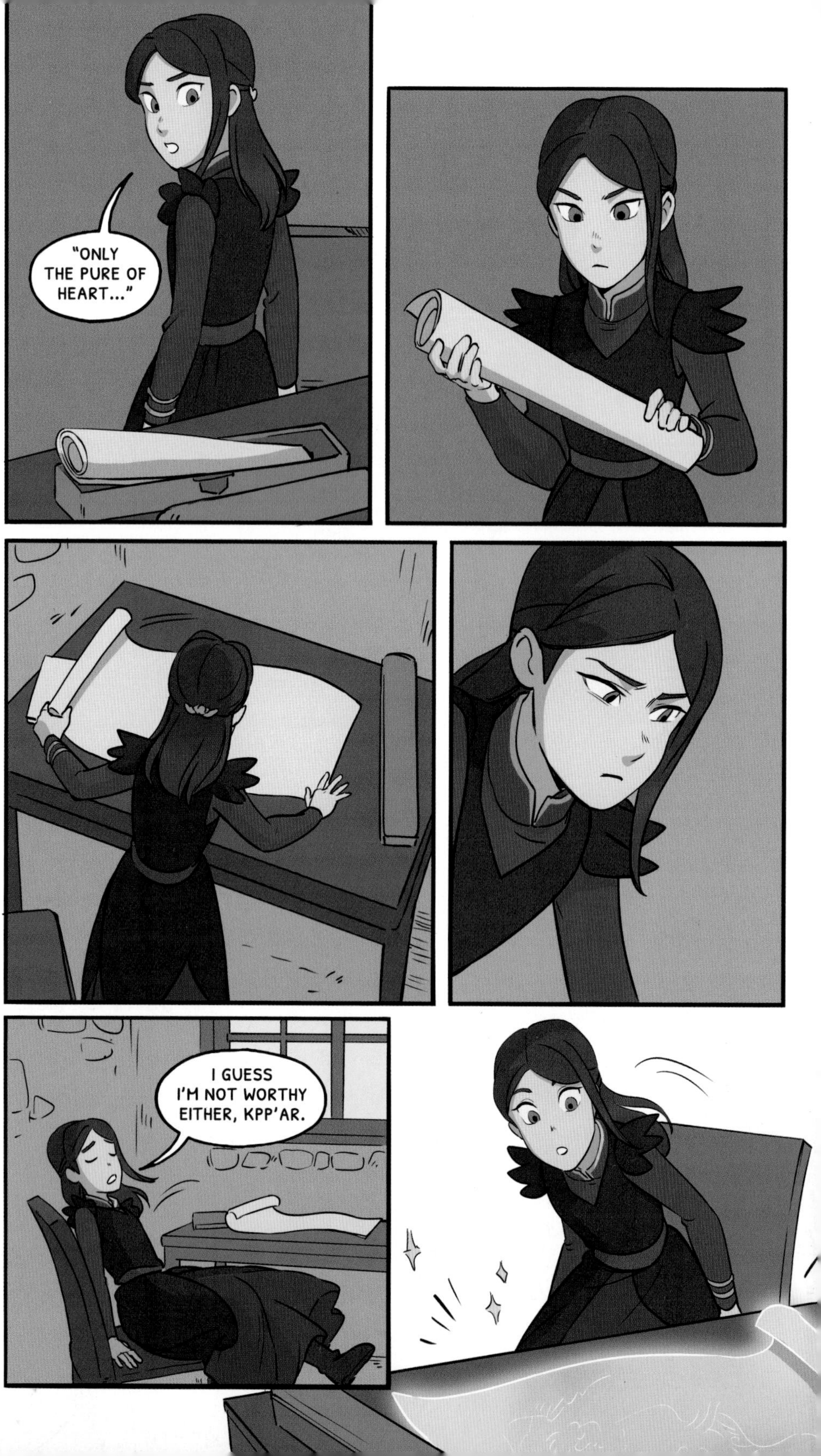
"ONLY THE PURE OF HEART..."
I GUESS I'M NOT WORTHY EITHER, KPP'AR.

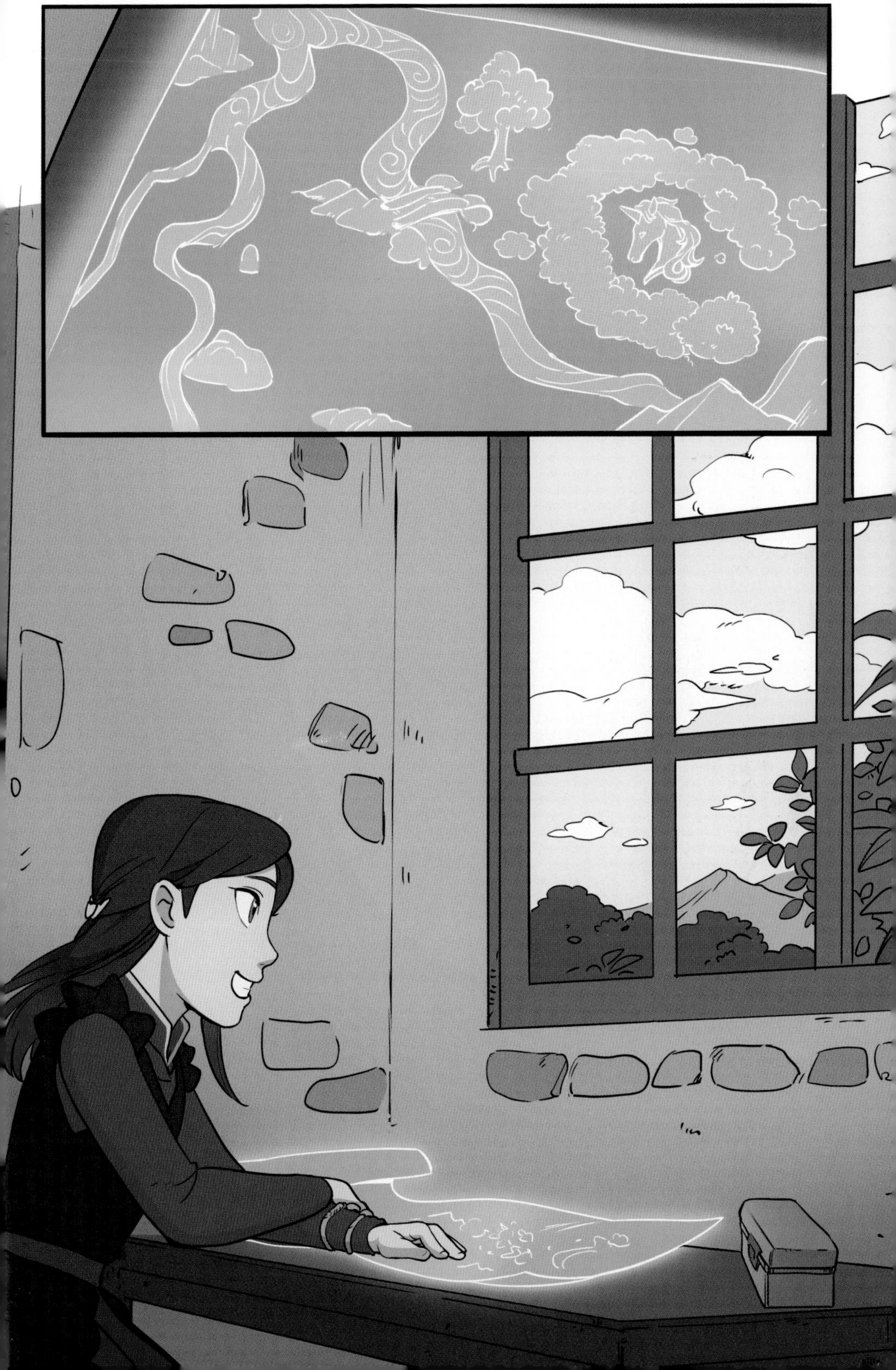

AARON EHASZ and **JUSTIN RICHMOND** are the creators of *The Dragon Prince* and cofounders of Wonderstorm, a media startup in Los Angeles, California. *The Dragon Prince* began as an original animated series on Netflix and is now being developed into a world-class video game by the same creative team.

Previously, Aaron was the head writer of *Avatar: The Last Airbender*, and Justin was game director on the *Uncharted* franchise.

PETER WARTMAN has been creating stories about monsters, robots, and spaceships since he could hold a pencil. He lives in Minneapolis, Minnesota, where he draws and writes comics pretty much all the time.

FELIA HANAKATA is an illustrator and comic artist based in Indonesia, where there is too much sun and rain. She believes storytelling breathes life and colors into the world. When she is not drawing, she reads, drinks lots of coffee, plays video games, and looks for inspiration in nature and her surroundings. You can find her online at feliahanakata.com.